DEDICATION

To those who have fostered my love of writing.

THE DECEMBER ISSUE

BY J. SHEP

PART I: CLASS

CHAPTER 1

In an otherwise barren office, two filled mailbags leaned against each other, both opened, exposing heaps of letters. This was Paul's old office, and his former editor-in-chief, Stephen, had ushered him in to see the mail. Finding the office so desolate, so unoccupied, startled him to silence, but not to the extent that the brimming mailbags did.

"This is what I wanted to show you," Stephen said, extending a hand toward the letters. When Paul did not respond, he continued, "This is the response to your November column. Do you believe it? And this doesn't account for the response submitted electronically."

His attention on the mail, Paul said, "It's not even November. It hasn't been on the newsstands for a week yet."

"And already—this."

"What are they saying?" He assumed Stephen had read a few and gauged their tenor as he always did, and he assumed most of them were fond farewells to Paul or to his column since readers knew of Paul's imminent retirement from *The Current Front*. In the August issue, the magazine had begun a countdown of the five final columns of Paul Scrivensby, so with only one more column after November's, Paul was sure the readers wished to extend their adieux.

"That's the thing, Paul. There are mixed reactions, really. Some of them are elated over your take on—what turned out to be—a volatile and timely topic." Surprised, Paul looked at the mailbags again. The topic was the decline of class, and he could not believe, first of all, that the content of his column elicited this much response so quickly, and second, that of all the topics on which he had written, this one—the decline of class—generated the heat. "Who would have thought, huh?" continued Stephen. "On the other hand, some of the reactions are—well—" and he did not wish to finish the sentence as forthright as he had delivered the first set of reactions, so he grasped for more gingerly wording. "They aren't as praising of your column, of your views."

Paul chuckled, suspecting Stephen preferred to act deferentially to his retiring employee and thereby soften the blow. "No need to mince your words with me, Stephen. I've been critically reviewed and I've been criticized before—you know that—and it comes with the territory. I'm no stranger to that."

"Maybe it was the unexpected tone. Your column normally offers hope. It's tinged with humor and playfulness, even amid the serious issues you've addressed. This last one was—it was a lament."

"And you think that put off some readers?"

"It's just that, you're near the end, you know? You've already officially retired, and the readers' reaction is in part negative. I'm just wondering, Paul, if this is how you want to end your career."

And in one sentence, the meeting in his old office became not about showing him the two mailbags but about something else entirely. He sensed ulterior motive where the sentence should have emitted concern.

"If? The columns are done. The November issue is already out, as you can see, and I submitted the December column weeks ago. Not much I can do about any of it now. Just let it take its course."

"Not if you address the readers—respond, sympathetically perhaps, to their grievances."

"What are you suggesting? That I write an apologetic letter to the readers in, what, the February, the March issue?"

Stephen sighed and glanced over Paul's shoulder. "What I'm suggesting is that you rewrite the December column and there, in your final column, offer an apology to anyone you may have offended in your November column. I already anticipate going down to the wire on printing December. We have some time before the December issue absolutely has to go to press—"

"Offer an apology? I've never had to apologize for my views—"

"The editors and I talked late last night before I called you in, and we thought the negative reaction might adversely affect our image. There's controversy that can be good for us, and then there's—. It's not the negative response that worries us; it's the volume of the negative response. We want you to go out on a high note. You've been with *CF* for forty-five years and have done the 'Partly Paul' column for thirty-five. We don't want your name and your reputation tarnished at the end, after so many years of solid work."

"You said some of the readers were 'elated' by my take on class, and you surely could not have scratched the surface of reading all these letters in such a short time. What if, by the end of the month, the positive reaction outweighs the negative? You may be worrying over nothing."

"We've sifted through hundreds of e-mails, and you're right, plenty of them are positive. But a whole lot of them are negative, Paul. Caustic, some of them. If this sampling is representative of the whole, then you've ticked off quite a few readers."

Paul looked again at the mailbags, this time wishing to tear through the letters and read each one, perhaps in an attempt to prove to Stephen that the praising ones did outnumber the disparaging ones. He wanted to challenge his former editor-in-chief by suggesting that the invitation to rewrite his final column had less to do with sparing tarnish to Paul's reputation and more to do with politicking to keep *CF*'s reputation from tarnish. He considered telling Stephen that he had turned in his last column and, as he had officially retired, would neither be writing nor rewriting columns for *CF*. Instead, Paul looked Stephen in the eye and said, "Stephen, I thank you for your insight on this and for the opportunity to redress things. Let me think on it a while, won't you? And if I decide to rewrite my final column, I will be sure to have it submitted within the next few days."

Stephen extended a hand. "Thanks, Paul. I really think it's in your best interest. I'll shoot you an e-mail with a deadline, and you do some thinking—some writing—and we'll get things squared away with the readers soon enough."

Paul shook Stephen's hand. "Thanks, Stephen. I have an afternoon flight back to St. Catherine's today, and I'll think on it back home."

"I'm glad you were able to stop in this morning so that I could show you—so that you could see with your own eyes—what I'm talking about." He sighed, placing a hand on each hip. "Paul, have a great trip back, and I'll be hearing from you."

"Mind if I sit here awhile and read a few of these?"

"Not at all. Take your time." Stephen made for the door. "Thanks again, Paul. Talk to you soon."

Alone now, Paul faced the desk chair pushed against the empty credenza and noticed the manila folders scattered on the desktop, as if someone had used the office to work on a project. He walked to the vertical blinds and adjusted them to let in maximum sunlight, and the room filled with the glow of late morning. He saw the same coffee stain in the taupe carpet from eight years ago when Boris Antonescu had been an intern and bumped into him one morning. The bare walls and empty credenza and unoccupied chair reminded Paul of the day he packed his belongings in late September, the memories he had reviewed while placing items in boxes, the hours he had spent writing, interviewing, discussing.

He had graduated from a reputable university with a degree in journalism and put it to work immediately at a small newspaper in Minnesota. He had grown up and lived in Saint Catherine's Cove on Lake Superior, not far from Duluth but over the state border, and the job in Minnesota proved just close and just far enough for a young man starting out. In that time, he had become engaged to and married his high school sweetheart Claribel Wheeler, a Saint Catherine's Cove girl herself, and months after accepting *The Current Front* position in New York, Claribel announced she was pregnant. Paul moved to New York City for the job at one of the most widely circulated magazines in the country, leaving Claribel in Saint Catherine's while he found a place for them to get settled. After their baby boy was born, Claribel and he moved to New York City with Paul, and there, they began to raise a family—three children in all—while making frequent visits to Saint Catherine's so that the children could enjoy the benefits of both locales. First an assistant editor and then a copy editor and minor contributor, Paul had worked his way up the ranks and in ten years had found his niche as a well-respected columnist. After only a year in this position, he and his family moved back to Saint Catherine's where Paul researched and wrote from home, making trips to the New York office at least once a month. He and his family moved into his father's place where they had always stayed for their shorter visits and helped take care of him until he passed away, at which point, the house became theirs. And through years of working with Claribel to raise Michael, Anna, and Pauline, he wrote and he mused and he wrote and he wondered and he wrote and he wrote and he wrote column after column after column.

All these years later and only a month after his retirement, he traveled back to New York for a gala honoring Rick Mendel, a verse columnist for *Cityscape*, an essayist and contributor to many well-known periodicals, a mentor to Paul when he had first arrived in New York, and now a friend. Rick's association with *Cityscape* had reached its fiftieth year, and the magazine held a banquet in his honor on Saturday. Paul, along with Glenda Armoring of *Pomp Magazine*, sat among Rick's other friends and family at the head table and enjoyed a lively evening celebrating, one filled with humorous reminiscences and warm sentiment. He enjoyed a nice lunch with Rick the next day, and Sunday evening, he received the call from Stephen asking him to stop by the office Tuesday morning if he had time before his flight.

He deflected an impulse to call Rick for advice on what had just been proposed to him by Stephen. Maybe pride obstructed a judicious step, but Paul decided that he had arrived at a point in his life when he should no longer be asking Rick for advice and that Rick had reached the point that he should be spared the bother. Paul would think this through on his own, with the insight of his wife only, and besides, he felt pretty sure he would not be writing an apology on which to end his tenure at *The Current Front*. But what were the readers writing?

Near the window was an armchair, and after Paul grabbed the top three letters from the mailbag, he sat in the chair, leaning forward to allow the sunlight to fall over his shoulder onto each letter in his hand. He smiled at the first envelope to his attention on account of the misspelling of "Current" with "Currant," an occasional occurrence in his letters. He pictured soldiers wielding bayonet-clad rifles, lurching through torrents of red and black berries on the "Currant Front."

He smilingly opened the envelope, hoping for a complimentary letter, and read the hand-written lines. "I have read your column for years, but I must say I find your views on the 'loss of class' in American society offensive. Your attack on classlessness is really an attack on most of the nation." The words in the letter poured over him like a viscous lava, and he became flushed, his forehead clammy. He was no longer smiling. A glance at the two bags, filled to the brim with letters, brought on another swell of heat. He finished reading the letter, its tone unchanging, and then opened the next envelope, not noticing that "Current" had been spelled correctly. He read, "Not all of us can afford to be classy, Mr. Scrivensby, and we do the best we can."

"I addressed that," he mumbled irascibly. "I said in the article I was not referring to social or economic class—that the class I'm referring to doesn't have to do with how much money one has or doesn't have—" and he scanned the letter for any admission to this important detail. There was none.

"You've endured criticism before, Paul," he thought. "You can do it again. Keep reading." He sighed this time, and the heatwave finally subsided. Resigned to more criticism, he opened the third envelope and began reading. "I have usually enjoyed reading your column, but this is the first time I felt moved to write you a letter. Thank-you for stating outright what so many of us have been noticing for years now—a deterioration of values and disregard for acting with class, and the significance of that." He still did not smile but sunk into the chair. He pulled a handkerchief from his pocket and wiped his forehead.

He considered reaching for another handful of letters. Three done with only five hundred more to go. He wanted to scour them all. One by one, he wanted to read every rant, every compliment, and in his free time, to reply to each. But the blaze that had accompanied reading the first few over-ruled this desire. Instead, he returned the three letters to their respective envelopes and tossed them on the top of the mailbag heap as he made for the door.

The pastrami sandwich had been calling his name since he had boarded the plane in Duluth. An obligatory stop on every visit to New York, the deli across the street from his office had become his favorite over the years, and he never missed an opportunity to stop in for the sandwich, the pastrami piled high beneath layers of fresh tomato, lettuce, onions, and the deli's signature sauce. He had a half hour before needing to head to the airport, and that was all he needed to enjoy this treat.

He sat at a table at the front window in the otherwise dim deli so that he could peruse the November issue—and, yes—reread his column. His priority, however, was taking a bite from the mouthwatering sandwich. The magazine next to his plate folded over to his column, a napkin on his lap, the plate before him, he said grace to himself and brought the sandwich to his mouth. He savored the deliciousness in this first bite before going in for a second. He glanced around, hoping to catch sight of the owner behind the counter so that he could offer a pleasant greeting but saw only a few employees he did not recognize and several patrons standing in line and sitting at tables. And as he enjoyed the second bite of his sandwich, he could have sworn he heard the words "did you read the article on class" coming from the one other table along the deli's front window.

The words shocked him. He stopped chewing. Two females sat at a table together, the mother facing Paul and the daughter's back to him. When he tilted his head, he saw the daughter holding a copy of *The Current Front* opened to his column. It was the daughter, a woman no older than twenty, who posed the question to her mother.

"I can't believe this," he thought, but he listened for the mother's answer as he slipped his own copy of the magazine under his plate.

"I did," she replied with unequivocal chagrin.

"He says he walked into a coffee shop and couldn't believe he saw patrons lying down on the couch and sitting with their feet up on the coffee table with their shoes still on—"

"I mean, get a grip, right?" interjected the mother.

"He said he saw a girl nestled in an armchair with her feet pulled in on the seat, but she had taken her shoes off and was barefoot. *I* do that! The whole idea is to get comfortable or they wouldn't provide that type of furniture in a public coffee shop in the first place, right?"

"Wrong!" thought Paul. "The whole idea might be to get comfortable, but other people use that furniture, too. Sink into the chair, sure. Read a book on the couch, fine. But don't sully the furniture with your bare feet or your shoes. Furthermore, it's not your house! Is there no pride in how you present yourself in public?" He had explained all this in the article.

"Right," her mother agreed firmly. "You know, I've read his column before, and I think he's a little uptight in general. This one was over the top, though."

A what-do-I-have-to-lose attitude accompanied an impulse in Paul to introduce himself and tactfully defend his stance, his "uptight" views, but he mustered the restraint to continue listening.

"I mean, he explains that there's a difference between getting comfortable in public versus getting comfortable in your own house—"

"Finally," thought Paul. She had indeed read that crucial component to understanding his gripe.

"—but who cares?" continued the daughter. "And who cares if someone sat in the same chair you're about to sit in with their shoes off? Unless the person is a total scumbag, it doesn't really matter."

He pushed the pastrami sandwich a few inches toward the middle of the table.

"Yes," thought Paul. "Who cares?"

He gathered his belongings as he heard the mother reiterate, "I told you he's uptight."

CHAPTER 2

After a comfortable flight, Paul arrived in Duluth where his eldest grandson, Mikey, met him for the ride home. In for his fall break from college, Mikey was spending most of his time at home with his family, for he genuinely missed them after a few weeks away. He volunteered readily when the topic of picking up his grandfather from the airport was discussed. He brought along his little brother, Eli, after having picked him up from basketball practice after school. Eli, an eighth grader at Greengate Grade School, took an understated delight in taking the ride to Duluth with the older brother he, too, had come to miss.

Paul threw his suitcase in the trunk and his carry-on in the backseat next to the often smiling but rarely speaking Eli. He greeted his grandsons, and in no time, they were on their way to Saint Catherine's Cove where a busy week awaited him. His wife still weak, he planned to do the grocery shopping tomorrow; tomorrow evening, like every Wednesday evening, he was going to take a walk with his good friend Roy; Thursday, he was being honored with an assembly at the grade school he attended—the grade school his grandchildren were currently attending; he was going to need to find time to rewrite the December issue, as well, if he so chose. But for now, he hoped to enjoy the car ride to Saint Catherine's Cove with the grandson he began to miss more and more after weeks away at a time and the shy younger grandson who shared his smile and kindness always but little else about himself.

"How was New York?" Mikey asked.

"Just the way I left it," his grandfather said, adding a chuckle. After so many trips back and forth, that became his staple response. "The ceremony for Rick was nice, and I treated myself to a pastrami sandwich at the deli across the street from *CF*. Got to take you there some day."

"Did you go in to *CF*?"

"I did stop in, yes." Only with Claribel would he discuss Stephen's proposition. He did not want to broach the topic with his grandsons. "No one in my office yet. It looks abandoned."

"Maybe they're waiting until your last column appears."

"Didn't really think of that."

"I read your November column."

"What did you think?" The question shot out like a jerk reaction, full of longing for a new and honest perspective on it. He was thinking, though, that his grandson had never mentioned reading his column before.

"I liked it." Then he grinned. "I think I still have class."

His grandfather smiled, too, and his shoulders dropped at the prospect of an easy conversation about it. "Anything in particular about it grab you?"

"I liked how you incorporated what Pat, Bill, and I told you about college classes." Mikey was referring to his boyhood pals discussing their first few weeks of college when they all had come in during Labor Day weekend. At the dinner table, they shared with Mikey's siblings, father, and grandparents their overall impressions of the college experience thus far. Mikey and Pat attended the same university, and Bill attended a different one. Pat brought up that he could not believe students showed up to class in their pajamas, as if having rolled out of bed, stepped into slippers, and schlepped across campus to class that way. All three boys agreed they had been shocked by that practice and discussed whether those students should have shown up to class or not if they weren't dressed appropriately.

"'Who determines the standard for what's appropriate to wear to class?' That's what they'll say," Mikey's father had said.

"Some of them don't even brush their hair or their teeth. That's not fair to the rest of us," Pat declared.

"I don't know," Mikey added. "Even if I woke up late one morning, I couldn't imagine running out of the dorm—to class or anywhere—without washing up a little and putting on clothes—like, real clothes—not pajamas."

"What do the girls think of all this?" asked Mikey's grandmother.

All three boys looked at each other. Then Mikey said, "Grandma, some of the girls wear pajamas to class, too."

The conversation had carried on in that way, and Paul, even then, sitting at the dinner table, had been mulling over the ideas to be presented in his column on class. At that point, he had still been brainstorming; he didn't draft and revise his October, November, and December columns until mid-September.

As he set the cruise control on the highway, Mikey continued, "You had been quiet about it at the dinner table, but I guess now we all know where you stand on that issue. The whole world does."

Eli started laughing at the thought of the whole world knowing what his family had been talking about at dinner one evening.

"What you were observing at college—I could tell it bothered you and your friends," Paul said.

"It's like your article said. I guess we just care about those things, and it's not a big deal to everyone else. I mean, the friends I made aren't bad people or anything, but some of them show up to class in rags. I take a shower before even my 7:30 class and put on real clothes."

"Is it just for classes they don't seem to care about dressing up?" his grandfather inquired.

"No! Go anywhere on campus and you'll find it—the library, the labs, the coffee shops—"

"Ah, the coffee shops," said Paul. "Another place I noted in my article."

"It's bad, Grandpa. People curl up on the couch in the Commons and fall asleep—I mean, drool-oozing-out-of-their-mouth-onto-the-couch fall asleep. It's a public couch! Pat and I walked into the library one day, and a kid using the computer for the online card catalogue had his bare foot on the desk with his big toe on the keyboard. Pat said he's going to start bringing bleach wherever he goes. People even take calls during lectures and labs. I try to assume they have a good reason to take them until I hear what they're talking about. It's bad, Grandpa. Some people really don't care about—" he wasn't sure of the word— "about what's appropriate, I guess."

Paul did not respond as he was ruminating amusedly over the bleach comment. Mikey had, over the years, more than amused his grandfather with a comment. He had brought rejoicing to his heart when he earned acceptance into the McGuinty School of Journalism, arguably the most prestigious college for which his university was known. He had brought his grandfather pride not only in his following in his footsteps as a journalist but in his commitment to learning grammar thoroughly and in his attention to developing personal voice and style. Years earlier, though, he had evoked in his grandfather a profound admiration over how stalwartly he had handled his mother's sudden death from a brain aneurism when he was eight years old, a stoicism uncharacteristic of a boy so young. Eli had proven himself a source of joy for Paul, as well, through his pursuit of music. Although the boy enjoyed athletics like basketball and swimming, he had revealed a natural talent for singing, one his teachers and family wished to encourage and develop after having picked up on a distinctiveness to his singing voice, a softness in perfect pitch and tone. Eli joined the church choir and the Greengate Grade School choir in addition to taking up guitar lessons. Despite the propensity for musical endeavors, he comported himself demurely through his natural timidity, always preferring to go unnoticed.

Sitting in the car with his two grandsons, Paul marveled about how good they were, a welcomed diversion from the prospects occupying his thoughts only moments prior. After a silent mile, he said, "I didn't know you read my column."

"I don't usually. Dad told me you were winding down with them, so I started to read them—the last five. Maybe I'll read the rest some day, too. They seem pretty good so far." Mikey grinned again and then hit the accelerator to reset the cruise control at a higher speed.

Mikey dropped off his grandfather by early evening and enjoyed a half-hour visit over a chilled spiced cider with his grandparents while Eli practiced guitar in the study. While Mikey sipped his cider at the kitchen counter, Claribel inquired about the gala honoring Rick Mendel, and Paul animatedly recounted stories from the evening.

"Throughout the evening, fifty different people stood at their table and shared a brief memory of Rick. They passed a mic around. He got fifty memories for fifty years with *Cityscape*."

"Did you give one?" Mikey asked his grandfather.

"Sure I did. I told the one about the prank Rick pulled on me when I first started 'Partly Paul,' the time he convinced me the wrong draft had been published before I had a copy of the magazine to verify. On account of something I had written in that draft, oh, was I panicking! The place got a rise out of it."

"Sounds like a pleasant evening all around," Claribel said. "Rick had a nice evening, and that's the important thing—I mean, after fifty years with *Cityscape*!"

"He did—for the most part, anyway."

"For the most part?" inquired Claribel.

"You won't believe what Rebecca Lewis said when she got the mic—the memory she shared."

"Rebecca Lewis? What was she even doing there?"

"I think Rick invited her as a courtesy."

"I would have graciously declined."

"Not Rebecca Lewis, nor did she graciously make an appearance and then be on her way. She shared a memory about Rick's divorce. Of all things to bring up—his divorce! That was probably the lowest point in his life."

Although Mikey hadn't been born at that time, he had caught wind through references since then to the sordidness of Rick's divorce and was astute enough to realize Rick had had an affair, a known detail in the New York circles.

"Hadn't dragged his name through the mud enough at the time it was going on? She certainly should be thankful to him for the mileage she got out of that scandal," Claribel said. Then she turned to Mikey and added, "She's known to be snide in her articles, and it was comments about Rick's divorce that really established that as her claim to fame."

"Published comments," Paul added. He couldn't help recalling that, two years after Rick's divorce, Paul had stumbled unfortunately upon the knowledge that Rebecca Lewis had taken up romantically with a married man, a restauranteur of whom Paul had recently made the acquaintance. How he wanted to run to Rick Mendel with this tidbit but instead shared the news only with Claribel. Paul kept it under his hat for nearly a year, even after the rumors broke, and when the news finally debuted officially, he never revealed he had known prior.

Claribel wanted to know what Rebecca Lewis had said about Rick's divorce at the gala but refrained from asking in front of Mikey in case it opened too many doors. So she concluded the conversation by saying, "If that was the only hitch, then I'm sure Rick had a nice evening. And I'm glad you did, too."

Paul had asked Claribel to join him at the gala, but she declined on account of her physical weakness. Only two months ago, her cancer had gone into remission, but after such frequent treatments, she still felt exhausted; getting dressed simply to lounge at home still felt like work. Taking a trip to New York did not appeal to her.

Eli's voice, singing accompanying his guitar playing, made its way through the lull in conversation and, although muffled through walls, sounded clear and on tune.

"Those years of choir are paying off," Paul said.

"You know it must be getting dark out when you hear our little nightingale," Mikey joked.

Before Mikey left to round up his little brother, he announced, "I'll take you to the assembly on Thursday morning when I take Eli and Gracie to school." While Eli began eighth grade at Greengate Grade School, their sister Gracie enjoyed junior year at Saint Catherine High School. Gracie could drive, but if Mikey dropped her off at school, he could have the car for the day. In for fall break, he assumed some of his father's responsibilities, including chauffeuring the kids. Paul looked forward to the ride.

When Eli entered the kitchen with his guitar to say good-bye, Mikey teased him about the reason he was practicing: Eli planned to ask Sunrise Walsh to the Halloween Dance at the assembly on Thursday by singing "Here Comes the Sun" to her, one of the boldest moves he had ever made but a safe one on account of knowing that Sunrise would say yes and having practiced the song so much. His grandparents welcomed the plan, hoping it might draw Eli out of his shell and boost his confidence in general. Paul was more excited about hearing his grandson serenade Sunrise than about being the focus of an assembly.

After Mikey and Eli had left, Paul and Claribel sat in the solarium sipping their second cider while the baked whitefish noodle casserole Roy's wife, Marni, had made warmed in the oven. Once Claribel had gleaned the details of Rebecca Lewis's comments at the gala, Paul transitioned to the events of this morning, presenting the phone call from Stephen and the meeting with him at *CF*.

"An apology?" Claribel interrupted Paul's story at least a full minute after he had mentioned the word. "An apology in the December issue? That'll be your last column."

From sitting in the room with the mailbags to the flight back home, Paul had been asking himself if an apology might indeed be the responsible way to handle this, but when his wife said the word, he ruled out the prospect.

"An apology!" he repeated, incredulous.

As many frustrated thoughts and as many angles on how to address her husband surfaced, no words rushed to the tip of her tongue. She sat with the cider in her lap, pulling the glass mug back and forth by its handle, knowing that her husband was beginning to simmer.

"So," she said at last, looking at him in the chair opposite hers. "To rewrite the December column or to keep it as is? That is the question."

Paul did not respond. Unless Claribel suggested otherwise, he was not going to write an apology.

"I'll have to think about this a little more, Paul, because I don't know that one course of action would be any better or any worse than the other right now. I see benefits of both. I can tell that right now you are inclined to steer clear of rewriting the column, and I'm behind that. And if you change your mind, I'm behind that, too."

He knew she would be supportive but wished for more of a push in one direction, and right now, the most comfortable direction was not rewriting the column. Looking at her, trying to ease some guidance from the eyes staring so lovingly back at his, he noticed her eyebrows sinking just barely—the way they do before she cries silently—and the gleam that accompanies her tears appearing in the corners of her eyes. Before the tears formed, she turned her head, and Paul said nothing.

The lull did not last long before Claribel, returning to a more comfortable vexation, spoke.

"You tackle issues that elicit a reaction. It's the nature of the column." The column's title, "Partly Paul," referred to its content, a combination of what was going on in America or elsewhere and what was going on in Paul's head as he reflected on it; once finished with his column, his audience had read what was partly Paul's take on it and partly the real-life situation. "Sometimes the subject matter generates fervid reactions and sometimes your views do—it's been happening this way for years. Like I said, it's the nature of the column."

"That's right. 'Partly Paul.' Thirty-five years of 'Partly Paul.'" He furrowed his brow reflectively. "I never even liked the name 'Partly Paul' for the column, but I went with it because they thought it coincided nicely with the purpose of the magazine." *The Current Front* aimed to keep readers *au courant* on timely issues but encouraged articles that emphasized what readers might struggle or battle with, as on a war front. "Now I publish an article that readers are battling over—maybe battling with themselves over—and I'm asked to offer an apology. I don't understand it."

Claribel looked at her cider and started to laugh as Paul wondered why. She explained, "It's ironic to me. Do you remember when *CF* turned seventy-five—you had been doing 'Partly Paul' for ten years—and the editors met to revamp the magazine—to discuss giving it a new look—and they considered changing the title of your column?"

Paul smiled widely and hung his head, as if embarrassed. The way he smiled was the way his grandson Eli smiled, free but bashful. He knew where she was going with this.

She continued, "They had narrowed it down to three titles and decided to go with something that complemented the title of the magazine. So they went with—" she started laughing too hard to finish.

"So they went with 'Full Frontal with Paul.' I remember." Paul blushed.

"You had to fight to keep them from changing it to that," she said once she caught her breath. "You never liked 'Partly Paul' but found yourself fighting to keep it! They didn't see what was wrong with 'Full Frontal.' They thought it was so edgy and witty, and you—"

"—and I," he completed, still blushing, still unable to look at Claribel, "thought it was so classless."

CHAPTER 3

"I had a quick talk with—be careful with that, Michael!" Paul overheard his daughter Anna saying to his son. He stood at the top of the stairs, listening to his children's muffled conversation in the kitchen. Assuming their parents were sleeping, they spoke with low voices, encouraging Paul's neck to protrude and his foot to take a few more stealthy steps downward. The movement enveloped him in the thick, sweet aroma of apples, a comfort more warming than the early morning sun beginning to fill the house.

"I am being careful," Michael returned.

"He's fine," Pauline said. "Who were you saying you talked with?"

"I was saying I had a quick chat with Father Soplido," Anna continued. "I ran into him on a walk on the promenade by the lighthouse—"

"How do you two always find the time to take walks?" interrupted Michael.

"—and he said he really liked Dad's article on class. He said he might use a line or two from the column in his Sunday homily."

At this, Paul quickly descended the remaining stairs and entered the kitchen. "If he wants to avoid anything being thrown at him, he might want to reconsider."

"Were you listening to us? I didn't even know you were up," said Pauline.

"Don't you eavesdrop on your kids?" Paul asked.

"I love listening to them talk when they don't know I'm listening," Pauline affirmed. "But it's cute when they're little kids. You're listening to full-grown adults."

"Your children are never too old for eavesdropping on them to be enjoyable," Paul said as his children smiled and cringed simultaneously, as they wondered what other conversations he may have overheard without revealing his presence.

Paul stepped to the stove as it was monitored by Michael. Simmering, sliced apples under just-baked pie crusts topped four burners, their flames turned off. While Michael wrapped a dishtowel around his already mitt-clad hand, the girls poured a small kettle of extra apple syrup into an ice tray. While Pauline poured the syrup into the tray, Anna topped off each cube compartment with a splash of milk. The early morning sun was beginning to illuminate their work.

"*Tarte tatin?*" Paul asked, recognizing the scene from Claribel's routine.

"Yes," Anna responded. "Mom said she was going to make one because she was getting the taste for it. So we beat her to it and made one for ourselves, too."

At least once a week, while Claribel was undergoing treatments and recovering from them, and now while her accustomed wellness slowly returned, Michael, Anna, and Pauline came over early, before their own work day began, to wash and fold laundry, to dust and mop, to make a few dishes that would last the next few days. Claribel and Paul both appreciated the effort and the care, but Paul especially enjoyed listening to his children interact—often banter—and share stories about their own children as they worked together to help their parents during a difficult period. Listening to them and witnessing their giving forced the challenges of Claribel's illness to revert temporarily to an unnoticed place, to a place re-established as joy and love.

"I love this recipe," said Pauline.

"Mom got the recipe from Oliver, remember? Oliver's mother used to make it, and when she passed away, he couldn't replicate it. He gave it to Mom, and she makes it as well as his mother did, he says. Even Peony Pilsen is jealous of it."

"That's why we're making extras," added Michael. He explained to his father that they would be leaving two tarts for Paul and Claribel, Anna and Pauline would be splitting one, and Michael would be taking one whole one. A hit with their own children, the treat would not last long in any of their households if they made it half as well as their mother did.

As his sisters pulled up stools to the island and settled in with cups of coffee, Michael glanced over the resting tarts in the pans, looking more like pies than tarts at the moment. "They're not quite ready to flip," he reported.

Everyone in the brightening kitchen turned when they heard the backdoor open. Within moments, Paul's good friend Oliver appeared, exaggerating a sniff of the aroma as his eyes widened.

"Oliver?" announced Paul. "Stopping by pretty early, aren't you?"

"I ran into Anna yesterday, and she told me the Scrivensbys were making Ma's *tarte tatin* this morning," he shared.

"I told him to stop by if he wanted," Anna said, rubbing out of her palm the pain of having peeled many apples. Pauline had rolled the dough.

"It smells as good as I remember." Oliver exaggerated a drawn out, loud sniff again, smiling through the delight of the scent. "I deserve a slice after sticking up for you, Paul. Got into a quibble at the marina with Ernest Hammacher over your column on class."

Paul dropped his head. If his good friend had been sticking up for him, at least he knew on which side of the apparent controversy Oliver stood. "Let's hear it, Oliver."

"I'm making it sound worse than it was—just to get that slice of *tarte tatin*," he chuckled. "But the long and short of it is that Ernest and his wife spotted me and said, 'You're good friends with Paul Scrivensby. You must be a little embarrassed of your friend after an article like that,' and I said, 'Not embarrassed at all.' They couldn't believe I had read it and didn't find it off-putting. I stood up for you, though, Paul."

"What bothered them about it?" asked Pauline before her father could. She had not yet learned of the controversy it had sparked.

"They had issues with what they perceived as a 'condescending' view, but they apparently saw themselves in a behavior you singled out as lacking class. I wonder if they would have taken issue with the article if they hadn't been perpetrators of it themselves."

"Which behavior?" asked Anna.

"The part about the theater and the opera."

Of course Paul knew exactly to what Oliver referred, but he had never witnessed Ernest and his wife doing it. He poured Oliver and himself a cup of coffee while Oliver explained.

"I remember," Oliver continued, directing the comment to Paul's children, "that this really bugged your father. I had met up with him once in Chicago, and your dad, your mother, and I went to the opera for an evening. And it happened again years later when we went to a musical in New York. Here's the issue: right as the show is ending, during the last number—before bows even—a few people get up and leave, hurrying to beat the crowds out. They interrupt—destroy—that final moment of the show that everyone else is caught up in. At the one in New York, the couple right in front of us rose, gathered their coats— one dropped his coat and had to pick it up—and then headed out, and seconds later, another couple in our row shuffled past us to get to the aisle. Killed the whole mood of the final scene! Your father doesn't get rattled that easily, but boy, was he fuming those two nights. I remember them distinctly. Your father is absolutely right."

"They could at least stay to show their appreciation for the performance. That's important to the performers," Anna said.

"Even if they didn't enjoy the show, they could still be respectful enough to acknowledge all the work the performers and crew put in. It's plain rude, otherwise," Michael added.

"What did Ernest have to say about it?" asked Pauline.

"He says, 'We do that to make less of a traffic jam getting out of the parking lot,' and I say, 'You're doing it to beat the traffic jam, not to help everyone else.' He says, 'One less car, along with the others who are doing the same, makes it easier on everyone,' and then he says, 'Scrivensby says class is about thinking of others, and that's exactly what we are doing—so who's to say our behavior isn't classy?' I didn't buy it, but I say, 'Fine, you're saving the masses from a huge traffic jam, but disrupting the end of a show for the bulk of the audience—a paying audience—isn't thinking of others.' He says, 'We pay like everyone else, and we can leave when we want.' So I say, 'You might pay like everyone else, but you don't appreciate art like everyone else, or you would stay to enjoy the final moment and stay to applaud.' 'So now we're *not* classy for *not* applauding,' Ernest's wife says. Boy, I wanted to push them into the lake."

Handing him the cup of coffee, Paul said, "It's not like you to have held yourself back."

"If they were about twenty years younger, I wouldn't have held back."

Everyone chuckled, in part from the comment, but also from how riled Oliver had grown over recounting the exchange.

"Thank-you, Oliver. I appreciate the support," Paul said. "But what you don't know is that at least two mailbags full of reactions like theirs are propped against the wall of my old office in New York. Just saw them for myself. I never imagined this topic would generate so much chatter."

"That explains fearing for Father Soplido quoting you in his homily," said Michael.

"That's the reason, Michael."

"All-righty, I was just popping in," Oliver said, walking to the stove for a closer look. "I have an early morning call. Save me a slice, will you?" He set the coffee down and headed for the backdoor.

"You sure do a lot of favors for someone who's retired," Paul noted.

"You don't ever truly retire, Paul," Oliver responded. "Besides, it's not like my skills suddenly turned off. I'm happy to use them here and there."

"Stop by my house later today," Anna said. "We'll share a slice of ours with you."

They heard Oliver say, "I'll hold you to that!" before the door shut.

"Michael," Anna began, "Mikey told us about Eli asking Sunrise Walsh to the Halloween Dance."

"I like Sunrise," interjected Pauline. "Great parents, too."

"I'd feel much better if Eli crossed girls off his agenda for now," Michael responded with a hint of despondency. "He's too young to add dating to his plate. He should be spending his extra time working on his guitar and voice lessons. And basketball season started."

"And swimming," added Paul.

"He's already so good at that—and getting faster," Michael said. "He's good at everything he does, that kid. You know the coach makes them swim in the lake?"

"I don't like that," commented Anna.

"Helps build up stamina," Michael justified. "I like to think it'll keep him too tired to pursue girls."

"They're just friends," assuaged Anna. "I wouldn't worry too much about it."

"All right, Michael," Pauline said. "I think you're on."

When Oliver had passed the recipe to Claribel and she had started making the *tarte tatin*, Michael, Anna, and Pauline were teenagers. Excited to take on the challenge when his mother lamented doing it, Michael volunteered to flip the apple tart from the pan into the plate; whenever she made it, she called on him for this crucial final step before the light sprinkling of powdered sugar and dollop of *crème fraiche*. All these years later, now an adult with teenage children of his own, Michael was relied on to do the same. Paul watched as his daughters gathered around their brother, who, donning the proper insulation on his hands and arms and the furrow of a serious task on his forehead, placed the first plate over the pan, grasped the two firmly, and flipped. As Anna and Pauline then carefully lifted the pan to maintain the *tarte tatin*'s form, Michael moved on to the next. Paul smiled, enjoying the delight they took in their roles, anticipating the smile it was sure to bring to Claribel's face.

With Claribel's shopping list in hand, plus a few tidbits of his own to buy, Paul grabbed a cart at Bud's, the local grocery store, and began the search for each item. The bigger grocery stores were located outside Saint Catherine's Cove, but this smaller one offered all the essentials the residents of Saint Catherine's needed, including produce from nearby farms, fresh fish from the lake, and run-ins with all the locals one might hope to see as well as all those who, despite one's best efforts, never seem to be avoided.

"They're flying off the shelf," said Sil, the cashier. Periodicals of *The Current Front* variety were not usually showcased in the check-out lanes, but on account of one of Saint Catherine's very own writing for it, it had for years been featured prominently on the top shelf there. Although most of Saint Catherine's subscribed to it, the stacks in the store always depleted quickly. At first, Paul thought the comment referenced the controversy of the column, but upon second thought, he realized that she was noting the pleasant rally over his column's imminent end. He smiled graciously and bowed his head at her before heading for the baking goods aisle.

Peony Pilsen, a stout woman his own age he had known since grade school, examined cupcake wrappers while her granddaughter, Petunia, picked just the right decorative sprinkles. Noticing Paul's cart moving toward them, Peony pulled her cart instinctively closer to ensure enough room to pass even though she had positioned it with this consideration to begin with. As he neared, she realized it was her old friend.

"If it isn't the talk of the town!" she shouted. "Petunia tells me you're being honored at Greengate Grade School. Congratulations!"

Paul blushed as he said, "Thank-you, Pee. Not sure I'd use the word 'honor,' though. Just an assembly where I get to talk about my career."

"Modest as ever. I'm hoping I'm the next Greengate alum to be honored. I want the Home Ec kitchen named after me!" Her jovial inflection invited a smile no matter what she said, and Paul did just that. Her wish reminded Paul of how delicious the cranberry pie she had made for him and Claribel last week tasted. "Petunia, for one, is excited about the assembly. They've been talking about it for weeks in class. I might pop in myself, Paul—maybe stand in the back and listen."

Petunia, a second grader at Greengate, pulled two containers of sprinkles from the shelf and extended them to Paul. "Grandma is helping me make cupcakes for Mommy's birthday tomorrow. I get to decorate them. I didn't have to go to school today so that Grandma can help me bake!"

Facing the girl, Paul crouched next to his cart to see the sprinkles. "Pink and yellow! Those are beautiful colors. Your mommy is sure to like them."

"I know. I'm going to make them so pretty for her!" She placed them in her grandmother's cart and returned her attention to different colors of sprinkles on the shelf.

Peony inched toward Paul as she whispered, "The sprinkles we have at the bakery apparently don't offer enough variety for Petunia, so she had to come here to pick them out." She referred to her family-owned bakery that Paul knew well.

"The grass is always greener. All right, Pee. I'm on a mission for Claribel. Maybe I'll see you at the assembly. Give my best to the family."

"And all my best to yours, as well, and to our dear Claribel. I'm hoping we will see you both at the parlor for ice cream one night soon. And don't get so nervous at the assembly that you say something stupid in front of an entire auditorium of grade schoolers!" She chuckled as Paul passed her in the aisle.

When he turned into the hygiene aisle, he noticed his good friend Roy reaching for shaving cream and gently bumped his cart into him. Roy turned to greet his friend.

"Glad I ran into you," Roy began. "Saves me a call. I have to cancel our walk tonight. My son needs a hand hanging a gutter that fell, so I'm going to stop by after dinner to help him."

"Picking your son over me. I see how it is," Paul said.

"How was New York?"

"It was good. It was nice to be back. Visited a few of my old haunts while I was there."

"Still can't believe you're friends with Rick Mendel. That's like knowing a celebrity!"

"We're good friends, but he and I don't go back as far as you and I. It was nice to see him, though. He had a few of us over for lunch the day after the banquet. Real nice time."

"Did you stop in at *CF*?" But before Paul could answer, Roy added, "I read your November column."

He braced himself despite standing amid the familiarity and the easiness of an old friend. He suspected that, on account of the stigma associated with it, tensing up might accompany every reference to this column, and he did not like that. Reason overtaking him, he relaxed but still asked, "What did you think?"

"Some of your best work. I say that without hesitation. I told my children to make sure they buy a copy just for that column. Really, Paul, some of your best work."

Relieved, he sighed. "Not everyone sees it that way, Roy."

"Who doesn't see it that way?"

Just then, they heard a sort of yelp, and a cart crashed into Paul at such a velocity that, as he moved to dart out of the way, he leapt awkwardly enough to land inside it! The cart came to a halt before striking Roy. All three men froze at the strange sight—Paul in another man's cart full of groceries, his legs and arms hanging over the sides, his mind spinning over what had just happened.

The owner of the cart, a man their age but with considerable more vim in his mien, looked into his cart and said, "Want to get the hell out of my cart, Paul?"

When Paul realized it was Dr. Drew, he flailed to get a grip and to find his footing and then propelled himself from the cart with Roy's help.

"I should have known," Paul said, shaking his head. He was not particularly amused but not offended either. He had known Dr. Drew, one of few family practice doctors in Saint Catherine's Cove, for as long as he had known Roy, although he had always been much closer friends with Roy. All three, along with Peony Pilsen and plenty of others, grew up together, having attended Greengate Grade School and Saint Catherine of Siena High School.

"What are you two ladies doing?" he asked as he glanced at the contents of the nearest shelves. "Ah, I see. Going to shave each other's—" and Paul swung a hand over Dr. Drew's mouth. Although muffled, the word "legs" sounded.

"What the hell is your problem, Paul? I shouldn't have called you two 'ladies.' Nothing ladylike about you. You're a couple of hussies."

"Would you knock it off?" said Roy.

"What for?" he asked.

Paul checked either side of them for patrons. "Because you're in public! And Peony Pilsen is in the next aisle!"

"Peony Pilsen can kiss my—" and Paul swung a hand over Dr. Drew's mouth and again wasn't quite fast enough.

"What's your problem, Drew? She's with her granddaughter."

The smile never leaving his face, Dr. Drew rolled his eyes. "Her granddaughter? On a Wednesday? What, it's okay for her to teach her granddaughter to ditch school, but she can't hear a few spicy words that add a little kick to any conversation? You should start sprinkling a few in your column, Paul. Might liven it up a little."

Both Paul and Roy laughed at Dr. Drew's ribbing but still stood at the ready in case he launched another expletive or two. Paul and Roy sometimes felt uncomfortable with him when not in a private setting among friends.

"In fact, Paul, I read your November column already."

"Here we go," thought Paul.

"I heard a few of my patients talking about it in the waiting room yesterday, so I read it last night—"

"Why don't you retire already?" Roy interjected.

"—and I want you to know that I don't give a flying—well, let me censor myself since I'm in the presence of polite huss—company. I don't give a flying—" and he said the word.

"I thought you said you were censoring yourself!" Paul said.

"I did censor myself. Anyway, I don't give—a flying fig—about molding myself to your idea of class or—"

"Really, Drew? I would never have guessed," said Roy.

"If class is not swearing in front of anyone I damn well feel like swearing in front of, then I don't want any part of it."

"Of course you wouldn't, Drew. When have you cared about doing anything you didn't want to do? Forget that some ears might find it unpleasant. Forget that children could be influenced by it. Swear away in any company you want and don't care one iota about anyone else." Pointed as Paul's words were, they came off as banter and were received as such by one with whom he went back so far.

"I'll tell you this, ladies," Dr. Drew continued. "When I don't hold back, people like me more. When I pickle my conversation with some tangy words, people see me as fun. I like being seen as a fun guy. I definitely like it more than being uptight."

Roy looked at Paul and dryly, decisively declared, "Despite who he offends, there's no denying he's fun to be around."

Paul had to concur. "The life of every party—always good for a few laughs." Well, sometimes, anyway.

Dr. Drew pushed his cart past the others as he said, "Thought you'd see things my way, ladies. Now let me go ram my cart into Peony Pilsen and berate her for teaching our young ones to ditch school." Paul and Roy shook their heads as Dr. Drew passed out of sight. From the next aisle, they heard him shout to them, "Have fun pulling the poles out of each other's—" and the expletive was followed by several gasps from nearby patrons.

CHAPTER 4

Claribel had been sleeping in later the past few months, so Paul was used to breakfasting alone or holding out until she was up. This morning, he sat at the kitchen counter finishing his bowl of oatmeal as he awaited Mikey's arrival. His grandson was going to chauffeur him to the assembly at Greengate Grade School that morning.

When Claribel entered the kitchen with an energy he had not seen in a while, he could not speak. Had he wanted to, Claribel would not have let him, for she was all a-chatter.

"Today's the big day!" she said before Paul saw her. "When's the last time you've been to Greengate? Eli's Christmas pageant last winter? I wonder if they'll let you see the classrooms. They can't have changed much since our kids attended."

She talked while preparing herself a bowl of oatmeal from what Paul had left on the range. Paul always made enough breakfast for two when he woke up before her, as she had always done for him before the cancer. The aroma of cinnamon invigorated the room—and him—as she ladled the oatmeal from the pot to her bowl. A combination of happiness and wonder characterized Paul's expression as he watched her, listened to her. Registering such marked energy a good sign, he hadn't seen this Claribel this early in the morning in months.

"You sure you don't want to join me?" he asked her, the hope in his voice unmasked.

She stopped to talk directly to him. "I do want to join you, but not this morning. I'll be cheering for you from home, Paul. You know that."

"I know that," he affirmed, and then watched as she resumed adding slivered almonds to her oatmeal, accenting the cinnamon with a fainter but pleasant fragrance.

"How about the column, Paul? Given any more thought to what you're going to do?"

"Honestly, I'm still not inclined to issue an apology in the December issue. I just can't bring myself to do it. I can't find a reason to do it. Yet sometimes, I think if I read all the letters, maybe I might change my mind." He sighed while she poured herself coffee. "I guess I still don't know."

"Your time is almost up—" and this strange wording resonated with both of them, suspending them in a tension, before she continued with her thought— "and you won't need to think about it anymore. I mean, once you reach the deadline and that issue is printed, it will be done. That day can't come soon enough, can it?"

Paul did not respond. The writer in him interpreted a metaphor in her words, a metaphor for herself, and he did not want to answer.

"Ready?" Mikey asked. His voice was accompanied by the sound of the door opening, footsteps, and Eli and Gracie's banter about Halloween costumes. Paul and Claribel had not heard the car pull up.

"Let me grab my jacket," Paul responded. He brought his coffee mug and empty bowl to the sink just as Claribel made a place for herself at the counter. All three grandchildren kissed their grandmother while Paul was out of the room grabbing his jacket, and after Paul kissed Claribel himself, they parted, loaded the car, and headed for Greengate.

After dropping off Gracie at Saint Catherine High School, Mikey elicited from Eli that he was nervous to ask Sunrise Walsh to the Halloween dance in front of the whole school. He at least basked in the consolation that he and Sunrise had discussed it in advance and, as they had been friends since first grade, were relieved to go as friends with each other. With this in mind, the stakes lowered for Eli. She did not, however, know he was going to ask her to the dance in front of the entire school with a song. A good friend, he really wanted to make her day and somehow was able to set aside his shyness in order to achieve this. Paul recognized himself in Eli and tried to pinpoint when he, too, had stepped out of his shyness. When he was Eli's age, most of the children who grew up to be his closest and longest-lasting friends were but easy acquaintances, for he had solidified true friendships with them after they had begun high school. Except for Peony, who, circumstances necessitated, had lived with his family for a month when she and Paul were ten years old, most of his other long-lasting friendships involved at this young age hours upon hours of playing, not so much developing that deeper knowledge and appreciation of the other that accompany teenage years. A glance into the backseat to wish Eli good-luck was received by a bashful smile from his grandson and a quick turn of the head out the window.

When they arrived at Greengate, the kids bolted for their homeroom as they normally did before the first bell, and Mikey and Paul remained at the front office. Just opposite the front office was the foyer to the auditorium in which the assembly was scheduled to take place. After a short wait, Lucretia Willows, the school librarian and old friend of Paul, arrived to escort him to the auditorium. Lucretia had devised the idea to bring Paul to the school and took the reins on organizing the event once she had easily gained the necessary approval.

"Paul!" she exclaimed and then hugged him. "Right this way." She was always all-business, wasting no time to lead him into the auditorium and onto the stage. Mikey followed, unsure if he should accompany them to the stage or lag behind to find a place in the last row of the house. He decided to remain behind, at which point Mrs. Willows said, "Also glad to see you, Mikey! I hope we prepared you well for college, dear."

Lucretia led Paul to one of several chairs arranged in the middle of the small stage, but he did not sit as she rattled off the agenda for the morning. "We have ten minutes before the students head down. The bell hasn't even rung yet. They will report to homeroom, teachers will take attendance, and within the first five minutes of class, they will assemble here. Once they're in, Principal Hines will greet the students and introduce me. Then I will introduce you. You can address the students, and your address will be followed by a question and answer session. After that, your grandson will offer a closing, and Principal Hines will dismiss the students. As we discussed, try to keep your address to no more than twenty minutes. Questions shouldn't take more than ten minutes. Any questions?"

"No, Lucretia. Sounds good."

She sighed, and with a noticeably different tone said, "Good. Straightforward as can be. Now, how's Claribel?"

"Doing much better. Still a little tired but in high spirits."

"Good! I've been praying for her. And how about retirement? You're amongst the first of us, Paul. I'm giving myself one more year." As if second-guessing herself, she continued, "I don't know. Sometimes I think about staying a few more years, but the older I get, the more I speak my mind. That gets me thinking that maybe it *is* best I retire next year or I'll be getting myself into trouble. I say what I think nowadays, and if that's not bad enough, I don't always bother to cushion it." She placed a finger on her closed lips as they formed a smile. "Retirement, Paul. How is it?"

"It hasn't sunk in yet, Lu. I can't offer much yet, but I know it feels good to have—time."

"'Feels good to have time.' That sounds so promising, Paul."

Principal Hines and her secretary Mrs. Janes entered the auditorium, followed by Mr. Bevel, the industrial arts teacher, all oblivious to Mikey sitting in the last row. Principal Hines, a portly woman in her fifties, wore a pale blue, tailored suit while Mrs. Janes, of similar stature in her early thirties, donned stretch pants and a long, purple sweater. Wearing jeans and a sweater,

Mr. Bevel was the hip, young teacher, no older than twenty-five, who always tried a little too hard to be the students' favorite; he was placed in charge of the auditorium, from building sets for the drama club to maintaining the curtains' cleanliness and functionality, from operating the lights and sound to organizing the stage for assemblies and events. They spotted Paul and advanced to greet him. Before they arrived, they overheard Lucretia say, "Wink, wink, Paul, but I'll have you know, I always use Great-Grandma's fine china for nice occasions. No paper plates for me on the holidays, and I host the big ones!"

"Ah, the November column on class," said Principal Hines. She, Mrs. Janes, and Mr. Bevel shook hands with Paul and then headed to the podium positioned stage right. Mr. Bevel raised the mic and flicked the switch. As she paged through a binder on top of it, Principal Hines continued, "I have to say, Mr. Scrivensby, I enjoyed the column. Dressing up for a nice occasion is to this day required in my household, even for my kids who have moved out."

As Principal Hines rattled off occasions requiring one's nicer apparel, Paul noticed Mrs. Janes and Mr. Bevel rolling their eyes upon making eye contact with each other. "Not fans," Paul thought before giving Principal Hines his full attention.

Taking the binder in her hands, the principal continued, "I'm not just talking about events out of the house. I mean the events I host at home, too!" The topic seemed to rile her.

Not to be outdone, Lucretia provided anecdote. "What drives me up a wall is the 'nice jeans' fad." Principal Hines scoffed in agreement. Mrs. Janes and Mr. Bevel crossed their arms in unison, clearly put off. Lucretia tilted her lean torso to the side and placed a bony fist on her hip as she continued with what she meant. "'Why are you wearing jeans?' I ask my granddaughter's boyfriend. 'We're going to Mass!' I say. 'But these are nice jeans,' he says. 'Nice jeans'? They're *jeans*, sweetheart! Wear your 'nice jeans' to a nice bar, but not to church!"

Principal Hines sighed in frustration, shaking the binder in her hand. Then, affectedly collecting herself, she carefully set the binder on the podium. When she turned to do this, she noticed the demeanor of her two employees. "What are you two pouting about?"

They looked at each other and did not respond.

"Well, what are you two pouting about?" she asked again, her voice evincing a hint of anger.

Paul chimed in, "I think they don't agree with your stance on how to dress for certain occasions. I imagine they don't agree with my thoughts in the column."

Lucretia Willows and Principal Hines turned slowly toward the sulky pair standing next to the stage curtains and glared at them.

"Did you read Mr. Scrivensby's column?" asked the principal.

As if caught not having done his homework, Mr. Bevel replied, "No," shakily as Mrs. Janes replied more firmly, "Yes, I did. I read it on the toilet last night. I knew you'd be coming today."

"And you don't agree with him?" asked the principal.

When neither responded, Paul said, "And it's perfectly fine that neither agrees. I presented my views—one man's views—on the topic, but that doesn't mean there isn't room for plenty other views—"

"Fine! I don't agree!" said Mrs. Janes, as if Paul were giving her the green light to counter.

"And I didn't read it, but I don't agree either," said Mr. Bevel.

"So you don't dress nicely at your family parties on Easter or Thanks-Giving?"

"Thanks-Giving? We go out and play football all morning and get home just in time for dinner. Heck, sometimes we're even late! We don't have time to shower and change," said Mr. Bevel, his arms uncrossed now and gesticulating.

"And we're all watching football or movies anyway," said Mrs. Janes. "What do you gotta get all dressed up for to do that?"

Lucretia, incredulous, asked, "But what about the church holidays that begin or end with a feast at home? What about Christmas? You need to wear your church clothes anyway!"

Principal Hines could not get past the football playing and before either could respond to Lucretia, she blurted out, "What if you smell after playing football all morning? How do you sit down with your family, sweaty and dirty and smelly, and subject them to that?"

Mrs. Janes immediately retorted with, "It's family! Who cares?"

Too familiar with that catch-all and growing more irked by that attitude, Paul still tried to pacify the mounting tension on the stage, especially when he noticed students and teachers entering the auditorium. As teachers ushered the first students into their rows, Paul clasped his hands gently and offered, "We can't confuse class with customs. Some of us simply have different family customs, and—"

Lucretia, oblivious to Paul's attempt to placate the situation, turned to Mrs. Janes and said, "She is your boss, you know. You could address her a little more respectfully." She raised her chin when she said this, which Mrs. Janes found particularly bothersome.

"She needs to show respect to earn it!" responded Mrs. Janes, directing her words to Principal Hines.

Principal Hines's eyes bulged, and after a shocked pause, she whispered, "How do you talk to your boss like that?"

"Because she has no class," whispered Lucretia, inserting her raised chin between the two of them.

As more students filled the rows of the auditorium, Paul grew more anxious about the scene on stage. "Perhaps we can continue this discussion after the assembly. The children are almost—"

"I'm sorry," Mrs. Janes said, although her face had reddened with ire. "I should not have said that." Directing her attention to Lucretia, she said, "And you're not helping."

Lucretia inhaled deeply. She looked more at Paul than at the others and said, "I should not have said that, either. I, too, apologize." Paul smiled, a sanguine air overtaking him as he felt a calm on the horizon, but his relief was short-lived. Lucretia added, "This started out as a compliment to Paul on his article. I simply wished to tell him that I enjoyed his latest column, and that I insist on using my great-grandmother's fine china for nice dinner parties and holidays."

"What is the big deal about which plates you use?" Mrs. Janes, heated again, reverted to the debate that had landed them at each other's throats to begin with. "Fine china just isn't practical!"

"Paper plates work just fine!" Mr. Bevel contributed. "And if you want to use the real thing, why fuss over china you have to be careful with? Use the everyday plates and bowls. It's just like she said—they're more practical."

"Hi, Mr. Bevel!" a group of fifth graders shouted as they found their seats. Mr. Bevel's scowl transformed into a bright smile as he absorbed the attention and waved at the kids.

Although she was whispering on account of the children, Lucretia's voice revealed a returning rancor when she said, "Since when is practicality the prized virtue? Practicality at the expense of elegance? Practicality at the expense of tradition?"

As if she had had it with Mrs. Janes and Mr. Bevel, Principal Hines declared, "There's a place for practicality, but what does neglecting decorum and tradition teach the children?" Her question had grown so loud by the last word that most of the children in the nearly filled auditorium stopped chatting and stared at her, scared.

The sudden silence in the auditorium served as a prompt for all on stage to halt. Lucretia and Mrs. Janes looked down, Principal Hines stepped back, Paul sighed, and Mr. Bevel continued waving to students. Then Lucretia whispered, "Let's find our places so we can begin."

Mr. Bevel and Mrs. Janes stepped into the wings while Paul and Lucretia took their seats on stage. Principal Hines stood at the podium and tapped the mic twice.

Mikey still sat in the back near the auditorium entrance, noticing his cousin Henry, Aunt Anna's son, among the fifth graders. His cousins Hannah and Paulie, Aunt Pauline's twins, sat next to Peony's granddaughter, Petunia, among the second graders.

From his seat, Paul scanned the house for his grandchildren, as well. At last, he caught sight of Eli entering the auditorium. As the other eighth graders found seats in the last few rows, Eli drifted from the class to sit in a reserved seat in the front row so that he could offer the closing speech. As Eli, guitar in hand, passed teachers standing in the aisles, Sunrise, too, drifted from the other eighth graders and rushed toward him. Paul could see from the stage that consternation marked her countenance and thought he saw her hands shaking as she faced her palms outward, flat, to avoid running into anyone in her hurry. Chatter had resumed, mostly from the eighth graders just entering, and Paul saw Sunrise's lips call Eli's name. He was in the front row already, and as she headed down the aisle to reach him, a teacher intercepted her and directed her back to the eighth grade rows. Paul saw that Sunrise persisted before acquiescing to the teacher's directive. Her forlorn trek to the back of the auditorium was accompanied by several aggrieved glances at Eli, who did not seem to grasp an import to her attempt to reach him.

Distracted by Eli and Sunrise, Paul failed to notice Petunia Krizman slip from her row and ascend the side staircase to the stage. Stepping in front of his view of the school children, Petunia presented Paul with a beautifully decorated box. Surprised, he smiled and accepted the box from Petunia into his hands.

"What's this, Petunia?" he asked her sweetly.

"Open it!" she said, and then swung her arms behind her back, clasped her hands, and swayed.

Paul untied the thick, purple ribbon and lifted the top of the box to find a tantalizing cupcake inside, one with vanilla frosting decorated meticulously with pink and yellow sprinkles in the shape of a pencil. He could tell each sprinkle had been placed deliberately and with much attention to form the pencil. He could tell she had given much thought about the image with which she chose to decorate it and appreciated the connection to his writing. She was beaming with gladness to have given this gift to him.

"It's a cupcake," Petunia said, still swaying. "Grandma and I made you one while we were making them for Mommy's birthday. I decorated it all by myself!"

"And you did a beautiful job!" He looked into the full house and saw Peony Pilsen standing in the doorway near Mikey. Amid whispers and shushes, she waved when they made eye contact, smiling at the moment between Paul and her granddaughter.

"Grandma decorated the box," Petunia shared.

"The box is beautiful, too! Thank-you, Petunia. This is wonderful." He hugged the girl as Lucretia took the cupcake from him, herself heart-warmed by the deed. By the time Petunia ran to her row, all the students were seated and quiet, awaiting the greeting from Principal Hines.

"Good-morning and welcome," began Principal Hines, and when the student body greeted her in turn as they had been taught, she continued with a few introductory words, making sure she thanked both Paul and Mrs. Lucretia Willows for allowing this event to take place. Once she had reminded the students to be on their best behavior, she called Mrs. Willows to the podium.

Lucretia, greeted by a quick applause, spoke about her friendship with Paul that had begun at Greengate Grade School many years before. Peony laughed from the back as Lucretia recounted the time shy little Paulie Scrivensby got dared to slide down the banister between the first and second floor, lost momentum halfway down, and, stuck in his trek, toppled sideways off the railing into Roy Palomer and Peony Babic's arms; they had positioned themselves for his rescue and were caught by Principal Thompson with a shaking Paulie in their arms. The principal gave all three detentions, but Drew Slate and Oliver Montgomery, the ones who had dared him, got off scot free as their complicity could not be proven. Mikey and Eli especially enjoyed this tale as they had never heard it. Then Lucretia rattled off his accomplishments throughout his career as a writer. Finally, she called Paul Scrivensby to the podium, where, after hugging his old friend, he found himself standing before the student body.

Perhaps it was the nerves of standing before a group of children—among them, his own descendants; perhaps it was knowing that he, years ago, had sat in those very seats and how much time had elapsed since those years, how much had changed in those years, how far he had come; perhaps it was seeing row upon row of the children's young faces and reminiscing about his own youth that finally stirred thoughts about his retirement. He—was—retired—and it finally hit him. He no longer had work to report to, Claribel survived the cancer, they planned to spend their days together, and it finally hit him—these will be *his* days. Claribel survived. But—how many days will he have with her, and how will he spend them?

The thoughts crossed his mind in the blink of an eye as they sometimes can. Intellectual as they were, they seemed to take the form more of a feeling that overwhelmed him than a string of thoughts. A quick survey of the audience called attention to the wide-eyed expectancy of his grandchildren—Mikey, Eli, Henry, Hannah, Paulie—all eager to hear their grandfather talk. Eli's wide smile finally pulled Paul from his musings to the business at hand.

"Good-morning, Greengate!" he said. They greeted him as they had Principal Hines, and then Paul continued, "Thank-you for welcoming me back today! I'm going to tell you a few stories about growing up here in Saint Catherine's Cove and my life as a writer. Are you interested in hearing those stories?"

In unison, especially the younger students shouted, "Yes!"

"Good! Then let me start with English classes at Greengate!" He talked about grammar and composition skills and their importance to communicating with clarity, and what a good job Greengate Grade School and Saint Catherine High School did with those. He took them through a typical workday while working for the paper in Minnesota and did the same with his early posts at *The Current Front*. He offered a few notes on how the magazine operated and his role as columnist—the search for topics, drafting, edits, and meeting deadlines. He concluded with encouragement to any students who wanted to write for the rest of their lives. And he completed his address within the twenty-minute parameter to a loud applause. His connection to families in the town and his familiarity with Saint Catherine's and Greengate helped him relate to the youngsters, as did his pleasant mien, so they received his presence and words warmly.

He returned to his seat so that Lucretia could field questions from the podium. Every student had prepared for Paul's visit in part by writing a question for him based on what they had learned in class. Mrs. Janes handed Lucretia a bag from which she would draw three names. Those students would be asked to read their question to Paul.

The first and second graders inched up in their seats to watch as Lucretia dug her hand into the brown paper bag, wondering anxiously if their name might be called. The older students, just as hopeful, tried not to show it.

"From Mrs. Peters's fifth grade class, we have Samantha Carlisle!"

Samantha stood and looked at an index card. Reading, she asked, "You retired from *The Current Front* after forty-five years. Why didn't you wait until your fiftieth year to retire?"

"Good question," Paul said, sitting on the stage but leaning toward the audience. "I thought about waiting another five years, but you see, as some of you know, my wife became ill, and I realized I wanted to spend as much time with her as I could without worrying about the deadlines and the trips to New York. And my grandchildren are getting older, and I wanted to spend more time with them, too. So I thought, 'I don't need a special milestone year. I'm going to retire now.'"

The teachers began the applause after his answer, and the student body followed suit. Then Lucretia drew another name.

"From Mrs. Mertz's third grade class, we have Eleanor Rowling!"

Eleanor stood and looked at her index card with the large, hand-written letters. Reading, she asked, "Did you want to write for *The Current Front* when you were in third grade? Will you still write when you retire?"

"That's two questions," Paul joked, eliciting soft laughter. "I honestly had not heard of *The Current Front* when I was in third grade. But when I was in fifth grade, I knew I wanted to be a writer. And yes, I will keep writing now that I have retired—" and, he thought, "I may have to if I follow through with this apology"— "but it will be freelance work, and maybe, just maybe, I'll write a book."

A short applause followed this answer as Lucretia pulled the last name. "From Mrs. Henkel's seventh grade class, we have Peter Unterbrink!"

When Peter Unterbrink rose, a flurry of grins and snickers trailed. A sneaky smile accompanied him as he looked at his index card and read, "I will be asking a question I heard my teacher Mrs. Henkel ask under her breath in class yesterday." Paul had no idea who Mrs. Henkel was but easily spotted her when half the auditorium turned toward her standing in the side aisle, flushed if not horrified. "Mrs. Henkel would like to know why you think it's so important to impress others by showing off how much class you have."

While the students who understood Peter's rascality snickered away, the teachers reacted with shock. Principal Hines placed her hands over her mouth in embarrassment. Mrs. Willows, on the other hand, took issue with Mrs. Henkel's remark at all, let alone her uttering it in front of the students, and grimaced from the podium.

Paul forced a chuckle and decided to try to make light of the situation. "You may have just landed yourself in hot water with Mrs. Henkel, Peter."

Some of the students laughed, but Peter, transitioning from furtive to temerarious, said, "I told my parents what she said at the dinner table last night, and they said she missed the point." He glanced brazenly at Mrs. Henkel, her face in her hand. She pulled her hand away and looked at Lucretia, Mrs. Hines, Paul, anyone for a lifeline.

"Well, okay, Peter," Paul stammered, deciding that quickly and politely addressing it and then moving on might spare Mrs. Henkel any more embarrassment. "Class has to do with taking a healthy pride in what you do so as to present something special for others, so as to consider how others might feel, so as to try to ensure others' happiness. I can't speak for Mrs. Henkel and how she interpreted it, but my point was that class is about *caring*, not impressing."

"And had Mrs. Henkel read the article with any attention," Lucretia said into the mic, "she surely would have seen that Mr. Scrivensby had spelled that out. He even illustrated his point with the example about those who do not use fine china for guests even though it would contribute a touch of elegance, about those who have done away with ceremony even though it would contribute a touch of honor for the guests and the occasion, about those who no longer decorate or even tidy up and dust before guests arrive even though it would contribute a more aesthetic and pleasant environment for them."

Mrs. Janes stepped onto the stage from the wings as she said, "Now, Lucretia, you're doing it again! You're not helping! You're making a difficult situation worse!"

"I am doing no such thing. I am fostering intellectual discussion!"

"Here's intellectual discussion for you! I don't clean my house before my guests come; I clean it afterwards. They walk all over the floors. They touch the furniture. What's the point if they're going to make it dirty again seconds after you clean it?"

Principal Hines stood now, herself enervated, and said, "So you neither wish to impress *nor care* about your guests? That's—lovely."

At her boiling point, Mrs. Janes blurted out, "All this talk about class is mumbo-jumbo!"

"My parents said the ones who are quick to dismiss the importance of class are usually the ones who don't have any!" shouted Peter to Mrs. Janes, his note followed by awestruck buzz from his peers.

"Do you have a single original thought?" shouted Mrs. Janes back to Peter. "Mrs. Henkel's question—your parents' thoughts—what about you?"

"It doesn't matter where it comes from," said Lucretia into the mic. "His views—their views—are correct!"

"Will somebody turn that microphone off!" shouted Mrs. Henkel, finally able to speak.

Mr. Bevel rushed from behind stage to the mic and flicked the switch off. When the students saw him, they called his name, so he smiled and waved, inadvertently flicking the switch back on in the motion. He fumbled to turn the mic off again.

"You're so quick to judge who's classy and who's not!" shouted Mrs. Janes to Lucretia. "Is it classy to be this judgmental? Who the hell are you to call any of us unclassy?"

Lucretia sauntered in front of the podium coyly—no need for a mic—before saying, "Me calling you unclassy? Me, Peter Unterbrink, Peter Unterbrink's parents—it makes no difference. Why do you care so much about being called unclassy *if you don't care about class?*" Although Mrs. Janes stood behind her on the stage, Lucretia looked into the audience at no one in particular, crossed her arms in satisfaction, and smiled.

"Well said, Mrs. Willows." said Peter, and then to Mrs. Janes, "Isn't it just mumbo-jumbo?"

"Will you sit down already?" admonished Mrs. Henkel from the aisle.

Paul couldn't believe what was happening—the students looking back and forth from speaker to speaker, reacting to the repartee and the indignation behind it, whispering and gasping; the school personnel losing any sense of restraint in their effort to defend their stance; himself unsure if he should take a side, chime in with his views, put a stop to the banter growing more and more caustic. Then he noticed Petunia Krizman, Peony

Pilsen's gift-giving granddaughter. She sat in her row twirling her long, brown hair with a finger, swaying in the cushiony auditorium seat, oblivious to the debate and the rancor.

"Excuse me," Paul said. "Excuse me." He stood at his seat on the stage and everyone, perhaps out of deference for the guest of honor, hushed. "I don't mean to single anyone out—" and right then, assuming the comment referred to her, deflecting pending ignominy, Mrs. Henkel burst into tears and ran out of the auditorium. "Sorry about that," Paul said. "I don't mean to embarrass anyone, but would Petunia Krizman please come to the stage?"

Curious as they were, the students remained quiet as Petunia blithely sidled through her row to the aisle and onto the stage. Peony, curious herself, took two steps down the aisle toward the stage. Even Peter Unterbrink finally sat. When Petunia arrived before him, Paul reached for the box with the cupcake in it.

Holding it before her, he asked the little girl, "Petunia, what happens when you eat a cupcake?"

"What happens?" she repeated. "You chew it and it goes into your tummy."

"That's right! And it looks yucky when you chew it, right?" Petunia smiled. "Yes! Yucky!"

"But it tastes so good it doesn't matter that it looks yucky when you chew it, right?"

Petunia clasped her hands behind her back, started swaying, and then nodded in agreement.

"Petunia, if we're just going to chew it up and swallow it and let it go into our tummy, then why did you take the time to decorate it so nicely?"

"Because I like decorating cupcakes. And I wanted it to be extra nice for you! Yours has a pencil because you are a writer."

"So it was about making it more special for me." Then he turned toward the house. "And Peony, why did you put the cupcake in a nice box, decorate it with lace and fabric, and tie it so perfectly with a ribbon? I'm going to ruin your beautiful work when I open it anyway, right? Wouldn't it have done just to give me a cupcake in tinfoil?"

Catching on, Peony jovially said, loudly for all the kids to hear, "A cupcake in tinfoil would have been a nice gesture, yes, but I take pride in everything I do. I take pride in making a delicious cupcake, and I take pride in decorating it, and I take pride in packaging it beautifully—because I want to be sure you enjoy it."

Then Paul addressed anyone willing to hear. "Petunia didn't have to take the time to decorate this cupcake down to the detail. She did it for me. Peony Pilsen didn't have to bother with putting it in this decorative box. But she did it for me. That's classy, kids. Class isn't about trying to impress others. Class is about being good to others—by giving them your best."

"Your best behavior," thought Mikey.

"Your best effort," thought Peony.

"Your best china," thought Lucretia.

The message settled in minds, in hearts, wherever it needed to. For some, it was swiped at and flung away. For others, it sunk softly into a comfortable spot. As the listeners allowed it to register, Mikey, from his humble seat in the back, began clapping, and within seconds, the entire student body was applauding.

Principal Hines stepped to the podium, flicked the switch on, and called Eli Scrivensby to the stage to make the closing. When Eli arrived on stage behind the podium, the applause recommenced for him.

Paul and the others returned to their positions on or off the stage, and Petunia ran to her grandmother in the aisle. Eli leaned his guitar against the podium, unfolded a piece of paper from his pocket, and smiled brightly at this grandfather.

"On behalf of Greengate Grade School," he said, "I would like to thank you for talking to us today. To honor your nationally recognized achievement of writing for *The Current Front* for forty-five years as well as your willingness to give back to your old grade school, Greengate will be framing and hanging in the auditorium foyer the first and last issues of *The Current Front* that your column, 'Partly Paul,' appeared in."

Mrs. Janes and Mr. Bevel stepped onto stage, both still miffed, the former holding a framed copy of the issue of *The Current Front* in which Paul's first column appeared, the latter holding an empty frame. While everyone clapped, Paul speculated about which version of December's final column would be "immortalized" in the Greengate display. Several times, he said, "Thank-you," as the applause subsided.

"Paul Scrivensby," continued Eli, "has always been a role model to the Saint Catherine's Cove community and has been a role model to my brother and sister, my cousins, and me. To everyone else, he is 'Paul' or 'Mr. Scrivensby,' but we get to call him 'Grandpa.' Thanks, Grandpa, for visiting our school today and for being the best grandpa we could ever want."

He had lived to enjoy many moments throughout the hours and days and weeks—his marriage, the birth of his children and grandchildren, word of Claribel's remission—but he sometimes wondered why he survived this long. Now he knew. He had, like this moment so full of pride in his grandson and joy in the knowledge of being loved, more moments to enjoy. The pride, the joy, the love overpowered him, and his throat tightened as his eyes fogged.

Some of the teachers murmured sweetly while the student body applauded again. Eli looked at Mrs. Hines for confirmation that he could move ahead with his plan, and when she nodded her approval, he reached for his guitar.

More collected, Paul noticed this exchange and looked for Mikey in the last row, hoping to make eye contact in order to relish in their prior knowing of the bold event to come. But Mikey's attention had drifted elsewhere. His brother's fellow eighth graders in the rows in front of him watched as Eli reached for his guitar and burst into whispered chatter.

"Did you hear Eli is asking Sunrise Walsh to the dance from the stage?" one boy said.

"Yeah! But Charlie McGregor just asked her on the way to the auditorium!" replied another.

"I know! Eli's going to sing or something, but he doesn't know yet!"

Several snippets of chatter revealed the same information: Charlie McGregor had just asked Sunrise Walsh to the dance before the assembly. Mikey reeled and reddened and—froze—immobile in his seat except for his heart, which felt as if it were retracting into his chest.

"Could Sunrise Walsh please come to the stage?" Eli asked in his characteristic, timid way.

Sunrise rose, one hand over her mouth, realizing Eli was going to ask her, of all times and in all places, in public. She looked at the ceiling and sighed, and then made her way down the aisle toward the stage.

Mikey could hear whispered phrases repeated amongst nearby eighth graders—"Eli Scrivensby"—"she was just asked"—"so awkward"—"he doesn't know yet"—"Sunrise Walsh"—"he's going to sing to her"—"Charlie McGregor just asked her"—and he unfroze at last to see his little brother, flushed already, stepping around the podium. His grandfather rested his hands on his knees, smiling in anticipation. Mikey shot up and bolted toward the far side aisle; he had to warn Eli.

As Sunrise stepped onto the stage, herself ruddy but still beautiful, still composed somehow, she said softly, "Eli, wait," but he had become too absorbed in what he was about to do to hear. The pained expression on her face alerted Paul that something might be amiss, and seeing Mikey soar down the side aisle confirmed his assumption.

Within seconds, Sunrise had called Eli's name, Mikey had arrived at the foot of the podium and stage-whispered his brother's name, and Eli—had begun playing the guitar. Seconds later, he was serenading her with the opening words to The Beatles' "Here Comes the Sun," gaining confidence on each line, glancing at her from time to time, assuming her blushing stemmed from his playful embarrassment of her. When he arrived at the first refrain, some of the students joined in. And something about the energy and the singing started to shift, especially for Eli, from agitation to invigoration, an energy that affected everyone, even the teachers. The sung lyrics paralleled the new feeling in the room as cheerful, sing-along smiles formed on face after face. The next time the refrain arrived, anyone who knew it sang along—sang vibrantly and joyfully—collaborating with the ever-calm Eli Scrivenbsy to serenade the ever-kind Sunrise Walsh. Even the gossipy eighth graders sang, helping him do what none of them had dared to do. And after a shortened version of the bridge, even the younger kids who hadn't known the words were singing along with the older kids and teachers during the final refrain.

Sunrise knew the song's end drew near—seconds away—as he strummed the last chords, and she looked again at the ceiling, inhaling slowly, this time with a sort of confidence replacing her worry. Mikey called Eli's name before the song ended, hoping to get his attention before his little brother spoke, knowing his next few words would include asking Sunrise to the dance.

And finally, Eli stopped. The song ended. Applause commenced. Paul wanted to be overjoyed, but he worried about the unknown instead. As the applause subsided, Eli placed his guitar against the podium, turned to Sunrise standing no more than five feet away, and said, "Sunrise, I—"

"Eli!" she interrupted. "I can't believe you did this!" She smiled, growing more flushed.

"—and I was wondering—" Eli tried to continue. Sunrise wouldn't let him.

"I can't believe you followed through on the dare. You see, Eli and I have been best friends since first grade, as most of you know, and we're always coming up with dares and jokes and stuff. And last month, Eli dared me to serenade him if he asked someone to the dance before I got asked, so I dared him to serenade me if I got asked to the dance before someone asked him. We shook on it. And when Charlie McGregor asked me to the dance on the way to the auditorium—" she made eye contact with Eli that was charged but loving, sad but hopeful— "I had no idea my best friend would follow through on his end of the deal let alone act so quickly."

She saw and Mikey saw and Paul saw Eli try to make sense of what Sunrise was doing, of what had just happened, try to fill in the gaps even as she explained them. His heart wanted to sink, but the realization that she was saving him sunk in instead. Reverting to the shyness with which he was most comfortable, he could but look down.

Then Sunrise walked next to him. "You didn't waste any time with this one." And she kissed him on the cheek. "Thanks, Eli."

The audience sighed a collective "Awww" and some of the boys irreverently hooted. "Probably Dr. Drew's grandchildren," Paul thought.

Always more comfortable smiling, Eli smiled widely as he turned red. Regaining his confidence, he said toward the audience, "You're a lucky guy, Charlie McGregor. If someone hadn't asked her soon, I would have."

CHAPTER 5

The peppered conversation of the car ride home between Mikey and his grandfather focused on Eli, not the Third World War that nearly broke out over class. Eli and Sunrise had stayed behind while the rest of the students were being dismissed from the assembly. While Mikey was studying the framed copy of *The Current Front* and Paul was thanking Peony and Petunia again for the cupcake, Sunrise explained to Eli that she had been asked by Charlie McGregor on the way to the assembly and, not wanting to hurt his feelings, had said, "Yes." She wanted to tell Eli immediately thereafter but couldn't get to him. She had never dreamed, however, that moments later, Eli would be asking her to the dance in front of everyone. She said she had to think fast, and with all this talk of class, she kept thinking of what the classy thing to do would be. Then she thought of Mrs. Willows's recollection about Eli's grandfather being dared to slide down the railing and, on the fly, somehow concocted the lie about the dare between Eli and her.

"I don't know if it was the classiest move, but I couldn't let you go through with it," she told Eli after the assembly.

"I think it was pretty classy. This way, nobody got hurt. Thanks for looking out for me," Eli said.

All of this had been said within Mikey's hearing, for he cared less about the magazine display than about Eli's situation. So he recounted all this to his grandfather during the short car ride home. His grandfather said he thought Sunrise's effort demonstrated class had she been successful or not.

Mikey dropped his grandfather at home and reminded him that he and Eli would swing by later that evening with the dinner their neighbor had made. This evening also marked Mikey's last night in town, for he planned to return to college with his friend Pat the following morning in order to participate in some of the Halloween fun on campus that weekend.

Paul entered a silent house, learning soon after his arrival that Claribel was napping in the solarium. He knew her never to nap and wondered how much longer she would feel drained so easily, yet her energy this morning had offered promise for a bright future.

Her napping gave him time to think after a busy few days, to think about whether or not to rewrite the column for his last issue. Despite encounter after encounter wherein the November column or the topic of class had been broached, discussed, debated, embodied, his mind had refused to think on it. Even now he couldn't bring himself to decide one way or the other and resisted thinking about the dilemma altogether.

Hours passed this way, Claribel still napping and Paul avoiding a decision by reading, looking in on the garden, loitering on the porch as the scent of autumn leaves sailed on the breeze and the faint sounds of Lake Superior waves greeted his ears. To stretch his legs, he meandered down the block and took in a view of the Saint Catherine's Cove Lighthouse in the distance, atop a cliff just northwest of the marina, a beacon, a guide, and a warning to nearing vessels. The hope that Claribel would awaken forestalled a whim to walk the few blocks to Samuel Park. Standing in the fresh air, he stared, still, for several minutes at the lighthouse. Is this what the rest of retirement might be like? Before long, the cupcake called his name as had the pastrami sandwich from the deli across the street from his office—his old office—but he resisted the urge so that he could show Claribel the masterpiece in its entirety. Instead, he returned home and rummaged the refrigerator for left-overs, oblivious to the dusk settling on the Lake Superior town, oblivious to the sleepy footsteps behind him.

"I caught you," Claribel said. "Snacking this close to dinner."

"You're awake!" he exclaimed, pulling his head from the refrigerator and shutting the door. "That was a long nap!"

"I woke up earlier today than I usually do," she responded. She glanced at the kitchen clock. "It's almost seven o'clock! Mikey and Eli should be here any minute with dinner. I didn't realize it had gotten so late." She crossed to the oven and turned it on. "I'll preheat it now so that it'll be ready to warm dinner."

"I have time for a drink. Been wanting one all day."

"Why? Didn't today go well?" she asked, concerned, as she sat at the counter. She was dressed now, and as autumn evenings brought autumn chills, she wrapped a sweater around her blouse, letting its sleeves hang unoccupied, and buttoning just the top button.

"Yes and no. So much to tell you. I'll tell you the good stuff first—" and recounting like the narrator of a good story, he explained about the ceremony, the speeches, and Eli's bold serenade, culminating, of course, with Sunrise's bold move to save him from embarrassment. Claribel, agog, hung on his every word and smiled by the end at what she foresaw as the beginning of a long-lasting love story.

"Those two will get married some day. Mark my words. There's something special about that friendship," she prophesied.

"It's crossed my mind," he agreed.

"Now what didn't go well?"

"I should have seen it coming when Lucretia warned me she's having trouble biting her tongue these days." He continued to share the issue over class and his column that broke out before and during the assembly, accounting for exchanges between Lucretia, Principal Hines, Mrs. Janes, and Mr. Bevel, the insidious question from Peter Unterbrink embarrassing Mrs. Henkel, and the example he tried to illustrate through Peony and Petunia's good deed.

"Good heavens! So much of that in front of the children? Can you imagine what the parents are listening to now at dinner tables around Saint Catherine's?"

"And Lucretia, why, she tried fervently to support me—my views in the column—but, by golly, she had a way of making things worse!"

"Your column struck a chord with some people, and you saw two mailbags full of letters to prove it. I guess you weren't expecting it to hit so close to home."

Just then the phone rang, and Paul rushed to the study to answer it. Seconds later, Mikey and Eli appeared in the kitchen with a casserole and an undressed dinner salad. Eli had his guitar, too. Before they spoke, Claribel brought her finger to her mouth to encourage them to keep their voices low while Paul spoke on the phone in the next room.

"Quite a day, I hear," she said, herself whispering.

Eli smiled and looked down as Claribel uncovered the casserole dish and placed it in the warm oven. She placed the salad in the refrigerator.

"Grandpa told you, huh? There's more we'll tell you over dinner when he's off the phone," Mikey added.

"I wish you'd be around next week, Mikey. I'm hoping to start cooking dinner, myself, again and not relying on Paul and everyone else. Was going to make the shepherd's pie you like—good fall food."

"More for Gracie and Eli," he said and punched his brother in the shoulder. "Just promise to make it one day over Christmas break!"

"Promise."

Mikey leaned over the kitchen sink, his face nearing the window. "I hope it rains tonight," he said.

"It's not expected to," Claribel noted. "Not that that means anything on Lake Superior."

"I want it to rain, too, but not tonight. Tomorrow. Why do you want it to rain?" Eli asked.

"I don't know. I like rain whenever I'm feeling—." He became less candid in the blink of an eye. "Why do you want it to rain tomorrow?"

"If it rains during swim practice, we won't have to swim in the lake. Coach says we have one more week in the lake before it'll be too cold, but when it rains, we use the pool." He strummed his guitar, letting the notes sing a hopeful arpeggio.

"Grandma, Eli's going to teach me to play the song from this morning. Can we practice in the solarium while dinner heats up?"

"Sure, honey. I'll call you when it's ready. Won't be long."

Moments after their exit, Paul entered the kitchen with a rocks glass of bourbon and a splash of Cointreau on ice. "I told you I needed a drink." His temper wasn't flaring—it never did—but he was evidently annoyed.

"What's the matter," Claribel asked. "Who was on the phone?"

"That was Stephen. He was calling to ask where I stood on the rewrite."

"What did you tell him?"

"I told him I hadn't decided. And I may be wrong—I don't know—it was over the phone and not face to face—but I got the distinct impression he thought I was out of my mind for not rewriting the December column. I asked him again, 'Do you really think an apology is the best route, Stephen?' and he said that it was really in my best interest—that he didn't see much difference in the readers' mixed responses the past few days. I told him I still needed to think about it."

"And he was okay with that? Paul, if you're going to rewrite the column, you're going to need to do it soon."

"He said I had better decide by tonight because they want it by tomorrow. He said they'll go ahead and publish the last column as is if I opt for the original, but a rewrite has been advised."

He took a sip of his beverage and followed it with another, bigger sip. He set the glass down and leaned his hands on the counter, staring at it. Claribel, stepping next to him, put an arm around his waist and her head on his shoulder.

"It's just so frustrating," he said calmly, resigning at last to the responsibility of making a decision once and for all.

"Everything was going so smoothly and then—this," Claribel commiserated.

"I keep asking myself, 'What is keeping me from apologizing?'"

"And what's the answer?"

"I never get to the answer. I keep reformulating the question. 'What's keeping me from apologizing for writing just another column?' 'What's keeping me from apologizing for presenting my own views as I have for the past thirty-five years?' 'What's keeping me from apologizing for defining class as I see it and commenting on ways I've seen it fall by the wayside?'"

He took another sip of bourbon and then turned to Claribel. He looked at her alone, a longing in his gaze, a fire that accompanies the youth that sometimes blazes in his eyes. Her eyebrows dipped and tears formed. She knew he needed something from her.

And finally, "You want my two cents?" She looked away after saying this.

And with the longing pouring into his voice, he said, "Yes."

"Good, because I'm going to give it to you whether you like it or not."

He wanted to smile but couldn't. He said only, "Good. I want to hear."

"Here's what I think. Your article helps people recognize there's always a higher standard. Why should you apologize for reminding people to live their lives by a higher standard? You're not holding anyone to that standard; you're illuminating that *there is* a higher standard. Does living by that standard make life more difficult? Yes, because it means we have to care more. But it also makes life more fulfilling, not just for ourselves but for others. You don't have to apologize for recognizing that."

The advice, forthright and clear and coming from his wife's heart and passing through her lips, settled over him pleasantly, like the pleasant fragrances and dins of the lake. Her perspective was solace, and not just because he wanted counsel but because—he wanted assurance that she was living.

As he deliberated how to respond and reached for another sip of bourbon, he and Claribel heard a noise from the solarium, a metallic but pretty clanging. They turned to see Mikey and Eli standing in the doorway to the solarium, the late dusk in the many windows surrounding them. Eli had bumped his knee into the strings of the guitar.

"I just realized I hadn't heard you practicing," said Claribel, wondering if they had been eavesdropping instead. She and Paul met the boys at the solarium, entered, and turned on two lamps.

"I didn't even know you were here," said Paul.

"We kind-of overheard what you were talking about," Mikey admitted. Eli, as usual, looked down and stupidly kicked his guitar again.

"So now you know," Paul said to the grandchildren. "My November column caused a stir with some readers, and the editors think I should rewrite the column I already submitted for December. You got a taste of how volatile it was today at the assembly."

"Are you going to take Grandma's advice?" Mikey asked.

Paul looked at Claribel. "I think I'm inclined to take Grandma's advice, yes. Do you have anything to offer on the matter?"

Mikey shook his head. "I'm with Grandma on this."

A hush fell on the room—until Eli accidentally kicked the guitar again. They all looked at him, and, flushed, he looked up. But this time, he wasn't embarrassed from hitting the guitar.

"I have a thought—or—I mean—I think I have a thought," he stammered, unused to speaking up.

"What are you thinking, Eli? I'll take any advice at this point," Paul said, trying to put him at ease, trying to encourage him to feel comfortable sharing his ideas.

"Well, you try to be classy with everything you do, don't you?" Eli asked.

"Yes, I feel I do try. Not always successful, but I do try."

"I think so, too. And after you've spent a lifetime trying to be classy, especially when you're as old as you are, I don't think you can just turn it off."

Paul, unsure where little Eli was going with this, asked shakily, "Are you suggesting that I write the apology?"

"No, I'm saying that if my hunch is correct, you never turned it off while you were writing the December column to begin with."

He involuntarily looked at his foot on which rested the guitar, spinning it a little. When he looked up again, his grandparents and Mikey were looking at him with smiles so wide that only Eli's could outdo theirs.

Following up on Eli's thought, Mikey said, "My stupid little brother is right. The original December column you wrote couldn't lack class and graciousness if you tried—the way you wrote it to begin with. That's probably the way you want to go out."

"Claribel, Mikey, Eli—they all agree," thought Paul, and perhaps they were all correct. He had striven to write a gracious farewell column, full of gratitude and gracefully rendered reminiscences and careful restraint and his characteristic hopeful outlook.

So he announced, "It's decided then. I'm not rewriting the column."

Claribel and the boys heard after he walked to the study Paul's part in a brief conversation over the phone with Stephen, one that ended, "Please keep my column as is. You can print the original December issue."

Part II: Offensiveness

CHAPTER 6

The autumn wind had been picking up throughout dinner, and as Paul, Claribel, and their two grandsons cleared the table, rain began to tap on the windows and roof. Strong gusts of wind blasted raindrops into the side of the house and the windows with such clatter that Claribel asked if it were hailing.

"You boys better get home quick. Grandma and I will take care of the dishes," Paul said to Mikey and Eli. Mikey, in from college for his first fall break, planned to leave in the morning with his friends back to school. For Eli, this Thursday night was a school night, and he needed to finish homework.

"Good-night, Grandma. Good-night, Grandpa," the boys said, pulling the hoods of their jackets over their heads.

"Don't forget your guitar," Paul said to Eli.

"It's at the back door," the boy said, making his way there.

As they opened the back door, Claribel shouted, "Be careful driving! It's dark, and the wet leaves will make the roads slick!"

"I will!" shouted Mikey, pulling the door shut behind him, the wind stirring resistance.

"At least it's close. They will be home in minutes," Paul said.

"I hope it will have stopped by tomorrow while Mikey's driving to school."

"I hope it will have stopped by bedtime, which, after today, should not be far off."

"Let's see how you feel when we're done with the dishes, and if you're up for it, we'll have a drink in the solarium." Claribel was the first to head to bed of late, and her suggestion for a nightcap warmed Paul's heart; the Claribel he had been waiting for was returning.

"Why don't you make us a drink and sit, Bel. I'll finish the dishes," he said.

"Got to get back in the swing of things. I took a long nap today." She looked at him assuredly. "Don't worry. I have it in me. Besides, it won't take long. The boys made a good dent."

They both made for the counter and started cleaning up, and within a short while, they had finished. A casserole and a salad, dinner had been far from elaborate and ensured minimal clean up, after which, the couple settled in the solarium, snug on opposite ends of the same couch.

Claribel looked at her husband curiously as he flipped through magazines from a basket at the foot of the couch. "You never sit on the couch with me."

"Is it throwing you off?" Paul asked, smiling distractedly while searching the magazines.

"It is," she admitted, looking at the empty armchair across from her. "You usually sit in the armchair with one foot on the ottoman." She thought it strange that whenever Paul was in New York for business and she sat on her corner of the couch, the armchair never appeared empty, but now, with his unaccustomed seat on her couch, she felt a distinct void, a vacancy, when she glanced at the chair, even though her husband sat nearby.

"Maybe I'm trying something new." Lightning illuminated the lamp-lit room for a moment, and Paul set the magazine he had finally chosen on the arm of the couch. Then he crawled on all fours toward—and then over—Claribel, whose shock forestalled a smile from forming. His face inches from hers, he smiled, melting her frozen amazement and revealing her own delighted smile underneath. And then he kissed her.

For a moment youthful, he sprung, it seemed, from the couch, grabbed the magazine, and sat in the armchair. After a few seconds of page turning, a glance over the magazine proved that a grinning Claribel still stared at him, wondering. He, too, began to wonder, never really reading the articles in the magazine. He wondered if this were the epitome of retirement for the next few years—sitting in the solarium with his wife, leisurely spending an evening without a plan for tomorrow, not thinking twice about acting impulsively. He wondered if he would spend these upcoming days flinging himself from the deep grooves his routines had burrowed or if he would snuggle in the comfortable ones, now that he could enjoy the ease they might bring—would that be wrong? He wondered what doors might open now that Claribel's health was returning, and he counted on joy behind every one of them.

Although he had officially retired days ago, he had never felt the changes it promised, and this past week had been more strenuous than some of the most hectic weeks in his entire career. During this last week of October, he had been to New York, had been told his November column was receiving pointed reaction from readers, had been asked to consider rewriting his December column—the *final* column—with an apology, had deliberated the decision for days, had watched his grandsons run to his assistance after he was honored at his former grade school, had announced to his former boss that he would not rewrite the December column, and had, at last, settled in for a quiet evening alone with his wife whose cancer had only weeks prior gone into remission. In fact, these were the first moments his retirement felt realized, inhaled, enjoyed.

Jolting him from a reverie of wonderment, the phone rang. The vim still in his being, he sprang from the chair to answer the phone, opting for the one in the study so as not to disturb Claribel's reading. He returned minutes later with his coat under his arm and a felt, gray trilby in his hand.

"You can't be going out in this weather," Claribel stated but in reality asked why he was going.

"That was Oliver. Said Lucretia had a heart attack this evening and was rushed to the hospital. She's awake and under observation. He wants to head over and check in on her—

wanted to know if I wanted to go with. He's going to swing by to pick me up."

"Lucretia? Good heavens! You just saw her today!"

"I know. I think my heart stopped a moment before he finished his sentence and said she was okay."

"Poor thing. Give her my best."

"I think she'd appreciate a quick visit."

"It's still coming down pretty hard, Paul. Be careful out there," cautioned Claribel, pausing between her words to confirm her pronouncement through the sound of the rain pounding on the house.

Oliver lived only a few blocks away, so his honking soon after the phone conversation surprised neither of them. Paul flung his coat and hat on, kissed Claribel good-bye, and ran out the back door. He scrunched the front of his coat with his hand instead of zipping it as the rain pelted him, and he held his other hand to his hat to prevent the fierce wind from robbing him of it. When he entered the passenger seat, Oliver greeted him and waited as his friend shook the rain off his hat and fastened his seatbelt. Paul, taking his time settling in, had not reciprocated a greeting when Oliver said, "Will you look at that? It stopped raining!"

Paul looked through the windshield and watched the wipers swipe at nothing. In a sudden, the rain had stopped and the wind had lessened.

"Well, I'll be—" said Paul.

"You're good luck, Paul. Now I can drive and actually see where I'm going. It was coming down in buckets for a while. I still want to hurry, though. I'm concerned they won't let us see her a minute after visiting hours, and we'll be cutting it close."

"Step on it, then. I'm in." He set his trilby on his lap, content the droplets of rain had been shaken onto the floor mat. Another glance out the window reminded him that he should have turned on the front porch light as this residential area was quite dim. The only streetlights in St. Catherine's Cove surrounded the perimeter of Samuel Park and, of course, lined

Main Street. Even the streets along Lake Superior lacked lights, although the glow from the few near the docks and marina reached the streets on clear evenings.

Once he had backed out of the driveway, Oliver leaned over the steering wheel, his neck inching toward the windshield like a turtle emerging from its shell. He squinted as he accelerated, trying to peer through the darkness, delineating the wet streets and curbs and trees.

"You can turn the windshield wipers off now," Paul said, chuckling as he spoke. He had preferred not to speak at all as he did not wish to distract Oliver from driving. Oliver did not respond as he switched them off.

Oliver accelerated cautiously through the dark streets, every few seconds shifting the head he had so intently positioned over the top of the steering wheel. Paul, however, leaned back, amused at the tension in his friend's pose but fully understanding of it, for he had noticed himself now driving the same way at night. He knew, too, that the destination lay not fifteen minutes away toward the outskirts of town and would make but a short car ride.

Content not to interrupt Oliver's concentration on the road, Paul mused over how volatile the reactions had been to his November column—he would tell Oliver all about it when they leave the hospital—how he had written the article about class slowly vanishing from society, how those who uphold the importance of class can be villainized for doing so, how some readers expressed elation over Paul's calling attention to this, and how some readers expressed scorn over Paul's stance. He had to tell him about the students' questions at the Greengate assembly and the tumult one question caused. And he had to tell him what his grandsons had said to encourage Paul to decide not to issue an apology in his last column.

As the topics to share with Oliver raced through his head along with reprimands for thinking of anything but Lucretia, he mindlessly gave his trilby another shake over the floor mat to eliminate any last droplets of rain but in so doing accidentally snapped the whole hat from his hand to the floor.

"Darnit," he said, trying to lean forward to retrieve it.

"What?" asked Oliver.

"I dropped my hat." And realizing the seatbelt was restricting him, he unfastened it. He was grateful they approached Samuel Park on account of the light it provided as they drove along its perimeter. The brightness brought to Oliver an increasing confidence as he accelerated and receded into the seat a few inches. As Paul bent to swoop up the hat, he noticed through the park shrubbery, beyond the trees, sitting on a bench, what looked like his grandson Mikey—sitting after a heavy rainfall, his hair wet, his head resting on a hand that covered his eyes and brow. They were passing the park quickly, and the dim streetlamp cast the faintest glow around the shape, rendering it hard to make out. Forgetting the hat a moment, Paul inched toward the window to confirm the identity of the figure when he heard the horn, when he saw the lights flash through the driver-side window. Oliver swerved toward the park. Skidding over wet leaves in the street and enduring an impact from the oncoming vehicle, Oliver's car flipped, crashing upside down on a patch of lawn in the park.

CHAPTER 7

The white gold of brilliant light cleared to the pressure of a soft voice, to a heavy sadness laced with hope, to a thick, white fog. When he felt the firm touch and movement on his forehead, a few speckles of the golden light sparkled through the fog. The fog did not clear as he discerned unfamiliar words.

"Per istam sanctam Unctionem et suam piissimam misericordiam, adiuvet te Dominus gratia Spiritus Sancti."

And when he heard a collective "Amen," he started! His eyes opened—the fog clearing immediately, the golden rays—gone, too—and he saw the priest in vestments at his side and Claribel behind him, along with his children and grandchildren encircling the bed—not his usual bed—in an unfamiliar room encumbered with harsh lighting. Black and white beads, spinning and sparkling, swayed gently from clasped hands.

"No, stop!" he said with shocking volume for his first words in nearly forty-eight hours.

"Paul!" said Claribel, stepping before the priest to lean over her husband, to make herself seen, instictively knowing it would comfort him to recognize someone, to recognize her. "You're okay, Paul. It's Claribel. We're all here. You're okay!"

"Am I dying? What's going on?"

"You're okay, Paul." She glanced at the priest who was smiling kindly on Paul. His smile was genuine and comforting, even to Paul. "You were being anointed. The Anointing of the Sick. You were in an accident."

"I thought you were giving me Last Rites!" Paul said, his voice hoarse and tremulous.

These words offered a relief to his family, and with tear-lined eyes, everyone laughed—at last. He was finally conscious. He seemed himself. He thought a simple anointing indicated his imminent demise. This was as soothing to them as blessed oil. The nurse, followed by Dr. Drew and another doctor, hurried in. The priest stepped back to make room, but Claribel took Paul's hand and smiled at him, her face close to his.

"I'm going to need everyone to step outside for a while," Dr. Drew said.

At this Claribel reluctantly released his hand. As the family shifted toward the hospital room door, Paul heard Claribel say, "He's awake now. Everything is going to be okay."

Later that night, after the doctors' visits, Paul's family returned to his bedside. His son Michael with Mikey, Gracie, and Eli, his daughter Anna with her son Henry, his daughter Pauline with her husband Brent and their twins Hannah and Paulie, and his wife Claribel crowded the small room. He had not had a chance to discuss the accident or his condition with Claribel until they all left feeling confident he was conscious for good. As his children and grandchildren departed, he asked Father Soplido, the priest from his parish who had been administering the sacrament, to stay. Preoccupying his concerns, Oliver's condition overtook most of Paul's questions, but before Claribel and Paul could discuss much, he grew drowsy and drifted into dreams of sitting in his New York office, the blinds opened, the sunshine streaming through, while he pored over the December column—his last—and glanced at the mailbags opposite his desk, on every glance the bags and letters increasing in number—first two bags piled with letters, then three, then five—all leaning against each other, tipping so that letters sifted out onto the carpet. And he suspected every letter issued a criticism over his column on class, over his lack of remorse, over his unmerited retirement. He could not budge from his chair behind the desk to read a single one.

He awoke from this dream to find himself in dimmer lighting within the same hospital room. A nurse stood over him, checking his vitals. She smiled when she saw his eyes open and whispered for him to go back to sleep. Before she turned off the light, he saw Father Soplido sleeping nigh upright in an awkward armchair beyond the foot of the bed. Lacking the strength to reflect on it, Paul immediately dozed off again.

When Claribel visited early the next morning, he finally learned about the accident and its aftermath. A pick-up truck driven by an out-of-towner smashed into them, hurling their car onto the lawn of Samuel Park. The paramedics arrived quickly and rushed Oliver and Paul to the hospital they had been heading to to begin with. An unconscious Oliver was examined and sent immediately into surgery wherein the doctors stopped some internal bleeding around his left lung. Paul, on the other hand, was examined and closely monitored; despite no worrisome indications on his cat scans, he had remained unconscious for an inordinate amount of time. In the meantime, the doctors recognized blunt force trauma to his right forearm, resulting in no broken bones but serious contusions. Paul's brazen friend from grade school, Dr. Drew, had been finishing for the day in his hospital office when he learned Paul had been brought in; he had stayed late after Lucretia's untimely interruption earlier that day. Dr. Drew, as Claribel explained, stuck around to make sure Paul, Oliver, and their families were well cared for and comforted. He was present while other doctors explained the situation to each family and to each patient.

Paul, to his embarrassment, also learned that his family had gathered in the waiting room the night of the accident. Mikey, Gracie, and Eli slept overnight in the waiting room as they were not allowed in Paul's hospital room. Father Soplido, the priest the Scrivensby family knew quite well during his many years as pastor of Saint Catherine's, had visited the last two nights, the second of which he began the Anointing of the Sick and stayed over night so that Claribel could get a good night's rest in her own bed. The worry and anxiousness and altered schedules that his situation had brought on for others truly disturbed the unassuming patient.

"There's something else, Paul." Claribel had not finished filling in Paul when Dr. Drew arrived, bright and early, to check on him. His caustic playfulness never diminished one bit, even while his old chum groggily recuperated in a hospital bed days after an accident.

"Are we still swipping in and out of consciousness, Pauwie Wauwie?" he asked belittlingly. "Are we still checking out of weality because we can't handle our wetirement?"

Even though he was cracking a smile, Paul said, "You're not funny, Dwew."

"Dishing it back at me?" he said to Claribel. "That's a good sign. Such a good sign I think we can get you out of here tomorrow afternoon and into your own house to recover peacefully."

"It's not too soon?" asked Claribel, more alarmed than relieved.

"There's not much more we can do for him here. We've been monitoring him, and Dr. Baumhauer sees nothing to be alarmed about from the brain activity. In fact, it's that arm of yours that's going to cause you the most trouble. Contusions to the bone—pretty painful—but we'll have a sling for you to wear to keep it immobile and from hanging at your side. The next six to eight weeks should be a blessing to readers everywhere who won't have to put up with your crappy writing for a while."

"Not sure how much writing—" Paul began.

"But that's right—you're wetired."

"Yeah, yeah, yeah," Paul rejoined. He had a more pressing question than sparring with Drew. "How's Oliver? And how's Lucretia?"

"Three kids from the same grade school and high school class all ending up in the hospital on the same night. Can you believe that? As a member of that class, I'm glad bad crap happens in threes or else I'd be worried about my own health. Thanks for taking one for the team, Paulie. Oliver is doing well—we got him taken care of real good. He will need to stick around a little longer, and his recovery will be painful—but a full recovery is expected. Lucretia's been discharged, but she's been ordered to take it easy. We kept her over night for observation and sent her home the next day."

"She gives her best, Paul," Claribel added smilingly.

"She sure as hell better!" said Dr. Drew. "This whole accident is practically her fault. You wouldn't have been out on that road if she hadn't had a heart attack!" Dr. Drew smirked at Paul. "You think I should stop by and tell her that on my way home today?"

"Drew! Of course not!" exclaimed Claribel. "Even if you're joking, that would tear her up."

"You're right," the doctor concluded. "I'll wait a week."

Used to the antics of his friend, Paul began to chuckle, a good sign to both present.

"All right, Paul, I'll be back a little later to confirm, I hope, that you will be discharged tomorrow. Until then, you might want to spend a little time thinking about how to honor me in your statement to the press—about my medical prowess and knowhow, the exceptional care with which I fulfill my livelihood."

"The press?" inquired Paul.

"That's the other thing I had wanted to tell you," Claribel said.

"That's what you get when Little Miss Celebrity Columnist gets into an accident—the press showing up. They've been asking when you're being discharged so that they can talk with you. I wouldn't be surprised if they try to catch you here before you go." Dr. Drew made for the door before adding, "So talk me up! I'll be back in about an hour."

Paul looked forlornly at Claribel, who stepped to his bedside.

"They were here the night of the accident, but we issued no statement. Even more showed up the next morning, but we still had no word on your situation. Lucretia's son said the accident had been mentioned briefly on the local news, but when I got home last night, I found several messages on the machine from reporters and journalists. They want the story. A few of them were from New York, and one message was from Stephen at *The Current Front.*" As she spoke, Paul pressed the remote to raise his torso in the bed. His injured arm reclined across his abdomen.

"I don't want to be conducting interviews throughout all this, and I don't want anyone badgering the family, either."

"They seem eager for the story, and most of them have been pleasant enough. Do you think Dr. Drew is right? That they might try to catch you on your way out tomorrow afternoon?"

Paul turned his head to its side, looking past Claribel to the new morning sunlight sparkling through the window. He knew that addressing the press would be inevitable. Still, he wanted to do it on his own terms and wanted to look presentable. The thought of visitors—even his own family—seeing him in a hospital gown with his teeth unbrushed and his face unshaved repulsed him.

"If I can walk out of here tomorrow, we'll have a press conference here. You or one of the kids can contact the reporters with the details. Bring a change of clothes and my toiletries so that I can shave and look respectable. We'll do it tomorrow, all at once, on our way out, and be done with it."

Claribel tilted her head, admiring the strength emanating from her husband—he was, indeed, on the mend. Her admiration overruled her concern about his decisive approach so soon after a serious accident. Avoiding an impulse to second-guess him, she said, "Sounds like a plan. Let's wait to hear from Dr. Drew about what time you might be released tomorrow, and once I know, I'll contact the reporters. We can leave word with the hospital, too, in case they've been contacted." Then she took his left hand in hers and held it, careful not to touch his right arm. "You scared me, Paul."

He looked into her eyes, but when he saw them well up, he turned his head toward the window again, using no words to speak.

"I kept thinking, 'You didn't come all this way through a battle with cancer—you didn't find out it's in remission—just to lose your husband, Bel.' I was so afraid of losing you, Paul."

His gaze did not meet hers. He had no memory of the accident. He still felt disoriented, unsure of his bearings. Yet, he remembered the column and the dramatic effect its reception had had on him, and he remembered Claribel—talking with her, crawling to her on the couch, loving her.

"You can't lose me," he said. "Not before I've had a chance to enjoy my retirement."

Claribel released a quick laugh. "I love you so much."

When she leaned in and kissed him, he replied, "I love you, too."

Later that day, Paul stood up and walked in the presence of doctors. Doctors and nurses entered and exited throughout the day, all checking on Paul in one way or another, all encouraging his discharge the following day. Dr. Drew discussed the press conference with Paul, arranging a time and an unoccupied hospital room as the location. He had coordinated with the hospital's public relations staff, to whom he planned to introduce Paul tomorrow, all the particulars. The hospital's public relations team worked with *The Current Front*'s public relations representative in New York to effect a mutually beneficial presentation of Paul's situation—not that much manipulation was necessary—and worked together to announce the conference. While Claribel phoned the reporters from home in the afternoon, Mikey and Eli, along with their father, spent a few hours with Paul; the boys' sister, Gracie, babysat their little cousins, Henry, Hannah, and Paulie, so that Aunt Anna and Aunt Pauline could spend time at the hospital, as well.

"I came bearing more visitors," shouted Dr. Drew, entering with friends Roy Palomer and Peony Pilsen. "Paul, I thought you should know—they visited Oliver first."

The visitors greeted the patient and his family, and Peony set a small arrangement of flowers on a ledge in the room. Roy held on to a gift bag. As it rested in his hands, Mikey tried surreptitiously catching a glimpse of its contents.

"What is this? A greenhouse or a hospital room?" asked Dr. Drew, taking in all the flower arrangements and teddy bears holding hearts and get-well cards that decorated the small room, including wishes from Rick Mendel, *The Current Front* staff, and Principal Hines from Greengate.

"I got you something you can enjoy when you get home, Paul," Roy shared, pulling a bottle of bourbon from the gift bag. I won't leave it here, but I wanted you to see it—an incentive to get well soon and get home."

Paul announced, "I can leave tomorrow, the doctors say."

"Great news!" Paul's son exclaimed, the relief evident in his tone. Unable to hug his recumbent father, he transferred his joy to his sons, swinging an arm around each of their shoulders for a few seconds. Mikey and Eli high-fived in celebration.

"I'm leaving after a press conference here at the hospital."

"I saw on the news that more details would be forthcoming," Peony said.

"More details about how exceptional your care has been, right Paul?" added Dr. Drew. "And if you don't extol my medical skills and gentle bedside manner, I'll be forced to reveal to the press the spectacle I saw under your hospital gown—well, more like lack of spectacle." The stunned, wordless reactions from all present only encouraged Dr. Drew to continue. "What? So I sneaked a peek. I'm a doctor—I'm allowed access—and if I should choose to expose your shortcomings to the press, boy, will *Current Front* columnist Paul Scrivensby have a lot to be embarrassed about. Or a little to be embarrassed about? I don't know how to put it—you're the writer."

Peony hemmed as she shook her head, establishing a reaction Dr. Drew could work with.

"Don't hem and haw. Like you don't agree?"

At this, Peony tried to shrug off Dr. Drew with a flip of the hand.

"Okay. Okay. I didn't sneak a peek," said Dr. Drew, as if to relent. "I didn't have to. Seen it a hundred times already. He likes showing it to me."

At this, Mikey, Eli, and their dad started laughing, used to Dr. Drew's ribbing, but Paul's mounting embarrassment elicited laughter from even Peony and Roy. He could not believe that Drew was joking this way in front of his grandchildren.

"He's my personal physician," Paul stammered. "He's talking about my yearly physicals." Paul surveyed the room, hoping to find understanding in the visages of his family and friends but finding instead only grins and laughter.

"Sure, I am, Paul. I'm talking about your yearly physicals," Dr. Drew said and then winked.

When he winked, Mikey blurted out a snicker, and Eli's eyes clenched in quiet laughter. Their father, laughing himself, just shook his head as Paul turned red.

"Take that back!" Paul shouted.

"Take what back?" asked Drew.

"That wink!"

"I will not!" Dr. Drew declared, feigning indignation.

"People might not know you're joking! They might think—"

"Think what? That maybe every now and then, you show up in my bedroom and drop your trousers?"

Paul, horrified and redder than ever, looked to see his grandchildren's reactions and found both keeled over laughing, tears streaming down their cheeks. Mikey's laughter sounded like a pant while Eli's emitted no sound. Something about the effect Dr. Drew's inappropriateness had on his grandchildren comforted him—seeing them laugh, even at his expense—and he lightened up. He turned to Peony and Roy, themselves smiling and shaking their heads, more embarrassed for Paul than appreciative of Dr. Drew's zany humor, and he said, "I give up."

Dr. Drew patted him on the left shoulder and said before exiting, "Just don't say the wrong thing at the press conference."

Paul enjoyed a nice visit with his family and friends, including his daughters Anna and Pauline who arrived moments after Dr.

Drew's exit, while Claribel made the phone calls from home. Before long, Paul's son Michael told Mikey that he had better be taking off for college soon; after all, tomorrow, a Monday, classes would be resuming now that fall break was hours away from ending.

"Tomorrow is Monday?" inquired Paul, panic-stricken. "Then today is Sunday? I missed Mass!"

To Paul's delight, Mikey, unsolicited, acted on his grandfather's concern and contacted Father Soplido, who arranged for a Mass in the hospital chapel later that evening. Paul, his family, and a few other patients and hospital staff attended the short Mass; Mikey, however, already off schedule, had begrudgingly begun driving to college at the insistence of his father.

Before the long day came to a close, Father Soplido, the last one to leave the room, bid Paul farewell. The main light off and the curtains closed enough to block exterior light, Father Soplido appeared wan, weary, yet a gleam in his eye and the whiteness of his teeth revealed by his smile called attention to his vitality. Paul did not know his age but had always assumed his priest neared his forties. Even in the dim light, tired and exhausted on account of kindly shepherding, he seemed youthful. Or maybe the chestnut hue of Father's eyes evoked youth as they reminded Paul of counting fallen chestnuts in the lawns along Steele Street as a boy. And now the man Paul had known for years but knew little about had just provided him with a bounty of kindnesses and was leaving for the night.

"I will visit tomorrow before your press conference. I'm happy you are doing so well."

"Thank-you, Father, for visiting, and thank-you for Mass today, and thank-you for relieving Claribel last night—above and beyond."

"Would you say it was the classy thing to do?" Father grinned when he said this, happy to see the smile it elicited from Paul.

Paul shook his head from side to side as if to say, "Not you, too," but instead said, "I'm truly grateful."

"Good-night, Paul. God bless you."

"Good-night, Father."

When Father Soplido left and Paul's head sunk into the pillow, words raced through his mind—phrases and sentences flashed before him—the statement he would give at the press conference needed to be well-put. More seemed to be riding on these words than others he had procured.

CHAPTER 8

Dr. Drew and the public relations staff led Paul, Claribel, and Father Soplido to the unoccupied hospital room, one more spacious and more private. Earlier, while Paul showered, shaved, and dressed with a nurse's help, so much more slowly than he was used to, the staff transferred the flowers and cards from Paul's room to the new one. Public relations had convinced Paul that hosting the press conference in a hospital room instead of a conference room would present a quaint feel, a sympathetic ambiance, and not one so austere. Paul, although he saw the hospital's benefit in this perception, found one for himself, too: in light of the varied reactions to his penultimate column, a warm scene might invite more warmth from the readers.

One of the staffers had informed Paul that the press was waiting in a holding area, soon to be allowed into the room. Paul glanced at a clock; still on schedule, the reporters would arrive within five minutes. After having been on his feet for so long in the shower and while dressing, in addition to the long walk to the new room, Paul felt weary and asked to sit. Dr. Drew helped him onto the hospital bed in the room, careful not to disturb his arm resting nervously in an unfamiliar blue sling.

Paul's only comforts came from knowing the press conference would translate to a mere fifteen seconds of news and maybe a five-line blurb in a newspaper here and there. At least he looked presentable—showered and clean-shaven, groomed and well-dressed in wool trousers and a cashmere sweater over a button-down. This sudden fatigue, however, could not wrest his mind from thoughts of the pending press, their questions, his statement—now garbled in his head—and Paul asked for Claribel to draw the blinds. When she did, he saw the gray glow of a drizzly fall day. He wanted to imbibe the fresh drizzle in order to dispel the rush of heat flushing his face, to swathe his head in the gray, fresh mist and inhale.

The public relations team and the doctors touching base, Paul, from the patient bed, lifted one leg onto the bed and reached for Father Soplido's hand. "Will you say a prayer for me?" Unused to such nervousness, the normally composed columnist was reaching for a last recourse.

"I'll say a prayer *with* you," Father Soplido responded, and with Paul made the Sign of the Cross. The chestnut of Father's eyes calmed Paul, lifting him to memories of walks down Steele Street with his father, holding his hand while tallying the chestnuts embedded in each lawn.

As Father said a prayer, the door was held open by someone in the hall, and reporters, journalists, and photographers entered, quick to set up but quick to halt when they saw Father Soplido in his white habit praying with Paul. Paul noticed the determined gait of Rhonda Turner, a local reporter, transition to a skulk, and Mickey Hall, another local reporter, shush his videographer. Ted Handly, a journalist for WBAM, barged to the front holding a mini-recorder.

"What's the hold up?" Ted Handly asked. The head of public relations looked at Paul, and Paul signaled for her to begin.

Dr. Drew, Dr. Baumhauer, and Claribel stood behind Father Soplido and Paul. The head of public relations, with her team beside her, made some opening statements before the press, introducing all those present, including Father Soplido. As she began an overview of Paul's current state, Ted Handly interrupted.

"We want to hear from Paul Scrivensby. Could Father Sopapillas over there speed it up?"

The room had been quiet before, but a fresh hush held its breath, calling attention to itself. The head of public relations stepped aside for all to see Paul and the priest and said, "It's Father Soplido. Mr. Scrivensby will make a statement and field questions shortly, after—"

Ted Handly sighed, glancing at other reporters for a face that shared his disgust. Not thirty seconds later, the head of public relations finished her statement and opened the floor for Paul, who slowly rose from the bed with the steadying hands of the doctors and Father Soplido, while photographers and videographers caught the moment.

Once to his feet, he leaned toward his priest and whispered, "What did he call you?"

Father shrugged, unsure. But Paul had distracted himself from his short speech by asking this question of Father Soplido, by wondering if he were not too weary to stand, by hoping he would not forget the short statement he had planned the night before. As he began to address the press, he stammered over his words until at last he could think of nothing to say except, "Thank-you for coming."

Rhonda and Mickey's smiles put him at ease, so he began to speak more freely, grasping for any word that came to mind from his thoughts the night before; just one word might give him something to expand on, even if not as eloquently as he had hoped.

"Thank-you for coming," he repeated. "On Friday night, a car accident sent my friend and me to the hospital, ironically while on our way to the hospital to see a friend who had been admitted earlier—"

"That's not ironic. Come on, he's a writer." The interruption came from Ted Handly, but Paul, concentrating on his statement, did not catch it and continued, although the looks on other reporters' faces indicated a displeasure with Ted.

"Despite the injuries, I am happy to report that my friend is no longer in critical condition, and I have been officially discharged today. We both expect full recoveries, thanks in large part to the extraordinary service and skill of Dr. Drew Slate and

Dr. Dieter Baumhauer, along with the nursing staff. I have no information to share at this time on the accident itself nor on my friend's injuries—nor on mine. We are grateful for our health, for the support of family and friends—"

"And fans!" added Rhonda, bringing a smile to everyone's face. Rhonda, solid, tall, all-business, and poised, commanded the part of the room occupied by the press.

"—and fans—and ultimately for the opportunity to live another day." Paul looked at Claribel, sharing in their mutual experience of the same feeling within weeks of each other.

"And maybe you can finally begin to enjoy your retirement now," Dr. Drew added this comment, eliciting more light laughter. Atypical of himself, Dr. Drew spoke out of nerves, and his lips even quivered after he spoke.

"A nice, classy retirement, right?" asked Ted rhetorically, unsmilingly.

"At this time, if you have a few questions my doctors or I might be able to answer, ask away." Paul fielded a few questions, some about his care, some about whether or not the accident had rattled him, some about his future writing, especially now that he donned a sling, and even some about his thoughts on his last column, expected to hit newsstands in a few weeks. He addressed them casually, respectfully, and succinctly, all the while maintaining composure.

As the conference drew to a close, a young reporter new to the field, Eloise Bernardi, double-checked on a few names when she asked, "Dr. Baumhauer, I didn't catch your first name and title."

"Dieter," he replied. "Head of neurology."

"It's in the press kit, little girl," Ted sneered.

Trying to appear unfazed despite her sudden blushing, she continued, "And Father Soplido. You're the pastor at Saint Catherine's Church. Your first name again, please? That one's not in the press kit."

"Poncho," Ted blurted out as he lowered his mini-recorder and began to pack up. No one responded. "Poncho Sopapillas. I like mine with *mole* sauce." He joined his photographer at examining some of the shots in the digital memory of the camera, oblivious to the hush he had once again heaved into the center of the room.

Father Soplido smiled not ashamedly but bashfully and looked at his shoes.

"Excuse me," said Rhonda, "but that is uncalled for."

"What?" asked Ted.

"I think you should apologize," she said.

Paul looked between Father Soplido, whose gaze remained fixed on the floor, and Ted, standing like a puffed rooster before the other journalists. Hoping Father would look up but spotting no indication that he would, Paul returned his stare to Ted.

"For what? Come on. Let's pack up," Ted said, directing his last words to the photographer.

"The derisiveness toward Father—as well as the condescension to—" Paul squinted to read Eloise's full name on her tag.

"It's okay," said Father Soplido, smiling graciously at both Rhonda and Ted. "I'm not offended. Let's just see to it that Paul enjoys a peaceful and quick recovery."

"Apologize!" persisted Rhonda.

Relieved, Ted replied, "He just said there's no issue. You're the one making an issue of this, Rhonda." He turned to the photographer and increased his haste in exiting, bumping into the others who loitered in their shock, some of whom were still on duty with recorders and movie cameras running.

Rhonda, stunned that Ted had turned this on her, scoffed and looked at Paul and Father Soplido apologetically.

"It's Fernando," the priest said softly to Eloise. "Father Fernando Soplido."

That evening, Paul watched from his bed and Claribel from an armchair nearby, as the news opened with Paul Scrivensby's press conference—"Scandalous comments from journalist Ted Handly spark outrage at a press conference held by *Current Front* columnist Paul Scrivensby." Paul and Claribel watched in shock as the two-minute story showcased footage of Ted's "ethnic slurs" and Rhonda's entreaty to an unmotivated Ted for "a reasonable apology." They listened as Rhonda, in a separate interview, voiced her "complete disgust" over Ted's "offensive comments" and as Ted Handly, cameras in his face as he entered his house, had "nothing to say."

They particularly enjoyed the closing line of the entire story incidentally sharing that "Paul Scrivensby is expecting a full recovery."

CHAPTER 9

Not much after 10:00am, Claribel eased herself from bed, slipped on her robe, and entered an empty kitchen. The lure of brewed coffee beckoned her to the mugs before curiosity over her husband's whereabouts could preoccupy her. While she was pouring her coffee, Paul entered hurriedly, dressed and holding his coat over his arm.

"I just got off the phone with—" he began.

"Paul, you're not going anywhere!" Her instinct to keep him from doing anything that might impede his recovery found form in vexed words.

He stopped at the counter, checking himself in his own haste. He set his coat over the back of a stool and rested his one free hand on it. "I just got off the phone with Father Soplido's answering machine. I'm going to visit him at the rectory. I think he could use my help."

Paul's phone had rung several times after the news yesterday and early this morning. He turned off the ringer on any phone close enough to the bedroom that might interrupt Claribel's sleep, and he answered none of them. In the morning, he listened to the messages, most of which involved requests for comment on the "ethnic slur" at his press conference. One message, though, came from a still jovial Father Soplido, wondering if Paul had any suggestions about handling all the calls he has been getting and the press camped outside the rectory hoping for a statement. Paul called him back, but Father

Soplido did not answer. He decided, then, that he must go straight to the rectory to assist however he could.

"Paul, I know you want to help, but you haven't been home from the hospital for even twenty-four hours. And, I'm sorry, but I won't let you drive with a sling on!"

"I'll take it off then. My arm's not broken."

"Paul, you're not going anywhere. I realize how much distress that news story caused you. You're not thinking clearly. Please, Paul, put the coat away and allow yourself some rest."

"Bel, I can't stay here and—recover—when Father Soplido could use my help. He reached out to me, and I want to come through for him. I mean, think about everything he did for me the past few days—spending the night so you could go home, celebrating Mass in the chapel. I can't do—nothing."

The phone rang, and Paul rushed to the study to answer it. A few minutes later, Paul returned to the kitchen, took his coat off the stool, and hung it by the backdoor. Claribel looked quizzically at him, hesitating to take her next sip of coffee until she heard an explanation.

"That was Father Soplido. He said he doesn't want me driving, so he's going to sneak out the back of the rectory and head over here to talk."

"I feel much better about that."

"I thought you might," he said with a grin. "Let's put another pot of coffee on so that it's fresh." Then he moved to the coffee machine.

"How did he sound? Stressed?" Seeing her husband begin to prepare a new pot of coffee, she crossed to relieve him of the chore. "Let me do that."

"I made it this morning. I can handle making coffee," and then, "Father sounded his usual self. Pretty upbeat."

"That, I have to say, is something else. To have to put up with what that Ted Handly said—and he's not even Mexican. Putting up with all this aftermath. It's something else that he can remain upbeat."

"It might be an air he's putting on to get through this. This is new territory for Father, I imagine—insults hurled at him publically from someone he doesn't know, the press camped outside his door. He may not be as upbeat as he's letting on."

Paul refilled his mug with coffee, holding the coffee pot awkwardly as he tried to make the use of his less dominant hand look carefree. Although Claribel hadn't finished more than half, he filled her mug as well until so little remained in the pot that he didn't feel guilty about pouring it into the sink. She stopped him, asking him to pour it into an empty ice cube tray instead; she would use it for iced coffee *granite* one afternoon. Then he started another pot of coffee, grunting as he pressed the new filter to the sides of the container, sighing after leaving a trail of ground coffee from the canister to the machine as he shakily added scoops to the filter.

Claribel noticed that her husband's movements were jerky, agitated. His haste only accentuated his struggle to adapt to using his left hand and carefully guarding his right. "You seem anxious," she commented.

"I am anxious," he confirmed. "I'm anxious to help Father out of this mess because—well, because I feel responsible."

"Responsible? How?"

He dropped the scooper in the canister, sealed the lid, and turned on the coffee machine. "He wouldn't have been at the hospital if it weren't for me, if it weren't for my name drawing some attention from the press. And he would not have been so conspicuous if I hadn't asked him to say a prayer with me, holding up the press conference. And, honestly, I just feel bad for the guy when he's so kind and good-natured."

"You can't blame yourself for this, Paul. You're not responsible for someone else's actions or words. I understand how you feel about wanting to help him. And you know what? If any good can come of this, it will be helping Father Soplido get through this as painlessly as possible, and I know you will do just that."

"I hope so."

A half an hour later, Paul welcomed Father Soplido and escorted him into the solarium after a stop in the kitchen for a cup of coffee. On the way, Father asked Paul how Claribel fared, referring to the returning strength and readjustment to better health he had noticed while at the hospital together. She had begun her toilette before Father arrived, and Paul hoped Father might see for himself the renewed energy in his wife when she joined them. He inquired about Paul's arm as they took their seats, Father on the couch and Paul in his armchair pulled near the ottoman between them. Claribel had set a tray on it with cream and sugar, spoons, napkins, and a plate of Peony Pilsen's sugar cookies. The men each set their coffee on the tray, but neither reclined into his seat. The morning, like previous ones, showcased the gray of an overcast sky as well as sporadic drizzle, but every few minutes, a ray of sunshine spirited itself free from behind the clouds and brightened the room for moments at a time. Paul and Father noticed but remained too absorbed in their musings to mention it.

Although he had known him from Saint Catherine's for over seven years, Paul, for the first time, studied his priest's appearance. His hands resting on his knees were olive—not a dark olive but a blanched variety matching the light tone of his face. His facial features did not seem characteristically Aztec, nor Mayan, nor what might prompt one to assume Mexican. His hair was short and black, neatly trimmed and barely capable of being parted, and Paul suspected from the shadow forming around his freshly shaved jawline that Father could be no older than thirty-five. No gray hairs mixed amongst his dark black sideburns; the skin around his always smiling lips was taut and the gleam in his brown eyes youthful.

Paul, still anxious, felt tired but wished to thwart a pending yawn, so as not to suggest to Father that he needed rest, that he was being put out, that he found this meeting remotely boring or taxing. Successfully avoiding the yawn, Paul quickly began to speak, hoping conversation would preempt another.

"So the press is camped outside the rectory? How'd you sneak out?"

"The front door of the rectory is on Main Street. I called Louise Sorrensen, the parish secretary, and told her to park on Steele Street, the street behind the rectory, to wait for me. Father Peychaud opened the front door to check for the mail and happened to distract the reporters while I dashed out the back door to Steele Street. Then I took Louise's car here while she walked around the block to the rectory. It was fun!"

"Sounds like an adventure," Paul said, glad Father could find a little merriment amid the woe. "I imagine you're not too keen on the press right now, especially after Handly."

Father's eyes dropped to his coffee sitting in the tray, and the smile never left his face.

"I'm afraid you had better address the press, Father," Paul continued, "so that you can move on—so that you can put this whole thing behind you."

"I have no issue with the press, Paul. And I'm in no hurry to move on. I wish to encounter each event and issue and interaction in my life as it presents itself, and I wish to address each as necessary. One might be quick, and another might take more time. I'm interested in bringing peace for anyone involved, not moving on just to be done, just for the sake of moving on."

"I see," Paul said, unsure how to respond. The words "interested in bringing peace" hovered in Paul's mind, suspended in a mist not unlike the precipitation outside. It was those words that preoccupied Paul to a muteness that stifled his further commentary.

He realized after hearing Father's words that he longed for more than rest. His retirement he wanted filled with peace— long, tranquil days in Saint Catherine's Cove with Claribel, his children, and his grandchildren—but he could not fathom quite how to fill a day with peace.

"I want to help you however I can, Father," Paul said at last. "I want to help you do whatever you need to do. How can I do that? Would you like to make a statement? I can take the lead on organizing that."

"Father Peychaud is taking care of that as we speak. I asked him to inform the press that they may pose questions this afternoon at one o'clock. I talked to the Provincial of the Order this morning and received his permission and advice. He suggested we hold it at the rectory, so Father Peychaud has arranged to host them in the rectory parlor."

"That's not too far off. Are you sure you want to do this so soon?"

"I am sure. I know they are anxious to hear from me; although, I am not so anxious to draw attention from so many more important issues they could be covering. The thought that I am a news item is a marvel to me still."

"They're most likely not covering important issues anyway, so don't feel you're pulling them from something significant. I wish they covered more of the positive stories in our community, but they don't. So may I make a suggestion?"

"Please," said Father, reaching for his coffee and taking a sip.

"Instead of fielding questions, you may wish to make a statement, thereby controlling the event and the information they receive. Do you have a statement prepared?"

"That, I do not, but I don't want to make a statement. I'd rather not volunteer any information they don't already know after having been present at the event itself. I just want to answer questions."

"No statement?"

"I have no fear of questions, Paul."

"But you don't know what you're going to get, Father."

"And that's why I would like your help. If you could brainstorm about some questions I might expect to be asked, I would appreciate it. I feel the exercise might help me at least feel more prepared if not actually collect my thoughts on the matter."

"Why do I have a feeling you already have some thoughts collected on the matter?"

Father grinned and looked at the coffee cup he held in his lap. A reserved strength exuded from Father, and Paul enjoyed that about his presence.

"No fear of questions, huh?" repeated Paul. A negative nod from Father received the question. "All right, Father. I think I know the angle a few of these reporters are going for, and I will ask a few likely questions. Please forgive me if I ask a question that may come off as offensive or intrusive. I'm only trying to prepare you for the possible worst, and some of their questions may be hard-hitting."

"I promise you I will not be offended. May I ask one other favor?"

"Of course, Father."

"May I request your presence at the conference at the rectory today? I know you must be sick of reporters after yesterday's conference, and I know you want nothing more than to settle in at home and recuperate from the accident, but I would feel more—reassured—knowing a respected parishioner and—friend—is there with me. I will drive you there and back. However, if it's the least bit taxing on you or even inconvenient—"

"I'd be happy to, Father." Paul recognized a formality in Father Soplido's delivery of the request and hoped to thwart the poor priest's conscientious deliberation over each word. "No need to feel embarrassed about asking me. You're not putting me out at all, and to be honest, I was going to ask if I could attend, anyway."

"Thank-you, Paul. Your presence will be a solace to me."

"You sure you want to take questions?"

"I'm sure." Father's response was typically upbeat and imbued with a joyful hope.

"Then let's start some question and answer."

Paul asked a series of questions that came so quickly to mind that he needed little deliberation, little floundering to concoct them. His knowledge of certain reporters likely to be present coupled with his understanding of the field provided insightful questions and topics for Father to consider. Before Claribel entered to greet the guest, Paul suggested that Father err on the side of brief answers, cautious ones without coming off guarded. Claribel's entrance prompted Paul and Father to explain the plan for the afternoon, nearing rapidly. Claribel concealed her displeasure at Paul's leaving the house, but Father detected it nonetheless, promising to return her husband by two o'clock.

The coffee had finished, and Father lifted the tray in order to bring it to the kitchen counter as they prepared to leave. Paul, steps behind his parish priest and hastening to leave for the rectory with plenty of time to set up, failed to notice that the gray had lifted as the solarium filled with sunshine. And Father Soplido never noticed as Paul released that yawn and never knew how badly Paul had wanted to sit, despite having been seated for the past hour and a half.

During the car ride to the rectory, Paul confirmed something he thought he had remembered hearing in a homily by Father—that he was born in Spain.

"Yes, born in Spain but emigrated to America with my parents when I was three. So all my schooling, from pre-school through high school, took place in the States."

He knew English fluently and had no accent, although certain intonations here and there might spur the question of being a non-native speaker, Paul thought. "Where did you grow up?"

"In Chicago. I went to a wonderful Catholic high school in a Chicago suburb. Then my maternal grandfather in Spain got sick. It was becoming difficult for my grandmother to take care of him, so my parents considered heading back to Spain to help her. Around that time, my paternal grandfather, also in Spain, took a fall and needed help with his recovery. That did it. My parents decided to move to Spain."

"And you went with."

"I had been accepted to several colleges, but I was still discerning the priesthood. So I went with and shortly thereafter joined the Dominicans in Spain. My high school was run by the Dominicans, so I was familiar with their ideology already. When my grandparents passed, my parents returned to Chicago. Because of my unique situation and upbringing in the States, I was transferred to the Central Province and eventually given the pastorate at Saint Catherine's."

As Father spoke less formally, Paul reflected on friendships, their forming so often during the in-between moments. When Father had visited Paul in the hospital, Father was on duty, in a manner of speaking. When Paul had spoken with Father at the house, Paul was on duty. Each in his own way had been working with the other, building a relationship but not necessarily a friendship. But now, in the car, without their role as priest or advisor, they simply spoke and listened and enjoyed each other's company. He found himself realizing that his friendship with Drew had developed during a car ride, too, and his friendship with Lucretia in the bleachers at a baseball game. He experienced a strange discomfort in realizing he had only now learned this.

Father's guard down, he spoke casually and freely, and Paul listened more freely, letting his imagination visualize Father in his youth, taking notes in a wooden seat and desk in a Dominican high school classroom just like Paul's, taking solemn vows in a dim, candle-lit chapel in Spain, staring out the plane window as he glanced at the patches of land in which he learned English, unpacking in a sparse bedroom of the rectory in Saint Catherine's Cove. Paul also appreciated Father's calmness and propriety, two characteristics that made forming a friendship easy for Paul.

The car ride ended quickly, and Paul eased himself from the passenger seat before Father Soplido could help him. They cut through the Standards' driveway on Steele Street to sneak into the rectory through the back door, hearing the reporters' voices in the parlor. Father Peychaud, who had pressed his hands and face against the windows in anticipation of their arrival, greeted them in the kitchen before escorting them into a small den where he relayed the status of things. Father Peychaud paced quickly while he read from a hand-written list of notes for Father Soplido to remember, to consider, to be aware of, some official from the Provincial, some reassuring about Father Peychaud's willingness to end the conference should a reporter cross a line. As he rushed through the notes, he reached for a mug of tea on a nearby stand and bumped his hand into it, nearly knocking it over. He continued to pace after he had read the notes, never taking that sip of tea. Once Father and Paul had freshened up, the two entered the parlor, announced by Father Peychaud. As cameras flashed and rolled and microphones drew near, Father Soplido stood behind a podium, with Paul and Father Peychaud steps behind him. Father Peychaud folded and refolded the sheet of paper on which the notes were written, and Paul, leaning against the wall, used his good arm to reinforce the sling holding his other arm.

"Welcome," Father Soplido began. "I see some familiar faces."

Whether he was referring to their celebrity or having met them at Paul's press conference, no one was sure, but they laughed nonetheless—controlled, nervous laughs.

"If you have some questions for me, you may ask them at this time. I promised Mrs. Scrivensby I would have her husband returned by two o'clock."

As Father had already done, Paul surveyed the faces of the reporters. Rhonda Turner stood front and center with her team, attracting expectant eyes to herself as the first to pose a question. Mickey Hall stood nearby with his team, always pleasant and affable. To Paul's surprise, Grant Joiner, a journalist for *Cityscape*, extended a recorder toward Father; his scrunched eyebrows revealed his constant constipation more than his quizzical longing for a good story, and Paul could not help cracking a smile, for he knew from several years of crossed paths the journalist's medical issue. Eloise Bernardi, fledgling and unconfident in her abilities, positioned herself on the perimeter of the press crowded into the small room. The size of the group surprised even Paul, who did not recognize all the faces. Some, he knew, might be new to the field as Eloise was, and others writers hidden behind their words.

As expected, Rhonda did not miss a beat in asking the first volley of questions. "Rhonda Turner, KARI-TV. Let's start with this. You're not Mexican."

Father responded with his bashful smile. "No, I am Spanish."

"And you were not born in the United States."

"No, I am an immigrant."

Cindy Carter, as the name tag on her lanyard noted, whispered to her cameraman, "Immigrant? I thought he said he wasn't Mexican."

Everyone heard. Rhonda, about to ask her next question, halted and closed her eyes.

"You can be an immigrant from other countries besides Mexico," whispered her cameraman. "He's an immigrant from Spain."

Cindy blushed. Amidst the tension associated with ethnic slurs and prejudices, she glanced down.

Rhonda continued. "As an immigrant from Spain who has clearly assimilated to American culture—to America—how rattled were you by Ted Handly's attack, by his reference to you as 'Poncho Sopapillas,' clearly a derogatory reference to someone of Mexican heritage?"

"I was not rattled. I believe I looked at the floor when he made the comment and smiled. I never once felt rattled."

"What, Father Soplido, went through your mind when you heard that egregious ethnic slur, likening you to a nationality you don't identify with by origin?"

"The Mexican culture, like the Spanish culture and like the American culture, is beautiful—one which embraces the Catholic Church. I did not initially associate the comment with an ethnic slur, as it has been labeled in the media. But somehow, I knew his comment lacked kindness. What went through my mind? I recall thinking his boldness was humorous to me. Inside, I laughed—"

"Laughed?"

"—laughed the way a teacher might to himself when a student does something uncouth that's amusing. The teacher doesn't want the student to know it was funny for fear of accidentally condoning the deed, but somehow, it still translates as funny to the teacher, who can't let on. That's how I felt."

"Ted Handly's comments were certainly on par with those of an elementary student and reflect a stunning immaturity, but the fact is, he's an adult. How does that weigh on your thoughts, Father?"

"It doesn't. Many adults have a childish side, immature impulses. I hear all about it in Confession week after week."

The press, anxious to find a reason to relax, laughed at this comment. Rhonda could but force a grin. She wanted more, but before she could persist with burrowing through Father's reactions to excavate the least bit of rancor or disapproval, Mickey Hall chimed in with a question.

"Mickey Hall, WLAK-TV. I tried putting myself in your shoes, and I imagine you never saw this news story coming. After all, the original story was supposed to be on Paul Scrivensby's car accident. Instead, Ted Handly's calling you a derogatory name has made headlines and the nightly news, eliciting strong reactions from people, locally and nationally. How do you respond to the sudden hype of which you are the central figure?"

"I honestly did not see it coming. I am still somewhat shocked by the turn of spotlight on me."

"Do you wish this whole thing would go away, Father?" asked Mickey Hall.

"I guess I have not spent my time wishing for that, Mr. Hall. I am happy to see this through, and I hope it will be addressed with tact and peacefulness by anyone interested. And I hope they will not forget the more significant feat—that Paul Scrivensby, a nuanced, delicate writer with a conscience, has escaped a serious accident with a minor injury."

As eyes shifted to Paul, he blushed and inadvertently squeezed his sling with his good hand. It stung, and, as he flinched, he stood upright, gently bouncing off the wall. The attention did not last long as Mickey continued with his questions.

"Father, is there anything you'd like to say to Ted Handly?"

"There is not. I wonder, though, if there might not be anything Ted Handly would like to say to me. If that were the case, I would like him to know that he is welcomed."

Mickey, leaving little time for another reporter to pose a question, asked, "Are you torn between a personal reaction to Handly's comments and a responsibility as a priest to turn the other cheek?"

"What do you think?" asked Grant Joiner directly to Mickey. "This whole thing has been a sermon."

Father Soplido smiled bashfully, squinting as he looked down. Father Peychaud accidentally tore the note he had folded nearly twenty times as he took a step into the room. But before his agitation could get the better of him, Paul said plainly, "I don't know, Grant, that he could separate the two." He said Grant's name as if he had known him for years, two professionals comfortable with each other's agendas, and the effect was calming.

"I just mean," added Grant, "that we're not getting much. I may be wrong, but I feel as if Father Soplido is placating if not holding back."

"I assure you, Mr. Joiner, that my responses are honest. I harbor no ill-will toward Ted Handly." When he spoke, he looked into Grant Joiner's eyes, and Grant Joiner looked down.

"The man viciously disparaged you, not once but twice, in front of others," he said to the floor. Then, with renewed conviction, he added, "You can't mean to tell me you were not offended. I don't believe it."

"I was not offended," Father Soplido reiterated definitively.

"I don't believe it, Father!" snapped Grant.

The delivery came off heated and aggressive, and Paul stepped in again to mitigate. But Father Peychaud interjected himself physically, wringing the ink out of the folded note. "Father Soplido has reflected and prayed on the events of yesterday, and he is not a liar. I'm afraid I cannot allow him to be subjected to more heinousness, so this conference must now come to an end."

Just as the grumbles stirred, as upset glances were exchanged, as Rhonda Turner murmured, "Just when we were getting somewhere—" Father Soplido said commandingly, "I repeat— with sincerity—that I was not offended. To be offended is a choice. And I chose not to be offended."

Paul stepped beside Father Soplido, an instinctive move to show solidarity with him, but the words "I chose not to be offended" struck him as they did everyone in the room. The energy in the room, teetering between tranquility and upheaval, stopped on the brink. While Rhonda and Grant reveled in the first emotional reaction from Father Soplido all day, Mickey and Eloise lamented his being brought to that point. But the words "I chose not to be offended" thwarted all from continuing as they contemplated the meaning, re-evaluated where this comment positioned their story, and grasped for questions to formulate.

"The idea of this conference was not for you to have to defend yourself," said Father Peychaud to his fellow Friar. Redirecting his comments to the press, he said, "We thank you for your time and questions and now request that this conference be adjourned. Thank-you."

A few reporters began packing while some of the photographers snapped shots of Father Soplido, Paul stalwartly at his side. Grant Joiner grumbled in a way that called attention to his displeasure as he jotted notes into a notebook, and then surlily asked someone for directions to a washroom. Soon, all but Eloise and Rhonda had left. Eloise approached the podium where Father Soplido stood, a stoic smile on his face, and extended her thin, dainty hand. "Thank-you for having us, Father. We know you didn't have to do this." A tenuous bracelet sliding down her arm looked less delicate than her.

"I was happy to, Ms.—"

"Bernardi. Eloise Bernardi, freelance journalist. I'm affiliated with Precision Press right now." She appeared anxious—eager to leave—but not with the ambition to write the big story, not with the hurry to tackle more exciting endeavors that beckoned. She looked like someone rushing to retreat, like someone defeated.

"Thank-you, Ms. Bernardi," Father said as the young journalist sidled away.

Her team heading to the door, Rhonda approached the podium next, knowing she was the last one and timing it thus. "Not the ending you imagined, I bet."

"I confess, Ms. Turner, that I thought it would run more smoothly," Father rejoined.

"I could offer you an opportunity to turn this around—to turn this into something positive—that is, if you'd be willing to sit down with me for an exclusive. What do you say?"

"An exclusive?" inquired Father Soplido. The question piqued the interest of Paul and Father Peychaud, who, on either side of Father Soplido, leaned in.

"I can offer you a chance to talk to me one-on-one without all the cameras or other press. It would give you a chance simply to tell your story."

"Why do I have the feeling," said Father Peychaud, "that there's more than 'an exclusive' in it for you?"

"You don't need to be cynical, Father. There's so much we didn't get to cover. I just want something to make a full story out of. I make no bones about that."

"I'm afraid you got all we are willing to give, Ms. Turner," said Father Peychaud.

"But doesn't the public deserve more? Doesn't Father Soplido deserve justice?"

"I'll leave what I deserve to God, Ms. Turner," said Father Soplido.

She looked at him as if to say, "Another one of those 'I'm a priest' answers," but instead said, "I see." While his comment tempted her to throw in the towel, persisting had become too much of a habit for her to back off so easily.

"Could I at least get a comment on your reaction to Anita Gonzalez-Shea's statement earlier this morning?"

The three men exchanged glances, and Rhonda knew she had something.

"You didn't hear?"

"I'm afraid I don't know what you're referring to," admitted Father Soplido.

"Should we know who that is?" asked Father Peychaud.

"Anita Gonzalez-Shea of D.C.—one of D.C.'s largest law firms—Worth, Sutton, and Gonzalez-Shea. Ring a bell now? They handled the Glen Harbin case last year. Gonzalez-Shea was the lead prosecutor."

"The name—the story—rings a bell," said Father Soplido, but he couldn't place it. Paul, however, could as he had heard it discussed at meetings the previous year at *The Current Front.* His friend and coworker Sorita Jennings had been covering it and shared plenty of tidbits about the trial. The trial involved sexual harassment allegations at a leading software development company. The case sharply emphasized that the CEO of the multi-million dollar corporation, amongst others, perpetuated the harassment by turning a blind eye. Paul knew that Anita Gonzalez-Shea's involvement in Father Soplido's situation did not bode well for an imminent ending to this ordeal.

"How do you know this? What did she say?" asked Father Peychaud ingenuously.

"I'd be happy to share that—and to cover your reaction—if you can grant me an exclusive." Rhonda Turner, as if holding all the cards, stepped to Father Soplido and extended a firm, strong hand.

Father once again smiled and said, "I am not ready to acquiesce to an exclusive at this time; however, I thank you for sincere, vested interest in representing my voice."

Rhonda lowered her hand and shook her head. Before turning her head toward her team waiting at the door, Father Soplido noticed her eyes redden with caught tears. Whatever angst she felt revealed itself in a sigh as she said to her colleagues, "That's it. We've got all we're going to get. Let's go."

When she turned to meet them at the door, Father Soplido said calmly, "I can tell you are frustrated. What can I do to bring you peace?"

She stopped and turned to him, her eyes still red with restrained tears. "I just wanted justice for you, Father. I wanted to expose the truth, and part of the truth is your real reaction to those words."

"Jesus said, 'I am the Truth.' And He is The Prince of Peace. It seems to me that the peace I wish for you and the Truth you wish to convey should go hand in hand then." He stepped in front of the podium toward Rhonda. "I did tell you my real reaction. If you can trust me—if you can trust that I have told you the truth—then maybe writing the article can bring you peace."

"But you're not admitting to the least bit of indignation. Can you understand my frustration, Father?"

"I think your frustration lies not so much in my not admitting to something I never felt, but in not finding the reaction you want from me for your story. You say you want to expose the truth, but when I give it to you, when I insist that I was not offended, it's not good enough."

Rhonda looked from Paul to Father Peychaud, unsure how to proceed.

"I'm not sure there's much more Father Soplido can do," interjected Father Peychaud amid the din of swelling voices outside. Rhonda turned again to her team and made for the exit as the voices grew louder, grew nearer. When Rhonda reached the door, the members of the press who had just left scurried back in, anxious to establish great locations. Reporters and cameras lined both sides of an aisle toward the podium in the middle of the room, behind which Father Soplido was retreating.

"What's going on?" asked Father Peychaud. "I kindly requested the conference come to a close."

"Anita Gonzalez-Shea just arrived," said Mickey Hall, positioned close to the podium. "All the way from D.C. She's on her way in right now."

Father Peychaud, Father Soplido, and Paul all heard the remark, and all froze in stupefaction. Then they heard Grant Joiner's voice as he spoke directly into his videographer's camera, "We are here live at the Dominican rectory of Saint Catherine's in Saint Catherine's Cove, Wisconsin where lead prosecutor of Washington D.C.'s Worth, Sutton, and Gonzalez-Shea, Anita Gonzalez-Shea, has arrived to make, we suspect, the recently maligned Father Fernando Soplido an offer to represent him in a suit against journalist Ted Handly. Father Soplido is currently poised to consider her request." With a sudden vim carrying his words, he announced, "And here she comes now. Again Anita Gonzalez-Shea entering the Saint Catherine's Parish rectory in Saint Catherine's Cove, Wisconsin."

The three men could not move from their position as the press parted for Anita Gonzalez-Shea's entrance. She stepped into the parlor smiling. Stout despite a petite stature, she wore an unpatterned, hunter's green tailleur with a cream, satiny blouse; gold, thick bracelets clinked on each wrist and called attention to a faceted emerald ring on her right-hand index finger, the faceted diamond of her engagement ring on her left hand, and the gold wedding band next to it; her black hair curved under her jawline, coiffed neatly, as if she had not just traveled across the country. Behind her, D.C. and national press extended their microphones and cameras to obtain footage; she had brought them with her.

The smile stiff and unfading, she walked the aisle made for her by the press with clunky but confident steps, and extended a clanging hand to Father Soplido. "Father Soplido? Anita Gonzalez-Shea. Pleasure to meet you."

She offered no epithet nor appositive, assuming neither was needed. The Glen Harbin trial had made national headlines and interrupted shows, and she had led the charge. He was sure to know the power in the hand he graciously shook.

"You couldn't have known I was coming," she whispered. "But did you hear my statement earlier?"

Father nodded that he had not. Rhonda inched toward them to capture their initial exchange.

Anita extended a hand to Father Peychaud, nodded as he accepted it, and then turned to Paul. "Paul Scrivensby, it is an honor." She used her left hand to hold his left hand, and before he could release it, she turned to the press, holding a pose long enough for a few shots.

Father Soplido maneuvered behind the podium, welcoming Anita behind it with him in spite of his quizzicality. Sharing the podium, the two stood front and center, and Anita wasted no time simultaneously addressing Father and the press. She commanded the conference as if it had been called for her.

"I apologize, ladies and gentlemen of the press, for the intrusion. Even Father Fernando Soplido—of Spain—did not know I was coming. If Father will allow me, I wish to make a statement—" and giving neither Father Soplido nor Father Peychaud a moment to respond, she continued, "—a statement reiterating the sentiment I voiced earlier today from my D.C. office. My utter disgust for Ted Handly's behavior not only remains but intensifies, as it must; however, I cannot let my reaction remain a feeling only. My conscience compels me to take action, to fight for justice. Outraged and offended by the unprovoked insults issued by irresponsible reporter Ted Handly, I wish to represent Father Fernando Soplido—*pro bono*—in a civil suit against Ted Handly and WBAM for emotional harassment and distress. We'll leave it at that for now."

A murmur amongst the press and renewed attention to Father Soplido provided enough opportunity for him to redden. Paul looked at Father Peychaud, wondering if they shouldn't end this conference again.

Anita continued, "Ted Handly is banking on a priest letting Ted walk all over him without consequence. I have a message for you, Ted Handly and the powers that be at WBAM who have let him go unreprimanded: you will not get away with this.

As a Mexican myself—and one who loves my *sopapillas*—I will bring justice for Father Fernando Soplido and the Mexican people who have suffered enough."

Facing Father Soplido while stepping backwards, she extended a hand over the podium toward him for all to see. Her stiff smile returning, she said, "What do you say, Father? Shall we work for justice together?"

Father smiled gently and turned to Anita. Warmly, cordially, he took her extended hand in both of his and held it before the press, not in a way that suggested a handshake or acceptance of her offer, but in a way that exuded graciousness. Maintaining the rigid smile, Anita flinched, not expecting Father to handle himself with so much poise and control of the situation. Not to the press but to her, he said, "Mrs. Gonzalez-Shea, I appreciate your concern and reflection on my situation, and at this time, I wish to say only thank-you for the offer. As I am sure you must understand, a decision like this warrants considerable reflection from me. As I would like to avoid acting in haste, I entreat you for some time to think on it. Will you grant me this?"

"Of course, Father. I know you are a wise and reflective priest and will come to the right conclusion before long." She used her free hand to touch Father's enveloping hands and then withdrew them, stepping again towards the podium.

Paul suspected Father had already made up his mind on the matter but felt relief at his pastor's diplomacy and composure. Father Peychaud, sweating now, sighed gratefulness as well. Assuming Anita would now bring the press conference to an end after accomplishing her goal, Paul and Father Peychaud seemed to sink into the wall behind the podium.

"Ladies and gentlemen of the press, that is not all I wish to say."

Paul and Father Peychaud tensed and locked eyes. Father Peychaud placed a hand over his heart as if to conceal its pounding from the cameras.

Anita began, "Father Soplido is not the only one victimized by the cruel hatred spewed by Ted Handly. Rhonda Turner, who demanded an apology—and received none—was victimized. Anita Gonzalez-Shea, a concerned citizen of Mexican descent, was victimized. The American people who witnessed his cruelty were victimized. But I cannot represent the American people, as I am so willing to do, because in such a case, proximity to Father Soplido, the object of Ted Handly's attack, is requisite. Not even Rhonda Turner had a relationship close enough to Father Soplido to allow me to take legal action on her behalf. However, another man does have that closeness to Father Soplido. So I would like to extend the same offer of representation as I have to Father Soplido—to Paul Scrivensby!"

More murmuring commenced as Paul emerged from the wall as much as he wished to recede further within it. Father Soplido looked back at him, but Anita never broke eye contact with the cameras from the press she had brought with her.

"Paul Scrivensby, as a parishioner and loyal friend to Father Soplido, as you have made clear by your supportive presence here alone, will you accept my offer to represent you in a civil suit against Ted Handly and the powers that be at WBAM for the third-party emotional distress and harassment inflicted by Ted Handly and his hateful words?"

When she said this, he immediately thought of Claribel, who had used the same word earlier that morning regarding his reaction to last night's news—"distress." His anxiety over how to help Father Soplido swelled to the surface of his memory, as did recollection of his shakiness making the coffee. And as the press aimed their microphones and cameras at him, a resentment swirled around his heart, raced past his throat, and settled like acid into his brain. How dare she put him on the spot like this! How dare she promote herself at his and Father's expense!

In this moment, as Anita stared at the cameras, never glancing behind her for so much as a glimpse at Paul, Paul found it hard not to be offended by her blatant self-promotion. But Father Soplido's maxim, "to be offended is a choice," echoed through his mind, and he believed him.

Miffed by her gall, he shook himself free from the resentful thoughts, from the impulse to be offended, and stepped toward the podium. "I, like Father Soplido, will address this—gracious—offer after some time to consider it. Thank-you." He immediately took a step back.

As if with a switch, she turned her smile on again as she said, "Of course. I hope to stay in Saint Catherine's Cove for the night and reach a decision with Father Fernando Soplido and Paul Scrivensby soon. Ted Handly's actions cannot continue to go unadmonished, nor can those who perpetuate such actions by looking the other way go uncorrected. I am confident the three of us can work together to arrive at justice and to send a powerful message to those who wouldn't otherwise think twice about spewing hatred. Again, I apologize for interrupting the conference, and I thank you, the press, the Dominicans at Saint Catherine's, and Father Soplido, for allowing me to speak."

Cindy Carter shouted, "Father Soplido! How surprised were you—" at the same time Mickey Hall shouted, "Anita! Will you pursue Ted Handly without—"

"That's enough!" interjected Father Peychaud, beads of sweat pouring down his forehead. "The press conference is done!"

More shots were taken as grumbles accompanied sinking shoulders and perturbed glances.

Except for those Anita brought, the press began to pack up again. She leaned toward Father Soplido and said, "*Nos reunimos pronto? Tenemos mucho que discutir,*" to which Father responded, "*Quiere volver a la rectoría mañana a las 10:30 para tomar el desayuno? Podemos hablarnos entonces.*" Then addressing Paul, Anita said, "We'll be in touch, Paul."

Paul noticed that only when they stopped talking, Anita's press stopped recording. Confident the conference had ended officially and non-officially, they, too, began to pack up. Rhonda Turner watched for any further interaction between Anita and Father, and when she realized Anita was accompanying her crew out, Rhonda then exited. Grant Joiner sidled to a nearby washroom for another attempt. Paul saw Eloise Bernardi shaking her head in disbelief, the last to exit. She stopped before leaving the room and headed toward Paul and Father.

"I don't know how to make sense of all this," she said, her exasperation and greenness evident. "But I just wanted to apologize for any distress this is causing both of you."

"Don't use that word," Paul said, making light of the situation and surprised that levity so easily replaced the flush of anger he had just experienced. "It has legal meaning now."

Eloise blushed until it hit her that he was joking. "Neither of you wanted all this hoopla. I know what it's like to want to escape something that feels so much bigger than you. This might be my last—." She paused. "I don't think I'm cut out—." Articulating her thoughts grew too difficult, so she closed, "Hang in there."

Paul sensed her discouragement but did not know how to respond in this moment, his mind leaping amongst thoughts on too many recent topics.

She crossed through the parlor and left as Father Peychaud followed, making sure the press saw themselves out, locking the front door after Grant Joiner's surly exit, and peering through the window as their vans and cars finally cleared.

In the parlor, Paul said to Father Soplido, "I guess we bought some time to think."

"I already made my decision, Paul. I can't speak for you, but I have no intention of suing Ted Handly."

"How are you going to break the news to Anita?"

"I invited her over for breakfast tomorrow."

Paul looked dumbfounded. Was that what had been established in Spanish minutes earlier?

"You act quickly."

"There's no use in belaboring this when I know my heart. You and Claribel are welcomed, as well. And speaking of Claribel," he added with a grin, "I can get you home to your wife on time if we leave now."

Father Soplido saw Paul into his house before heading back to the rectory. Claribel waved from the front door when she saw her pastor pull away and then met her husband in the kitchen to inspect his wellness and his spirits. Paul schlepped from the kitchen to the solarium and plopped into the armchair while Claribel followed, announcing that he looked exhausted.

"I am exhausted. I've been dying to sit down since the moment I left the solarium with Father Soplido this morning."

"You're sitting now. Why don't you put your feet up on the ottoman?" Before sitting on the couch, she pushed the ottoman toward Paul's armchair.

"I'm not going to get comfortable here, I'm afraid. I'm heading straight upstairs for a nap. I just want to tell you about the press conference first."

Claribel could not bring herself to sit back as Paul's story reeled her curiosity toward him. Neither could Paul rest his legs on the ottoman as he narrated about Cindy Carter's embarrassment, Mickey Hall's perspective, Rhonda Turner's offer and dejection, Grant Joiner's vocal dissatisfaction, and Father Peychaud's nerves getting the better of him.

"So that's why it ended early and you arrived home on time," Claribel said, as if Paul's story were coming to an end.

But he continued, as if capturing an entertaining anecdote in his column, about Anita Gonzalez-Shea's surprise arrival, about her stealing the lime light of the conference with a press team she brought with her from Washington D.C., about her offer to represent Father Soplido and his announcement to think on it.

"That is a twist the media will have a field day with. Coming all the way from Washington D.C. to make the offer—publically! If Father hadn't given them enough to work with, Anita Gonzalez-Shea certainly did." Once again assuming Paul had brought his story to an end, she sighed.

But Paul carried on with the final twist and the actual conclusion of the story—that Anita publicly offered to represent Paul, too, in a third-party emotional distress suit, that the conference abruptly ended again, and that Anita and Father Soplido planned to meet tomorrow morning. "I think I should be there to give her my response, as well."

"She offered to represent you?" Claribel repeated, the prospect spinning in her mind.

"Offered to represent me," he reiterated. "I'm not sure I know what a 'third-party suit' is."

"Why don't you call Brent or Roy? I'm sure they could shed some light on her offer."

"I'm sure they could, and I may do that," he said reflectively. Then, shifting to firmness, he said, "But I'm not accepting her offer."

"You're not accepting," Claribel echoed, nodding a sort of approval and consent with her head. "You're sure?"

"I'm pretty sure, yes."

"'Pretty sure' isn't sure, Paul." Then she added, "You *were* distressed." Her grin revealed her enjoyment over complicating the matter for Paul, an enjoyment he appreciated.

"This offer isn't about me or my rights being violated or my 'distress.' It's about her. It's a way for her to make herself relevant again now that the Glen Harbin trial is old news."

"That's what I would assume, too—"

The phone rang, so she did not finish her thought. She answered it in the study and called Paul in to take it. "It's Stephen."

Stephen, the editor-in-chief at *The Current Front*, had already sent flowers for the car accident so was perhaps checking on Paul's recovery. Perhaps he was calling for business. Paul put the phone on speaker, encouraging Claribel to remain.

"Paul, how are you feeling?"

"I'm tired, Stephen. Got out of the hospital only yesterday."

"And already an eventful afternoon!"

"You've heard."

"Paul, we know a story is breaking soon about Anita Gonzalez-Shea's offer to represent you."

"Word travels fast in this business. Let me guess—you want to know my answer before anyone else?"

Stephen chuckled. "That would be nice. I have a bigger request to make of you, though."

Paul and Claribel's eyes connected, using the held contact to share speculation over the possibilities.

"Go on."

"We're wondering, no matter what you decide about the case, if you'd give us a feature story about Father Soplido, Ted Handly, and the entrance of Anita Gonzalez-Shea on the scene. We want it for the December issue."

"The December issue? It's already November. That can't give me much time to write it."

"We know anything you give us will sell. The controversial column helped a lot, but after *the accident*, the November issue's sales are soaring. We want the same for the December edition."

"Don't you think my final column might do that itself, now that I've been in the press for other matters?"

"Your final column is likely to ensure established readers will not neglect the December edition, but the feature on Father Soplido that so many journalists are vying for right now could broaden our audience. We're sure to gain attention from new readers, and the feature—as written by you—could secure that."

Paul looked at Claribel again, and she crossed her arms and stared at her husband's as she said, "Stephen, you do realize Paul is wearing a sling on his right arm and can't write."

"Claribel?" asked Stephen. "I should have realized that. I saw it in the press footage from the hospital, but Paul's got another hand, doesn't he? Paul, you can type with your left hand just this once, can't you?"

"You made your point, Stephen. You want me to write this thing. You've got a lot of nerve asking for this right after asking me to rewrite my final column." His tone playful, he noticed Claribel's glower.

"I respected your decision, Paul. That counts for something, doesn't it?"

"All right, Stephen. I will think about it. I'll get back to you soon."

When they finished the phone call, Paul and Claribel returned to the solarium still brimming with sunlight. More comfortable there, they stood this time, too preoccupied to sit.

"You have a lot of thinking to do, don't you, Paul? Letting Anita Gonzalez-Shea represent you. Writing a feature for *The Current Front*'s next issue. Who would have ever thought you had retired?"

"'A lot of thinking to do.' I'm tired of thinking. I'm just plain tired," he said, the exhaustion and exasperation clear. "I wanted to visit Oliver and Lucretia today, but all I want to do right now is sleep."

He left the room and headed for the stairs. From the bottom, Claribel watched him climb them slowly. Once in his bedroom, he kicked off his shoes, lay on the made bed, adjusted his sling-held arm on his abdomen, and fell asleep before he could fully entertain thoughts on his rekindling resentment for Anita Gonzalez-Shea, blaming himself for Father Soplido's media frenzy, reprimanding himself for not asking Claribel how she was feeling, wondering when he would get to see Oliver and Lucretia, and giving ample consideration to writing a feature for the yet-to-be-printed December edition.

Paul did not wake that night—did not wake before morning—along with Claribel, who gently inserted herself under the sheets and covers beside her husband only an hour after he had lain down for his "nap." Together, they missed the news that evening showcasing Father Soplido's statement, "I was not offended. To be offended is a choice. And I chose not to be offended," and the addendum about Anita Gonzalez-Shea's arriving to offer representation to both Father and Paul. A long, deep sleep protected them from recycling thoughts on these turbulent issues, but would it revitalize them enough to endure whatever else Paul's first days of retirement had in store?

CHAPTER 10

On the ride to his house the day before, Father Soplido had informed Paul of the plan to meet Anita for breakfast at the rectory at 10:30am, so when Paul awoke at 8:30am after sleeping undisturbed through the whole night, he did not feel panicked about arriving late. He let Claribel sleep as he carefully showered and dressed, put on coffee, and, seated at the island in the kitchen, read the local paper. Drizzle emitted simple sounds and grayed the morning but could not pelt the vibrant yellow and crimson leaves from the trees. Saint Catherine's Cove still looked heartily vibrant in mid-autumn, not winter-stark. From Paul's second-floor windows, he could see nearby Lake Superior and the lighthouse on a winter's day; as of yet, he could barely see them through the fiery foliage.

Claribel's footsteps on the floor above pulled him after a short while from his blank stare at the newspaper opened to the article on Father Soplido, the caption under the photograph reading, "To be offended is a choice. –Father Fernando Soplido, O.P." He was thinking not about yesterday's press conference nor the decisions he would have to make concerning offers from Anita Gonzalez-Shea and Stephen at *The Current Front*, but about Father's maxim. Just as Paul was concluding that the words indeed offered good advice, the back door opened and ambled footsteps heralded his grandchildren's arrival.

Eli and Gracie walked in the kitchen and greeted their grandfather as he wondered to what he owed this morning visit on a school day.

"We slept through our alarm," Eli said.

"Eli set it for the wrong hour," revealed Gracie.

"I did not!" Eli was ticked and backed away from arguing about it as if, at this point, he were tired of arguing about it.

"Shouldn't you be on your way to school then?" Paul asked.

"We'll both get detentions if someone doesn't call us in," Eli announced.

"And Eli is afraid Dad will kill us when he finds out we got detentions for oversleeping and getting a tardy," revealed Gracie.

"So you thought you'd stop here on the off chance that I might call you in late? As if there were a good reason for being so late to school?" inquired Paul, acting doubtful but thrilled to come through for his grandchildren.

"I guess so," responded Eli, a mild embarrassment pinking his face.

Paul laughed and said, "Let's find the schools' numbers."

Eli had Greengate's number on hand, Gracie Saint Catherine High School's, and the grandchildren waited delightedly while their grandfather called the schools, announcing their late arrival. They marveled when their grandfather hung up each time without having given a reason for their tardiness.

"You're good to go. Just stop in to see the attendance secretary before you go to class."

"Thanks, Grandpa," they both said.

"But you have to do your grandmother and me a favor. If you can wait another fifteen minutes or so, we could use a lift to the Saint Catherine's rectory. I can't drive in this thing." When he said "this thing," he lifted his arm in the sling and grimaced on account of the sudden wave of pain that rippled from his hand and wrist somehow to his stomach.

Eli cringed sympathetically and replied, "We'll take care of the lift, Grandpa." Gracie had received her driver's license not too long ago.

Until Claribel had readied herself, Paul chatted with his grandchildren in the kitchen and enjoyed every moment of it. He had wanted to spend more time with them, and the encounter reminded him he wanted to call Mikey at college, too. Yesterday, he had wanted to do so many things and pulled off none of them; he wasn't accomplishing nearly as much as he had planned in what was supposed to be free time, not the least of which included sitting on the solarium couch reading, listening to the birds and the rustle of the trees, and just plain resting.

Once Claribel entered the kitchen and had a few sips of coffee, the grandchildren drove their grandparents to the rectory by 10:20am. Father Soplido in an apron greeted them at the door and waved to Eli and Gracie as they rode off joyfully late to school without repercussion.

Two pans on the stove awaiting completion would soon join an assortment of breakfast items on the counter, and the round table in the small kitchen proffered five place settings along with a pitcher of orange juice and a coffee pot atop a trivet. Father Soplido insisted Paul and Claribel help themselves to coffee and to sit wherever they liked. As they reached for their mugs and Father turned his attention to the stove, the doorbell rang. Father Peychaud descended the stairs to let in Anita Gonzalez-Shea and escorted her to the kitchen. She, like Paul and Claribel, took a moment to take in the bounty on the countertop.

"It's not too often I get to cook something special for guests," Father Soplido said while placing freshly seared *botifarra blanca* and piping hot *croquetas* onto a platter. All the food prepared, he enumerated each treat, from the *coca de llardons* and the All Saints' Day *panellets de pinyons* to the *truita amb suc* with plenty of what he said locals in Spain call "*xup-xup*," a bed of tomato sauce. The guests served themselves and found a place at the breakfast table. Claribel took a moment to cut some of Paul's food for him. After a grace led by Father Peychaud, they began eating and vociferating their taste buds' delight of each bite. Father Soplido glanced down on each compliment and repeated, "Thank-you. It was my pleasure." Although no one waited to learn about them before enjoying, he spent a few moments explaining each dish, noting that certain foods and ingredients peculiar to Catalonia, like the *botifarra blanca*, a type of sausage, and the *serrano*, a cured ham for the *croquetas*, can be imported, to incorporate a taste of authenticity to each bite. The recipes for the ham and cheese *croquetas*, or "*croquetes de pernil*" in Catalan, and the spinach-omelette-like *truita amb suc* hailed from his mother's family while the baked goods recipes like *the coca de llardons*, a slightly sweet bread, and the pine nut cookies called *panellets* descended from his father's. The intriguing flavors and the fervent explanations of traditions, history, and technique interested everyone gathered.

Father Peychaud, on a sudden recall, rose from the table and pulled a wooden trinket box from a drawer. He showed the guests a light-blue anchor charm and announced he had found it yesterday after the press conference. The golden charm inlaid with faceted jewels sparkled despite the drizzly gray illuminating the room.

"Cute," said Anita, in a way that somehow belittled the charm.

"It's not yours then?" double-checked Father Peychaud, turning on the kitchen light to brighten the room a little.

"Mine? No." A disgust for something so small sounded in her voice as she glanced at her heavy, gold bracelets and her emerald ring from yesterday. Today she wore another tailored suit, only in paisleys but still a forest green.

"That belongs to Eloise Bernardi, the young reporter off to the side of the group," Paul interjected, resting his new eating arm so unused to so much work. "I saw it on her wrist when she shook our hands. It was one of three—that anchor, a cross, and a heart."

Father Soplido and Father Peychaud smiled. "We will have to contact her today about returning it," Father Peychaud said.

Brief discussions on the autumn in D.C. as compared to the autumn in Saint Catherine's Cove, Paul's last trip to New York, and the difference between Spanish and Mexican chorizo broke the ice before the morning's order of business leapt to the fore.

Father Peychaud and Claribel remained silent but attentive. Father Soplido thanked Anita for her offer and tactfully declined it. Anita, as if expecting this response, refused to accept that he had adequately contemplated it.

"The thought of a long trial, I'm sure, is daunting and scary—" she rejoined.

"—and would deplete my energy for more necessary work here," added Father Soplido.

"But that's my point. Don't you need to put aside your own desires to accomplish a better good? The sacrifice of your time and taking on something this challenging could pave the way for a more caring generation of people."

"It's not *my* desires I'm necessarily putting first. I am obedient to the ministry I have been called to perform by superiors, and my vow of obedience obligates me to follow through. The ministry I'm performing is about others, not myself. So it is not my 'own desires' that I am placing before what you want to accomplish."

"I'm afraid the message this sends is that it is okay to offend—that you, Father, are okay with letting others be offensive."

"I am not okay with others using their mouth to spew venom, but again, to be offended is a choice."

"This morning's headlines," Anita reminded herself. "Let me tell you a story, Father. A few months before the Harbin trial hoopla, one of the younger lawyers on my team, Burton Main, openly homosexual, was walking among the security and lawyers escorting a client out of the courthouse as a few reporters and photographers met them on the steps. Somehow, as the lawyers made their way to the car through the press, Burton and a photographer, Jethro Kimms, bumped into each other and started bickering. The photographer, Jethro Kimms, called Burton Main a derogatory name, a known slur against homosexuals. And Burton was clearly bothered by it when he brought the story back to the office but was willing to let it slide. 'Why should it?' I thought. 'Why sweep this under the rug?' And so I talked with Burton about it, and we pursued Jethro Kimms, intent on not letting him get away with it. And while it wasn't highly publicized, Jethro had to attend sensitivity training. He may have gotten off light, but he won't make the same mistake twice, I'd guess, after a few weeks of sensitivity training."

"It sounds to me like you are the one who needed the sensitivity training." Father Soplido's comment prohibited any movement at the breakfast table.

"Of course using words deliberately to injure another human being is wrong, and Jethro Kimms was wrong to do such, but you were the one who was overly sensitive to those words," Father explained.

"Am I hearing you correctly?" Anita looked around the table for an ally but was met with no eye contact.

"Even Burton Main was willing to let it roll off him, choosing not to be offended, but you are the one who reacted in a way that made it an issue."

"I made it an issue to prevent it from being an issue in the future. Am I the only one who sees this?"

"I suppose I see human nature differently than you see it."

Anita took a sip of coffee and swallowed slowly to regroup after Father's unforeseen response. Then she continued in her characteristic no-nonsense manner. "My point was that something was done in that small, basically unknown incident, and something should be done in this big, now public incident. What Ted Handly did was offensive, and we have a responsibility to act."

"Here's the part I'm struggling with, Mrs. Gonzalez-Shea," said Father Peychaud, speaking for the first time since he displayed the anchor charm. "Let's assume being offended isn't a choice. Or let's say it still is. Doesn't matter. Isn't being offended somewhat subjective? What's offensive to one might not be offensive to another."

"Being called 'Father Sopapillas' is *debatably* offensive? That slur might *not* be offensive?"

"It's offensive to you. It wasn't offensive to Father Soplido. What's the standard for what constitutes offensive or not? Has the Court set a standard on this? To me, something so clearly subjective and ambiguous makes this whole proposal moot, not to mention that Father Soplido has publicly voiced his view on the matter—that he chose not to be offended."

Dropping Father Peychaud from the conversation like a piece of lint from her pocket, Anita turned to Paul. "I will assume that Father Soplido does not speak for you, Paul. Anyone sitting here at this very table can see how visibly distressed you are for your dear friend and priest—" Paul glanced at Claribel in part to ask "Do I look distressed?" and in part to declare, "I do not look distressed." The look accomplished both but also cemented their awareness of Anita's stratagem. "—and this unnecessary distress caused to you should not go unpunished. You, at least, see that, Paul. Don't you?"

"Anita, I'm afraid you don't have a client in me either. And I'm grateful for your flying out this way to talk to us in person and for your interest in repre—"

"They say," Anita interrupted, her eyes now fixed on Claribel, "that behind every great man is a great woman. Could I entreat you, Claribel, woman to woman here, to get through to your husband? Woman to woman, could I entreat you to talk some sense into this stubborn man—" and she chuckled to make light of the comment, to trim the adjective of any sharp edges— "to do the right thing?"

"My husband is a great man because he has a good heart and a good mind, and if I have anything to do with his greatness, it's because I've let him love and think for himself and have supported him along the way."

"So humble of you, Claribel, but history tells us otherwise: Napoleon's Josephine, Roosevelt's Eleanor, Wash—"

"MacBeth's Lady MacBeth, Ahab's Jezebel," added Claribel.

Anita stared in Claribel's eyes and emitted the faintest forced chuckle. "I thought as one woman to another, *you and I* could get something accomplished here."

"Then that was a mistake, Anita. I don't want to get embroiled in hollow alliances. There are great men in their own right. There are great women in their own right. Each has supported and encouraged the greatness of the other through the centuries, certainly. 'Woman to woman'? If I were Mexican, would you have said, '*Latina* to *Latina*'? It's a frivolous sense of unity that makes for so much division. It's what pits groups against each other instead of truly bringing groups, individuals, together. What do you think is more likely to beget peace? A clash—in the courtroom, over the airwaves, wherever—or forgiveness? Forgiveness is bigger than a group sharing the same gender or sharing the same ethnicity or race or religion."

"Then like Father Soplido, you, too, see human nature differently than I do."

"We need to leave room for hope," Father Soplido added, looking at the blue anchor charm in the trinket box. "Which is another thing that connects us as humans, not divides us into groups within groups. A perspective on human nature without room for hope is more cynical than history illustrates, too."

Resilient, Anita surveyed those at the table, her unflinching eyes meeting each of theirs. With strong, direct delivery, she persisted, "I think we've lost sight of the point. I am trying to achieve something good here, and I need your help to do it. I am trying to show *all people* that hate crimes in any form are intolerable. Why is it so hard for you to get on board with that?"

"Please do not confuse my directness for rudeness, but I think it's because everyone here sees through you," said Claribel, clasping her hands on the edge of the table as delicately as she spoke. "This is about Anita Gonzalez-Shea, not thwarting defamation and hatred. And if we hope to bring awareness to the intolerability of spewing hatred, there are other ways to do so. Your approach is rooted in fear, in scaring people to behave nicely through fear of consequences. We are simply willing to explore other ways at this time, Anita."

"If by exploring other ways, you mean doing nothing, then I don't know how you hope to accomplish anything."

"Choosing not to be offended *is* doing something. And it's just one step," Father Soplido said. When nothing but a metallic stare met his statement, he continued, "But forcing someone to behave how you want—dragging them through a trial, sending them to sensitivity training—isn't always effective or lasting. And for those who witness it on television and in the papers, it's enough to scare them into behaving a certain way for fear of similar consequences, but do we want to build a culture of fear?"

Anita backed her chair from the table just enough to indicate that she wished to depart. "I think it's safe to say we are on very different pages on these matters. We're in different books, perhaps." Before rising, she looked across at Claribel and said, "But I expected more of you, Claribel."

"By 'more,' do you mean seeing things the way you do?"

"I suppose—" and instead of offering clarification simply admitted, "Yes—I am surprised by your perspective."

"Spending five weeks straight wondering if you're going to survive treatment, wondering if you're within days of your last breath, might change your perspective on a few things—might help you see a bigger picture."

The D.C. prosecutor, lifting her napkin from her lap in anxious haste for departure, stopped. More slowly, she placed the napkin next to an unused spoon alongside her plate. Anita smiled, perhaps the first yielding smile since she had arrived, and said, "You've been through a lot, haven't you? Both of you have." She included Paul in her gaze and then rose at her seat. "I am happy you both have fared so well. We have reached an impasse, I think, so I better go. Thank-you, all of you, for your time and for this wonderful breakfast. If you are ever in D.C., I will host a traditional Mexican breakfast for you. I don't cook much anymore, but I might enjoy an opportunity to tap into the skills of a younger Anita of Durango, who used to cook with her *abuelita*. I think you would all enjoy it."

Smiling himself, Father Soplido rose and said, "We would like that. I recognize, as you do, that we differ in our views, but I thank you for receiving our differing views and our declining your offer so graciously."

"Let's say I chose not to be offended," Anita responded.

"And of course, no offense was intended," added Father Soplido.

Everyone stood now, and walked Anita Gonzalez-Shea to the door. They exchanged farewells, and Anita walked to her waiting car and driver. Once her car had pulled away, Father Peychaud excused himself, leaving the other three to wrap up breakfast at the table.

"That started to get heated," Paul remarked.

"I give Anita a lot of credit for maintaining her composure—and her persistence. She must have seen a lot to be so unbothered by our denying her offer over and over, on grounds quite different from hers," said Father.

"But boy could she be relentless! Putting you on the spot like that?" Paul said to Claribel.

"Claribel," Father Soplido said, "I apologize you were pulled in in that way. While it certainly affects you, the offer to represent Paul and me, I thought, would encompass Paul and me only. You handled yourself much better than Paul and I did."

"Behind every great man is a great woman," Paul said, smiling at Claribel. Claribel, however was not smiling. She was staring at her coffee and, only when she realized a response was expected of her, forced a grin with closed lips, offering no eye contact.

"Paul, there is something Anita and I agree on, though, but for different reasons," announced Father Soplido.

"What's that, Father?"

"Generating awareness. I think we can agree that, while bringing her name back to the attention of the nation might be her primary aim, a secondary goal is to make people think twice before speaking hatefully to another. I feel that this issue has been so muddled by different agendas and different presentations by the media, that a few important things are being lost, including the story of what actually happened—of what is happening. I had thought the press conference yesterday might be a forum to share my story and put this issue to rest, but that did not happen. I was too naïve, I believe. So Paul—"

And Paul knew what was coming next. Should he simply start expecting, just when he might find himself with free time, that something requiring his attention will present itself? "—I was wondering if you would be willing to write my story. An 'official' article." Paul wanted to look at Claribel but had already sensed something amiss with her, so he, too, stared at his coffee. "There is no one I trust more to be true to the story and to my perspective. And you witnessed most of it yourself—even this behind-closed-doors meeting with Anita Gonzalez-Shea." Father Soplido picked up on Paul's inability to commit as he listened to silence and watched his parishioner's immobility. Respectful as ever, Father said, "And please do not decide now. Think about it at your leisure, and let me know when you have thought it through. Of course, I will be grateful even for your consideration."

"Thank-you, Father," Paul said at last. "I will not rule it out." Before they rose to depart, Paul's gaze landed on the light-blue anchor charm, and a sudden idea sparkled in his eyes.

Peony Pilsen arrived at Paul and Claribel's minutes after they had shut the door. Father Soplido drove them home, and before Peony's knock, Paul had been telling Claribel that he already felt tired. His wrist throbbed in pain, and Claribel wondered if he didn't need a painkiller. But Paul didn't want to talk about his pain. Once alone, he was intent on checking on his sullen Claribel. Just as she suggested a painkiller, he said, "You never told me you were afraid of dying." She looked at him, aware her mien had changed after she announced the reason for a new perspective on life, and corrected him. "I never said I *feared* dying." When Peony knocked, they sighed in a will-it-end disbelief before returning to the front door, recognizing Peony, and politely opening it.

"I won't keep you," she said off the bat. Rays of sunshine were penetrating the overcast sky, landing on the Scrivensbys' porch. The residents of Saint Catherine's Cove held their breath for a brighter day, for they knew the town radiated in an autumn sun. "Just strolling along the lake and wanted to stop by to invite you to see Oliver at the hospital tonight, and Lucretia, too, if you're feeling up to it."

"I've been wanting to stop by for a while now!" exclaimed Paul, happy to receive the invitation. "Let's do that, Bel."

"Wonderful, my dears. How about I drive? I'll pick you up around seven o'clock, okay? Roy and Nora plan to be there, too. And if you have the energy, we will all go to my daughter's for ice cream." When Peony referred to her daughter's, she meant the ice cream parlor on Main Street that her daughter owned and ran, the same one that Peony and her husband once owned and ran and Peony's father before them, the same one that doubled as a coffee shop and bakery from the early morning until the early afternoon, the same one that for over fifty years featured Peony's baked goods, her father's strawberry phosphates, and her husband's root beer floats. On many an evening, Peony's friends, including the Scrivensbys, met there to play cards, to eat ice cream and pie, and to share banter and gossip and laughter and secrets and friendship, always sitting around the one big table toward the back.

"I think we might muster up the energy," Paul responded, looking to Claribel for affirmation. She forced another grin.

"You feeling okay, Claribel?" asked Peony.

"Just a little tired. It's already been a long day, and it's not even noon."

"Get your rest, my dears. I need you back to your old self, Claribel, so we can take our walks together once a week. And just because you've retired doesn't mean you can join us, Paul."

"What makes you think I'd want to, Pee?" responded Paul.

"That makes it easy then," Peony chuckled, happy to avoid a defense of husband-free time for the wives. Besides, she knew he took his strolls with Roy. "I'll let you get some rest then, and I'll swing by around seven."

"Pee, why were you strolling along the lake? You don't usually walk along the lake, do you?" inquired Claribel.

"I do on occasion. You know, I usually walk along the lake when—this is going to sound so strange—when it's misty and gray and drizzly, when I can't see the lake from my window. I like to walk through the mist until it comes into sight and then, since I'm so close, I just keep walking and stroll the promenade alongside it past the lighthouse to the docks. Guess I need to make sure it's still there or something." When no one spoke, she chuckled and added, "But the sun is coming out now, so I'll be taking a different route home. Get some rest, you two!"

She turned and waved behind her, and once Peony had reached the sidewalk, Claribel stepped onto the porch, next to the idle, swinging loveseat. Paul stepped behind her, and the noon sun coddled them both. "The last walk I took, which was a few days after I had been diagnosed with cancer, I walked alone."

"You only walk with Pee once a week. You usually do take your walks alone, or with me."

"But on that last walk, I went to the lake, too, and standing at the foot of the lighthouse, I felt the strangest impulse to go to the top. And Blake Carroll didn't deliberate for one second over letting me up—just said, 'Don't see Claribel Wheeler in here all that often' and I said, 'Claribel Scrivensby, Blake' because he's always forgetting what's happened over years' worth of time. Sometimes, it's as if time stopped for him. And I climbed the steps, round and round, until I came out on top and met a clear afternoon—cloudless. And I stared for a good hour at the lake, watching the water's tiny crests and valleys as they shifted—millions of them moving and moving and moving like nothing was wrong, like time *doesn't* stop. And then I walked to the other side of the gallery deck and saw the whole town—all the houses built on the sloping green, the streets and walkways, the lights turning on as dusk turned to evening. And I saw the movement of people—men returning home in their business suits or work uniforms, women pulling sheets off the laundry lines in their yards, children—all the children—running and riding bikes and playing on the sidewalks and in the streets and in the yards. And then I saw our house. You were out of town, and I hadn't turned on the lights before I left. The house was dark. And the suspended loveseat on the porch barely swung—and was empty. I had no laundry hanging in the yard. And that was the first time it occurred to me—that I might die. All the other houses were bright and bustling, and ours—ours—. It was the first time I felt scared. And then, just like that, I shook it off. Just like Mrs. Larson's five-year-old granddaughter snapping the sheets from the line, I shook it off. I knew at that moment I could never voice that fear—the fear that I could die in a few weeks. *Voice* it? I could never *acknowledge* it. I knew if I acknowledged it, that fear would become more than an idea—one that could take over—and I couldn't let that fear become a reality, or death might become a reality, too. So yes, I did fear dying—once. The rest of the time, I *wondered* here and there if I might die or if I would make it, and after a few seconds, I'd push the notion from my mind. Wondered—often during those weeks. Feared—only once."

Still standing behind her, Paul wrapped his left arm around Claribel's waist and rested his chin on her shoulder. They stood together, still, in the sunlight.

"You never told me," Paul said.

Claribel did not respond.

After a moment, Paul spoke again. "Fear of dying? Imagine waking up after a two-day coma to the sound of a priest chanting Latin in your ear and oil smudged on your forehead." Paul had hoped to make Claribel laugh, and he succeeded. He didn't want his wife feeling remotely sad and acted to lift the mood. "I thought it was Last Rites!"

Claribel smilingly turned, careful not to move Paul's injured wrist, and encouraged him to take a nap. "And maybe we can find a painkiller."

"I'll ask Dr. Drew about a painkiller if I see him tonight. But Bel, you said you wanted to rest, too. Head on up and I'll meet you. I want to make a few quick phone calls first."

Claribel did head up as Paul sat in the study next to the phone. He had two phone calls to make, the first to his grandson Mikey.

"Mikey! It's Grandpa!"

Paul caught up with his eldest grandson for ten minutes, enjoying spending time with him, filling him in on Eli and Gracie's tardiness, and listening to Mikey's stories about parties and classes. When Paul inquired specifically about Mikey's journalism class, his grandson revealed that the professor had given an assignment in relation to Rhonda Turner's statement about a journalist's responsibilities; the students in the class must write a reflection on responsibility in general. "I've been formulating some thoughts on it," Mikey told his grandfather, "but it doesn't really matter what I write about it. The professor won't read it. He hasn't read or passed back any of our writing. I'm getting more feedback on my writing from the professor in my creative writing class than in my journalism class."

"I'm sorry to hear that, Mikey. An introductory class like this is the place to establish a strong foundation."

"Someone asked about the papers, and the professor avoided answering whether or not he had read or graded any by telling us that the important thing is that we're writing at all, that that's the way to improve writing skills. He said the point isn't that our writing is read, but that we're always writing."

"I think it's a shame, but I'm glad you're at least getting something out of the creative writing class."

Mikey shared a few more quick stories, including one about classy behavior and one about its absence, and after requesting that his grandfather not call in for Gracie and Eli anymore so that they can enjoy detentions, he thanked his grandfather for the call and bid him adieu.

Without wasting a second, driven both by mission and by the desire to sleep, Paul dialed the phone again.

"Stephen, it's Paul. I've come to a decision about the feature article."

CHAPTER 11

Gracie stared at the ten photographs she had laid on the kitchen countertop next to a school notebook and pen. Paul saw as she lifted one photograph, lowering her face for a scrutinous look.

"What are you working on?" Paul asked her. He had awakened from his nap and entered the kitchen to inspect the sounds he heard.

"I had to give a presentation on the Saint Catherine's Cove Lighthouse in history class, and Mr. Gunder asked me to present on it at the lighthouse sesquicentennial anniversary shindig they're having soon. So I started writing, and I have all these photographs of the lighthouse from my project."

"That's quite an honor. Congratulations!"

"Thanks. But I think he just picked me because he knew I had done the bulk of the work for it already."

"Still an honor. Hoping those photos will provide a little inspiration for your speech?"

"Yes, but I keep focusing on this one, and it has nothing to do with the speech."

She passed the photograph to her grandfather, and he could see that it captured an inscription that ran along the first floor molding near the entrance, one he, himself, had seen upon entrances and exits into and from the lighthouse over the years. The inscription's black ink against the white molding coincided with the black and white exterior of the lighthouse and the Dominican shields inlaid throughout the edifice, but an orange-red hue outlined the words on this particular quotation of Saint Catherine of Siena.

"It's one of Saint Catherine's most famous maxims. It's in the entrance of the high school, too."

"I know," she responded, lost in thought. "It's got me thinking."

"'Be who God meant you to be, and you will set the world on fire.' Are you thinking about who you are supposed to be?"

"In terms of my career, yes," Gracie responded. "I've been thinking a lot about becoming a lawyer, especially as our academic advisors talk more and more about applying to colleges next year."

"I think you'd make a great lawyer. You have a good mind for it. You're quick, too," Paul said with affirmation, assuring her of his support as he handed the photograph to her.

"But I'm not sure—" and she set the photograph down, staring at it again.

Trying to interpret her concern, Paul said, "But you're not sure if it'll be the right choice, or if you'll make a good lawyer, or if it's what you're truly meant to do? All those worries will fizzle away."

"No," she said softly. "I'm pretty confident I will make a good lawyer. I'm not afraid of studying and working hard, and I really feel it's in me. I have for a while now. I'm just afraid that—that Grandma would be upset, or that my mom wouldn't approve."

While Paul had initially been intent to flit through this conversation, her statement thwarted him from continuing to his study.

"I'm sure your grandmother would be thrilled to see you pursue a career in law. Why would you think anything else?"

"Because my whole life, she has told me that strong women, like my mom, led fulfilling, full lives as wives and mothers. She always said we need good wives and husbands and good mothers and fathers before we need good businessmen and businesswomen. She not only talked about the dignity of being a good wife and mother but proved it through how she lived her life, and I know my mom did the same. Neither of them had careers. So maybe she'd be disappointed in me for not being a housewife, too. Maybe she wanted to teach me everything she knows so that I can raise a family well. If I become a lawyer, which I feel strongly about, she might disapprove. And so would my mom."

"Gracie, your grandmother is a wonderful wife and mother and grandmother, but that's in large part because she has taken such pride in doing what, for her, was what God meant for her to do. And for you, that may be something else. Your grandmother will see that and will not be disappointed, especially as you set the world ablaze with the way you live your life." He smiled, and she smiled, too. He hadn't realized that uncertainty about the future, for Gracie, pertained less to her calling and more to how her own family might react. That she was grappling with something that could induce such angst touched him, his sympathy bubbling to the surface of his heart so that he had to hug his granddaughter with his free arm. "And your mother would be nothing but proud, Gracie."

She reciprocated his hug, and when she released herself from it, a purposeful smile enlivening her face, she pulled a locket pendant from the chain around her neck. She opened it to show her grandfather.

"I've started to wear this locket you and Grandma gave me for my sweet sixteen."

Paul could see two tiny photographs, one in each side of the locket, one in color, the other in black and white.

"This side is my mom, of course. Mikey keeps her rosary in his pocket, and I've always kept this photo with me. I thought the locket was the perfect place for it now. And on the other side is one of you and Grandma on your wedding day. Dad had it in a picture album, and I asked him to make a duplicate for me. Then I trimmed it to fit in the locket."

"That was taken in front of the doors of the church right after the ceremony," Paul said, smiling at it, not one he had looked at in years.

"Even though I want to be a lawyer, I still hope I can start a family that's as good as the one you and Grandma raised."

As she closed the locket and let it dangle from the chain, Paul realized his granddaughter had come to the point, despite her youth, that she dwelled on such issues—the woman, wife, and mother she wanted to be, the career path she needed to take— and that he and Claribel served as her exemplars. "That's terrifying," he caught himself thinking before swallowing in fear, wondering if whatever mistakes he and Claribel had made could adversely influence his grandchildren. He had considered the importance of leading by example, but the import of it suddenly became closer—and real.

"I'll probably need your help wording this speech, Grandpa," Gracie said, returning her attention to the notebook, as if the conversation were degrees from serious.

On account of Peony's apple pies for sale and the rarity of seasonal cinnamon-honey ice cream, the parlor bustled with more activity than an autumn late evening usually afforded. Peony's daughter, Poppy, shuffled between the register and the patrons' tables, always dawdling as long as she could at her mother's table of friends. A lone employee of seventeen carried three root beer floats to Gracie, Eli, and Sunrise's booth; they would work on homework until their grandparents beckoned for a ride home. A few other patrons occupied booths and tables, but the large table in the back belonged to Peony Pilsen herself and her coterie comprised tonight of Paul and Claribel, Roy and his wife Marni, Lucretia's daughter Laura, and Nora, another classmate of Paul and his friends, who was also Lucretia's closest friend. They conversed over slices of pie and scoops of ice cream while sipping coffee. Nora fidgeted with a copy of the local paper opened to the photograph of Father Soplido. Roy shuffled and reshuffled a deck of cards that was sure to go unused tonight as those gathered preoccupied themselves with discussion of pressing happenings amongst Saint Catherine's Cove's finest.

"I feel bad that Lucretia wasn't up for visitors tonight," Peony said to Lucretia's daughter Laura. The plan had included visiting Oliver at the hospital and then popping in to see Lucretia at home; however, shortly before leaving the hospital, Laura's brother Greg informed them from home that Lucretia seemed to have fallen asleep early and wouldn't be having visitors. Paul in particular felt disappointed, the only one not to have visited yet. The group caravanned to the ice cream parlor where Gracie, Eli, and Sunrise met them—root beer floats in exchange for a ride home.

"Her sleep has been erratic," shared Laura. "She gets winded just getting in and out of bed."

"I've spent a few hours each day with her," Nora said. "Even this soon, I can see she's getting stronger."

"She'll be back to her old self in no time, Laura. We'll all be keeping an eye on her." Claribel spoke to comfort Laura who she could sense felt uneasy about her mother's heart attack and recovery.

"I wish she had stayed awake," Laura continued. "It was important to her that she talk with Mr. Scrivensby. She had been asking for him since she was in the hospital."

The note piqued Paul's curiosity. Claribel interjected, "Don't forget that Paul has been recuperating, too, but I'm sure they will talk soon."

"He's got lots of free time now—to visit Lucretia, to play cards with us—don't you, Paul?" announced Roy, happy to have a fellow retiree in his longtime friend, one with whom he planned to spend much more time.

"Doesn't feel like I'm retired," Paul said, pushing his bowl of ice cream a few inches away.

"We wouldn't know you are officially retired, either," said Peony, "because you haven't had an official retirement party."

"He doesn't want one," said an incredulous Claribel.

"Your achievements and all that's ahead should be honored, Paul. We—your friends here—would love an occasion to celebrate that," offered Peony.

"Pee just wants to party. Doesn't care what the reason is!" declared Roy jovially.

"Wants a reason to drink!" added Poppy, leaning on the back of her mother's chair.

"I don't need a party to drink," winked Peony.

"No party, please," Paul said. "I don't want any hoopla over me. I'm retired. It's done. It's official. No party needed."

He seemed to have the final say on the subject, which warded off more discussion on the matter. Nora, returning her attention to the newspaper, changed the subject ingenuously.

"'To be offended is a choice,'" she quoted. "I think Father is right, and I have known that all along. I never thought about it in those words, *per se*, but I have lived it."

"Did some patrons return their books late, and you didn't snarl at them like you do to me all the time?" asked Roy. He referred to Nora's title as head librarian at Saint Catherine's Cove Public Library.

"You never get them in on time, Roy! I should stop letting you check them out!" she snapped. Then calmer, "No, I choose not to get offended all the time. Just the other day, that nasty Lydia Schnutt traipses into the library to return *The Crystal Candlestick* by A. M. Aelwright, which just happened to be my contemporary fiction pick of the month. Sets it down on the circulation desk in front of me and says, 'I couldn't even get through half of this.' I don't say a word and politely take it when that wretched Lydia Schlutt, she says, 'I don't know how you could recommend it. Did you even read it?' I don't say a word. I politely nod, indicating that, yes, I did read it. And then that hideous banshee, knowing she's not getting anything out of me, traipses out of there, and I could see that her tacky skirt was of that cheap fabric you only find—"

"Okay, Nora," interrupted Roy. "You're a veritable paragon of virtue."

"But there's more," she added. "When I glance again at the book, I see the title is *The Crystal Chandelier* by Sandra Romanciere! That dingbat Lydia Schmuttface checked out the wrong book! Wasn't my pick at all. Surprised she didn't like it, though. It was poorly written trash. But I wasn't offended one bit by her rudeness."

"That's minor," said Peony. "I refused to be offended years ago for an offense much greater. It's no secret I don't get along with the parents of my daughter-in-law Chase, the one married to my Billy."

"Here we go," said Poppy. "The wedding shower."

"Wedding shower?" inquired Laura. "I don't think I know this story."

"Chase's mother, Hunter, had Chase's aunt, Trap—that's Hunter's sister—throw the wedding shower for Chase and my son, and—you won't believe this—didn't invite me."

"What?" gasped Laura.

"Didn't invite the mother of the groom," Peony confirmed.

"It had to have been an oversight," speculated Laura. "A glaring oversight."

"That's what Billy thought, but I knew better all along. So when Billy brought it up to Hunter and Trap, they said that in their circles, the mother of the groom was never invited to wedding showers, and since they were the ones throwing it, theirs was the protocol to be followed."

"I don't believe it!" exclaimed Laura.

"I told Billy not to make an issue. Shower or no shower, I would still send a gift, and I didn't want my Billy in the middle of any disharmony. But I wasn't offended in the slightest. I'm cordial as ever to them. To this day, I choose not to be offended."

"Except when Hunter came into the parlor a week after the shower, and you accidentally tripped while holding a blueberry pie that ended up in her face." Poppy patted her mother on the shoulder once she had announced this.

"Such an unfortunate accident," confirmed Peony. "That was a perfectly good blueberry pie just wasted. But I maintain, I was not and to this day am not offended that I wasn't invited."

The parlor door flung open. Dr. Drew flew in and marched right to the back table.

"I see I didn't get the invitation to this auspicious gathering of enlightened minds, Peony Pilsen. That's downright offensive!"

The group erupted in laughter, calling Gracie, Eli, and Sunrise's attention, as well as a few other patrons'. When Paul stopped laughing, he could but shake his head and pull his ice cream back before him. With his left arm, he fumbled for the spoon and began eating.

"I did invite you, Drew, while we were in Oliver's hospital room. Maybe you were too busy listening to yourself to hear me," Peony stated.

"Maybe you shouldn't invite me when I'm talking. That way, I might hear it."

"Maybe that was the whole point," Peony said under her breath.

"We were just talking about how preposterous it is to be offended," said Nora, holding up the newspaper for Dr. Drew.

"You're telling me," said Dr. Drew, grabbing a nearby chair and inserting himself between Paul and Claribel. "I just got called 'offensive' by a patient last week!"

"*You?*" The feigned incredulity in Paul's voice called Eli and Gracie to their grandparents' table with Sunrise in tow, for Dr. Drew was sure to have a great anecdote in store.

"Me," reiterated Dr. Drew, yanking Paul's ice cream toward himself just as Paul was about to dip his spoon. "Can a guy get a spoon in this place?" he asked Poppy. "Never mind—there's one right here," and he grabbed the spoon from Paul's hand. He dunked it into Paul's ice cream, ate a heaping spoonful, and then began his tale.

"Last week, a patient—this middle-aged woman—a real 'negative Nora' and a complete fat ass—tells me I'm offensive for calling her a fat ass!" He enjoyed another spoonful of ice cream while everyone stared at him in disbelief. "Can you imagine? Telling your doctor he's offensive? And you know what? I wasn't offended in the slightest. I chose not to be."

Eli and Gracie, in stitches, glanced between Dr. Drew munching away on his stolen ice cream and their grandfather debating whether or not reclaiming his ice cream was worth it.

"Just when I think you've shared the worst, you give us another doozy," Roy said.

"It was that Mrs. Janes from Greengate," Dr. Drew announced.

"Drew!" shouted Peony. "You can't say that! It's unethical!"

"Needless to say," Poppy said, "she's not a patient of his anymore."

"No, and good riddance. That woman pooped all over the place. Couldn't control it. She's another doctor's problem now. I don't need that irritating hag pooping all over my office."

Here was an instance wherein all gathered wanted to be offended—at his rudeness, for his revealing her name, over his disgust at her medical issues—and couldn't bring themselves to stop laughing long enough for a trace of offense to set in.

"How about you, Roy-Boy?" asked Dr. Drew. "Ever walked away unoffended?"

"I certainly have," declared Roy. "Back in college, I had a roommate who—" he searched for a word and then continued— "well, it's a strong word, but who *slighted* me."

"Oooh 'slighted'! Almost knocked me off my chair with that one, Roy," Dr. Drew said, rousing Eli to another bout of quiet laughter.

"The last week of the semester, we had made plans to go to the burger joint after our last exam. I was looking forward to it all week because I knew Marni was planning on being there—we weren't even seeing each other yet, but I had been smitten since high school—"

"Yack!" whispered Dr. Drew to Paul.

"—and last minute, he comes into the room and says he got invited to hang with some of his friends on the football team. Left me without a—without a—"

"A wingman," offered Eli.

"Sure, a wingman! I was on the football team, too, and turned down their invitation to hang out because I had made plans with my roommate already, and because I was hoping to see Marni. But, angry as I was at the time, I wasn't at all offended he picked other friends over me. Of course, this wasn't the first time he had slighted me, but it sure was the last. I never spoke to him again."

Everyone looked at each other perplexed, for it sure sounded as if Roy had been offended and retaliated.

"You were clearly trying to punish him, which suggests you were offended," concluded Dr. Drew.

"I was not offended."

"If you really wanted to punish him, you should have *stayed* friends with him." Dr. Drew laughed at his own joke.

"Punishing him at all shows that you were indeed offended," posited Peony.

"Maybe we could all work a little harder at truly choosing not to be offended. But what about when the offense is deliberate? When someone *means* to offend or insult you? Do you think Father Soplido's advice still applies?" asked Marni.

"I think it especially applies then," declared Paul, "for a variety of reasons."

"I think the offense was deliberate in my case," said Peony. "Although, they tried to lessen the blow—perhaps in hindsight but too late—by saying 'this is how it's done in our circles.' They still meant to offend me."

"They got off lightly with nothing more than a pie in the face," said Nora.

"And the only thing my mother felt bad about was her blueberry pie going to waste," said Poppy, reiterating that her mother had, indeed, chosen to be offended.

"If Pee was within one mile of that fallen pie, I'm sure it did not go to waste," whispered Dr. Drew to Paul. "I'd put money on it."

Somehow Peony managed to crack Dr. Drew in the back of the head with her open hand without alerting Claribel, who sat between them.

The door to the parlor opened again, and Laura's brother Greg entered, holding his toddler son in his arms. He set the boy down and nudged him towards the counter to pick out an ice cream while he sidled toward the large table.

"Greg, did you just leave Mom's?" asked Laura.

"I did. Promised the little guy some ice cream on the way home, but I'm glad I caught you all still here. Mom woke up before I left and asked me tell you, Mr. Scrivensby, if I saw you here, to 'implore' you to visit her tonight on your way home. She's been asking for you since she was in the hospital."

Paul looked at Claribel. "Tonight?" he repeated, not to make sure he had heard correctly but to convince himself that this was urgent, at least to Lucretia.

"Tonight," replied Greg. "She came all the way downstairs and was reading in the living room when I left. I imagine she will be up awhile."

"All right," Paul said. "Eli and Gracie, why don't you take your grandmother home, and I'll hitch a ride with—" He scanned the table for a willing face, and Drew reacted quickest.

"I'd be happy to take you, old friend. I came on my skateboard!"

"Look at you," Lucretia said, concerned about her friend when she saw him wearing a sling. "I feel just terrible—just terrible—that all this happened to you and Oliver on your way to see me. None of this would have happened if—"

"It's not your fault, Lucretia," Paul protested.

"I wasn't going to say it was my fault. It was Derek Braynard's fault."

"Derek—? I haven't heard that name in years except for the incidental article here and there I've come across."

"He's the reason for all of this."

"How is Derek Braynard the reason for my car accident? What does he have to do with any of this?"

"Sit down, Paul, and let me tell you."

As Paul eased himself onto the couch next to Lucretia, he cared less about not moving his wrist than allowing his thoughts to be preoccupied by Derek Braynard. Derek had grown up with Paul and all his friends but tended to keep to himself. Paul had always been reserved in his own way, but his affable and congenial disposition endeared him to his peers. Derek, more withdrawn than any of the other kids, distanced himself, observing them from afar. After graduating from Saint Catherine High School, he seemed to disappear, never keeping up with anyone, including Claribel for whom Paul knew he had a fondness. Derek, the group learned years later, went on to write as a freelance journalist for various magazines, mostly of a travel or adventure variety. Despite sharing the same field, Paul's path had never crossed with Derek's since their Saint Catherine's Cove youth. The prospect of his resurfacing now in any significant way puzzled him.

"Comfortable?" Lucretia asked. She pulled a pillow from behind her back and passed it to Paul in case it might help mitigate any discomfort.

"I'm fine, Lucretia. Let's hear this story."

"All right, here goes. It all goes back to the day you were honored at Greengate Grade School. The ceremony ended, the school day ended, the work day ended, and after I had finished a few tasks, I went home. Some time after sunset—and my sense of time as I recollect that day is off on account of everything that happened—after dinner—I realized I had left my embroidery behind the circulation desk at the school library. I had brought it that morning thinking I might have a little free time to work on it and never got to it. I needed to get it done for Mercy Wagenknecht's baby shower and didn't want to risk putting it off, so I drove to school in the rain to get it. Of course the place was deserted at that hour. I parked my car in the lot, walked in, found my embroidery, and then, on my way out, while still in the building, as I approached the glass doors, I noticed another car in the lot—a shiny, beige sports car. It wasn't there when I had pulled up, and I didn't recognize it. It was curious to me, but I didn't think much of it as I opened the glass door. It shut, and I made sure it had locked behind me. When I turned toward my car, he appeared. Derek Braynard. Standing right next to me. I wasn't expecting someone to be standing next to me, and I certainly didn't recognize him after all these years, and I jumped. And then he said my name. 'Lucretia Leitner,' he said. 'What are you doing here?' I didn't respond because I didn't know who he was at this point. My heart started racing, and I was wondering if I could reach my embroidery needle. 'You don't recognize me, do you?' he said, and then introduced himself as Derek Braynard from way back. Never dawned on me at the time that he was actually able to recognize me after all these years; of course, I've changed the least of all of us, I think we would all agree."

"What was Derek Braynard doing at Greengate after dark?" inquired Paul. "Standing outside *in the rain?*"

"He said he was just visiting Saint Catherine's Cove after many years. Said he wanted to stop by Greengate before he left. A little calmer, I asked if this was his first time back in Saint Catherine's Cove since he moved away, and he explained that he had come through every now and then over the years. He said that he was spending 'fall break' here in Saint Catherine's Cove and would be heading back to school the next morning. It struck me as odd—I don't know what I thought when he said that because he hadn't revealed yet that he worked at a university. Anyhow, he said he was feeling nostalgic and wanted to peek in."

"No harm in that, I suppose," Paul mused aloud.

"I explained that I had been the school librarian shortly after earning my library science degree, which is not easy to come by, as you may or may not know. Then I don't know what got into me, but I thought he might want to know that Greengate honored you that morning. I just thought he might enjoy hearing that, us being Greengate classmates and all. Well, Paul, a change came over him. His face kind-of contorted as if he were struggling to keep me from seeing his grimace, and he got fidgety and serious all of a sudden. I didn't know what to make of it, so I talked right through it, telling him how a few candidates were in the running to be honored but that we unanimously agreed on you, especially in light of your retirement and your continued presence in Saint Catherine's Cove. Well, Paul, he grew more and more irritated, and his reaction veritably scared me. Between being startled by him before and witnessing this strong reaction, my heart started racing again. And then, in this soft, raspy voice, he murmured, *'unanimously? Paul Scrivensby?'* And I stopped and confirmed, 'Yes, Paul Scrivensby, our classmate who writes for *The Current Front*, was unanimously selected for the honor.' And that's when he lost it. Started ranting about how he's been all over the world writing about mountains and villages or something, and no one recognizes him, how he's been the dean of the McGuinty School of Journalism for five years, and no one wants to acknowledge that—"

"The McGuinty School of—that's the College of Journalism at my grandson Mikey's university," Paul interrupted.

"—but that the whole town doesn't think twice about honoring Paul Scrivensby, who writes 'a safe column' once a month for the 'country's most boring citizens!'"

"What?"

"And, Paul, he said, 'I've had it with Paul Scrivensby!' and marched to his car in a huff, stomping through puddles, leaving me stunned and horrified. His car screeched out of the lot, and my heart kept racing. I probably shouldn't have driven, but the ride was so short, I knew I'd be home in no time. I was upset the whole car ride home. I parked in the driveway that night. As I stepped out of the car, my heart wasn't just racing but pounding, and then I felt the sharp pain under my arm and fell right back into the car seat. A neighbor saw me and, well, that was my heart attack happening."

"This is just bizarre," Paul said, circumspectly observing Lucretia who had mildly riled herself in the recounting of the tale. But she had disclosed it now, and he found relief in hearing her issue a long sigh.

"I've been wanting to tell you since it happened. I thought you should know."

Paul looked at his lap, his left arm lying across it, his sling-supported arm tensing. He consciously dropped his shoulders to relax it in response to the pangs of pain. The pain offered a mere distraction from musing on the incident just narrated. Derek Braynard not only held a grudge from something that had happened in high school but could not bring himself to conceal it. Lucretia Willows had been so rattled by the encounter that it sent her only to the hospital with a heart attack and luckily not, Paul dared to imagine, the grave. Did this result reflect an over-dramatic reaction on the part of Lucretia or how filled with unexpected ill will Derek Braynard reacted? But as the thoughts raced through Paul's mind faster than Lucretia's heart that night, they kept returning to his title as "Dean of the McGuinty School of Journalism" at his grandson's university. He had no idea and had really paid no heed when, years ago, he had learned of Derek's articles appearing here and there—never reading one of them.

"You've been quiet a full minute, Paul," Lucretia announced.

"Just taking it in, I guess."

"Nora's the only person I've told, and she wasn't nearly as quiet as you. She can't wait until Derek passes through again to give him a piece of her mind. Any thoughts you care to share?"

"I keep thinking he's the dean of Mikey's school of journalism, and I'm wondering if the reason I keep thinking about this is that I need to pay Derek Braynard a visit when I drive over to see Mikey, which won't be for several weeks now—" and he tilted the arm in the sling to indicate the reason— "to clear the air with him. Didn't think I needed to clear the air with him, but after what you just explained, it would seem there's some bad blood between us—at least on his part."

"Maybe such a gesture would go a long way. It seems he's offended by the esteem we hold you in, or maybe he's offended by something you've done that you don't even know."

Paul wondered how much Lucretia had been following the news to have brought up being offended but assumed she had done it unwittingly. Suddenly, Paul played the part of Ted Handly as a finger had pointed at him, as a voice had called *him* out. Now, someone was offended by Paul, and it was not the faceless readers of his column.

"Maybe I need to do what Ted Handly couldn't do— apologize, even though I don't see the point."

"Ted Handly! I just saw today's paper, and boy have you been in the thick of that mess!"

"So you do know about Ted Handly and Father Soplido. Whatever is going on with Derek Braynard would not be an issue today if he had done what Father is suggesting—not get offended. The more I think about that, the more sense it makes—practical sense but spiritual sense, too."

"It was Derek Braynard's choice, then, to be offended by you, but that doesn't mean you have anything to apologize for. Ted Handly *does* have something to apologize for, and Father Soplido is not even offended. You have *nothing* to apologize for, and Derek *is* offended. How inane!"

"Needed or not, if an apology might bring Derek some peace concerning me, then an apology, or at least a chance to talk, he will get." As he spoke, Paul recalled another of Father Soplido's adages from the past few days: "I'm interested in bringing peace."

"Paul, would you ever believe we would be applying these new lessons now? That we would still be learning valuable ways of living from Father Soplido and—each other?"

"I keep waiting to start my retirement, Lucretia. Maybe there are a few things I didn't count on having to do now that I'm retired, and your story is an indication to use this time to expect the unexpected, because I have time for things to pop up now. And I have no excuse not to address them—seeking out Derek

Braynard and spending a few hours to visit recovering friends among them."

Lucretia placed an arm on Paul's shoulder and a hand on his good hand. She smiled at him and then looked down, not saying a word.

"Well, Lucretia, I better take off. Dr. Drew is waiting in the car."

"Dr. Drew? He drove you here? Why on God's green earth did you drive with him?"

"I thought you might feel this way, which is why I made him wait in the car."

She chuckled before saying, "You know, he's crass as can be, but he has been so good to me through all this heart attack business. Checked on me in the hospital a few times. Even makes me laugh every now and then. You could have let him come in."

"He did want to check on you while he was here, so I can tell him now to stick his head in and—"

"Not a chance! You tell him I'm fine and to drive you right home to Claribel! He's been good, but I can do without listening to him right before going to bed."

"All right, Lucretia. Thanks for sharing the story. I'm sorry all this resulted."

Lucretia maintained that no apology was necessary and saw him out. Dr. Drew made sure Lucretia saw him waving from the car before pulling away with Paul.

"I'm sorry to make you wait," said Paul. "We weren't all that long, I hope."

"You got a quickie in, huh?" Drew said, winking. When Paul scoffed, Drew poked him in the ribs and laughed. Paul's exasperation with his friend's crudeness never kept Drew from laughing at his own jokes.

The short ride to Paul's provided enough time for Paul to recount Lucretia's encounter with Derek Braynard. He was concluding as Dr. Drew pulled into Paul's driveway.

"Derek Braynard?" Drew was jogging his memory. "Wasn't that the creepy kid who got cut from the boxing club?" He started to chuckle as he added, "Imagine that—getting cut from the boxing club."

"*I* got cut from the boxing club!" Paul affirmed.

"You did? That's right. *You* were that creepy kid who got cut from the boxing club."

Paul ignored the dig. "Derek and I *both* got cut. But yes, that's the Derek that Lucretia saw the other night."

"Now I seem to recall something else—something involving Derek and Claribel—"

"What you're thinking of involves Derek and *me*, Drew. And I'd love to reminisce about it, but I have a long day tomorrow and need to make some calls and then get some sleep."

"Long day? You shouldn't be having long days right now. You need to take it easy."

"I was presented with an opportunity from *The Current Front* yesterday, and I need to call the office about it. I need to meet with Father Soplido, too, because it involves him. And I want to visit Oliver and Lucretia again, too."

"Take it easy. That's a doctor's order. You don't have to do it all tomorrow."

"I'm just trying to get to a point where I have nothing before me and can start enjoying my retirement. Thanks for the ride, Drew. See you soon."

"See you soon, you-couldn't-cut-it-as-a-boxer wimp," replied Dr. Drew cordially.

CHAPTER 12

Claribel, wont to sleep late these days, never realized just how early Paul had risen from bed that morning. With much on his plate, he knew his slower movements warranted an earlier start. His gingerly activity allowed Claribel to drift back into sleep easily.

Showered and dressed and re-wound in his sling, he descended the stairs and, once in the study, sifted through the many messages Claribel had written from Stephen at *The Current Front* requesting a call but leaving no reason, from Rick Mendel offering his support, from Rhonda Turner with KARI-TV wishing to get another statement, from Lucretia hoping to speak with Paul about the night of her heart attack, from concerned neighbors, parishioners, and former coworkers, from sundry others. At least he had addressed Lucretia's message last night. Anticipating no time to brew coffee, he put his coat over his right shoulder and slipped his left arm into the sleeve in time to notice Peony Pilsen's car pulling in. He hurried through the drizzle into her car.

"Looks like another walk to the lake for you, Pee," said Paul upon entering.

"Maybe it'll clear up by walk time. Buckled?"

When he confirmed, she drove to Saint Catherine Church with Paul. Peony attended early morning daily Mass, followed by coffee at her daughter's coffee shop with a small group of parishioners who also attended. Aware of Peony's daily ritual,

Paul saw in Peony an easy way to get to the rectory without any fuss. He attended the short Mass with Peony beforehand.

By the time Father Peychaud finished celebrating Mass, it wasn't yet seven o'clock, and Paul strolled with Peony through the drizzle to her car to thank her for the ride and to see her off. Then he walked to the rectory where Father Soplido greeted him at the door.

"Good-morning, Father!"

"Good-morning, Paul. You are not a minute too early nor a minute too late!"

A car pulled up in front of the rectory, and Paul and Father Soplido could see a young woman taking a moment to primp herself using the dropdown mirror prior to emerging from the driver's seat.

"That is Eloise Bernardi," Father said. "She must be stopping by to pick up the charm she dropped at the press conference."

"I know. I called her last night right before I called you and asked her to join us at this hour."

Father looked at Paul quizzically as Eloise approached. "Good-morning, Father. Good-morning, Mr. Scrivensby."

Father led them into the parlor after exchanging greetings and taking their coats and then reached for the trinket box, proffering the dazzling blue anchor charm. Using the arm bedecked with the same bracelet, Eloise reached for the charm. "My anchor," she said cheerfully, placing it in her palm. "The link broke. I don't remember it snagging on anything. I have to get it fixed so I can have all three back together again."

"Faith, hope, and charity," declared Father Soplido.

"Yes." Eloise lifted her arm, and before the bracelet could fall down her forearm, she held it near her wrist. A small, gold cross inlaid with yellow gemstones and a small, gold heart inlaid with pink gemstones dangled from the bracelet. "I received each for a different Sacrament. The cross was for my Baptism, the heart my First Communion, and the anchor my Confirmation. They're all three set with different varieties of topaz."

"They're beautiful," Father mused.

"Thank-you. I'm just happy to have hope back. I had thought I lost it," she said, reevaluating the blue anchor. "Thank-you, Father, for holding on to this for me. I'm grateful you found it." Then, placing it in a small coin purse, she put them in her purse. "Mr. Scrivensby, you've had me wondering for hours. What did you want to talk to me about this morning?"

"I wanted to talk to both of you at the same time about an opportunity that might interest the two of you."

"Shall we sit? I have coffee made right over here." Father pointed to a couch and chair surrounding a small coffee table. Paul and Eloise sat on the couch while Father poured three espressos from a service on the table. Then he sat in an upright chair adjacent to the couch.

"Let me provide some background on the opportunity I'm about to present," began Paul. "The morning after the press conference, you may or may not know, Ms. Bernardi, that Father and I met with Anita Gonzalez-Shea to discuss her offer to represent us both. Of course, between the press conference and that meeting, the press had had a field day with the situation, as they continue to do."

"I suppose I'm part of that field day, in the most minor of ways. My stories don't seem to amount to much," Eloise said, self-deprecating and sincere.

"Your approach tends not to be as sensational, more devoid of emotion—at least devoid of the anger attached to many of the stories—and that, I feel, is a strength of yours. Unfortunately, no one gets to appreciate its subtly and truthfulness because it doesn't stand out amongst the louder versions of the story."

"Sometimes I wonder what the point is of telling a story that gets trampled on by the other versions."

"Hold that thought, Ms. Bernardi," Paul said with kind firmness. "Some time after I returned home from our meeting with Anita, the editor-in-chief of *The Current Front* called me. He asked me to write an article on everything that's been going on, from the first press conference with Ted Handly to Anita Gonzalez-Shea's offer to represent us in a civil suit. Who better to tell the story than me, right?"

"You are the best person to tell the story, Mr. Scrivensby!" exclaimed Eloise, truly happy at the prospect. "No one else's story could hold a candle to yours. So you're writing the story?"

"I told him I'd think about it."

"So you haven't decided to write it?" inquired Father.

"I decided to retire," Paul stated with relief in the breath that followed. "I had an idea that might let me do that while doing something meaningful for the two of you, as well. Father, I think you'd like a chance simply to share your views on this incident—maybe to elaborate on the views you voiced at the press conference before it got a little volatile. Ms. Bernardi, I think you'd like a platform to share the story in a way that captures the humanity of all parties involved and, dare I say, shows compassion. I know I'm taking a leap here, but I'd like to suggest that you, Father Soplido, discuss your story—because this really is *your* story in so many ways, not mine—with Ms. Bernardi in an official capacity, and I'd like to suggest that you, Ms. Bernardi, interview Father Soplido for a feature article in *The Current Front.*"

Father Soplido and Eloise Bernardi froze, each with a saucer glued to a palm and a demitasse handle glued to two fingers. Each gaze did not budge from the other.

"So you know," continued Paul, "I talked it over with the editor-in-chief of *CF*, and he supports it. There are some conditions, but he's behind it. All you have to do is give me the greenlight, and I'll pass the word along that Eloise Bernardi is writing a feature on Father Fernando Soplido."

Movement finally melted the freeze in the form of blushing from Eloise and smiling from Father Soplido. And while Father lowered his cup and saucer into his lap, Eloise nervously took a sip, realizing too late that it hadn't cooled enough. Panicking, she gulped it down and opened her mouth to let in cool air.

More embarrassed than ever, she looked at the two men seated nearby and slumped forward, placing her coffee on the table and turning even redder.

"What do you say?" asked Paul.

"I say, 'I like the idea,'" exclaimed Father.

"I—I—don't know what to say. Are you sure I'm the one to—? I understand that you don't want to write it, Mr. Scrivensby. You want to begin your retirement. But are you sure you want *me* to be the one to write it instead?"

"I have given this plenty of thought—even did a little research late last night on your work—and I am confident you are the one I want to write this. Your writing shows promise. This story affects me, too. I wouldn't ask just anyone."

"I don't know," she said.

"I think you do know," Paul said. "I think you know you want to run with this opportunity, but you're doubting yourself. Remember, Ms. Bernardi, you found hope again. And you already have faith and charity. You never lost those. What do you say?"

She smiled—a slowly formed but confident smile. "Thank-you for taking this chance on me, Mr. Scrivensby. This is a once-in-a-lifetime opportunity. Yes. Yes, I'd be honored to write this article for *The Current Front!*" She started waving her hands in front of her face as if to ward off tears.

"I'm glad to hear it," said Paul.

"As am I," agreed Father. "I'm curious to hear what these conditions are, Paul."

"The main condition is that I oversee all the written work. I work with Ms. Bernardi on mechanics, grammar, style, the angle—but, as I mentioned, I've seen your work already, and, after speaking with you a few times, I'm not too worried—and once written work gets my stamp of approval, I pass it along to the editors at *CF*."

"Absolutely! I'd be honored to work under your guidance!"

"And—" and Paul cringed for a moment, not from pangs of pain in his wrist but from their possible reaction to the next condition— "they want the article printed in the December issue, which means we are under the gun."

"It's already November," stated Father Soplido.

"Absolutely! We will work hard and get it completed as soon as possible!" Eloise, too elated to let even the news of imminent deadline crush her, stood up, unable to contain her joy.

The other two stood. Father extended his hand to Eloise, who enthusiastically shook it. Then they each shook Paul's hand.

"Maybe I can take a first sip of coffee," Paul said, leaning toward the table to clasp his cup. It shook in his trembling left hand still unused to dominance.

Father Peychaud, with a grave countenance, entered through the front door, making for Father Soplido. His seriousness infringed on the merriment conspicuously.

"Father, a moment with you," and he guided Father Soplido to a side hall where he whispered something. Paul and Eloise had but exchanged glances before the two priests returned to the parlor.

"Father Peychaud informs me that, while walking from the church to the rectory, he intercepted Ted Handly on his way up the front walk. He asked to speak to me. Father asked him to wait on the front porch."

"Are you going to see him?" asked Eloise, breaking a short silence.

Father Soplido looked at the floor, a barely perceptible smile forming. "Yes. I'd like to welcome him in. Could I trouble you, Paul, once again, to stay?"

"I'm happy to stay, Father," replied Paul.

"I better leave then," said Eloise, reaching for her purse on the couch.

"No, Ms. Bernardi," Father said. "Given our new arrangement, I think this might be a fitting time to stay—if you could."

"Yes, of course I could," and she returned the purse.

Father Peychaud saw this as a cue to let in Ted Handly, thus walking to the front door. Father and Ted entered the parlor within moments. Ted wore a navy business suit, but his white button-down shirt hung loosely over the waistline of his pants, about to fall out, his collar button was undone, and his black and blue plaid tie, still knotted, drooped below his second shirt button. His face unshaven and his eyes lined with puffy circles, he appeared sleep-deprived but excitable, even in a perceptible sulk. Father Peychaud stepped next to Father Soplido and crossed his arms.

"Father So—" Ted began in an attempt to greet Father Soplido. Then he nodded respectfully and said only, "Father."

"Mr. Handly," Father Soplido said, extending a hand. Ted took it and shook once.

"Miss," Ted said, acknowledging Eloise. "And Paul Scrivensby. Wasn't expecting to find you here this morning."

"Good-morning, Ted," Paul said as he lifted his left hand in the air to wave.

"What brings you here today?" asked Father Soplido.

"I'd like a few moments of your time, sir—or Father." In an embarrassed, grouchy way, he added, "If you'll allow it."

"I will allow it, Mr. Handly; however, I'd like my friends, Paul and Eloise, present, as well."

Ted looked at the four figures in the room and, picking up on a unified front of sorts, did not protest. "Sure." Without a moment to transition, he blurted, "I got fired yesterday—on account of—everything."

"Fired?" Father Soplido repeated, his head tilting, his eyes squinting.

"Anita Gonzalez-Shea made it known in that press conference that she would be representing you and taking action against me and WBAM for not acting. WBAM acted. They fired me."

"I'm truly sorry to hear that."

Ted shook his head, unsure what to believe. To Ted, Father Soplido's sadness over any misfortune befalling him seemed unlikely, impossible. Yet, Ted noted the gentleness in Father's mien and had heard the comment and had read the caption as many other citizens had; Father Soplido chose not to be offended. He had made it public. He is a priest. The words had to hold weight. They had to be true.

"I came to ask—and I know I have no right to ask you, but I hopped in my car and didn't think it through because I was so consumed with knowing—I have to ask—are you going to sue me? I don't care about the station anymore, but are you coming after *me*?"

"No," Father said immediately, wishing not to prolong Ted's anguish. "I'm not going to sue."

"Scrivensby?"

An impulse urged Paul not to give Ted Handly the satisfaction of a definite answer, but, dissuading himself of anything beneficial deriving from this response, he replied, "No, I'm not suing, either."

Ted sighed as his hands ran through his hair, pulling it back.

No one spoke; everyone felt it should be Ted who spoke next. But the pause turned into more than a pause, filled only by the sound of a few heavy breaths from Ted.

Then Ted spoke. "All this for nothing. You're not even going to sue."

Father Peychaud's stalwart stare turned icy as he said, "I heard those sighs, and they sang relief. Instead of being grateful for that relief, you get upset that you were fired 'for nothing'? You ungrateful—"

"I am grateful!" he erupted. "But I can't bring myself to believe I lost everything over—" He didn't know what to say for fear of saying the wrong thing, for fear of offending.

"Over something so minor," Father Soplido said, to finish his thought.

"Is it true, Father?" asked Ted. "Is it true you were not offended?"

"It is true. I was not offended. But I was—" Father stopped before the last word. He looked at Ted, then at Paul and Eloise, and found no point in revealing it. Realizing no good could come from Ted knowing that last word, that truth, he simply said again, "I was not offended."

"He was hurt," Eloise said, reading the word in Father's eyes. "There's a difference, you know. Being offended is a choice. Being hurt isn't. You stung him with your words, and he shook it off and got over it, choosing not to let you or your words get to him. But you hurt him. Even if it was minor, even if it was for no more than a moment—that kind of moment that in reality lingers—you hurt him."

Paul looked at Eloise and knew she was right. He knew why he entrusted the article to her.

It was Ted's reaction that preoccupied him, though, or his inaction, rather. Once again, Paul, like the others, found himself waiting for Ted to utter the next comment, to say the right thing, but no words issued from his lips this time.

In a flash, parts of Paul's conversation with Lucretia replayed in his head, and he recalled his willingness to apologize to Derek Braynard just to make the peace. Maybe his apology would lack a requisite sincerity or maybe, after talking with Derek, it would possess that sincerity, but he knew an apology might beget peace. And now he recognized that Ted stood face to face with that same opportunity. Before Ted stood a man who disregarded an offense in a heartbeat, a man who could have retaliated in a way that sent a powerful message to the nation, a man who might appreciate an acknowledgement let alone a display of remorse or gratitude.

So Paul broke the silence. "Ted? Anything, Ted?"

Ted looked at him blankly.

"How about 'thank-you, Father, for not suing,' or 'I'm sorry, Father, for bringing this mayhem into your life by my carelessness or deliberate insult'? How about any sign that you care, Ted?"

"I'm not looking for forgiveness. I'm not going to pretend that I'm suddenly religious," Ted said, conflicted amid traces of anger.

"You don't have to be religious to apologize or to say thank-you. It's the decent thing to do."

"The classy thing to do, Paul." This came from Father Soplido, referring, of course, to Paul's controversial November column. It wasn't the surprise of the comment that elicited the unforeseen reaction, nor the potential it had to be rife with insult amid an uncomfortable situation that sprang from insult, nor even the unexpected speaker. Paul and Eloise started laughing when they saw the big grin on Father's face after delivering it. Father Peychaud, shaking his head in disbelief, smiled, too. And then Ted Handly, unable to refrain, closed his eyes amid the lifted tension and exhaled audibly.

"I couldn't resist," Father Soplido said between snickers.

"If this doesn't prove how unoffended Father was, I don't know what will—making light of a situation like this." Eloise's smile did not fade.

"Paul, you're right," Ted said at last. He pulled his tie a good inch lower for no good reason before running his fingers through his hair. "Father—"

"Hold that thought, Ted," Paul interrupted. "I think you and Father should have this talk alone. Father, we'll show ourselves out."

Paul retrieved his and Eloise's coat from the closet and let the two Fathers lead him and Eloise to the door.

"Thank-you, Paul," Father Soplido said.

"We'll all be in touch, starting this afternoon. We have a lot to get done in little time."

"Of course," agreed Father.

"We are committed to this," added Eloise.

When the front door closed, Eloise extended a hand to Paul, a steady, firm left hand. Paul shook hers with his left hand, noting the difference in the unsure reporter from the press conference. "Thank-you," she said. "I'm looking forward to working with you, and I won't let you down. Thank-you."

Paul glanced at the front door of the rectory, knowing that behind it, the prospect of peace loomed. And he felt good about that. While the giving and accepting of an apology begot peace within, the giving and accepting of hope begot peace without. He saw that offending and choosing to be offended do not bring peace to another, and that it's easier to be offended than to choose not to be. And here he stood, before a young reporter who had just thanked him for the peace in the hope he had renewed in her, hope in a promising future as a journalist of meaningful work. But did she realize, he wondered, the peace she was handing to *him* by choosing to accept this responsibility? Did she realize that his peace derived from the hope she renewed in him—the hope for new good writers, the hope for persons to take on the more difficult deeds, and the hope for his own free days ahead?

"Thank-*you*," Paul responded, "for helping me finally start my retirement."

Eloise drove Paul home, and as he peered into the drizzle, he smiled, anticipating that after a few more days working with Father Soplido, Eloise Bernardi, and the editors at *The Current Front*, he would be on the phone with Stephen celebrating the completion of the December issue.

PART III: RESPONSIBILITY

CHAPTER 13

"The verge of retirement." Claribel used this expression, and he fixated on the thought. Should he be past the verge by now?

An accomplished writer, one held in high regard by readers across the country, reclined in an armchair in his solarium with a draft of an article on his lap. No sunlight was radiating through the windows. Paul had had to turn on the lamp before he began reading on account of the overcast, fall morning. The forecast, Paul recalled, had indicated sunny days ahead, but he knew not to trust forecasts; everyone had told him retirement would be restful and relaxing. He had yet to see this.

The surprise of a controversial column, the car accident, and the press conference debacle that had hurled Paul and his pastor into the limelight not only renewed fervor in the author but strengthened it. How, then, could he have crossed the threshold over the *verge* into retirement?

The article on Paul's lap this morning was, however, not his own. It couldn't be, for he had retired. Stephen's request that Paul write an article on the controversial press conference and its aftermath tempted him, but he was still grimacing through the recovery of a bruised wrist. Instead, Paul's plan *to oversee* the writing of the article by an ingénue with whom Father Soplido was comfortable working allowed days of leisure to appear more imminent. Soon, the masses would know Eloise Bernardi, and Paul saw a warmth to her approach and a vibrancy in her writing that he knew would present an honest telling, relate a truthful story, and touch readers. Stephen wanted the article for the upcoming December issue, despite the proximity to printing. The article could not reach the editors of *The Current Front* unless approved and submitted by their beloved Paul Scrivensby, so the seasoned writer found himself this morning reviewing Eloise's first draft, which she had sent before he had awakened.

The day before, after returning home from an interview with Eloise, he had met his wife Claribel in the kitchen preparing dinner. Her strength was returning more quickly these days, and Paul sat on a stool at the kitchen island happy to see her making dinner for the first time in weeks—a fall dinner, at that—for he smelled the thick aroma of her laurel beef stew and the lacey, spiced scent of baked apples. Large kettles occupied four burners, one a hearty, beef stock reducing to a *consommé*, another a *remouillage* using the bones and vegetables from the first stock, the third the laurel beef stew, and the last a cinnamon caramel sauce for the apples. Simmering broths and stews and baking sweets warmly blanketed the room on a cold, dreary evening in early November. While she cooked, Paul made himself his before-dinner drink, bourbon on the rocks with a splash of Cointreau, and discussed the long day with Claribel, noting his new task of overseeing the upcoming article.

"At least you're on the verge of retirement, Paul," Claribel said.

"I suppose so," he replied, watching her pour cooled stock she had set aside into an ice tray; Claribel often saved a portion of a robust broth or stock and froze it in ice trays, using a cube to add depth to side vegetables and other dishes throughout the season.

As his mind began to reflect on Claribel's words "the verge of retirement," he noticed the abundance of food she was preparing and felt reassurance at the surety of her recovery. Prior to her illness, he wouldn't have given the sight a second thought. Now, he observed it with hope and satisfaction and relief.

"While you were out today, Michael called," she shared. Michael, their widowed son, lived with his three children. "He got called out to Europe on a project—had to leave today."

"To Europe?"

"To England. He had planned to leave the kids with Pauline, but Gracie and Eli asked if they could stay here. He checked with me, and I had no objections. They wanted to be useful and help us out, especially with your bum wrist and arm after the accident."

Paul would have to continue wearing a sling for up to eight weeks. The wrist, neither sprained nor broken, emanated pain on account of severe contusions to the bones. The skin turned bright red but never swelled, and when left undisturbed, lying in the sling, the wrist and forearm generated little to no pain. One week since the night of the accident, the pain had gradually subsided.

"So the kids are staying over then?" Paul inquired.

"Yes, Gracie will bring Eli over after basketball practice, once they stop at home to pack a few things. Michael needs to leave for the airport tomorrow morning before dawn, so he won't be joining us for dinner. I'm making dinner for four tonight."

Dinner for four comprised the two of them and only two of Michael's children. Gracie and Eli's brother Mikey was currently enjoying his first semester at university. He had come in for fall break the week preceding Paul's accident and had remained in town until his grandfather was cleared for release from the hospital. While Gracie showed interest in law and little Eli began to consider music more seriously, Mikey had been accepted to the prestigious McGuinty School of Journalism at his university, studying the craft of writing as his grandfather had.

Paul sipped his bourbon and pulled his supported arm to his side. "Can I help with anything?"

"You can keep sipping away. You've had a long day and started early. I, at least, slept in. It's nice not to put anyone out for dinner—finally feeling up to making a full meal myself, although I may have gone overboard. I have a *remouillage* simmering that we can use for soup tonight. I'll just add some *ditalini*. I've had a brisket braising in the oven most of the day that we can enjoy tonight, too. I'll make a salad when the kids get here. After dinner, the *consommé* and laurel beef stew will be done, and I'll store them away. I put together an apple cobbler and can warm that for dessert tonight. We now have food for days." She had said all this while opening the oven for a peek and giving the broths a few mindless stirs, but when she finished itemizing the dishes, she turned to face Paul, anticipating the big smile on his face. Claribel knew she was indeed returning to her old self, and his smile validated that, as did the productivity before her in the kitchen. "You have barely rested since you returned from New York, and the car accident didn't help. It's time for me to take care of you."

"'Time for me to—'? As if you are reciprocating. I don't feel as though *I* adequately took care of *you* during your treatments. I was still flying back and forth to New York, wrapping things up at the office there."

"And every second you were here you spent doting on me, bringing me to appointments, letting me sleep, cooking for me, coordinating meals for us that our family and friends volunteered to make. You have nothing to feel guilty about, especially considering all the projects and the loose ends you were trying to tie up at *CF*. So let me take care of you while your arm is in that thing."

She did not convince Paul that he had done enough. As he saw it, he had not scratched the surface of doing what a loving husband should have done, yet here he was taking pride in her first foray back into the kitchen to cook a full meal.

Claribel gave the broth a last stir and, upon setting the ladle on the trivet, sighed. Then she sat on the island stool beside Paul, sneaking a sip of his beverage. "Don't have much to do until the kids get here for dinner."

"So 'the verge of retirement,' huh?" he repeated.

"Are you ready to spend more time with Roy? I have a feeling he has been waiting to spend more time with you."

Paul, a lifelong resident of Saint Catherine's Cove, Wisconsin, was not the first of his lifelong friends to retire, nor would he be the last. In fact, he, along with these friends, took pride in working beyond typical retirement age.

"Let's see. Who from the Greengate days has retired and who has yet to do so?" Paul asked, serious about the undertaking of enumerating the friends belonging in each category.

"And who never will?" joked Claribel.

"There's Roy and Oliver. They may dabble in their fields still, but they've officially retired. And technically, Peony—"

As thunder struck in the distance, the first they heard of it all day, the backdoor opened, and Gracie and Eli entered, lugging large duffle bags and backpacks as well as a guitar.

"Hello, kids!" shouted Paul, happy to see them.

"Have enough to last you a few nights?" asked Claribel.

"We have enough to get us through school tomorrow and then the weekend." Gracie spoke more for herself. As tomorrow, Friday, was a school day, she needed her Catholic school uniform plus recreational clothes for Friday night and the weekend. Eli, who attended Greengate Grade School, could wear almost anything.

The grandparents kissed their grandchildren, and Claribel dove into preparing dinner. Gracie stayed with Paul at the kitchen island, chatting with them and working on homework while Eli practiced guitar in the study. At one point, as Claribel dressed the salad, Eli shouted, "Grandpa, you have more messages on your desk now than I have seen here my whole life!"

Claribel had listened to many messages and taken plenty of calls during Paul's absences, including while at the hospital, during press conferences, and during his interview. As was her custom, she left each message on a notecard, staggering them on his desk alphabetically by caller. Eli's announcement reminded Paul of all he had to do in addition to overseeing Eloise's article.

"I'm going to need your help tonight, Eli! I have a lot of thank-you cards to write and can't do it with my good arm in a sling. So I will dictate a few to you to write for me. Sound good?"

"Sounds good," shouted Eli from the other room.

They said grace and dined together, Claribel rekindling the delight she used to take in her grandchildren's reaction to her food. Paul's injury did not diminish his appetite one bit, joyfully prompting Claribel to offer seconds sooner than she had anticipated. After the exchange of stories during dinner and the washing of pots and pans, Claribel retired to bed early, leaving Paul and the kids to finish up. Eli wrote five thank-yous as Paul dictated to him and then turned his attention to algebra homework. Paul made sure Gracie and Eli were comfortable before heading to bed himself.

Early the next morning, Paul readied himself slowly, found Eloise's draft among his e-mails, and printed it out. The kids rose and showered before enjoying a light breakfast of cereal and fruit. They left with their grandfather's cautions against driving too quickly on slick, leaf-covered streets in the morning drizzle. With a coffee in hand, Paul entered the solarium where he had left Eloise's draft on the armchair, flipped on the lamp, and, once relatively comfortable for a man in a sling, began reading, reflecting, and revising. He smiled regularly throughout the process, for Eloise's work showcased fine perspective and writing. His faith in a novice's ability had not only gone undashed but increased. He noted questions on the draft in scratchy, left-handed penmanship and made the few needed revisions and edits.

In his study, as he typed his notes to Eloise with one hand, he heard Claribel enter the kitchen and pour herself coffee.

"Need a refill, Paul?"

"Sure," he shouted back. "I'm sending Eloise an e-mail with my notes on her draft. It was good!"

Claribel brought in the pot of coffee and poured Paul a refill, then gave him a good-morning kiss. She wore her pajamas and robe still, easing slowly into the morning as she usually did.

Although he had been up for hours already, Paul was happy to see Claribel moving about early.

Paul finished and sent the e-mail, and then glanced at the notecards on the desk. He would have to put off enjoying free time in his retirement for a few days in order to tackle the responsibility of returning calls and sending thank-you cards. The "verge of retirement" translated to an indefinite, extending while of fulfilling obligatory tasks, tying up loose ends, and following through on responsibilities of all types. As Paul opened his mouth to comment on the number of cards, they heard a knock at the front door.

Dr. Drew greeted Paul and, awaiting no invitation, showed himself in. "Oh, this is awkward," he said to Paul.

"What's awkward?" Paul asked.

"That you're here. Claribel said you wouldn't be around this morning." He winked at Paul. Claribel had remained in the solarium and didn't hear.

Paul, who managed to blush even to this day at Dr. Drew's insinuations, refused to entertain his waggery. "What are you doing here?"

"Just a quick house call on recovering patients," he announced.

"We didn't call," Paul joked.

"I'm calling on you," Dr. Drew responded. "I have a light day at the office. Just popping in on my way. How are we feeling?"

Paul led Dr. Drew into the solarium as Claribel offered him a coffee. He had been generous in his house calls to Saint Catherine's Cove's recovering outpatients and old classmates, and despite his crassness, they appreciated his concern and his expertise. As Paul explained that the reddening in his wrist and forearm had lessened, the phone rang. Since Claribel was pouring coffees, Paul excused himself to the study to take the call. A short while later, he returned to the solarium, hurrying, agitated, and oblivious to interrupting Dr. Drew's question to Claribel. He had his coat on, the right half resting over his shoulder.

"I have to go to the university. I have to get to Mikey," he said.

"What are you talking about?" asked Claribel, perplexed as ever.

"That was the president of Mikey's university. Said he couldn't reach Mikey's father, so he called us as the back-up contact. I need to be there for him. I need to leave right now!"

"What? You can't drive! What happened to Mikey? Is he okay?"

"Mikey's been suspended."

CHAPTER 14

They had been driving for almost two hours at this point, Dr. Drew at the wheel and Paul in the passenger seat. Tension had subsided to anticipation of arriving at the university, talking to Mikey, and extracting some information.

Paul had insisted he would not let a sling stop him from driving to the university and only flinched, impervious to the pain that stung him, when he tried to fling off the sling too abruptly. Dr. Drew, quick to intervene, stopped Paul from yanking it off and readjusted it, announcing that he would gladly drive Paul. Immune to the protests, he called his office to have his few appointments rescheduled, and Paul convinced Claribel, who had been voicing interest in accompanying them, to hold down the fort since Gracie and Eli were in their care. Claribel told Paul she would call Mikey to let him know to meet his grandfather in his dormitory in a few hours as Paul and Dr. Drew hurried into the gray morning.

Paul thanked Dr. Drew several times once en route, and Dr. Drew reassured each thank-you with how glad or excited or thrilled he was to help. Once they had been traveling for a good while without music or conversation, Dr. Drew said, "Aren't you glad I didn't come over on my skateboard?" The comment put Paul at ease, replacing the angst over his grandson with a temporary levity.

A glance at Dr. Drew driving, casually resting one hand on the top of the steering wheel, the other hand on his lap, his shoulders relaxed and eased into the seat, reminded Paul of the first ride he had taken with Drew when they were kids. Paul and Drew had grown up together in Saint Catherine's Cove and attended Greengate Grade School and Saint Catherine High School together but hadn't traveled in the same social circles all those years. Drew hung among a more popular crowd and had established his closest friendships with his football teammates, friendships he maintained to this day. While Drew played football, golf, and baseball—and boxed—Paul played only baseball, allowing for more interaction with Drew in spring than other times. The acquaintanceship, always amicable, turned into a friendship when, as juniors in high school, Paul announced to the baseball team that he thought it might be a kind gesture for the team to visit Otis Carroll in the hospital; Mr. Carroll, a local fisherman and an avid fan of Saint Catherine High School's varsity baseball team, was recovering in the hospital after a boating accident. This invitation before practice managed to silence a team unwilling to commit to giving up an hour or two of their time, until Drew, the team captain, said, "That's a great idea and would mean the world to him. I'll drive with Paul there after practice today. Anyone who wants to join us can follow." Sure enough, after practice, Drew invited Paul to hop in his grandfather's pick-up truck, and the two led a small caravan of the team to the hospital. In addition to Drew, only three other boys had use of cars, so each vehicle was packed. Paul felt special, singled out by one idolized by most of the school, to join him in his car. He felt special sitting in Drew's car, leading everyone else toward an idea Paul had come up with—an idea Drew approved and respected. Paul and Drew had entered Mr. Carroll's hospital room first, so Paul witnessed the man's glow radiating brighter and brighter as his smile widened and widened as player after player entered, crowding into the small room. Drew was right. The visit made Mr. Carroll's day.

On the ride home, Drew asked Paul if he wanted to stop for an ice cream at the parlor, at that time owned and run by Peony's father. The idea enticed Paul because he had already missed dinner, and the thought of ice cream without dinner was just cockamamie enough to lure him into spending another half hour with Drew. Drew hadn't spoken much on the drive to visit Mr. Carroll, but Mr. Carroll's elation seemed to invigorate Drew into chatting the whole car ride back to town, and his crassness budding then, he brought Paul to tears with laughter as he commented on Lucretia's likely reaction when she finds out Chris Rainier, a self-professed hater of books, likes her; the surprise that Blake Carroll, Otis's nephew and the lighthouse keeper, caught Roy and Oliver drinking behind the oil house and joined them before walking them home to their parents; and how funny it was that Father La Tour fell asleep in the school chapel and Father Duchamp gingerly tied his shoelaces to the kneeler. Although imbued with passion and gusto, he belted one-liners and humorous anecdotes casually, just like how he drove—how he still drives.

While each had established better friends in his own circles, the two had become chummy ever since. In fact, since that car ride, Drew began to blurt out his zingers in class from time to time, always looking at Paul for approval in the form of a smile, a blush, or an all-out bout of laughter. Prior to that ride, he had never made quips out loud in class for even the teacher to hear, ones that earned him more than a few reprimands. And when Paul read an original composition for class or the class poem at the commencement ceremony, Paul's first concern was often Drew's attentiveness. Prior to that ride, he had not shared his writing with many outside his family and close friends.

Drew attended a Grand Fourteen university on a football scholarship and excelled on the field and in the classroom. He then continued through med school, completed a residency in Chicago where he married Ella and started a family, and began his career. Not too long afterwards, he returned to Saint Catherine's Cove where he opened his private practice and assisted at the hospital. Ella died in her sixties, and all five of Drew's children moved to Chicago, interacting often with their mother's side of the family, visiting Saint Catherine's Cove as often as they could, as well. Nowadays, he kept up with the family still residing in Saint Catherine's Cove, siblings and their descendants, and the friends he had made over the years. He gradually transferred patients to the younger Dr. Dreves, freeing up time little by little.

As annoying as each could be to the other, they enjoyed a pleasant history together, and now, over seventy years since playing as toddlers, found themselves inscribing yet another story into their history.

"I'm going to ask something that raises an eyebrow for me, Paul, and I don't want it to rile you," Drew said, maintaining his gaze on the road ahead. Paul noticed he had to inch toward the windshield to read the signs and knew it wasn't just the drizzle that necessitated the squint-accompanied tendency.

"Go on," encouraged Paul, wondering if the question were but a set-up for a prank or if it were legitimate.

"Why did the president call you about the suspension? That can't be typical, can it? Wouldn't the dean or an authority a little lower on the totem pole be the one to call?"

"The dean, huh? I see where you're going with this."

"We know who the dean of Mikey's college is now, don't we? You don't think there's a connection to—I mean, in light of Lucretia's story—"

Drew referred to the story that their friend Lucretia had related two nights ago. The recovering Lucretia explained to Paul that an unexpected visit from an old Greengate Grade School classmate, Derek Braynard, triggered the heart attack that had her rushed to the hospital the night of Paul's car accident. He had stopped by Greengate that evening and had run into Lucretia. When Lucretia shared that Paul Scrivensby had been honored at Greengate earlier that day, Derek erupted in anger, scaring Lucretia. He sped off in his beige sports car, and Lucretia, rattled by his vehement reaction and indignation toward her announcement about Paul, returned home to endure a heart attack before stepping out of her car. A detail that came to light, in addition to the odd hatred of Paul, included Derek's securing the deanship of the McGuinty School of Journalism at Mikey's university.

"It crossed my mind." Paul wanted to leave it at that, wishing their suspicion would come to naught, settling like useless ash at the bottom of a fireplace. But a restlessness compelled him to wonder. "I can't imagine that this man who I didn't even know was holding a grudge against me would take it out on my grandson. It can't be."

"For his own sake," Drew said, "he better not have."

"All right, Mikey. Let's hear it."

Paul and Drew had arrived on campus, parked, and found Mikey and his best friend Pat, also from Saint Catherine's Cove, waiting for them in the dormitory lobby. After a hug between Paul and Mikey and without many words, the four walked to an on-campus café at Mikey's suggestion. The drizzle had ceased though the clouds never cleared, and before long, they found themselves taciturn, staring into the gray through the window of their isolated table in a nearly vacant café. Sipping their coffees in order to stall broaching the topic was not an option as they had come out too piping hot to consume.

"What did they tell you?" Mikey asked.

"Not much," Paul returned. "The president of the university called me himself—said you had signed a document granting him permission to call your family with this information. He couldn't get ahold of your dad. He's probably still on the plane, and I know there are several legs to that trip."

"I've tried calling several times, and I keep getting his voicemail. Maybe he will check when he lands. I hope this doesn't screw up his business plans." He pulled towards him the cellphone he had set on the table under his money clip and keys. He wanted to see if any texts from his dad had come in. When he lifted the cellphone from under the other objects, the money clip rolled over, revealing the first item clipped on top of his cash, credit cards, and ID cards to be a small photograph of his mother. When he saw no notifications on his phone, he placed it on top of the money clip.

"We won't worry about that right now. Anyway, the president explained that you had written a paper that caused a stir, that you had been issued certain sanctions and warnings but felt they were unwarranted. He didn't say who, but he said that certain university personnel found your protest of such sanctions an act of defiance and moved for suspension. He said that normally there's a hearing before suspension, but that they temporarily suspended you from classes before an official hearing in order to avoid any disruptions in your classes—something like that. If I understand correctly, there are two types of suspensions: an official one and a temporary one as the college determines how to proceed in certain situations. Yours is the temporary one. I asked a few questions, which he skirted or answered vaguely, so I announced I would be coming to campus to get you and planned to stop in to see him for more information. He said he would be expecting me and wished me a safe trip. So before I meet with him, I want the story—and don't leave anything out."

"And don't tell any lies or omit something because you think we'd be ashamed of you," Dr. Drew added. "Your grandfather can accomplish more with the full, honest-to-God truth."

"I won't lie, Dr. Drew. I don't have anything to lie about."

"Would you like me to go away while you tell the story, Mikey? This is private and none of my business."

"No, you can stay, Dr. Drew." Mikey exhibited a controlled calmness, one Paul had seen at other times in his grandson. He came off not only as stoic but as mature, capable, strong, and everyone at the table admired him for this mien. But Paul had witnessed it in Mikey even as an eight-year-old, amid profound devastation.

Mikey led the group in taking a first sip of his coffee, careful not to burn his lips or tongue. Once everyone else had followed suit, he began sharing his tale. He wrapped his hands around the coffee mug and turned it back and forth slowly as he spoke.

"When I came here for orientation, I signed up for my classes at the same time. I had to take Introduction to Journalism, and my advisor told me that every professor in the School of Journalism is required to teach it on a rotating basis. There were three sections of it, and not knowing any of the professors, I just signed up for the one that fit my schedule the best, the one taught by Professor Simms. Later at orientation, talking to some of the older kids, I heard that anyone who knows anything tries to get his classes because it's an easy A. So on the first day of class, when he passed out the syllabus, I saw that a short composition of some sort was due every week, along with readings, and I wondered just how easy this A was going to be. I soon realized that nothing turned in was ever read—not my work or anyone else's. After the first three weeks, I just assumed he was a slow grader. For the fourth assignment, he required a meeting with him beforehand, which I thought was promising. I met at the scheduled time, and we discussed my approach to the assignment. He actually gave me some good insights. Then I wrote it, turned it in, and never heard about it again. So this went on the entire semester, and some of us would ask if anyone had gotten anything back, and the answer was always 'no.' One kid even asked Professor Simms during class, and he just said, 'The important thing for a journalist is to be writing—always writing,' and maybe he was right about that, but I was expecting some guidance and feedback on my writing. So this past week, in light of everything that was happening with you and Father Soplido in the press, Professor Simms told us to write a two-to-three-page paper voicing our views on the topic of responsibility—anything we wanted—not even in relation to writing or journalism. He said we would talk about the concept in relation to journalism in a class discussion later this semester, after some assigned readings. For now, he just wanted our general views. So I gave him my views on responsibility, noting that when one signs up for something, the responsibilities of the commitment are inherent in the *commitment*, in the act of committing. I said, 'For example, a man who commits to teaching a class needs to be responsible, then, to assign work, to grade work, and to ensure learning needs are being met.' I never even mentioned his name; I just gave it as an example, and I'm the first to admit that my example was inspired by Professor Simms's not following through on his responsibilities as a professor, but I also knew he would never read my paper. He had never read anything."

"Why do I get the feeling he read this one?" asked Paul.

"What a fluke," Pat said, "that he read *this* one."

"The next day, I received an e-mail from Professor Simms requesting that I see him in his office, which I did. When I got there, another professor, Professor Heel, was present as a witness. I sat down, and Professor Simms said that it had been brought to his attention that I had written a derogatory statement about him and his teaching, possibly defaming his reputation or something. He had my paper on his desk and had the passage circled. He read it out loud and asked if I had indeed written that. I said I did. He said that he found the statement 'accusatory' and 'offensive.' I said that to be offended is a choice, and I was sorry he chose to be offended. He didn't really respond to that but said that he had spoken with the dean, and they decided that I would be issued an official warning that would go into my file."

"Defaming his reputation? You didn't broadcast it. You wrote it for his eyes only," noted Dr. Drew.

"What were you being warned about?" asked Paul.

"That I was showing 'egregious disrespect' toward a faculty member, and that such disrespect would not be tolerated in the future—that it would lead to suspension should I disobey the warning. They said it would be expunged from my record in a year if I maintained a clean record, but they added the 'sanction' that I be officially dropped from the Intro to Journalism class on the grounds that I posed the threat of disruption to the learning environment based on blatant antagonism toward the professor. I said that I had been nothing but respectful in the classroom, and that having to retake the class would set me back an entire semester since the introduction class is a prerequisite for any of the other journalism classes. The other professor, Professor Heel, said that they have found in these circumstances, when a student has voiced a grievance with the professor and been called out on it, that animosity in the classroom has led to disruptions. She said it would be best for all parties, so they would be dropping me from the class, with a grade of 'incomplete' appearing on my transcript until I retook the class. So I said that reacting this way—barring me from the classroom for writing a comment—is an infringement on my freedom of speech, and perhaps a professor of journalism should be more tolerant of others' views, including those in opposition to his inadequate teaching. They looked at each other, and Professor Heel said that I could meet with the dean to discuss how to appeal the warning. I said that I would like to do so, and that I harbored no ill will toward Professor Simms; however, I would have liked to see my papers graded. So then I left—"

"You know what's bothering me about this whole thing? Your professor said that it had been '*brought to his attention*' that you included that comment about his teaching," said Dr. Drew. "Were those his exact words? Does he have a t.a. perhaps?"

"He doesn't have a t.a., and yes, those were his exact words. I guess I never really thought about it."

Paul had fixated on another part of the story. "Did you meet with the dean?" he asked, attempting to mask his anxiousness.

"Yes, I went right to his office and asked his secretary if he was free. She checked, and I guess he said I could come in. So I went in and sat down. Just when he was about to sit, there was a knock at his door, and he went to answer it. It was the president of the university. He was with the secretary when I had asked her to see him, but I really didn't realize it was President Cringle until later in the dean's office. He talked with Dean Braynard in the hall for a minute, and then they both came in. Dean Braynard said that the president had asked to sit in on this conference, and I didn't know why or anything, but I didn't object. I told the dean what Professor Simms had said, and he said that he was aware of it all. I told him that I disagreed with the official warning and the additional sanction of being dropped from that class for the semester. Then he got really irritated and out of nowhere said my attitude could result in something more severe, like a suspension. I said that I didn't have an attitude, and he said, 'Sure you do. You have an attitude of entitlement. You think just because you're Paul Scrivensby's grandson that you can do or say whatever you want.' I don't even know where that came from. I didn't even know anyone knew I was your grandson. I mean, I know you've been on the news and we have the same last name, but no one asked me about it. I just assumed that maybe people thought I was some distant relative or something. The only ones who would know about it are the Admissions Committee because I referred to you as my grandfather in one of my application essays—"

"—which, no doubt, the dean of the school you were applying to saw, or at least learned about from someone on the committee," chimed in Paul.

"I told them that I didn't have an attitude of entitlement. I said I just wanted to learn about journalism, and my professor wasn't offering anything for me to work with—wasn't even reading our compositions. The dean cut me off and said something like, 'Hold it right there.' He said he had heard enough and wouldn't let me defame a great professor. He said on account of that comment, the warning and sanctions stand. I said I simply wanted to know the process to appeal that warning and sanction. He said that I was being belligerent, turned to the president, and moved that I be suspended. The president looked shocked and said that I needed a hearing and all this other stuff before I could be suspended. The dean said he didn't care what it took—that this type of disrespect shouldn't be tolerated. I said that I didn't see where disrespect came in—that in fact, I was trying to respect their system and protocol by inquiring about the process to appeal. Then the president asked to have a minute with the dean alone, so I stepped outside. About a half hour later, the president called me in, and the dean stomped off."

"So it was just you and the president in the dean's office?" asked Dr. Drew.

"Yep, and the president said that in the future, if I wished to file a grievance about a professor that I contact the ombudsman. I said that I didn't wish to file a grievance about the professor, and if I had wanted to address the grievance at all, I would address the professor directly. It was weird because the president smiled when I said that. And then the president said that they had reached an impasse and that the dean was persisting in moving ahead with suspension. He kept saying 'the dean wants' or 'the dean wishes' and never said 'we want' or 'we wish,' so I wasn't sure if the president was on my side or if he didn't want to admit to anything or what. He said that he would discuss the issue with the Judicial Affairs Committee but would likely temporarily suspend me until they reached a decision about moving ahead with a hearing. The temporary suspension was insisted on by the dean, he said, to keep me away. I told the president that I would be missing out on classes then, and if professors knew about it, it could adversely affect my reputation. I think he was conflicted because he sighed several times without saying anything. After a while, he asked if I would be willing to sign a document allowing him to release the goings-on of my situation to my family. I said that I didn't have a problem with that, so he asked me to stop by his office early this morning to sign it. I did, and then I guess he called dad and eventually you."

"Belligerent, huh?" said Paul, steadying himself and growing pensive.

"Grandpa, I swear, I went out of my way in every situation to keep composed and to be respectful. When the dean said I had an attitude, that I was entitled, that I was being belligerent, I don't even know where it was coming from. I was being calm but also stated my disagreement with their position. I can't believe a few sentences turned into this!"

He put his elbows on the table and leaned his face into his palms. No tears issued from his eyes, but his exasperation after two days of unforeseen drama finally surfaced. Pat, sitting next to his best friend, patted him on the back, while Paul and Drew looked away from Mikey to study their coffee.

"I think you handled this very well for a kid your age. And I think there's more than meets the eye on this one, Mikey," said Paul.

"I swear, I wasn't expecting any special treatment because I'm your grandson."

"I know that, Mikey. I have a few things I'll need to fill you in on. But for now, let's finish our coffee. Then I need you to lead the way to the president's office. He's expecting me."

CHAPTER 15

When the four finished their coffees, they strolled to Mikey's dorm where Mikey printed his composition at his grandfather's request. Paul sat a moment in the lobby of the dorm to read it quickly, then folded it and placed it in the sling. Pat remained at the dorm as Paul, Drew, and Mikey walked to Presidents' Hall, the central building on the campus housing the Bursar's Office, the Registrar, and the administrative offices, including the university president's. A long, gray walk, tree-lined and leaf-strewn, led to the entrance of the building. A flint tint to the windows did not permit them to notice the eyes monitoring their arrival from the second-floor picture windows.

Upon arrival, the three were shown upstairs, and pleasantries were exchanged between President Cringle and the visitors. President Cringle, comparable in age to Paul and Drew, donned a dark gray suit, a French blue button down with gold cufflinks, and a thick, gray and blue tie of silk. He cordially shook hands with all three, passed their coats to the receptionist, and listened as Dr. Drew announced his necessary presence as personal physician on account of wanting to keep a close eye on Paul, who shouldn't be out after his accident. Paul shared that they went way back. He made sure to explain that Mikey's father was en route to England and therefore unreachable, and that he appreciated being notified of Mikey's situation once Mikey had granted consent to disclose the information. After some polite inquiries about the accident and press conference drama, President Cringle said that he wished him a quick recovery and insisted on beginning a discussion on the issue at hand so that

Paul could return home soon. He escorted Paul and Drew into his office; Paul had suggested that Mikey wait outside the office until needed. Mikey sat on a bench in the hall leading to the president's office's tall, wooden double doors. President Cringle shut the doors behind them and led them to two large, leather armchairs opposite his desk. The office, spacious and spanning two floors in height, mingled the classical with the modern. Deep mahogany bookshelves lined the entire height of walls, portraits in oil hung from the few eyelets within the shelves and on the few open spaces of wall, and contemporary area rugs accentuated separate spaces including the president's desk and chairs, a reading area with two other leather chairs, coffee table, and leather couch, and a functionless, open area near the back wall and shelves. Doors leading to his personal restroom and closets could be spotted between bookshelves behind the president's desk, and a modern picture window rose from floor to ceiling in the middle of the office adjacent to the desk.

The conversation began, and as soon as he could, Paul inserted a question about how the president came to be involved in this matter, noting he thought it might not be typical. The president admitted that when he got wind of the happenings from his secretary who had lunched with the dean's secretary, he felt, given the connection to Paul Scrivensby, a noteworthy name in the press and one currently entertaining plenty of attention from the media, that he had better monitor this particular situation closely in an effort to keep it from escalating to "any proportion we, the university, would want to avoid." Paul read between the lines and did not persist in verifying his suspicions that the president feared a media frenzy. Paul said instead, "Why don't you tell us the chain of events from your point of view to make sure we are accurately up to speed, if you wouldn't mind."

"Wouldn't mind at all. We want to be as transparent as possible about how we have handled it thus far and as we go forward. This is the best way, I feel, to ensure no ill will or reason for animosity from either party." He then explained the happenings as Mikey had, corroborating Mikey's version but accounting for administrative reasons and university protocol that Mikey had not mentioned or did not know. That he picked his words carefully and made visible effort to articulate his story and reasons clearly were evident to Paul and Drew, yet his exactitude amounted to gratefulness on the part of Paul, relieved that the stories aligned well and that he could understand the measures. Paul, however, found himself wondering the same thing Drew had wondered upon hearing Mikey's story—how the professor found out about the paper's contents.

Without shaking a finger at Professor Simms's reputation for not reading papers, Paul told the president, "When Professor Simms called Mikey into his office, he used the words 'it has come to my attention.' I find this bizarre, President Cringle. What could Professor Simms have meant?"

Thinking that Paul was trying to force admission of incompetence in a professor, he stammered, "How else could he have known? I would simply assume it was an error in wording or his way of saying he noticed the passage upon reading it."

"President Cringle, I'm not trying to impugn Professor Simms in any way, but I also can't settle for that assumption. The same assumption crossed my mind, but there's just something about that wording that doesn't mesh with that explanation."

"I can't offer much beyond guesswork or assumption, I'm afraid."

"And I would prefer you not leave it at guesswork or assumption. I would like you to ask Professor Simms—just to put my mind at ease. Would you mind?"

He stalled, but upon realizing the request might be minor, and in an effort to show his cooperation and goodwill, he assented. "I'll call right now."

"We'll gladly step outside if you prefer to call in private," offered Paul.

"No need. Help yourselves to coffee if you'd like." He pointed to a silver coffee service on the table. Paul and Drew meandered to the coffee table but took no coffee. President Cringle asked to be connected to Professor Simms. Paul and Drew returned to their seats as President Cringle explained his question and listened to the answer. They heard a good five minutes of grunts and "ahhhs" before the president thanked him and hung up.

"It would seem you were correct. I think it lacks bearing on the issue before us, but in the interest of transparency and, as you had mentioned, putting your mind at ease, I will gladly share that it appears that Dean Braynard—that's the dean of the McGuinty School of Journalism—requested to read those particular papers." Paul and Drew exchanged glances, and Drew shook his head disgustedly as the president, oblivious, continued. "He had wanted to read some of the new students' work before he popped into the class to address them—thought it might add a personal touch to be able to refer to their own work. So it was Dean Braynard who pointed out the passage to Professor Simms, and the two together discussed the offense before proceeding in the manner I explained prior. In fact, it was the dean who insisted that action be taken."

"You answered my next question, too, President Cringle. I was going to ask how the dean ever got involved prior to Mikey's visit to learn about appealing the process. As I see things more clearly now, it was the dean who initiated the drastic action, and it is the dean who is advocating for worse recourses."

"I'm afraid so, Mr. Scrivensby. He is laid-back in his own way, so for Dean Braynard to embrace this so passionately, he truly must have found it offensive. And he is adamant about not brushing something so egregious under the rug."

"And you fully support this course of action?"

The president stammered again. As if lifting with tweezers each word he used, he said, "We are following the protocol outlined in the university documents that are clearly listed on the university's website and in the student manual distributed at orientation."

"I understand your need to support your staff, and I'm not going to ask you to say otherwise," Paul said, aware of the tightrope the president probably felt he was walking. "I'm not going to ask you to admit that there's something off about this—something rather extreme. I know you want to find a fair, judicious resolution as much as Mikey and I do. But I think my grandson is absolutely correct in wishing to appeal the warning and sanction for something so minor, and a simple visit to inquire about the appeal protocol turning into grounds for suspension is asinine. I know I can't get you to admit it, but I hope you can get through to the dean on our behalf that his judgment has been out of line from beginning to end of this whole unnecessary debacle."

"I will relay your concerns to him when we meet to discuss this further."

"And for him to say that Mikey has an attitude—why, that's also asinine. Mikey doesn't even use sarcasm lest he *accidentally* offend someone."

"Your grandson has indeed handled himself exceptionally graciously," the president admitted.

"*You* see that, but the dean sees an attitude? That doesn't make sense—"

"Dean Braynard may—" he did not know how to finish his thought without possibly suggesting the dean had gone too far, but instead of searching for the right words, he began another train of thought. "I know it's easy to fixate on certain details, but I wanted you to be aware of the whole story before I present some possibilities to you—"

Before the president could move into safe, objective territory, Paul continued, "I was going to say that it doesn't make sense unless you know there's more to the story."

"More to the story? Has Mikey shared something else with you?"

"No. This extra information is something that only Derek and I could know."

"Derek? Derek Braynard?"

"Dean Braynard and I go way back."

"Us, too," chimed in Dr. Drew, smiling widely at this reveal. "Dean Braynard has it out for me, and I'm afraid that's the source of all this needless fiasco. I don't want to get into the details and the history of it all, but not so long as a week ago, Derek made it known that he's out to get me. Keeping in mind that Derek has it out for me, does it now make more sense that the dean of the school, out of the blue, asked to read the papers from my grandson's Intro class? Ask the other Introduction to Journalism professors if he read any of their students' work. Does it now make more sense that the dean recommended the professor take action against my grandson? I get the impression Professor Simms would have been perfectly content to avoid any issues with his students, or frankly, any contact with their papers at all. Does it now make more sense that the dean called my grandson out for being 'entitled' as Paul Scrivensby's grandson, and is the only one who seems to be persisting in worsening the consequences for him?"

"Then you are suggesting that Dean Braynard has targeted your grandson in retaliation against you for—for whatever reason. I find that hard to believe."

"I find that hard to *stomach*, President Cringle, but it all makes more sense now, doesn't it? Again, I'm not going to put you in the uncomfortable position of admitting to anything in front of me; I'm going to ask you to use sound judgment in getting through to Derek Braynard about how bogus and extreme his charges and course of action are."

"I will keep this information in mind when we discuss the matter further."

"And if he denies it? Then it becomes his word against my word. I'd like you to keep this information in mind when you discuss the matter further, yes, but I'd like you to call in Derek Braynard right now so that you can hear for yourself. And I'd like the opportunity to speak directly to the dean about my grandson's situation. Can we arrange that?"

"If there's an issue between the two of you—"

"—One that Derek apparently neglected to mention to you," added Dr. Drew.

"—then might inviting him to join us make matters worse? How heated will this get?"

"I can promise you that I will keep my cool. I can't speak for Derek, though."

"All right," the president sighed. "We can arrange that right now, Mr. Scrivensby. In the event that you wished to speak directly to the dean or that we needed verification on any topic, I had called him in prior to your arrival. He is waiting in the vice-president's office next door."

"That would be swell. And for this visit, I'd like my grandson present."

The cheeks and nose of President Cringle reddened. Paul rose, as did Drew, and headed for the double doors to let in Mikey. The president phoned for Dean Braynard. Once he entered, Mikey cordially greeted the president again and wandered to the picture window with his grandfather and Dr. Drew.

"Paul, you stay focused on Derek," whispered Drew. "I'll work on President Kris Kringle if I can. He's on our side. I'll just reinforce that." Then to Mikey, he whispered, "The old 'divide and conquer,' Mikey."

Paul nodded in agreement as he heard President Cringle rise from behind his desk. The president joined them at the window. They looked out on the walkway leading to Presidents' Hall, the remaining red leaves of the maples rustling periodically in gusts of wind. At the end of the walk, a fountain showcased a statue of the university's founder. The window offered a partial view of other university buildings and parks and the tips of pine trees dotting the gray horizon.

Staring out the window provided a diversion in what proved a brief wait. Footsteps heralded Derek's entrance, accompanied by his initial words that turned them all away from the window.

"It's a beautiful view. Reminds us of Saint Catherine's Cove, doesn't it? Before you arrived, President Cringle and I watched you walking up. I couldn't believe my eyes when I saw Paul Scrivensby and Drew Slate. Still buddies after all these years. That's nice. You never really left Saint Catherine's Cove, you two."

"Derek," Paul said. "It's been a while."

"But I heard you recently spent some time in Saint Catherine's Cove," Drew said.

Derek approached them, and no one extended a hand to shake. When no one spoke, Drew added, "It was the day Paul was honored at Greengate Grade School, where we all went to school together."

Derek maintained eye contact on Paul, feigning resilience to Drew. As no one spoke and no one moved, Mikey extended his hand.

"Dean Braynard," he said. The dean reluctantly shook Mikey's hand and released it quickly.

"How about we all take a seat," the president said.

By heading for his chair, President Cringle encouraged them to move. The others sidled to in front of the desk, opting not to sit. A click abruptly lured their attention to the double doors. Derek hadn't pulled them shut, and one slowly creaked open. No one budged to close it.

Returning his attention to Paul, Derek said, "It's unfortunate that we have to meet under these circumstances involving your grandson."

"Unfortunate? I'd say it's unnecessary."

"How can you say it's unnecessary? I'm sure President Cringle has apprised you of the events that transpired—of Michael's comments in his paper directed toward one of our most-requested professors and his belligerence in refusing to accept a simple warning."

Paul, ready to erupt right there, looked at his sling, inhaled severely, and said calmly, "It's unnecessary because this isn't about Mikey."

"Michael's comments in his paper and his behavior in my office speak for themselves, and the action he compelled me to take was indeed, and unfortunately, necessary." He looked at Mikey with an expression that said, "You have to admit I'm right."

Paul saw as Mikey looked at the dean, perhaps wishing he could address the dean but suppressing his words, relegating them to thoughts only, and then looked down, clenching his jaw. "Okay," Paul began. "Before we get to the bigger-picture items, let's take this point by point. You came across a passage Mikey wrote about professors having the responsibility to carry out the duties they are being paid to carry out. That's a sound statement I think we would all agree to. Does that warrant a warning? Does that warrant dismissal from the class, which you failed to mention just now?"

"When the statement is directed at his current professor, it breeds animosity, and yes, warrants the warning he received. Professor Simms felt very uncomfortable about Michael's comment and knew it could cause disruption in classes to come."

"I didn't get the impression from President Cringle that Professor Simms felt uncomfortable about it," said Dr. Drew. "Am I wrong?"

Dean Braynard glanced at President Cringle and swooped in with "The decision to require Michael to drop the class was meant to benefit them both. Professor Simms could carry on teaching worry-free of upheaval from an antagonistic student, and Michael could choose another professor with whom he, I would hope, has no issue."

"I have to disagree with you on this because I think your reaction—not Professor Simms's—*your* reaction made a mountain out of a molehill. But fine. Everyone here disagrees with your decision, and that doesn't seem to matter to you—"

The dean glanced again at the president who remained unresponsive to the comment as Paul continued his thought.

"Mikey wisely disagreed with the decision, and instead of starting up with the professor, as a belligerent student might do, simply asked how to appeal the decision. When told to see you, he simply stated that he disagreed with the punitive action you and Professor Simms meted out and wished to learn the appeal process. Hearing that he disagreed with your warning and sanction really irked you, and you turned around and announced that he had an attitude of entitlement—entitled because he is Paul Scrivensby's grandson. Is that correct?"

The dean did not respond.

"I know it's correct because that's what Mikey told me, and that's what President Cringle told me. Now aside from how out of line that was—you're not the one on trial here, right? Aside from how out of line that was, you moved for suspension, the next most serious course of action in a disciplinary situation, because you didn't like his attitude. As I understand it, Mikey asked what the system for appeal was because he disagreed with your course of action, which, to you, equates to belligerence and entitlement?"

"President Cringle, you acknowledged Mikey's composure and comportment in that meeting. You were privy to it." Dr. Drew worded it in such a way that it came off as a harmless statement, not a question asking the president to confirm. This time, when Dean Braynard glanced at President Cringle, the president turned away with visible disgust.

"My grandson is not allowed to disagree nor ask for a way out? Not without being told he's asking for a suspension?"

"Again, my response to your grandson's offenses follows university procedure."

"But you single-handedly decided that my grandson's actions were egregious offenses when indeed any rational person in this room aside from you, along with Professor Simms, himself, would not have seen the passage in his paper as that serious, nor would have fabricated 'attitude' and 'belligerence' in an attempt to make the punishment more severe."

Turning to President Cringle, Dean Braynard said, "I assure you, that is not what I did. You were there when Michael came in to appeal. You heard him disparage Professor Simms after he denied that he had an attitude."

"By the way, Mikey, did you ever get the process for appeal?" Paul asked.

Mikey nodded no.

"You didn't? Mikey came in asking about the process to appeal and instead got blasted by you. Mikey wasn't the one with the attitude. You were. And you had an attitude toward him since your run-in with Lucretia back in Saint Catherine's Cove. That's why you asked to read Professor Simms's papers. That's why you made Mikey's comments out to be more serious than they were. And that's why you are seeking such severe consequences. It's about a vendetta against me that you betrayed during your interaction with Lucretia last week."

Mikey looked at his grandfather perplexed, and Dr. Drew surreptitiously placed a comforting hand on his shoulder. Mikey then looked at Dr. Drew, whose countenance signaled that there was indeed more to this story.

"Now that's insane!" Derek shouted.

"The timing was impeccable. You go off the rails about me to Lucretia and days later contrive a reason to censure my grandson."

"You've lost it, Scrivensby!"

"Then tell me why your actions toward my grandson are well beyond the measures of any level-headed person. Seeking out his paper?"

"I did no such thing! I requested all Professor Simms's papers before I made an informal address to his class!"

"What did anyone else's paper say?"

The question came from Mikey.

No one spoke.

"Go on," said Paul. "What did another student have to say?"

When the dean didn't respond, Mikey said, "Gladice Miller. Tom Flake. Brandon Barker. Sarah Gusterson. I'm just naming some of the other kids in class."

"Let me remind you that the topic of the papers was responsibility. Does that help jog your memory? Or maybe Mikey's happened to be the first and only one you read. Just got that disgusted you couldn't keep reading, right?"

"I don't have to take this. Mikey is the one who violated school policies, and Mikey is the one who needs to make restitution. We're not asking for the world. We're asking that he abide by the procedures outlined in the university guidelines."

"The issue isn't Mikey's punishment, nor his—and his family's—refusal to accept that punishment. The issue is that you targeted Mikey because you have it out for me and are making his actions seem serious enough to warrant these punishments."

"I mean, can you even deny what you said to Lucretia?" asked Dr. Drew.

Derek stared at Drew, and his face contorted with anger as it reddened. His breathing became loud, grunt-like, and a glance at the president assured him only that he may have lost his footing. The lack of support from the somewhat confused and all-too-silent president melded with the accusation that he deflected his animosity for Paul onto a boy, and these got the better of him. And trying not to lose his composure, he said, "I should have known the two of you would be out to get me. I saw you both walking up the path to Presidents' Hall like some kind of dynamic duo. And just like in school, you are gunning for me."

"We were never gunning for you," Paul said.

"All right!" shouted Derek. "You want to take the gloves off?"

"As I recall, you could never even get them on," said Drew with cutting directness.

"You can call me out for snapping on Lucretia about Paul. Fine! But the facts are the facts! Your grandson violated university policies by attacking a professor in his paper and needs to face the music! And his belligerence in my office escalated the consequences. That wasn't my doing! Those were Michael's actions, and there are consequences I must enforce—and the university must enforce!"

"All right, let's all take a breath," President Cringle interjected. "There's a lot more at play here than meets the eye, and tempers are starting to get the better of us. We won't be able to accomplish anything if we're acting on piqued emotions and not sound reason. Let's take a breath."

"So you're not budging?" Paul asked, still incredulous. "You're not going to see the light?"

"If Michael is as upright as you're making him out to be, then he should respect justice."

Paul looked again at his grandson, and in that brief glance, admired the grace behind his silence, the stoicism beaming from his eyes, the courage straightening his posture. At the same time, his soul wept at the innocence of a boy standing tranquil, the youthful light sparkling in his eyes, the virtue holding his chin high. And the sight of his grandson suddenly overwhelmed him, and a pride in his bloodline suddenly overtook him in a way he had only known when he held Mikey, his first grandchild, for the first time. His grandson, who would gladly respect justice, was under attack. A grandfather wishing initially only to exonerate his grandson became a grandfather ready to take down anyone who might try to assail his descendent. Then the clouds of conviction parted just enough for the single ray of an idea to pierce through them, and in that ray, that thin, bright passage, Paul found clarity.

He pulled Mikey's paper from his sling and unfolded it. "Where in Mikey's paper did he disparage or attack Professor Simms?"

"You can't be serious. Mikey owned up to it," Derek said, furtively gladdened that Paul picked the wrong road to ride down.

"I am serious. And my point isn't whether or not Mikey owned up to it. I'd like to know where in Mikey's paper he called out Professor Simms."

The dean didn't answer. He wondered if he shouldn't ask for the paper to read the passage aloud.

"I'll read the section to you," Paul said, holding the paper before him. "'For example, a man who commits to teaching a class needs to be responsible, then, to assign work, to grade work, and to ensure learning needs are being met.' Did we hear any mention of Professor Simms's name?"

"No, we did not," Dean Braynard said, "and that's irrelevant because Mikey already admitted he was referring to Professor Simms."

"I'll give you that," Paul said. "But, as the first one to read the paper, how did you know he was referring to Professor Simms before the meetings with Mikey?"

"It was a paper for his Introduction to Journalism class. Which other professor would he be referring to?"

"Derek, Mikey gives other examples of responsibility to one's duties. Why assume this one about teaching is specific?"

"I think his indictment of Professor Simms was obvious. Again, that's not the point, and you're steering us away from the real issue here." Dean Braynard with regained composure looked at President Cringle as if to be the one to return sanity to the discussion.

"I'm steering us away from the issue you want us to focus on and steering us toward a double standard that you're about to find yourself in the middle of. You see, the fact is that my grandson never once referred to Professor Simms in that passage, and you assumed it was him, so sure of it that you ran to him with the paper and initiated all this rigmarole. How were you so sure, and how was it that Professor Simms didn't question it either? It's because you both knew that it was true. You both knew that Professor Simms doesn't read his students' papers, nor grade them, nor hold students to their readings. You assumed it was about Professor Simms because you knew he doesn't do his job."

At this point, everyone in the room knew where Paul was going with this, and neither the dean nor the president could stop him.

"As the dean, shouldn't you have addressed Professor Simms's ineptitude? Or are you as irresponsible as he is?"

"Now you're crossing a line," Dean Braynard said. "I'll tell you what I told your grandson. Professor Simms is an esteemed member of this faculty—"

"—who doesn't do his job. That's an unfortunate reason students are so eager to sign up for his classes. Fine. But it seems that a little slap on the wrist is all it would have taken to address this issue, to ensure the student learning my grandson wrote of. Now if you can call my grandson out and bind him to the most extreme of consequences, I think *you* should be called out for not fulfilling *your* obligations—contractual ones, I'd imagine—as a dean. It's a shame that as a result of your ineptitude, my grandson and his classmates had to be deprived of the exceptional education they thought they were getting— that we thought we were *paying* for."

"That's it Scrivensby! You've gone too far. You can't turn the tables on me. Again, President Cringle, I wish to call your attention to the real issue here!"

"We seem to disagree on what the real issue is. You think it's my grandson's violation of policy, and I think it's you—you and your grudge against me, you and your outrageous response to a minor offense, you and your incompetence as a dean."

"You arrogant—! You think because you're Paul Scrivensby, you can waltz in here and get what you want? Clear your grandson's name and throw me under the bus in front of the president of the university? I didn't become the dean of the School of Journalism by accident! I earned it as a journalist, writing for periodicals you could never hope to contribute to. I have a name, too! People know Derek Braynard! And people are going to know what Paul Scrivensby did to try to railroad me here at the university!"

"Now, Derek—" President Cringle for the first time exhibited worry as a frantic air overtook him. Paul had surmised that media attention was the last thing he wanted, and now his own employee was hurling the university in that direction.

"No, President Cringle! Paul Scrivensby thinks he can strong-arm me into lifting the consequences to his grandson's actions, and that kind of arrogance is going to cost him his reputation."

"*Arrogance?*" said Dr. Drew, shocked that Derek could use that term on anyone else.

"Mikey, may I borrow your cellphone?" asked Paul, calm as ever.

"My cellphone?"

"Yes, I'd like to make a call."

Mikey handed his grandfather his cell phone.

"How do these things work?" Paul asked, as Mikey helped him manipulate it. Paul started dialing, awkwardly holding the phone in his left hand while hitting the numbers with the index finger sticking out of the sling. When it started to ring, he held the phone to his ear.

"Stephen? It's Paul." Lowering the phone to his chest, he whispered to the others, "It's the editor-in-chief of *The Current Front.*" He raised the phone back to his ear and began, "I have a favor to ask. I need to get a story in the December issue if we haven't gone to print yet. Oh, good! I'll give you the details a little later, but it'll be quite the breaking story, and one only I can tell. You see, my grandson just got railroaded by the university's dean of his school of journalism because of his relation to me, and I want this exposed. Sure, we can talk length and details later today. Thanks, Stephen. Good-bye now."

He handed the cellphone back to Mikey as he said, "Come on, boys. Let's get home. Mikey's been suspended, and I have another article to write."

Derek stood dumbfounded, glaring first at Paul and then at President Cringle for succor.

"Mr. Scrivensby," the president implored. "Let's not jump to that. I think we can work this out. You're a reasonable gentleman. I'm a reasonable gentleman. I think we can reach an understanding."

"I tried to reason," Paul rejoined. "And I hope you are what you say you are, President Cringle—a reasonable gentleman. But the problem is Derek Braynard, who is not only unreasonable but just plain vindictive. You two work it out and give us a call when you've decided. You know our stance on the matter."

"You can't change the facts," Derek said softly. "Your grandson violated—"

"My grandson did not violate university policy no matter how much you want to contrive it. He exercised his freedom of speech in a way that might get his professor to think—had he bothered to read the paper in the first place—without singling him out by name. And you—you abused your power as dean and tried to abuse your power as a journalist in an attempt to get back at me for something that happened over fifty years ago! For a dean of a prestigious school of journalism, you sure have a lot to learn about the power of the press. I guess now you're about to see what happens when you abuse your power as dean on the grandson of a man who holds the power of the press and *doesn't* abuse it."

Dean Braynard glared at President Cringle once more, and upon being met with the same muteness, grew irate. He inhaled deeply and stormed out of the room, slamming one of the large, wooden doors shut.

Paul faced the president who stepped toward them and extended a hand. "I guess you have some thinking to do. Once you've talked it out with all parties involved, please give us a call. You know where to reach me. Mikey is concerned about his reputation with other professors in the School of Journalism as well as missing class, so I trust you will make haste without rushing. I also respect the position you're in—having to defend university personnel and witnessing personnel go too far—but I know you will do what's right. And I want you to remember that my grandson has been nothing short of respectable in all his interactions. The comment in the paper might have benefitted from editing if not omission, but his comportment prior and thereafter has been exemplary."

"That is one thing I have to echo," the president said. Turning to Mikey, he continued, "I have worked as a dean and principal of several prep schools out East and in administrative positions at two universities before becoming president of this prestigious university. And I have had dealings of a disciplinary nature with young men and women over the years, some exonerated and some guilty as could be. Not a single one of them maintained the composure you have maintained throughout this ordeal. No snide comments. No evasion. No tears. How is it that you can carry yourself with such remarkable equanimity in the face of what must be a particularly trying ordeal for you?"

All eyes turned to Mikey, who looked out the picture window into the drizzle falling.

"As a parishioner of his, I took Father Soplido's message to heart and chose not to be offended. I also tried not to offend anyone else, especially after what I wrote in the paper. And as a reader of columnist Paul Scrivensby, I tried to act with class by caring enough to think about how I was representing myself, my family, my religion, my hometown, and even my school."

"I guess you got hit with a lot of those messages in the past few days," Paul said. "But I'd say you've been a class act for years."

"I think your efforts are admirable," the president said. Then he sighed and said to Paul, "Yes, Mr. Scrivensby, we will be in touch. I hope to reach a resolution soon."

"And we—" Paul placed an arm around Mikey's neck, and Drew did the same as they headed for the double doors— "have a long drive back to Saint Catherine's Cove."

The darkness that settles on early November evenings arrived in the company of jagged streaks of blue that revealed in split-second flashes the grumbling, sinking clouds hovering over Saint Catherine's Cove. The roars of thunder announced Paul and Mikey's entrance into the house. Dr. Drew hurried to his nearby home before the rain.

Claribel rushed to the door to greet Mikey with a hug. "Our trouble-maker returns!"

Gracie and Eli had returned from after-school activities not even fifteen minutes ago, and they rushed to see their brother and grandfather in. Claribel had filled them in, as vaguely as possible, about the call that had come from the university and their grandfather's willingness to bring their older brother home. Thrilled to christen his settling in to comfort and familiarity with their joyful welcome, Mikey hugged them each.

"Smells good!" he shouted, tossing two duffle bags under the kitchen island. Dr. Drew had stopped at Mikey's house on the way to Paul's so that he could gather a few things. A second duffle bag contained odds and ends from his dorm room.

"That's chicken pot pie filling. It's been simmering for hours. And you, Mikey, know better than to toss the bags under the island. Bring them up to your room."

The admonishment alighted pleasantly on Mikey's ears, affirming his presence in comforting and safe territory. He dragged the duffle bags from under the island and schlepped with them up the stairs to his Aunt Pauline and Aunt Anna's former room in which he would be sleeping with Eli while Gracie took her father's old room.

Paul made himself a bourbon on the rocks with a splash of Cointreau while Claribel prepared dinner, and within an hour, they all sat for grace. Paul could tell Mikey acted more at ease now. The car ride home had helped relieve him of angst as they all discussed the meeting, and Paul made it clear to Mikey that he—and Dr. Drew, for that matter—completely sided with him. Mikey had asked few questions but absorbed the information he garnered from fervid palaver between his grandfather and Dr. Drew. And now a home-cooked meal by his grandmother while sitting across from his brother and sister temporarily alleviated him of anxiety.

Claribel eschewed mention of the happenings at the university lest the topic engender indigestion while eating. She announced that they could discuss everything after dinner. She had wished to limit the discussion to a short while before insisting the kids do their homework, but today was Friday and she knew she wouldn't get much mileage out of that, nor could she send them on an ice cream run on account of the storm.

The kids cleared the table, washed the pots and pans, loaded the dishwater, and put the left-overs away after dinner. Claribel monitored from a stool at the island before pulling Paul to the solarium, thinking she might not have another chance to talk to him alone before the houseguests went to bed. He was walking in from the study when she corralled him.

"Did you see how many calls came in today?" Paul was astonished.

"Did I see? I took the calls and wrote the messages. Eloise said she sent you the revised article in an e-mail. Did you see that one? I imagine that's the most pressing."

"I did see it. I will read through it again tonight. Any word from Michael?"

"No. I'm hoping he will call soon, at least when he lands in Dublin."

"He couldn't find a direct flight to London?"

"Not when his employer is penny-pinching, Paul."

From the solarium, they peeked at the kids working in the kitchen.

"Mikey seems to be in good spirits," Claribel observed, lowering her voice. "Did it go well?"

"I think it will *turn out* well, but I can't say it went well. Bel, there's a lot I have to fill you in on. You won't believe when I tell you who the dean of the McGuinty School of Journalism is."

Claribel waited for Paul to say it, but he was apparently waiting for her to respond to the statement.

"Who?" she asked at last.

"Derek Braynard."

Claribel stared at her husband. Then she literally shook the shock off and stared at him again. "Is that a good thing or a bad thing?"

"It's a bad thing, and if it hadn't been for Lucretia, I wouldn't have suspected how bad, going in to this situation today."

"How does Lucretia figure in to any of this?"

"That's what I have to fill you in on. How long do I have?"

Claribel glanced at the kids working and shouted, "Please don't forget to wipe the table and the counter tops."

"We won't!" Gracie responded.

"Okay," Claribel said to Paul, "we have about five minutes before we'll have to hold them off."

"Why don't you sit."

Within the five minutes, Paul reminded Claribel that Lucretia, after her heart attack, had been requesting to see him and what she told him when he finally visited her; he recounted Lucretia's story about running into Derek Braynard outside Greengate Grade School, revealing that Paul had been honored at an assembly, and witnessing his envious and indignant reaction to the news before he hopped in his car and sped off; he explained what Mikey had written in his paper and how the ordeal unfolded from there. He stopped short of his visit with the university president and subsequently with Dean Braynard, himself, for the kids ambled into the solarium.

Claribel had been shocked to learn of Lucretia's encounter with Derek and his outburst against Paul. In fact, she barely attended what Paul said after that until its connection to Mikey's situation struck her.

With their grandchildren present, Paul decided to continue the story about his visit to the university president's office. Everyone listened in rapt awe as Paul, with helpful interjections from Mikey, replayed the scene nigh verbatim. Paul paused to comment at times, reiterating his distaste for the dean's handling of every facet.

When the story seemed to reach its end, the inevitable question came.

Gracie asked, "What happened that caused Dean Braynard to resent you so much?"

Paul and Claribel glanced at each other before Claribel looked at her hands in her lap. She never suspected this evening's conversation would head to this place, to that time.

"I bet I know," said Eli. "I bet you got a writing award or something that he wanted, and he has been jealous ever since."

"Unfortunately, Eli, it goes back even farther than that, and the reason might be even pettier, given how young we all were. You see, Dean Braynard grew up in Saint Catherine's Cove with us. He moved to town when we were in fourth or fifth grade and attended Greengate and then attended Saint Catherine High School with us, too. After that, some time when he was away at college, his parents moved to one of the Dakotas, and we never really heard from him around here again. Until recently, I didn't know he was a writer, to be honest. And when I did find out, I had never seen his work."

"So it goes back to when you were in grade school?" asked Gracie.

"High school," Claribel said. "Our junior year."

"To make a long story short, I asked one Claribel Wheeler to the May Festival the first weekend of May, and she said she would be honored to go with me—it was a date! And then, well, Derek Braynard asked her to go, not knowing that I had already asked, and she had to decline his invitation. He was wounded by it at the time, we could all tell, but I guess we just assumed that after all these years, he had gotten over it."

"That's kind-of like what happened with Sunrise and me, only Sunrise really wanted to go to the Halloween dance with me, not Charlie McGregor," Eli said.

"Yes, there's some similarity, but Sunrise handled it so well that no one's feelings got hurt. And your situation was very public," Paul reminded them.

"Grandma! Winning the affections of two guys? You were a vixen!" shouted Gracie. Mikey and Eli laughed, but Claribel could only purse her lips into a forced smile. Her mind grappled with other details that reappeared no less vivid now than when she had lived them over fifty-five years ago.

"Grandma, are you okay?" asked the intuitive Eli.

"She just—" Paul stuttered, catching the hopeful look from Claribel that he field the question. "We both just can't believe that, not only has he held on to it this long, but he directed a long-building anger about it at our grandson. That's the crazy part of this. Mikey, I can't tell you how bad I feel that our actions are coming back to haunt *you*."

"It's not your fault, Grandpa," Mikey said. Claribel looked again at her hands in her lap, her lips still pursed, her poise eerily still. Mikey could see that his attempt at consolation did not seem to affect his grandmother. "It's no one's fault except the dean's. I mean, some sores don't heal, or the scar is so big you can't forget it. You had no way of knowing it would have that effect on him, and you couldn't have known he would turn out to be the type of person to hold a grudge."

"Mikey, don't worry about the Derek Braynard and Paul Scrivensby clash. That's its own thing between the two of us—"

"—and me," interposed Claribel without making eye contact.

"All you have to do is let us get you through this university ridiculousness. I'm confident President Cringle sees things our way and will side with us. That's why he went out of his way to call us personally. I can't say they will retract the warning, but my guess is they will allow you to finish the class and not even consider an official suspension."

"I hope you're right. I'm still really nervous, though."

"I know you are. But for now, we have to play the waiting game."

The rain started thrashing the roof and windows, and lightning illuminated the darkness beyond the walls.

"I guess we can stop playing the waiting game for the storm," Gracie said. "No one can go out tonight, so I'm going to go upstairs and work on my speech."

"Did Gracie tell you, Mikey? Gracie is giving a speech at the Lighthouse Ceremony this Thursday night. You've probably missed all the hype about it. It's the sesquicentennial anniversary of the Saint Catherine's Cove Lighthouse, and they're having a ceremony and reception. I imagine you'll be back to school by then, but it should be a nice affair." Paul hoped the change in topic or the bright tone towards Gracie's role in the ceremony might draw Claribel back, but neither pulled her from her pondering.

"How did you get to give the speech?" asked Mikey.

"Everyone in history class got assigned a presentation on something in the area. We had to draw topics at random from a hat. I got the lighthouse. I gave the presentation already a few weeks ago. Then I guess Mr. Gunder volunteered me to speak at the ceremony. He knows someone on the planning committee. I'm basically modifying my presentation. It's mostly the history of the lighthouse with a few stories. Grandpa said he would look at it when I'm done."

"You might want to talk about it with Oliver the next time we visit. His grandfather was on the construction team that helped build the lighthouse. So was Blake Carroll's father. We old-timers will be at Pee's parlor tomorrow night if you'd like to stop in and ask questions."

"Thanks. Maybe I'll stop in if my friends aren't doing anything." While Eli mimicked her to Mikey and Paul's amusement, Gracie lazily rose from the ottoman she had plopped down on and headed for her bedroom. The boys decided to follow, although unlike Gracie, they lacked any specific agenda.

"I guess I'll go be nervous about the outcome upstairs," Mikey said.

"Now, Mikey, I told you. Don't spend the waiting game being nervous over something you can't control," Paul said.

Mikey reached into his pocket and pulled out a chain of black and white beads. "You're right. I could be more productive by praying for my case."

"I saw you holding those beads when I came to from my accident. You were praying for me," Paul said.

"It's Mom's rosary. I keep it with me all the time." He walked to a credenza behind the armchair and lifted a framed photograph of his mother and father standing in the yard, Gracie sitting at their feet, baby Eli in his father's arms, and Mikey nestling his head into his mother's side while she rested her hands on his head and shoulder. "I'll try calling Dad one more time, too." He set the photograph down and headed for his room with Eli in tow.

"I'll go practice my guitar," the latter said as he exited.

When Paul and Claribel found themselves alone, Paul scooched next to his wife and held her in his arm.

"Mikey was right," she said. "He's a smart boy. He really is. Some sores don't heal, or their scars are so big you can't ever forget them. They sit there staring you in the face. And I'm the reason for Derek's wound."

"Bel, you can't blame yourself."

"When you think about it, it really is my fault. All of this is happening to Mikey because of me." When she said this, she looked away from her lap and into Paul's eyes, hoping he would nod or shut his eyes or offer any gesture that might affirm her statement. He instead shook his head to contest it.

"Paul," she said, "you have a lot of messages to follow up on. Let me use the phone first, though. I'll be quick. I want to call Father Soplido for an appointment."

"With Father Soplido? You don't mean—?"

"For Confession, Paul. It's long overdue."

CHAPTER 16

While the kids ate breakfast after sleeping in, Claribel entered through the back door. Paul had been up and loitered in the kitchen with the kids, poking fun at their birdlike eating habits— Eli picking at his milkless cereal and chopped banana, Gracie munching on her two tablespoonfuls of cereal and milk in a bowl, and Mikey chomping on his banana only. He sipped his coffee and offered some to his grandchildren when Claribel plopped down at the island with the kids, setting two grocery bags on the floor next to her stool.

"Why don't you eat at the kitchen table?" she asked.

"I don't know," responded a groggy Eli, reading the back of the cereal box.

The kids declined coffee, but Paul knew Claribel would enjoy some. He poured her a cup full and passed it over the countertop to her.

"Peony drive you to the church this morning?" Paul asked.

"No, Lu drove. Stopped at the grocery store quickly beforehand to get some ingredients for shepherd's pie for Mikey. I know it's his favorite. I'll make it for dinner tomorrow."

His eyes widened when he heard her say this and gave her two thumbs up, almost losing the banana in his hand. He would have shouted something enthusiastically had his mouth not been full.

"There was a line around the church for the regularly scheduled Confession this morning, from eight o'clock to noon.

Father Peychaud was hearing them. Lucky I had an appointment with Father Soplido so that I didn't have to wait."

"You look like you're in better spirits," Paul remarked.

"I don't know," she said without elaborating in front of the grandchildren.

An hour later, while the kids were getting dressed for the day, Paul saw Eloise to discuss the article. They made a call to Father Soplido from the study and agreed on how to proceed. Following the plan, Eloise expected to have the article completed by the evening so that Paul could submit it for the December issue to the editor-in-chief, Stephen.

When Eloise left, Paul sat with Claribel to recount what had been discussed in the meeting. Then he shared his concern over the possibility of writing another article for the December issue.

"I have no reservations about going ahead with this article about Derek Braynard—Dean Derek Braynard—and how he railroaded my grandson. I have a few ideas about how to approach it. I just don't want to waste my time writing it if I don't have to, and I'm hoping the university will call soon, indicating a course of action."

"I'm happy Stephen has been willing to accommodate you," said Claribel.

"When I followed up with him on the car ride back from the university, he was responsive to it. He joked that the whole issue could be devoted to me at this point."

"He's been great, I have to say. And let's face it—you're still a hot topic. Did you see the paper this morning? Anita Gonzalez-Shea still hasn't announced that you and Father Soplido declined her offer for representation, and Father's statement about *choosing* to be offended is gaining momentum in the press." The reference prompted Claribel to recall the magazines in the checkout lane at the grocery store. "The new edition of *American Generations* features a headline about you I thought you might like: 'Paul Scrivensby: Class Personified.' I noticed a few others along the same lines. I think if you told

Stephen you were going to sneeze in public, he would arrange to catch it on camera and do a story on it."

Paul fidgeted with his sling and grinned humbly.

What felt like a long, sunny day gave way to an early dusk. Around the dinner hour, Claribel served left-overs from the past two nights, chicken pot pie and braised brisket with leeks, along with a lemony steamed broccoli side and a salad. She prepared the dishes with her daughters, Anna and Pauline, who had stopped in for a half hour. They helped their mother with the salad and broccoli while sharing a few stories about their kids, noting their excitement for the upcoming lighthouse sesquicentennial ceremony. Mikey, Gracie, and Eli cleared the table, washed the dishes, and wiped the counters in record time as their grandparents rested a few moments in the solarium. Before hitching a ride from the grandchildren to the ice cream parlor to meet with friends, the phone rang. Mikey, elated to learn his father was calling from London, tried to convince him to stay in England and not to worry about coming home for him. His father, however, said that he would be home as early as tomorrow evening. He told Mikey not to worry about picking him up at Minneapolis - Saint Paul International Airport as the company would arrange to send a car for him. After the call, Mikey drove his grandparents and his siblings to the parlor owned by Poppy, the daughter of Paul and Claribel's close friend Peony.

Peony's eight-year-old granddaughter Petunia opened the door of the parlor as they entered on the cold November evening and then ran to a small round table adjoining the old-timers' large table. At the small table, she picked the perfect colors of crayon to decorate the Thanks-Giving drawings in her coloring book. Poppy, as usual, oscillated between manning the register, working the counter, and hanging at her mother's table, chatting with her mother's friends.

A group of Gracie's friends sat at the counter enjoying strawberry phosphates with squiggly straws and practically swooned with giggles when Mikey entered; that he had been away at college only added to his heart-throb mystique. They welcomed Gracie over and made comments that had her hushing her friends and admonishing them with "Don't say that" and "He's my brother!"

Mikey sat with Eli at a small booth inches from their grandparents' table of friends. Within minutes of their arrival, the Walshes stepped in, Sunrise and her parents. Mr. and Mrs. Walsh ordered an ice cream for Sunrise, Eli and Mikey, and themselves, and then left the kids to enjoy a Saturday evening together, confident they were safe under the nearby watch of Eli's grandparents. Before leaving, they confirmed that Mikey would drop them off on the way home.

Peony Pilsen held court at the table already occupied by Lucretia, Nora, Roy, Marni, and Drew, reacting vociferously to Drew's quips, laughing raucously at Lucretia's rants. Every few minutes, Peony leaned over Petunia's shoulder to ask her how her coloring was going. She welcomed Eli and Sunrise and the unexpected Mikey, greeted Gracie with a holler across the parlor, and made room for Paul and Claribel at the table. Poppy cajoled Petunia from her coloring to request her assistance with serving the newcomers' orders, and then rested on her mother's chair back to enjoy some conversation as Petunia resumed coloring.

Eli and Sunrise recapped their mornings to each other, somewhat oblivious to Mikey's presence at the same booth, but more importantly, they tuned in every so often to the conversation at the table nearby. They all enjoyed spending time with the whole group of Saint Catherine's Cove's most established denizens, and Eli secretly anticipated a snarky Dr. Drew comment so that he could fold at the waist in a fit of quiet laughter.

Broaching the situation involving Mikey and Derek Braynard did not take long, especially since Claribel had mentioned the story to Lu earlier that morning and since Drew, though exercising discretion out of loyalty to Paul, had accompanied Paul to the university. Once the gist of the story had been recounted by Paul, the floor opened for commentary.

"Is that ever strange?" mused Nora. "We've all faced rejection—"

"Don't speak for us all, Nora-Bore-a," said Drew.

"We've *all* faced rejection in one way or another, and none of us became this bitter about it."

"We probably shouldn't compare, though," Claribel said. "It could affect us all differently. But it doesn't justify taking it out on our grandson."

"I have a question," stated Mikey. "During the meeting, what did you mean, Dr. Drew, when Dean Braynard said, 'Let's take off the gloves,' and you said, 'As I recall, you could never get them on?'"

Dr. Drew chuckled as he glanced at Paul. "Back then, Saint Catherine High School offered boxing—kind-of a club thing run by Father Duchamp—and Derek tried out for it but got cut. Kid was awful." He saw that Mikey grinned in his better understanding of the quip.

"And you brought that up at the meeting yesterday?" asked Nora. "Shame on you."

"Is getting cut from boxing off limits? I guess I won't mention that Paul got cut, too, for being even worse."

Taking less issue with getting cut than with being called worse than Derek, Paul protested, "I at least could get the gloves on, and I got a few good upper-cuts in."

"There was always something off about that boy," noted Marni. "I don't know that it was his fault. He did have to go home every day to that drunkard of a father."

"I think he was downright embarrassed of his father, and that's what made him try a little too hard to fit in at times and to keep to himself at other times," Roy evaluated.

Poppy, leaning on the back of her mother's chair, said, "Growing up and fitting in can be difficult at that age."

"It's not like we were an unwelcoming lot," said Lucretia. "I was something of a loner until Paul included me in some activities, and Claribel and Pee welcomed me warmly."

"And it was Lu who always made me feel welcomed, and we became closest of friends," added Nora. "Remind me, Claribel. What did he do? He asked you to that Swedish smorgasbord night, right?"

Peony chuckled. "No, Nora. That was my Roger! First date he asked me on."

"I didn't give Roger a lot of credit for his judgment in women, but I give that man credit for knowing how to get what he wanted. The surest way to Peony's heart is through her stomach," Drew said. He didn't have a moment to check for reactions before the crack to the back of his head landed.

"Derek asked me to May Fest," Claribel reminded them.

"May Fest! That's right!" said Nora.

"Derek sat with me the weekend before at a baseball game. It was a Saturday, and I was sitting alone in the stands by the third inning. Pee, you had been sitting with me and then had to go to work. And by the fourth inning, Derek had wandered over and sat next to me. I think it was a big move for him, but we got along just fine in class, so why not at the game? We talked, and I remember it was the longest fifth inning in the world—Paul went up to bat twice!"

"Struck out both times," Drew whispered to Mikey and Eli.

"And he really was quite pleasant," Claribel continued. "But then on Monday, everyone was whispering about May Fest the following weekend, and who was going with whom. I just assumed we'd go as a big group of friends, but people started pairing up." Claribel looked at the butterscotch sundae she hadn't touched yet and grew maudlin. "Then I had learned—"

Paul, as if picking up on the change in her mood and wanting to prevent her from having any time to wallow in it, lifted the tenor of the story by interjecting, "She had learned that Paul Scrivensby wouldn't mind going with her, and lo and behold, he asked her."

Everyone smiled at the recollection.

"I remember you two at the festival," said Marni. "That was your first date, wasn't it?"

"We think of it as our first date, yes." Claribel pursed her lips into a smile, carefully avoiding eye contact with Paul, with anyone.

"That was a fun night. It was really a fun time," recalled Roy.

"Derek asked you to go the day after Paul had asked," continued Lucretia. "He asked you at another baseball game after school with Pee and me right next to you. It was terribly uncomfortable. Who would have seen it coming, though? And you had to tell him you were going with Paul Scrivensby already."

"And the look on his face," said Peony, shaking her head. "He was embarrassed—flustered—but angry, too. He didn't say anything. He just reacted with all these emotions and marched away."

Claribel never looked up.

"I understand that in terms of his development and perhaps his outlook on life, all this is probably significant. He had a difficult family life. He had an awkwardness socializing. He got turned down to May Fest. But he still chose to harbor resentment for me for fifty-some years. Maybe he couldn't control his outburst in front of Lucretia, but he could control targeting my grandson in the most heinous of ways." Everyone noted Paul's attempt to find any reason to show sympathy for the man, but they saw the sensibility of his statement, too. Until he concluded his thought, a few glances at Mikey sitting within reach reminded them that a human being, a boy, a close relation of Paul's, had been directly affected by this one man's grudge. "We *are* responsible for our own actions."

"A level-headed person would have shaken this off years ago," said Nora. "Makes me wonder about him."

"We hope everything works out for you, Mikey," Roy said across tables. "I have a feeling things will turn out just fine. We'll all hop on the prayer wagon for you."

"Thanks, Mr. Palomer," Mikey said to Roy. Mikey had been dipping his spoon in and out of his root beer float since the moment little Petunia had served it, just as maudlin as his grandmother. Despite the optimism at dinner earlier, the puppy love right next to him, and the encouragement from his grandparents' friends, his mind relentlessly wandered to worst-case scenarios of having to face the university's Judicial Affairs Committee, learning he was going to be suspended or expelled, cleaning out his dorm room, explaining to his friends that he had gotten kicked out.

"Can we change the subject, please?" asked Paul, noting the persistence of Claribel and Mikey's sadness. "Can we talk about something more upbeat?"

"Good idea!" reiterated Peony.

"Poor Oliver," said Nora. "Still not well enough to join us. Recovery is going slower than they thought."

"Thank-you for that uplifting change in conversation," said Roy.

"I plan to visit him tomorrow if anyone is interested. I think I will go to early Mass and head to his place afterwards. At least he's home now."

"I may join you, Paul," said Lu.

"He's actually doing quite well," said Dr. Drew. "It's just that sometimes, recovery can go a little slower when you get to be our age. He's still doing well, and he was in great shape prior to the accident, which helps."

"Let's see if we can't get him to the Lighthouse Ceremony!" said Peony. "I bet he would like that."

"I bet he wouldn't miss it whether he's ready to get out or not," said Paul.

"I'd like to organize a group photo of you all while you're all dolled up," said Poppy. "I'd like to hang it in here. Don't you think the lighthouse would be a nice place for that? Maybe on the steamer. Or maybe at the lighthouse itself—the garden outside. Might be too cold on the gallery."

"There's always the promenade pier," said Nora.

The Saint Catherine's Cove Lighthouse rested atop a sandstone cliff. The cliff rose to about fifty feet above the lake water, and the lighthouse itself ascended to ninety feet. The base of the lighthouse featured a few other small structures, including the oil house and the storage shed, but around the facilities and cliff wound a promenade that descended eastward about a quarter mile to the marina and docks at water level. A small branch of the promenade followed the façade of the cliff down a staircase to a wide but short pier about twenty-five feet above the water. The pier, a favorite spot for stargazing and reflecting and shenanigans, jutted about thirty feet into the lake; it offered a close view of the lighthouse from the bottom up, and it provided a wooden rail for younglings wishing to enjoy a prohibited night-time jump and swim.

"Ah, yes, the promenade pier," echoed Drew. "Maybe instead of getting all dolled up, we could wear the same outfits we wore the weekend we finished junior year of high school when we went there."

Drew and Roy grinned, Peony covered her mouth, Lucretia scoffed, and Paul and Claribel blushed. Marni and Nora looked perplexed.

"Skinny-dipping?" asked Poppy, terrified of receiving confirmation.

Peony made sure Petunia's attention held fast to her Pilgrim drawing. Paul glanced at his grandchildren to find the boys and Sunrise avidly awaiting a response. Luckily, Gracie was oblivious as she chatted away with her friends at the counter.

"Did we embarrass poor little Paulie?" said Drew. "And when I say little, I mean *little!*"

"You went skinny-dipping, Roy?" Marni asked.

"A bunch of us football players—me, Drew, Oliver, a few others—were down on the pier with Betsy, Kathy, and Sheila, and then Paul, Claribel, Lu, and Lu's George met up with us. It was the beginning of Memorial Day weekend, and it was such a nice night. School had finished hours ago. And someone got the idea to—well, to jump in."

"Naked?" asked Marni.

"It probably happened with teenagers before us, and I'm sure it's happening now," Roy said, looking at Mikey for verification. Mikey smiled bashfully and affirmed the statement with a nod.

"You've gone skinny-dipping there, Mikey?" asked Paul.

He nodded again and then quickly added, "It's not like we went every weekend, but yeah, every now and then. But get back to your story, Grandpa." Mikey winked, happy with his prowess at repositioning the spotlight off himself and onto the old-timers.

"So we went skinny-dipping when we were seventeen," said Roy. "What's the big deal?"

"The big deal for Paul was more his little deal," said Drew, chuckling.

"Is anything off limits in front of my grandchildren, Drew? He's joking by the way."

"You have every reason to be embarrassed, Paul," Drew said.

"As I recall," Claribel interposed demurely, her spirits higher now, "you are the one who should have been more embarrassed that night."

Her comment teased laughter out of everyone present as the tables turned on Drew, not a regular occurrence, and not one usually maneuvered by Claribel.

"And how would you know what I have to be embarrassed about?"

"It was a clear, spring night—tragically clear."

"Most of us jumped in in our underwear and didn't fully disrobe until we were under water. You couldn't have seen anything."

"I couldn't resist, Drew. I did a swim-by under water. Let's say I never swam back."

Everyone erupted in laughter as Drew found himself on the receiving end of the jocularity for once. Paul's complexion remained ruddy despite his appreciation for his wife's defense of his—honor.

"Ironically," said Lucretia, "do you remember who the only one resistant to the whole skinny-dipping idea was? Take a guess, kids." She directed the question to Mikey, Eli, and Sunrise.

"Mrs. Scrivensby," said Sunrise. "For sure." Mikey and Eli nodded in agreement.

Lu shook her head no. "That wouldn't be ironic." Then she turned her head to Dr. Drew and pointed a spindly finger at him.

"Guilty," Drew said.

"That's right!" Claribel said as fog around the memory lifted. "You didn't think we should be doing it in May."

"It was the Month of Mary, and we had a few more days until June. I didn't think it was appropriate. And why is it ironic that *I* was the one who thought that?"

No one addressed his question before Roy noted, "In the end, it didn't seem to stop you."

"Blake Carroll stepped onto the watch room gallery at one point and just shook his head at us. Then he turned around and walked back in," Paul said. "I bet he used to skinny-dip himself when no one was around."

"Where was I for all this?" asked Nora.

"Gee, where was Snora for all this?" mocked Drew. "I'm pretty sure that was the day you decided to unsnuggle with a book for five minutes and lodge a pole so far up your ass you've never been able to get it out. Still shows up on your x-rays and everything."

This time, when everyone laughed, they were responding to Drew's attempt to turn the tables back around on someone else, unable to bear being the brunt of a few jokes.

"You're somewhat right, Drew. Now that I think about it, that Memorial Day weekend is the weekend I began and finished Dante's *Paradiso*." Then looking at the kids, she added, "I know the date of every book I've ever read."

"That's completely normal," Drew said wryly, eliciting a convulsion of laughter from Eli.

"I showed up late—I'll never forget that!" said Pee. "I had to work here at the parlor, and when I got to the pier, I saw all your clothes in piles, and I saw your undergarments floating in the lake, and all of you were laughing in the water. Can you imagine my surprise upon walking into that scene? I'll never forget it!"

"*You'll* never forget it?" said Dr. Drew. "Every town along the Lake Superior shore and ten miles inland will never forget it when you decided to cannonball in!"

Now tears started streaming down Eli's face while everyone else keeled over laughing, including Pee. Gracie and the girls at the counter stopped chatting in an effort to catch a strand of the jovial uproar. Shaking her head but unable to stop laughing, Poppy strolled to behind the counter. This climactic bout of laughter brought the conversation to a sighing end.

As her laughter subsided, Peony noticed Sunrise hand Eli a cloth napkin to wipe the tears from his face. The only one whose laughter did not relent, he lacked, in his fit, the coordination to hold the napkin, so it fell to the table. Sunrise lifted it and, smiling from fresh laughter herself, wiped the tears off Eli's face.

Touched by what she witnessed, Peony said, "It's nice how we all enjoyed our youth together here in Saint Catherine's Cove, went our separate ways—some to college, Drew to Chicago for his residency, Paul and Claribel to New York for *The Current Front*—and still carried on with friendship as we regrouped and raised our children and played with our grandchildren and retired. It makes me think—" and she stopped as if stuck in the thought she was about to share— "It makes me *wonder* what Saint Catherine's Cove will look like fifty years from now—when we're gone."

Everyone saw that she was staring at Eli and Sunrise when she said this, and this time, when Claribel pursed her lips, it helped to repel tears.

Roy said, "In fifty years, Eli and Sunrise Scrivensby will be grandparents enjoying a few laughs with Mikey and Gracie and Petunia and all their friends. And all *their* grandchildren will be occupying the tables around them, eating techno-flavored ice cream."

"Techno-flavored?" asked Marni.

"And by that time," Drew added, "little Petunia will be holding court at the table in the back while the ice cream is being served by her granddaughter Pineapple."

"Fifty years from now," Lucretia said, "we'll be long forgotten, relegated to a few stories like the ones we tell about Blake Carroll and his father and his uncle."

"I won't forget you," Mikey said. "I have a hard time forgetting the people who are the most important to me."

No one responded to Mikey with words but instead with eyes full of lake-drenched memories of laughter and sorrow, autumn-night fears of what floated on the waters before them, and star-illumined love for each other and for their children and for their children's children—and for the children they would never know.

Wading in the silence of their responses, no one noticed Mikey releasing the black and white rosary in his pocket and fighting the urge to remember.

When the evening wound down, Mikey, Gracie, and Eli drove Sunrise home for her early curfew and returned to the parlor to pick up their grandparents, who had been in mid-conversation at the time they needed to depart with Sunrise. When the Scrivensbys arrived home, everyone headed to bed and turned off the lights. Paul had only begun to drift into sleep when he heard a crack on the creaky wooden staircase, sure to have been caused by one of his grandchildren's steps. Although he would have let himself drift into sleep normally, a feeling nudged him to roll from bed, careful not to hurt his arm and careful not to rouse Claribel, to step to the top of the staircase, and to listen. On the stairs, he heard from the study a sound that he too surely recognized, having himself caused the same sound many an evening before dinner—the sound of the crystal decanter stopper sliding out of the aperture and the long pour of bourbon filling a glass.

CHAPTER 17

Mikey drove Paul and Claribel to church on Sunday morning, staying with them for the hour-long Mass celebrated by Father Soplido. They left at ten o'clock and headed for Oliver's house. Happy to visit him at home instead of the hospital, they brightened to see him open the front door himself upon their pulling in to his driveway. Oliver lived alone and had hired a caretaker while he recovered from the accident.

Just before Claribel exited the car, Paul said softly to her, "Give me a minute with Mikey, will you? Tell Oliver we'll be in shortly."

She looked at him quizzically and then met Oliver at his front door. When he had ushered her in after learning that Paul needed a moment with Mikey, he kept the door open for them to enter.

"What's up, Grandpa? Did you hear from President Cringle?"

"No, I'm afraid not. I think we won't hear from him until tomorrow at the earliest. I wanted to talk to you about last night—after we got back."

Mikey did not respond, unsure where his grandfather was going with this introduction.

"You were drinking in the study after we went to bed," he declared. "Pretty sure you helped yourself to the decanter of bourbon."

Could the issue be his age? Mikey was not sure why his grandfather would call him out on this and could not tell if he was bothered by it or not.

"You know I drink, Grandpa."

"Yes, I know you drink. I have no objections to having a drink once in a while. I'm just curious—why? Why did you have a drink after we all went to bed?"

Mikey looked out the car window, sighing as he gathered his thoughts. Then he began the process of coming clean. "I've been torn up about how this college stuff could turn out. I was thinking about it all day and all night. Having dinner with you and hanging out at the ice cream parlor took my mind off it every now and then, even though I caught myself wondering what I would do if I got expelled, but when I got home and was all alone, there was nothing to distract me from my thoughts."

"So you decided to drown your thoughts?"

"I don't know," he said. "I just decided to have a drink, maybe to take my mind off it, maybe to shake things up inside— my thoughts—so that they got so disoriented I couldn't think. I don't know."

"You could talk to me about it, you know. You could call your father."

His leg started to move up and down rapidly. Then, as if pained to share, he said, "I just want—"

His leg stopped.

"There's no one I can talk to and feel good about it. I'd feel like a bother talking to you or Dad at this point."

"You're never a bother, Mikey."

"I'd still feel like one."

"Look, Mikey. The only reason I'm bringing it up is that I want you to drink because you feel like enjoying a drink once in a while, not because you are turning to alcohol to help you through something, or help you not think about something. That's when alcohol becomes dangerous, as far as I'm concerned."

"I wasn't turning to alcohol. I just—I needed it to—" He couldn't finish the sentence without proving his grandfather correct, so he stopped talking. He didn't want to let on that he was getting worked up.

"Mikey, why don't you tell me what's bothering you?"

Mikey sighed again, this time releasing exasperation and mild anger. "You keep saying that I have to play the waiting game, that there's not anything else I can do. By while I wait, I keep wondering about every possible outcome, and they're all awful!"

"The likely outcome is that you won't get suspended and that you'll be admitted back to class. That's not awful."

"You say it's likely, but you don't know for sure. Until I hear the words, 'you're not suspended,' I won't be able to stop speculating about it."

"Let's look at the facts, then. The fact is that the president of your university called us. I feel this gesture is an indication that he wants to mitigate the situation as much as possible. He didn't have to call us."

"I know. I know. I saw his reaction to Dean Braynard when he accused me of being entitled. He thinks the dean was drastic. But it doesn't mean he can't be swayed by the dean or the Judicial Affairs Committee or whomever else he has to consult. What if it's in the university's best interest that I'm not a student there?"

"It's the president of the university you're talking about. He holds some pull."

"You can be as reasonable and sensible as you want, but it won't stop my mind from racing to the worst possible outcomes. I try to be reasonable to myself, and my fears get the better of me." He was speaking fast as if his heart had begun racing, and he didn't want to think about the worst outcomes anymore. He didn't want to think about waiting patiently for word anymore. "I just want my—" His exasperation culminated in a sentence he could not finish out loud. He did not want to admit the word to himself let alone out loud for anyone else to hear. He wasn't supposed to want this anymore, so he could not voice it, could not even think about it.

"Mikey?" Paul asked in a way that tried to tug the missing word out of his grandson.

Mikey looked out the driver's side window.

"Mikey, is there something else?"

"Can we go in to see Mr. Montgomery? I'll be wiser about drinking in the future." He didn't wait for his grandfather to respond. He opened the car door and exited the car, watching to make sure his grandfather didn't need a helping hand getting out. Then the two entered Oliver's house, joining Claribel in the family room. Paul suspected his conversation with Mikey would need to continue, but he thwarted himself from persisting with it at that moment, hanging on to the hope that an imminent call from the president of the university would expunge any more of Mikey's consternation.

Oliver responded to Mikey's presence as effusively as he did to Paul's, and then they both sat next to Claribel on the couch. Oliver's caretaker helped him sit in a recliner.

"I'm mobile. I can move around all right. I just get a little pain in my chest and lung, and I get exhausted if I'm on my feet too long. But I'm doing well."

"You look well," said Claribel.

"Drew says my recovery is going smoothly, so I'm happy. I'm feeling better every day. I'm planning on making it to the Lighthouse Ceremony Thursday night."

"I knew you would!" announced Paul.

Oliver had always done well for himself through autonomous, independent work and living. Growing up blocks from each other, Paul and Oliver spent summer afternoons playing imaginative games about Chippewa Indians making peace treaties with the Menominee before sailing together down the St. Croix River as new allies, building forts in each other's backyards, and occasionally fishing on the lake with their fathers. They trick-or-treated together in autumn, built snowmen together in winter, and judged a pie contest together in spring, all before turning ten.

They enjoyed many classes together from kindergarten through high school and worked on homework after school at the library or at one or the other's house. Oliver often turned to Paul for help with grammar while Paul turned to Oliver for help with mathematics. Playing baseball as teammates helped them rely on each other in a different way and provided plenty of fun afternoons with the whole group of local kids. When Paul went away to college, Oliver stayed in Saint Catherine's Cove continuing the work he had done through high school: he assisted his father, an electrician for the area. Working as an electrician, undoubtedly his vocation and passion, led to running his father's business for years until his retirement last year. Oliver never married and seemed perfectly content single. From when they were young, nights out as couples at the ice cream parlor, the pictures, games, Apple Harvest Fest, May Fest never stopped Oliver from attending and enjoying everyone's company, and they enjoyed his. Not boisterous or bombastic, he made talking easy for anyone, made gatherings fun by laughing quickly, and made everyone feel valuable by denying no one his kindness. He was also shockingly unabashed. Once, as a grade-schooler, he slipped in the early morning dew and landed in the ashes of the bonfire from the previous night. Paul, Drew, Oliver, and a few other friends had spent the night in Roy's backyard around a campfire and then slept on Roy's porch. When Oliver pulled himself up, blackened from the ash, everyone burst into laughter. Oliver simply shrugged, wiped a little soot off his brow, and went half the day sullied. And when Betsy Balou that night in late May had suggested skinny-dipping, Oliver was the first to strip— completely—and dive from the pier into the water. Unembarrassed, independent, and kind—these traits characterized him as a boy and only grew more pronounced as he aged.

"It gives me something to look forward to," Oliver said, "so I will be there."

"I like Poppy's idea," Claribel said. "Last night, she said she wanted us to take a photograph together so that she could hang it at the parlor. I think that would be nice, and you need to be in that photograph or it won't be worth hanging anywhere."

They chatted briefly and then rose to depart, Oliver standing on his own as they rose. On their way to the car, Lucretia pulled in, sorry to have missed a visit with Paul, Claribel, and Mikey.

Albeit a short ride home, Mikey never spoke.

They walked in to their house to the sight of Eli and Gracie at the kitchen table eating breakfast in their pajamas. The squint in their eyes seemed yet unadjusted to the streams of late morning sunlight rushing through the windows onto the table.

"Are you two just getting up?" asked Claribel.

Eli nodded groggily, and Gracie voiced a faint "Yes."

"Your father is coming home tonight. Does anyone have an idea of what time he's getting in?"

"And it's my fault he has to cut his business trip short and come home this soon at all," huffed Mikey, tossing his money clip, keys, and cellphone on the island counter. Then he took off for his room, leaping two stairs at a time.

"What was that all about?" asked Gracie.

"He's just in a lousy mood," Paul said. "He's got a lot on his mind."

"That makes both my brothers in bad moods," Gracie intimated.

"Gracie!" Eli said.

"Why are you in a bad mood, Eli?" Claribel asked.

"I'm not in a bad mood." But the way he said it expressed otherwise.

"You're not in a good mood," Claribel said, trying not to pry with questions.

"Mikey and I dropped Sunrise off last night, and Eli walked her up to the front door," Gracie began, but Eli protested.

"Gracie, stop!" he said. When she kept going, he put his hand over his eyes, not wanting to see a reaction but really not wanting to hear the story told.

"Mikey parked the car two houses down to give them a moment of privacy, and when Eli got back in the car he told us that they hugged good-night. But when Eli went to leave, Sunrise didn't release him from her hug. She closed her eyes and leaned in. Eli didn't know what to do, so he kissed her—" Gracie chuckled before adding— "on the forehead!"

Eli placed his head in his arms on the table.

"He's really embarrassed. He thinks Sunrise is going to dump him or something."

"Sounds like a typical Scrivensby male," noted Claribel, unfazed by the story.

"Eli," Paul said, "you have nothing to be ashamed of. Girls mature faster than boys. You just didn't see it coming so soon, and another time, you'll be ready."

With the muffled voice of a mouth inches from the tabletop, Eli said, "I kissed her on the forehead and ran down the block to the car. I don't think there'll be another time."

"This kissing stuff happens too soon these days," Paul said.

"Your grandfather and I didn't have a first kiss until our last year of high school."

"That's gross," Eli said.

Claribel pulled a tray of striped Halloween ice cubes from the freezer made from separate layers of orange pop, water, and root beer. She had made them the week before Halloween when Mikey was in for fall break. A tall glass of water called, and she figured she should use this ice to free an ice tray. While she poured her water, Paul inquired about calls and messages.

"Did you catch any calls this morning or did you sleep through them?" he asked.

"Dr. Drew left a message about joining him and some friends in a scrimmage of flag football and then remembered out loud that you couldn't play because your arm is in a sling," Gracie said.

"That pain in the neck," Paul said.

"He was definitely rubbing it in," Gracie added.

"Don't tell Dr. Drew about what happened with Sunrise!" Eli blurted out.

"Why not?" asked Paul.

"I don't want him to think I'm a dork," Eli said.

"You care what Dr. Drew thinks?" Paul was incredulous.

"I don't know what's worse," Gracie said. "Kissing Sunrise on the forehead or idolizing a seventy-two year old man."

Eli ugh-ed. "You're not helping, Gracie."

"Look, Eli. She will never forget that you serenaded her in front of the whole school," Gracie said. "Take it from a girl. If I were Sunrise, I'd only have to remember that once before remembering what a catch you are."

Eli raised his head finally with the hope that rose in his heart at Gracie's comment. Unconfident in her prophesy, however, he stood and walked forlornly up the stairs.

"I think it's official," Gracie declared. "I'm the only Scrivensby child without major issues."

"The boys are going to have major issues with their grandma," Claribel announced, "if they keep leaving their things everywhere I turn." She pointed to Eli's empty cereal bowl on the kitchen table and the contents of Mikey's pocket on the island.

"Go easy on them. They're going through rough times," Paul defended. "Maybe go a little harder on Eli—for caring what Drew thinks."

Then Eli hurried down the stairs, still in his pajamas. "Mikey's gone! The bedroom window is open, and he's not upstairs!"

"What?" Claribel set her glass of water on the counter and looked at Paul, who blanched.

Gracie ran upstairs to double-check and then rushed down. "He's not up there."

Paul, the most fretful of them all, somehow doubled as the calming presence, encouraging everyone to stay put when he noticed Eli and Gracie's impulse to run outside. Eli and Gracie threw on some clothes, and Claribel grabbed Mikey's cellphone from the counter, convincing herself that it would ring. Paul called Billy and Pat's parents, wondering if Mikey had stopped by to see them, although leaving through the bedroom window suggested Mikey was not making social calls to his friends' parents. In the meantime, Eli ran down a few blocks, peering up driveways and down streets for a glimpse of his brother, and Gracie drove around the area, checking four ways at every intersection. After about twenty minutes, the kids came back to report no trace of their brother.

"Listen, he probably just went for a walk or a jog to clear his head and didn't want to explain himself to us before he left. I'm sure he will be back any minute, and when he gets back, someone should be here. Eli, stay with your grandmother here. Gracie, can I bother you to take a drive down Main Street? He may have stopped at the coffee shop. I'm going to walk along the docks and up to the lighthouse promenade. I wish I had a way for you to contact me when he returns."

"Here, Grandpa," Eli said. "Take my cellphone. Call if you find him, and we'll call if he shows up here." Then he gave him a quick tutorial on how to make and receive calls.

Grateful for the cloudless noon, the absence of rain, and the radiant sun cutting the chill, Paul still walked hastily toward the lake, glancing every which way for his grandson. On occasion, he took walks alone, but most of his entailed brainstorming about column topics and ways to present a particular idea. His walks took him along the water's edge, so maybe Mikey's did, too. Claribel recently told him that when she had learned of her cancer, she walked to the lighthouse. Maybe Mikey had headed there, too, especially amid the buzz about the Lighthouse Ceremony.

As Paul hurried, he noticed Samuel Park ahead on his right where the quiet t-intersection he was approaching had been the site of his car accident. Until this moment, he hadn't remembered much of the accident, but the combination of seeing the park and nearing the intersection roused the flash of a dormant memory. On the night of his accident, when he dropped his hat and swooped to pick it up, moments before the crash, he thought he saw Mikey sitting on a bench in the park. Since the accident, he remembered nothing beyond jolting from the impact, waking up in the hospital to Father Soplido's

Anointing rite, and his family's inching toward his bed. And now he remembered this—that he thought he saw Mikey sitting in the park the evening of his accident.

Without talking himself out of it, he crossed the street and entered Samuel Park. Sitting on a bench under two maple trees, Mikey slumped, his elbows resting on his knees and his face resting in his hands.

"Mikey," Paul called softly after a few unnoticed steps near him.

Mikey quickly wiped his eyes and looked at his grandfather. A solemnity Paul had never seen filled his grandson's eyes like a rapidly rising tide. Streams of sunlight bathed his head when he lifted it from his hands and sparkled on the remaining smears around his eyes.

Erecting his posture, not allowing even a crack in his voice, Mikey said, "You found me. Were you just walking by or did you know I come here?"

"Walking by? I've been searching for you. We got worried."

"How did you know I was here?"

"I remembered seeing you sitting here the night of my accident. It's still foggy, but I think noticing you was the last thing I did before the crash. Is that a memory or my imagination?"

"I was there. I always come here to sit and think. Whenever I went jogging in high school, I ended up here. I'd just sit awhile on this bench and then walk home. That night, I slipped out to sit and think, storm or no storm. I heard the crash and saw the car roll onto its side. I'm the one who called the police—that was before I even realized it was you in Oliver's car. You didn't know any of this?"

"No one told me any of this." Paul, a bit shocked by the news, inconsequential as it was, could not overlook the sun sparkling on Mikey's tears, and those became priority. "So you came to the park again today, without telling anyone."

"I was hoping I'd be home before you noticed I was gone. I hope I didn't alarm anyone."

"You could have used the door."

"I just wanted to leave and return unnoticed. I didn't give using the window a second thought. Guess that was pretty stupid."

"What has got you so preoccupied that you didn't give climbing out a second-floor window a second thought?" Paul spoke delicately, aware of an unaccustomed fragility about Mikey, cognizant that something agonizing had been emerging, something capable of overpowering his uncertainty about the university president's decision.

Mikey looked at his grandfather for a moment, his eyes still laden with gravity, and then the weight of them pulled his head away and shifted his gaze downward.

"This morning, you were about to say something. You said, 'I just want my— ' and then stopped. I think I know what's bothering you, and I think this ordeal with the suspension is magnifying it."

Paul stepped to the bench and sat beside his grandson. Mikey stared ahead, hopeful his grandfather would say it out loud for him, the word he could not say. Yet he listened intently to the rustling maple tree leaves to distract him from the dread of someone's knowing the word, knowing him well enough to guess at it.

"I think you've been away at college for over half a semester, and you're in a new environment there. And you've missed home. Then, when you get home for a problem that never should have happened, your father is on a business trip, and home suddenly isn't giving you the comfort you need. I understand that you don't want to admit it, but you've been homesick, and now that you're home, you miss your father. That's what you were going to say but got too embarrassed, wasn't it?" He spoke gently, letting Mikey know he didn't need to feel embarrassed about missing home and about missing his father, even as an eighteen-year-old boy. "You were going to say, 'I just want my dad,' weren't you?"

Mikey started shaking his head from side to side slowly, closing his eyes in exhaustion. "No," he said airily, ruefully. "I was going to say—." He stopped himself again. Then turning his head toward his grandfather, the solemnity overflowing from his eyes, he said it—out loud—for the first time in ten years. "I was going to say that I just want my *mom.*"

In the stream of sunlight, sorrow poured from his glistening eyes, but no tears accompanied it.

"Your mom?" Paul's inflection delivered a question, but he was repeating Mikey's statement to help it register with himself. While mention of his deceased mother had always involved only the fondest of tones and memories, and while stories about her were always welcomed in conversation, wanting her back—an innermost, unspoken wish—had never been voiced.

"I know," Mikey said gently. "I know you must be mystified that I want to turn to her after all the years she's been gone. I know it's surprising because someone my age should be beyond relying on his mom at this point. I know you're probably so disappointed in me because I'm supposed to be the mature one, the oldest one, and I'm asking for my mom like a kid younger than Gracie and Eli."

The leaves shivered gently, as gently as Mikey spoke, and shook the chill from their reds and yellows in the soft sunlight.

"Disappointed in you? For wishing you could talk to your mother when you need her?"

"My mother who's been dead for ten years."

"Why would you think—"

With a fast-paced, fretful speech but still mild, Mikey interrupted him without thinking. "It was the night of your accident—that's when I started thinking about her, but not like usual—more a strong feeling of needing her. When I looked through the window of the flipped car and saw it was you, I thought you could be—dead. And for the whole ambulance ride and all the time in the hospital you weren't waking up, I kept thinking that I could lose you, too. And it kept reminding me that I had lost my mom—just as suddenly. When it turned out you were okay, I was relieved, but I never stopped wanting my mom as badly as I did. Then all this mayhem happened at school, and I just—I just want her here."

Paul castigated himself for being so wrong—for thinking that the threat of suspension and being away from school made Mikey miss home and his father. Where were there any signs of that? He had fabricated the theory out of thin air with no basis in reality. And he castigated himself for not noticing earlier that the issue stemmed much deeper, triggered by his car accident and prompting a resurgence of the pain surrounding the boy's mother's death.

"I could see how my accident may have aroused all those fears you experienced as an eight-year-old boy—seeing your mother collapse, waiting in the hospital, hearing about the aneurism, learning—" It was difficult for Paul to recall, too, especially the recollection of witnessing his son Michael deliver the tragic announcement to Mikey— "learning she had passed away."

Mikey turned his head away and after a pause turned it back toward his grandfather with the same tormented visage.

"Mikey, why would you think I'd be disappointed in you for wanting your mom right now?"

He slowly pushed his hands from his thighs to his knees and stopped them there, his arms stiff, his fingers extended. "She's been gone ten years. I'm eighteen years old. We both know I should have come to terms with her death by now. And here I am, wishing I could turn to her for advice or—or just—something. I don't even need advice from her. I just want *her* here."

"I think there's no set age a child comes to terms with losing his mother, especially when he loses her so young."

"I'm the oldest child. I've always been the one who needed to be strong for Gracie and Eli, and I had to step up to make things easier, better, at home."

"And you did do all that. To this day, you lead your brother and sister through their mother's absence, and you go out of your way to help your father. But asserting yourself as a strong leader doesn't mean you don't get the right to miss her."

"Yes, it does mean that! Someone who has come to terms with his mother's death wouldn't be feeling this way ten years later. Everyone said it when I was little. Everyone said how proud they were of me for how I was handling it. Everyone said how grateful my father was that I was acting like a grown-up, like a man, about it. You even said, Grandpa—" He lost his words in the difficulty of the memory and then pushed them out as if he didn't want the memory to linger on his tongue anymore. "At the funeral, next to the casket, you said my mom would be proud of me for being so strong." When Mikey gulped, Paul gulped, too, as the words and the casket and the gray-white winter day at the cemetery and Mikey's little reddened face all resurfaced. "So I knew I had to be strong, and I still do. I should be stronger *now* after all these years. And look at me. This isn't strength."

"You are a human being, Mikey, and human beings feel. You don't have to be ashamed of that at any age."

"I don't have a right to want her back! I don't have a right to miss her. I got to spend eight years with her—I hung out with her and talked with her and had a relationship with her. I got a chance to love her. Gracie was only six and barely remembers her. Eli was only three and never got to know her. So you see, Gracie and Eli have a right to want her back and to miss her. They're the ones deprived of the chance to develop a relationship with her. I got so much more than they got—years more—and I'm the one missing her? It's not right."

The qualities Paul so admired in his grandson, including his stoicism and strength, seemed in this moment flaws, and the angst that, like a flying carpet, carried every one of Mikey's recent speeches, lacked a pilot or a guide. It propelled his words and crashed them into his feelings. It collided with his reason and dented his virtues and stirred his capacity for delusion. Paul worried more about this angst than the frenzy of words zig-zagging haphazardly like leaves on a windy fall day; the leaves on the maples above clung tightly and merely flickered on their branch.

Before him sat the little boy he was proud of for being so strong, the boy to whom he had told his mother was so proud. It struck Paul, like the sunlight striking Mikey's countenance when he had pulled his face from his hands, that in his grandson's strength, he had not permitted himself to mourn; he had become strong so that everyone else could mourn. In a selfless attempt to assume a leadership role for his family, he had, at some point, recused himself from emoting, from feeling sad, and had curbed the acceptability of missing his mother. A grandfather's words the day of the funeral had been absorbed in an unforeseen and lasting way; the strength Mikey believed would make his mother proud built a thickening wall, separating him from feeling connections to her. But the love he had for her chipped away at it until it eventually formed a narrow, jagged tunnel all the way through. And Mikey could feel the love of what radiated through the tunnel from the other side of the wall he had built. He wanted to reciprocate the feeling, but he didn't know how to feel in that way anymore.

"Mikey, when your mother passed and your father told you what had happened, I'll never forget how you looked away from him and stared blankly. Then, after a few seconds, you lowered your head and closed your eyes. That was all. The night of the funeral, I went into your room to check on you after you had gone to bed, and a single tear was rolling down your cheek."

Mikey looked away again, into the stream of sunlight. The maple trees shaded his grandfather, and only Mikey sat in the sun.

"I think you were grieving, Mikey. We all were at that time. But I'm beginning to think you have never let yourself mourn. And there's a difference, at least as I see it. Grieving you do for weeks and months after a death. Mourning you do after the death, yes, but mourning is on-going and life-long. I lost my mother when I was fifty-five, and I still mourn her. I think you've set up some kind of expectation others have for you— one that's not necessarily there—and in the process of trying to meet this expectation, you've denied yourself the opportunities—and even the right—to miss your mom and mourn. And even though you placed this importance on what you think others expect of you, it's you who have had to live without your mother. Others can sympathize with you for missing your mom, but only you can know what it's like to miss her as a son. Only you live what it's like not to have a mother around."

"Everyone thinks she's been gone for ten years, but no one seems to understand that those ten years have been full of hours and minutes and seconds without her, and I feel every one of them—but I can't let myself miss her." His voice grew more frangible. "But all those seconds are getting the better of me."

"Mikey, you need to know—it is okay for a boy to miss his mother."

The boy's hand clutched a tuft of his hair. Then he pulled his hand away, oblivious that it was shaking. He wanted to believe it but could not convince himself. When his grandfather said it, the lesson seemed obvious in its simplicity. It seemed possible.

"Mikey, look at me."

The boy turned his head slowly and with utter difficulty looked into his grandfather's eyes.

"Mikey, you are allowed to miss your mother. And you are allowed to cry for her."

And at last he did. As if needing an invitation, he put his face in his hands and, in the presence of another, he sobbed. His chest heaved. His throat convulsed as he gasped for air between bouts of sobs. Ray upon ray penetrated the tunnel in the wall, chipping it wider, forming a fissure from top to bottom, cracking it until it toppled. Paul, one tear dripping from the corner of his right eye, sat with his grandson for second after second and minute after minute while he did nothing but weep. He placed his left arm on his back and helplessly sat beside him.

Many minutes later, when Mikey unslouched and sat upright, he inhaled and wiped his eyes. The maple leaves rustled in a strong breeze, and the crisp fall air tingled his wet eyes. And the laving sunlight washed him.

While Mikey caught his breath, unable to speak, Paul suggested he give himself moments to mourn, explaining, "When you miss your mother, let yourself mourn her. It might last a few minutes. It might last a few days. You might come here to do it, or you might go to the cemetery or the church or that armchair you used to sit on her lap in and listen to her read to you. But just allow yourself to mourn, Mikey. It is normal for a boy to need his mother. The thing is, for a lot of your life, when you needed her in the many ways a boy needs his mom, you couldn't access her. It's okay that that hurts. It's okay that you want her around. And it's okay to mourn. Mikey, can you promise me you will mourn whenever you need to?"

As a new wave of pain swelled from his chest, he did not answer with words and solely nodded.

"And whenever you need to, talk to your father or me, okay? You can talk to us about it."

Mikey nodded again.

As Mikey collected himself, he stood, and Paul stood with him, stood by him.

"Think we can walk back to the house?" Paul asked.

Mikey nodded and started walking with his grandfather, both much more slowly than how they had arrived at the park.

"Don't tell Gracie or Eli, okay?" Mikey requested.

"Not a word. But I do need you to dial this darn thing and tell them I found you." He passed Eli's cellphone to Mikey who smiled faintly and dialed for his grandfather. Within fifteen minutes, they had arrived home to the swinging loveseat swaying on the porch, to the silent welcome of his grandmother and siblings, and to the calming anxieties of wondering what the verdict on his suspension would be.

CHAPTER 18

Mikey barely spoke the rest of the evening although Claribel's shepherd's pie cheered him up through dinner, and jabs at Eli's misstep prompted smiles. After dinner, Gracie tackled homework while Mikey and Eli took turns writing thank-you notes that their grandfather dictated. Paul hoped it might take the boys' minds off *their* woes; however, the process made *him* feel no less overwhelmed as the list of thank-you cards seemed unending. While dictating one to Eli, their father arrived just after ten o'clock. Exhausted himself from travel, he sat at the kitchen table with the family to enjoy left-over shepherd's pie and to hear about Mikey's situation.

"Maybe you should hold off on the rest of the story," he said, and later, "I might need you to stop telling me this story right now," for he kept getting upset enough to lose his appetite. He exclaimed a few times that Mikey was being railroaded and that he planned to call President Cringle first thing in the morning. Paul convinced him to let him continue to work with the president, noting his optimism for a favorable outcome. When Michael acquiesced, he redirected his anger to Dean Braynard, deciding to target him with a call. Paul again convinced him to wait things out lest he inadvertently worsen Mikey's case. Mikey contributed to the story rarely, only when asked a question.

"Mikey might not let on," Paul said to Michael once Claribel and Mikey stepped out of the room, "but he is incredibly grateful you cut your business trip short to see him through this ordeal. He says he feels bad you had to come home because of him, but he really appreciates it. He needs you here."

"Not being here for my son—it wasn't an option."

Paul placed a hand on his son's shoulder. For that moment, both men looked vacantly at the floor.

Then Michael made a stride toward the sink with his and his father's plates.

"Besides, it wasn't 'because of' Mikey that I flew back. *He* didn't cause this," Michael added.

"You're right about that."

"That honor belongs to the dean."

Near midnight, after catching up and packing, the kids left with their father for home. Monday brought work for Paul as he returned calls, dictated cards to Claribel, and spent hours on the phone working with Stephen and Eloise on the Father Soplido article. He felt bad that he didn't have time to visit Oliver, and every task he took on was beset with thoughts about Mikey's pain and the outcome of the suspension issue. When no call came from the university on Monday, Paul began seriously to consider writing an article for *The Current Front*. Stephen graciously waited on finishing the December issue until Paul confirmed writing the article, for luckily, Stephen found the latest ordeal captivating and knew the readers would, too. "We'd miss current news if we printed too early," he reminded his devoted columnist, the joking in his tone not concealing the truth of the statement.

The only reprieve from the stresses that plagued his "free time" during retirement arrived in the form of a phone call from Eli, who, feeling more optimistic about his future with Sunrise, enlisted his grandfather's help for an idea he had concocted. The nightingale was at it again. Paul liked the idea and fulfilled Eli's request for assistance promptly, promising to keep the details a secret.

Tuesday morning demanded the final work on the Father Soplido article, and no sooner had he completed his part in the process, ready to sigh triumphantly and to shout to Claribel, "All done!" did the phone ring with a request from Lucretia to meet her on the lighthouse grounds at noon. As noon neared, Paul and Claribel decided to walk despite the somewhat steep ascent to the lighthouse cliff. They walked down the street on which their house was located, leading past Samuel Park to the docks, marina, and promenade along the lake. From there, they headed northwest up the promenade, passing the walkway to the infamous pier and arriving on the lighthouse grounds. The steady rise beleaguered them less than the bursts of breeze from the lake. Along the walk, they noticed activity involving workers and construction vehicles. Passing to the front of the lighthouse through a tree-lined park, they spotted Lucretia and Nora.

Next to a truck-mounted aerial lift, the ladies stood in the street, which ran parallel to the trees lining the park in front of the lighthouse. They were speaking to a worker who, as Paul and Claribel drew nearer, they realized was Lucretia's son Greg, a worker for the Village. When they arrived at the vehicle, they saw Peony sitting in the driver's seat of the truck, delighting in lowering the lift. Another worker standing on the lift gave her a thumbs-up as she descended him from the treetops.

"What have we been missing?" asked Claribel, noticing the gathering of friends. She could see Roy and Marni down the street discussing something as they pointed to the top of the lighthouse, and she saw strands of lights dangling from the golden sugar maples.

Greg greeted them cordially and then Lucretia explained. "Greg and his team are decorating for the Lighthouse Ceremony this Thursday, but as you know, the festivities will continue through Sunday. So all the trees along the park perimeter here will be lit, and later today, they'll start erecting a heated tent in the park."

"Sounds like it's going to be quite an event," Claribel said.

"The event of the year," Paul said.

"The event of the century for the lighthouse," Lucretia joked.

"Thursday, the ceremony will take place in the lighthouse. Then anyone interested can board the steamboat from the marina where, from the lake, we will watch the Saint Catherine's Cove Lighthouse characteristic, which Blake Carroll is very excited to flash," Nora revealed, referring to the particular flashing light pattern that allows mariners to distinguish one lighthouse from another. "And the characteristic will be filmed and photographed from a helicopter!"

"Yes, I heard about the helicopter," Paul said. "Nice touch!"

"I hope it doesn't storm, at least not while we're on that boat," said Lucretia.

"It'll be chilly, but it's not supposed to rain until Friday, if at all. Besides, we'll be on the steamer for all of a half hour," Nora assured.

Peony stepped out of the truck, thrilled to have just lowered the worker using the gears on the panel. "That was so much fun! Thank-you, Greg!"

"I guess sometimes it's the little things, huh?" he said.

"Listen, Paul. We summoned you up here for a reason," Lucretia said. "Everything will be decorated for the Lighthouse Ceremony for Thursday night, and the lighthouse will be open the whole weekend. Most of the activity will take place in the tent from Friday to Sunday. So Nora, Pee, and I got to talking—and we pulled Roy, Marni, Oliver, Drew, and a few others in on this, too—and we'd like to do a retirement toast to you on Friday here at the lighthouse."

Paul felt himself blushing and quickly insisted, "Now Lu, I said I don't need a retirement party—"

"—which is why we're doing a retirement *toast*," she explained in a way that indicated finality. "We think your lifetime working in the same field, in the same place, should be honored. And you have to admit, you're something of a celebrity now. So we are hoping you will allow your friends to indulge you in a ten-minute toast here at the lighthouse."

Paul looked at Claribel, and her expression evinced approval if not contentment.

"All right," Paul said. "As long as it's only a quick, ten-minute thing."

Lu, Nora, and Pee looked at each other in unison, excited at his agreement.

The excitement on their faces took Paul back to an afternoon when he was Eli's age, an eighth grader at Greengate Grade School. He, Roy, and Oliver headed to the library after school one Thursday in April to complete their English homework, a poetry lesson, and Lucretia, with whom they had classes, was volunteering as a clerk. She walked by their study table and, as they scoured page upon page of the poem, heard them trying to answer a homework question about foreshadowing the grandeur of the Holy Grail in James Russell Lowell's *The Vision of Sir Launfal.* "It's in the fourth stanza of the prelude to the first part," she offered. Roy kept questioning the answer Paul had been announcing about a buttercup, so Paul felt vindicated when all three could pinpoint the answer in the first prelude's fourth stanza. When she walked by again, they thanked her and commiserated about having to memorize it by May. Paul asked her if she worked until close, and, pointing to a sign advertising a lecture that evening beginning at five o'clock, she revealed that she had to stay through the presentation. Paul said that he and a few friends planned to watch the Saint Catherine High School varsity baseball team play their opening game of the season that night and invited her to join them if the lecture finished any time before eight o'clock; the game started at seven o'clock, and Claribel's older brother would be pitching. At the game around seven o'clock, Roy pointed out Lucretia walking toward the bleachers, a book in hand in case no one showed up, in case it was a prank. Paul waved her over, and when she sat with him, Roy, Oliver, Peony, Claribel, and a few other kids, she smiled the brightest Paul had ever seen. It struck him as strange that he had known her through all of grade school and never saw her smile that way. Peony passed a plate of homemade oatmeal raisin cookies resting on her knees to Lucretia, and she gratefully took one. After that event, they all spoke more easily and met up regularly, through high school and beyond. While working at the public library, she married George Willows with whom she had two children, Greg and Laura, and years later earned a degree in Library Science in River Forest, Illinois. When Greengate Grade School built a library as part of its extension, Lucretia became its first librarian and worked there since. Four years ago, her husband passed away, so, after a year of withdrawing from opportunities to socialize, she spent most of her time at work and with friends. Nora had become her closest friend in high school when she, too, began volunteering at the library. Nora had moved to Saint Catherine's Cove with her family several months before freshman year began at the high school. She worked at the public library and remained there for years, never marrying despite an engagement, and, like Lucretia, opting not to retire.

Peony's relationship with Paul developed markedly differently. She grew up a block away, the daughter of a close friend of Paul's father. When Peony's mother was sent away for vague mental health reasons, Paul's father took Peony in while her father adjusted, an adjustment period of over a month that, to Paul, felt just as nebulous as her mother's incarceration in an asylum. Peony and Paul were only ten then, and he, under strict orders from his father, included her in all playful endeavors. Classes together had made acquaintances of them, but living under the same roof made friends. A lasting friendship developed not only with Paul but with Paul's friends. As soon as Peony returned home, she assumed more responsibility at her father's coffee shop and ice cream parlor. Working closely with her father over the years, she learned how to make pie crusts and fillings, muffins, breads, cookies, and pastries. The first week she left the Scrivensbys' household, she learned to make apple muffins, and she learned how to make them after requesting guidance from her father—specifically apple muffins. A month living with the Scrivensbys magnified many idiosyncrasies and illuminated many behaviors, not the least of which included their eating habits, and she mentally logged Paul's pleasure eating an apple muffin from the coffee shop. So within the first week of her reinstallation at her own house, she brought a batch of apple muffins to Paul, so grateful for his kindness during a vulnerable and potentially traumatic period of her life that she resorted to this humble offering of thanks. Paul could not believe he could enjoy not one muffin for one breakfast but an entire plate of them. Through Peony's assuming so many responsibilities within her house and shop, she emerged a leader who drew on similar skills when it came to socializing and school. She established herself within the Saint Catherine's Cove community as a fun-loving, grand-laughing, hard-working friend to all. Roger's courtship of her caught the attention of the entire town, not only on account of Roger's boisterous personality, but more so because no one knew, between the two, who had met whose match. Peony devoted most of her time to helping at the shop and parlor after high school, and eventually divvied her time between work and raising a family of three children, Poppy, Billy, and Teddy. Her daughter Poppy helped her as she grew older until she eventually ran the place herself. Peony never stopped baking, but she redirected her time to attending daily Mass, meeting with friends and clubs, and watching her granddaughter Petunia. She always enjoyed a party, and when there was no occasion for one, she took great joy in simply meeting with friends or in organizing impromptu gatherings, somewhat like the one she collaborated with her friends on to honor Paul's retirement.

"I can see Pee is excited for yet another opportunity to partake in drink," Paul joked.

"I am excited to partake in an evening honoring my old friend. The champagne is a pleasant perk, though!"

"You know, Paul," Nora added, "it will last ten minutes or as long as you let it. It could go a little longer if you wish to say something yourself. There will just be a few of us."

"I'll think about it," Paul responded, feeling the weight of a new responsibility pressing on his shoulders—a short speech by Friday.

When Lucretia shivered and pulled her fall coat tighter, Peony encouraged her to step into the truck. The heater was on and would likely warm her in minutes. Lucretia used her son's hand to step into the driver's seat of the truck, and Nora, too chilly for comfort herself, stepped around to the passenger side door and entered.

"Much better," whispered Nora to Lucretia, who nodded in agreement.

"Will you look at that," Lucretia said, peering through the windshield down the block. "That's Mrs. Janes. What's she doing down there?"

Just distant enough to be unclear, Mrs. Janes, a leash in one hand with a small dog pulling on it, bent over near some maples near the street. All five leaned forward to make out her actions, and when Mrs. Janes rose and examined something in her other hand, they realized she had been picking up a certain unpleasant something with a baggy.

"Think it's the dog's or hers?" asked Peony.

Lucretia covered her mouth to prevent the burst of laughter from sounding, as if her coworker might hear. Her friends could not refrain either.

"I hate to say it, but Drew has been rubbing off on you, Pee," Nora said.

"Don't let him hear you admit that!" cautioned Claribel.

"Whosoever it is, at least she's picking it up at all," offered Nora, unable to bring Lucretia's laughter to an end.

"Paul, Claribel," Peony said, "why don't you see if Greg will let you sit in the lift for a nice view of the trees and the lake and the town." She lightly nudged Greg in the ribs with her elbows.

"I don't think we need to get in the—" Paul said.

"Hop in if you'd like!" Greg offered. "You can wind a strand of lights around a tree."

Paul looked at Claribel and shrugged. Neither finding reason to protest, they accepted the invitation and let Greg lead them into the lift. He helped them in before running back to the truck, stepping in, and leaning over his mother to operate the lever that raised the arm and the lift. Within a minute, Paul and Claribel stood eye level with the top of the maple tree next to them. Before accounting for the view the lift provided, Paul placed his arm around Claribel's waist, and she responded in unison. Paul looked to his right toward the lighthouse and Claribel looked to her left toward the town.

"How do you like it up there?" Lucretia asked from the driver's seat of the truck. Greg jumped out and wandered toward another worker to help him pull strands of lights from a crate plopped near the curb.

"The view from the lighthouse might be a little better, Pee," Claribel shouted, "but we're close enough to the tree to trim it if you'd like." The second clause she directed to Greg. He didn't hear her as he rifled through the crate.

Claribel, wrapped in Paul's good arm, looked ahead and saw Roy and Marni arm in arm down the street. She waved from on high and smiled at the reciprocated wave from their friends.

Lucretia turned off the truck. "Now you're stuck up there!" she joked. Paul and Claribel could see Nora laughing at Lucretia's gesture and Greg rolling his eyes smilingly.

"You know," Paul began, "I was a little upset that the first second I thought I had to enjoy my retirement got interrupted by a call from Lu, but now that we're here, I'm glad."

"Me, too," Claribel said, looking into his eyes.

"Paul!" shouted Lucretia from the truck, half-standing in spite of the truck's low roof. "Paul, it's that beige sports car!"

A beige coupe accelerated in the direction of Roy and Marni, and Paul and Claribel followed it with their eyes as it passed Lucretia in the truck and then the lift.

"It's Derek Braynard!" shouted Lucretia! "And he's not getting away this time!"

She truly believed Derek responsible for her heart attack, and learning of his deplorable attack on Paul's grandson did not diminish her resentment any. Suddenly, without a second thought, Lucretia turned the key in the ignition, flipped the truck into drive, and hit the gas.

Nora yelped as the truck jerked forward, as did Lu, herself. Greg heard the engine turn, saw the wheels spin, and ran toward the truck. Paul and Claribel, befuddled beyond belief, gripped the rail of the lift with one hand, flung the other arm around each other, and involuntarily screamed as tree branch after tree branch seemed to swing at their heads. They ducked, they pushed branches away, and they screamed again and again. Claribel dodged branches while trying to keep Paul from losing his balance as he struggled to use and not to use his supported arm.

When it came close enough, Roy shouted, "What the—?" while Marni screamed, "Lucretia!" The couple dove into shrubbery as Lu swerved to avoid them. The turn jolted Claribel into the side of the lift and propelled Paul into Claribel's arms.

Greg sprinted to the truck, grabbed the driver's door that Lucretia never bothered to close, and jumped in. He pushed his mother toward Nora, who was screaming "Lu" over and over while clutching her heart, and he pulled the parking brake.

Paul and Claribel jolted again, their heads stuck in a cluster of maple leaves. They looked at each other and saw the other's shock, daze, and wind-tossed, leaf-and-stick-strewn hair. They could hear Roy and Marni's overlapping groans as they tried to pry themselves from the bushes below. While Lucretia shouted that Derek Braynard had gotten away, they started laughing and never stopped until the lift had descended. In that moment, it didn't matter that Derek Braynard may have returned, nor that Lucretia could have killed them all trying to catch him. What mattered is that they hadn't laughed that hard together in months over adventures that could still find them.

Night fell, and with each darkening minute, Paul's joy over his friends' invitation diminished. The rush from the run-away lift and dodging tree branches had abated hours ago as speculation over the outcome in Mikey's ordeal replaced it. The lack of a verdict—or any word at all—disheartened him. He so wanted to deliver great news to his grandson. At first he felt helpless, but then he decided that a call to the president of the university might be in order. He grew more impatient and anxious as he reconsidered calling, fearing it might incite ill-will toward Mikey. Yet he knew that Mikey, in addition to grappling with the surfacing pain over his mother's death, was growing more impatient and anxious over his future, and Paul couldn't bear to see his grandson endure this. "And I can't forget," Paul thought, "that this is happening to him because of me!"

With no reason to believe a verdict imminent, Paul revisited his proposition to write an article for the December issue on Dean Braynard's targeting his grandson over a years-old grudge he held against Paul. Unable to dissuade himself, he stepped out of bed, out of the spinning concerns over Mikey's health, Derek's grudge, the university's judgment, and set himself up at his computer in the study. With his good hand, he started typing, word by word, the article on the dean's railroading of his grandson. His slow pace enervated him, the angle of the article—without knowing what the university will have decided—evaded him, and thoughts of Lucretia and Oliver's recovery interrupted him. Frustrated, he typed faster only to catch more mistakes.

He stepped away from the computer at one point in the middle of the night, paced, and found himself waking in his armchair in the solarium as the sun rose. He took a shower and dressed, hoping to feel refreshed. Then he put on a pot of coffee and headed back to his article, to his exasperation, to his unclarity.

Claribel found him typing animatedly and, before calling his name, heard a grunt. The aberrant sight gave her reason for concern, evident in her voice when she asked, "What is going on in here?"

He did not turn to answer. Continuing to type, he said, "Thought maybe I should write that article after all, and I don't have much time if I want to get it considered for the December issue. Derek is not getting away with retaliating against our grandson."

"How long have you been up, Paul?"

"I never went to bed."

"What?" She looked at the screen over his shoulder to get a sense of how much he had written. He had stopped typing to reread a passage. To avoid distracting him, she did not speak.

"No," he said, reading intently. "No, this isn't any good. I need to scrap this whole part." He stood up, his eyes still fixed on the screen. "I need to scrap this whole article!"

"Paul," Claribel said. "Why don't you step away for a minute, let your eyes rest, and then you can go back to it."

He stepped away from the computer, shaking his head, responding partly to her suggestion and partly to the criticism he had with the draft. Then he walked determinedly to the solarium. Claribel saw that he had neglected his cup of coffee and followed him with it. He had mechanically walked to his armchair but did not sit; with his left hand rubbing his head, he faced the chair. Sensing Claribel behind him, he turned toward her and accepted the mug from her outstretched hand.

He held it for a while without taking a sip and then turned toward the solarium windows behind the armchair. He watched the sun make silhouettes of the far trees and watched the peaceful movement of the yellow and red leaves of closer trees. Claribel, he knew, must be expecting some sort of explanation and was waiting patiently for a cue to address him.

"This isn't how it's supposed to be," he said.

"What isn't?"

"My retirement. This isn't how I was supposed to start my retirement."

"I'm sure you had some ideas about how to spend your time, but you could hardly have anticipated everything that's happened. Could you have predicted the reaction to your column? Did you know you were going to get into a car accident? Or that Ted Handly was going to spark a controversy at your press conference?"

He did not think to agree with her point that these unforeseen occurrences thwarted the simplicity he thought would accompany retirement but instead fixated on the occurrences. "Stephen asks me to rewrite my final column;

Oliver and I get into a car accident; Lucretia has a heart attack; Ted causes a controversy at the press conference; Father Soplido needs my guidance; Mikey gets suspended to determine whether he's *officially* suspended; Derek comes *from out of nowhere* with a grudge he's been holding against me for the past fifty years that I never even knew about! All in two weeks! And so little is resolved yet!"

"It will be. You have to be patient. There's no deadline on this, and there's no special date for when your retirement gets to be spent exactly as you want."

"I don't know how it's supposed to be spent. I feel like everything is slipping away from me—like my life is slipping away—right now, when I'm supposed to be living it and enjoying it the most. I'm supposed to be writing essays and vignettes for leisure, not defending my grandson to the Dean of the McGuinty School of Journalism! I'm supposed to be enjoying no schedule and strolling to the coffee shop to read the newspaper, planting garlic in the garden, sparing myself concern over not being able to sleep because I know I can dawdle through the next day with nothing planned. I'm supposed to be making up for lost time with my wife, not—"

"Making up for lost time?"

A swell of burning guilt for mentioning this rushed through his chest. "How much time did I waste all these years? How much time didn't I see you while you were taking care of the kids and even the grandchildren?"

His feeling this way over this issue baffled Claribel. "None of that was wasted time. Paul, what has gotten into you?"

"I've just been thinking. And now when I have a chance to make it up to you, time is being frittered away by all these— ordeals. Let's face it. My life has been rather prosaic for the most part—my entire life—and then in two weeks, all this!"

"But our life together? Paul, you did nothing wrong. We've had a good life together."

He flung his hands in the air. Even the arm in the sling lifted without his registering pain. As he spoke, he walked to the window. "Okay, sure, we were never unfaithful to each other, never got into fights the way some couples do, never mistrusted one another's competence, but that's because we gave each other space to do our own things. I wrote and traveled back and forth. You ran the household and kept our life organized."

Claribel crossed to her husband quietly. "Is that what made us work? I like to think it was love."

"We can still hurt the ones we love, Claribel. Love is there— we could never deny that—but it's not what makes us work. Didn't the nights without me, with just you to watch the kids, get to you? Didn't it hurt you to see how much time I put in in New York? How loving was it of me to be in New York four days out of the week sometimes?"

"You're confusing me, Paul. You just said what made us work was giving each other space. Now you're upset for my allowing you to travel to your work space in New York, to hold down a job, a career, without complaining about it?"

He flung his arms in the air again and sighed.

Realizing how riled he was getting, she smiled and gently turned him toward her. "Paul, when you went into the study to write for hours at a time and flew off to New York to work in the *CF* office, you were making sure the kids and I were provided for. I never saw that as anything other than love—not to mention, you loved what you were doing. And my taking care of the kids and doing the housework and making sure you had a meal on the table gave me an opportunity to show my love for you. When you would get rattled about something and would go outside for a brisk walk to work off your anger before you could take it out on me or the kids, wasn't that love? And when I'd get irritated, I'd rush outside and start hanging sheets on the clothes line, as taut as I could make them—and one time, I didn't have any sheets to hang, so I grabbed the basket, took out the sheets I had just ironed and folded, and re-hung them on the line! All that to spare you a tirade. That's love. And what about the times—?" She didn't need to continue with examples. She didn't need to prove anything to him or to herself. And she knew this topic wasn't where Paul was supposed to be right now. He had disoriented himself by over-thinking and landed here. "Paul, you know all this. Something's got you shaken. You got to thinking—and thinking and thinking—and managed to get yourself overwhelmed. You don't have to question how good you've been to me throughout our life together. No one has been better."

He turned back toward the window to observe the sunlight on the trees.

"You've gotten yourself all confused on account of so much going on when you're trying to close a chapter of your life and begin a new one."

"I feel lost," he said. "I feel as if I'm standing in this unrecognizable place that I just want to get out of, and there are all these roads around me. One of them, I know, will lead to the normalcy I could find comfort in, but I don't know which one it is. So I barrel full-throttle down one only to realize it's not taking me where I want to go. And I have to backtrack to that unrecognizable place in order to try another road. I do, and it's full-steam ahead down another road that doesn't work out. I threw myself into writing the article on Mikey's suspension. I threw myself into the notion that I had to spend every remaining moment with you to make up for my time away in New York. Nothing seems right. And now I'm back at that place, knowing there's a risk attached to taking the wrong road again and not wanting to waste the time it takes to make a mistake and head back." Then, as if defeated, he added, "So to avoid the wrong road, I'm tarrying here. The only problem is, I don't know this place either. I don't even like this place much."

"The place you keep finding yourself in is transition. It's hard to be between places, between points in your life. Believe me, Paul. I just found myself there." She glanced out the window so quickly that no tree or leaf or streak of sunlight registered with definition, yet she saw them all. "I found myself there unexpectedly as I took on cancer. You're going to see a light turn on, illuminating one of those roads for you. You're going to hear a call, a beautiful voice summoning you down one of those roads. And when you conclude that the light and the call aren't enchantment but sincere summons, you are going to walk down that road and find yourself in the right place, in a good place."

Inspired now by his view of the shimmering maple leaves, he grew calmer at the image of that right and good place—an English garden on a fall day with lavender and phlox and climbing rose bushes in the cooling shadow of maples and their yellowing foliage, or a quiet park lined with cobblestone paths, leaf-strewn in persimmon shades, amid evergreens and ashes. As the leaves in his sights rustled, thus the idyllic vision shook away.

"What if it's me? I feel as though the light and the call might be there, but I can't see or hear them because something is wrong with me. And I want to shake away this confusion or whatever is blocking me from seeing and whatever is clogging me from hearing." Looking into his wife's eyes with longing for solace, he asked, "Is it that I need to be more patient with that light, that call, or is there something wrong with me?"

"You need to be more patient with yourself. Paul, I think you need to take a breath and not be so hard on yourself." She took his left hand and held it in hers.

He watched her hold his hand and caress the top of it with her palm. He recognized that before him stood a model of forbearance and upbraided himself for how sorely he must have just tried her patience. Yet here she stood, facing him, holding his hand in hers. He glanced out the window at the trees and said, "I think taking a breath might be a good idea. A breath of fresh air. If you don't mind, I'm going to take a walk."

Reluctant to pull his hand away, he leaned forward and kissed her. She closed her eyes, and when she opened them, he was still standing there. His face captured the exhaustion his whole body and psyche felt, but his eyes still smiled at Claribel. And then he departed for a walk.

His thoughts, now laden with concerns over encumbering Claribel with too much of his angst, preoccupied him to the point that he disregarded the arduousness of the ascent to the lighthouse. A wave to Blake Carroll granted him access to the lighthouse stairwell spiraling to the watch room gallery. He stepped onto the terrace and hoped the breezes might carry away his angst and even his thoughts.

The sunny morning and the breezes off the lake refreshed him. He wished he could lean with both hands on the railing, but when the cold from the metal raced through his bones after only one hand's touch, he experienced a silver lining in carrying one arm in a sling. Above him, engraved into the molding, Saint Catherine of Siena, the laywoman surrounded by black and white Dominican shields, watched over him and the lake. He peered into the distance of Lake Superior, and then something caught his attention. Below him, on the promenade pier, he saw the waving arm of Dr. Drew. When he protruded his head over the railing to make sure it was Drew he saw, Drew held up a single index finger to indicate that he would be joining him. Paul watched as he walked down the pier toward the lighthouse.

During the wait, Paul wondered if he could take Claribel's advice—if he could be patient with himself instead of darting down a particular path. Could he be confusing the need to rush into retirement with his desire for an immediate resolution to Mikey's situation at the university? Could the fear of almost losing Claribel to cancer have tricked him into thinking he had to bask in the freedom of retirement the second it began? The answers did not come to him before an over-arching embarrassment for acting childishly overtook him. Before having a moment to beat himself up for sharing his confusion with Claribel, he heard Dr. Drew say his name.

"What brings you up here, Paul?" asked Dr. Drew, stepping to the railing beside him.

"I didn't sleep much last night. I needed to clear my head."

"This is a good place to clear your head—or at least to get your hair all messed up in these breezes."

"Are you coming to the Lighthouse Ceremony tomorrow night?" Paul asked. "Poppy wants to take that group picture."

"I'll be there." He leaned over the edge of the lighthouse and looked straight down. "Funny to think all that's happened around this place in its one hundred fifty years. Do you remember that night the first weekend we got back from freshmen year of college for summer?"

Paul started laughing. "I know where you're going with this. The night you asked Roy and me to distract Blake Carroll—"

"—while I got 'together' with Cindy Hauser in front of the lighthouse. That's the night."

"I remember all right. You took longer than we thought. You said you'd be fifteen minutes, and we were talking with him for an hour. We were struggling to come up with things to talk about after a half hour, and Roy wanted to kill you. We finally got him on the story about the tender approaching and capsizing in the sudden seiche, and that kept him going for a good twenty minutes."

"Cindy and I were standing directly below where we're standing right now. I took her there wanting to romance her a little, to show her the stars and listen to the waves. Boy did I get more than I bargained for."

"What do you mean?"

"I mean she wanted more from me than just a display of interest."

"You mean—?"

"Yep, that's what I mean. That's what took so long."

"You and she—?"

"All the way. Standing up. My first time."

"You never told us."

"I couldn't." Paul realized Drew's cheeks reddened not from the harsh breeze but from something else, from something within. "First of all, that would have ruined her reputation—although, turns out I cared more about that than she did—and second, I was ashamed. I never wanted it to happen—not like that—not with someone I barely knew. Believe it or not, I knew better. But when it started, I went with it—gave in—couldn't stop."

He leaned on the railing and looked at the lake, releasing a forlorn sigh.

"You sound like you still feel guilty." Then Paul chuckled. "I think you can let go of it at this point." Paul felt the strange sensation that Drew *needed* to share this, that Drew was grappling with some interior struggle and anguish of his own.

"The next day was the worst part of it. I had done the deed Saturday night and couldn't get to Confession before Mass Sunday morning, so I couldn't receive Communion. I knew my family would wonder what I had done."

"I'm sure they never suspected that."

"Didn't matter. *I* knew. And when I did go to Confession, well, that didn't go so well. Not only did I have to confess what I did, I felt compelled to say I did it against a lighthouse named after a saint."

Paul placed his head in his hand, unable to refrain from laughing and unable to keep from blushing. Why this story was surfacing now, over fifty years later, crossed his mind, but then again, everything seemed to be happening now, at this strange, dilating moment in his life.

"Not something *you've* ever had to confess, I imagine," Drew said to his blushing friend. "No doubt yours was on your wedding night."

Paul confirmed with a nod, his head still in his hands.

"Same with Roy and Billy and George."

"You've been to Confession, and you've unburdened yourself to me half a century later. I think you can put this guilt behind you now."

Drew inhaled the breeze. "It's your turn, Paul. What brings you to the top of the lighthouse? What are you pondering?"

Embarrassed enough for having irrationally ranted to his wife, at this moment, Paul wished to contain the many loose threads of thought from developing into the tapestry of another rant. Without lying, he answered with the vague, "Just have a lot on my mind. Trying to sort out a few things."

"Any word from the university on Mikey's situation?"

"No word. Not even a call to say, 'We're working on it.' That's partly what's driving me up a wall. I just want this addressed for Mikey's sake."

"You know, Paul, I have to hand it to you. When retirement crosses my mind, I always talk myself out of it. The way you've been spending your retirement—well, it's admirable."

Paul's mouth could have hit the floor—could have hit the lake. For starters, his retirement hadn't begun as far as he was concerned, and "admirable" was not among the words he would use to describe any vestige of it. He could not find a word to respond with, so incredulous was he at the comment.

"You've spent your career helping others by inspiring, teaching, encouraging through your column. Now that you've been retired, you've found a way to keep doing the same— helping others. You threw yourself into helping Mikey at the drop of a hat, threw yourself into helping Father Soplido when you probably preferred to recede from the limelight, threw yourself into taking on another article in order to help Eloise, practically a stranger to you. That's how to do it, Paul. I've spent my career helping others, too, in a different way—making sure they are healthy, that they can take care of their loved ones, that they can lead lives in a way they feel is good—but I don't have family around the way you do. I don't have as much family who rely on me here in Saint Catherine's Cove. So I'm terrified of retiring, Paul. I'm terrified of not having anyone to live for when I retire, like you do. Living our lives to benefit others— that's the whole point of *living*, not just our careers. And I don't think I'll be able to do that when I retire, not after watching how giving you have been only a few weeks in."

Ineffability continued to manifest as Paul's response. Drew had turned his attention to catching the breeze on his face and pulling the zipper higher on his coat, and Paul could but stare into the lake water. They stood in silence for several minutes— quite atypical for Drew, but he sensed he had touched on something significant for Paul and let him rest with it in the bracing breeze and calming movement of the water.

At last, Paul spoke. "Thanks for saying that, Drew."

"You said you had a lot on your mind, and I never let you explain." Then, before Paul could speak, "I didn't realize it, but I think I've had a lot on my mind of late, too, and explaining my thoughts on retirement and life may have helped me a little. I should call you 'Dr. Scrivensby.'" They both laughed at the prospect. "But I apologize. Besides waiting for the verdict on Mikey's situation, what else do you have on your mind?"

"To be honest, what you just said—well, I think it just *cleared* my mind." Months had been spent trying to figure out how to live for himself in free time unknown to him, but situation upon situation had stepped in front of him, blockading his ability to do this. And now, as viscerally as his cheeks felt the breeze, he felt the irony of growing angst-ridden over misspending his retirement when he may have been spending it correctly all along.

"I'm glad I could say something to help. You may not realize this, but you've been a help to me these past few days. Being able to drive with you to Mikey's university, watching you defend your grandson to the president and the dean—it invigorated me—it renewed me—and it made me feel like there's still plenty of life left to live meaningfully. And let's face it. We all have to answer to Someone some day. I've spent my whole life believing that, and I'm not about to stop now. Maybe that's why some of my past transgressions have come to mind. And I think that's why I'm not willing to retire just yet. I'm still capable, but I want to maximize how much benefit I can be to others. I want my final years to be spent giving of myself the way I have for most of my young life."

"Our 'final years,'" Paul repeated, shaking his head. Had they crossed the threshold into these years?

"Well, I have to pop in to the office, so I will leave you to your newly found clear-mindedness. I'll see you back here tomorrow night at the ceremony."

"Thanks again, Drew. I'll see you at the ceremony."

The sunlight twinkled on the shifting water. Never in a million years would he have expected to gain perspective from

Drew; having experienced an enlightenment of his own, *Drew* helped dissipate the turmoil in Paul's thoughts over misspending his retirement. The breeze chiseled Paul's face smooth like marble. Spending a few moments with Drew revitalized him now just as the car ride to visit Otis Carroll had sparked a friendship many years ago. The trees below rustled, and Paul saw some tenacious golden leaves finally relinquish their desperate hold and soar with the gusts beyond the lake.

"Mikey," Paul said into the phone, "Come over right away. President Cringle called."

"Did he give you their decision? Are they still deliberating?"

"I'll explain it all when you get here."

Paul had just gotten off the phone with President Cringle and spent minutes relaying the conversation to Claribel before immediately calling his son and then Mikey. He could not get ahold of his son and left a message, but he knew Mikey would be at home waiting for any news at all.

The call from the president, before even having had the conversation with him, was music to Paul's ears, although his spirits were already high after his talks with Claribel and Drew. He had, in fact, returned home with no compunction to attend the article, but instead turned his attention to brainstorming and beginning to draft a short speech for his retirement toast. His writing was interrupted to address a few details in the execution of Eli's plan to win back Sunrise, although Paul knew she had never been lost.

When the backdoor opened, three Scrivensby grandchildren entered, and Paul realized school had been let out. Gracie and Eli had just arrived home when their grandfather's call came in, so they joined Mikey, nearly as anxious as their older brother.

Seated on the couch and chairs in the solarium, the gathering gave stiff-backed attention to Paul, who relayed the story holding a bourbon on the rocks with a splash of Cointreau in his free hand.

"President Cringle couldn't get ahold of your father, so he pursued me since most of the conversation had taken place between the two of us anyway."

"What did he say?" Mikey asked.

"The temporary suspension has been lifted, Mikey. And there will be no further hearing or suspension. It's over. You can go back tomorrow if you'd like."

Although it seemed impossible, Mikey's back stiffened more for a few seconds as his grandfather delivered the news, and then collapsed with a sigh into relief. His hands clasped his forehead as his lips murmured, "Thank-you."

"President Cringle and Dean Braynard met with the Judicial Affairs Committee, and together, they concluded that neither a hearing nor a suspension is warranted. You can return to classes immediately, under two conditions."

Mikey sat up, removing his hands from his head, stopping them mid-air, as if the conditions might rattle him with another jolt of unexpected woe.

"The first condition is that you must apologize in person to Professor Simms for what you wrote in the paper."

"Done," said Mikey automatically.

"And the second is that you must rewrite the responsibility paper."

"Done again!" said Mikey, thrilled with the repercussions. "Done and done!"

"You will not have to drop the class, and no warning will appear on your record. He never outwardly expressed it, but I have a feeling they know this whole thing was rooted in Derek Braynard's grudge against me. Even if they didn't believe that to be true, they probably didn't want to take the chance of it coming off that way should the public learn of this debacle."

"This is such good news," Mikey said, seeing the joy in his siblings' eyes. "But—" and suddenly a few things started occurring to him— "what if Professor Simms isn't so happy to have me back? Or Dean Braynard."

"Those very concerns crossed my mind, too, Mikey, and I brought them up with President Cringle. President Cringle assures me there will be no ill will from Professor Simms; he's just anxious to put this behind him and continue with the semester. Keep in mind, Mikey, that this wasn't his issue to begin with. Derek Braynard made it your professor's issue. And to boot, President Cringle assured me that Professor Simms will be returning all work graded from now on."

"That'll be a nice change of pace," Mikey said, eliciting a few laughs from the family.

"The president had a request of me, as well. They asked that I do not write an article—not in the December issue nor any time in the future. I said that they won't see an article from me as long as the dean or anyone else doesn't publish anything about it."

"So that's it," Mikey stated as his emotions gained a momentum. "I'm going back. I have never been so happy to deliver an apology and rewrite a paper!"

Claribel inched over to Mikey on the couch and hugged him. Unable to contain his energy, he stood, leading all to do likewise.

"So I'm going back, and I can finally stop worrying about this." His smile—the whole of him—glowed like the autumn maple leaves in sunlight.

"Congratulations, Mikey," Paul said. "I'm happy this all turned out for the best."

"Me, too," Mikey said, as he and his grandfather hugged. "I think I'm going to hold off on returning to school, though."

"What do you mean?" asked Claribel.

"I think, as long as I'm in, I'm going to stick around for the Lighthouse Ceremony tomorrow and Grandpa's retirement toast on Friday night."

"Are you sure you want to miss that much school? That has to be several classes, and you're already behind three days," Paul stated.

"I'll get caught up. I really feel I should be there for your toast—I mean, you got me through this whole thing. The least I could do is stick around for your big night."

"Mikey, you don't owe me anything. You're my grandson. I'd do it if you had nothing in the world to repay me."

"No, I want to stay in town, Grandpa. Besides, a million ideas are already zipping through my mind about the new version of my responsibility paper, and I want to take my time writing it. I can do that over the next few days. And I need to think of a way to apologize to Professor Simms so that he will see how sincere I am instead of rushing into one tomorrow morning."

"Why don't we discuss this with your father when we get ahold of him," Claribel interposed. "In the meantime, let's celebrate with— hmmm." She had wanted to celebrate with a piece of pie, but they hadn't eaten dinner yet. She wasn't sure how to compensate.

"With a group hug," Gracie announced, stepping toward Mikey with open arms. The rest followed suit, and all hugged Mikey.

Afterwards, while Claribel prepared dinner, Eli touched base with his grandfather about their plan. Everything was in order, according to Paul, and he encouraged his grandson to continue practicing with the choir.

When the grandchildren had left and Paul and Claribel had finished dinner, Paul called Stephen in New York. Stephen could not be reached, so he left a message: "No article coming from Paul Scrivensby for the December issue."

CHAPTER 19

"The tent is going to be heated, right?" double-checked Pauline.

"Lucretia assured us it would be heated," Claribel responded. "And it should be warm inside the lighthouse, too."

Paul and Claribel stood with their family in the solarium. Their eldest child, Michael, had arrived with his children, Mikey, Gracie, and Eli; their second child, Anna, with her son, Henry; and their youngest, Pauline, with her husband, Brent, and their twins, Hannah and Paulie. On the cusp of sunset, they were pulling shawls and wraps tight, buttoning overcoats, and straightening children's sliding bows. Many of Saint Catherine's Cove's families were forming similar gatherings in anticipation of the Lighthouse Ceremony that evening.

The event included a short ceremony in the lighthouse, a half-hour steamboat ride onto Lake Superior for a view of the lighthouse characteristic, and a cocktail reception in the heated tent on the lighthouse grounds. Some time after the ceremony, Paul and his friends hoped to take a group photograph in or outside the lighthouse.

"Are we all ready to head out?" asked Pauline's husband.

"I think so," responded Pauline. "I'm just wondering if we shouldn't bring umbrellas. The rain is expected earlier than they thought. They're saying around midnight now."

"The whole evening is supposed to end around ten o'clock, so it shouldn't be an issue," Claribel said.

"Just as long as it doesn't rain while we're on the boat," Michael added.

"I won't bother with umbrellas then," said Pauline.

"Listen, everyone." Paul's call quieted everyone and turned their attention to him. "It's a night out for us all. I've been getting a lot of attention from the press lately. You have all done so well through this already, but let's be our most gracious tonight. I know I don't have to tell you this, but there will be more eyes than usual on us, and so much will be recorded. Let's have a fun night out and remember we are Scrivenbys!"

"Here, here!" Michael punctuated the speech.

And they gathered their belongings, rounded up the children, and headed to the ceremony.

Upon arrival, they joined the many attendees walking to the heated tent, checking their coats, and progressing into the lighthouse for the ceremony. Although the space was limited, guests managed to find open alcoves and nooks, congregating tightly but comfortably. Many of the town's denizens, especially the younger ones, made their way to the upper floors of the lighthouse until, after a half hour, people occupied every tier and even steps on the rounding staircases. Paul and Claribel remained on the main level, noting a small platform on the second-floor tier where Father Soplido, Blake Carroll, Gracie Scrivensby, and the president of the Lighthouse Preservation Society gathered. To the left of the small stage, a string ensemble had set up, and to the right, the Greengate Grade School and Saint Catherine High School choirs had assembled. Several reporters grouped together opposite the stage on the same tier. When Paul looked up, he saw the merry, laughing faces of Saint Catherine's Cove's residents peering down from behind the railings lining every tier of the lighthouse, and his heart leapt at every smiling recognition of his family and closest friends. Nora and Lucretia, surrounded by the latter's family, nestled with the choir; Roy and Marni stood with their family on the tier above, with Dr. Drew inching toward them when he noticed Roy; Peony, Poppy, and Petunia chatted on the highest tier, laughing away as they took in the light-hearted air. When Peony waved at someone excitedly, Paul followed her gaze to the main floor to find Oliver cautiously easing his way in, balanced by his caretaker.

A subdued refinement in the garb and accoutrements of the many guests accompanied the merriment. Paul donned a dark gray suit, a white shirt, and a navy blue tie speckled with gray and white polka dots reminiscent of a star-studded sky. Claribel wore a floor-length, midnight blue gown with a gray-turning-blue scarf wrapped once around her neck, both ends of which reached the hemline of her dress, one strand behind her, one before her. Roy and Oliver wore sleek, plaid suits in metallic browns, ecru shirts, and gold-tone ties; Roy's shirt boasted French cuffs with gold cufflinks inlaid with pearl while Oliver accented his suit with a vest matching his plaid. Lucretia wore a dark purple gown with violet tassels spiraling from collar to hem, and a matching purple wrap draped around her back, while her best friend Nora flaunted a forest green dress hitting mid-calf and a shawl of contrasting dark and light greens. The soft pink button-down that Dr. Drew wore with his classic navy blue suit formed a glow around his solid navy blue tie; white gold buttons and cufflinks accented his suit nicely. Peony stole the show in her Victorian bouffant-style gray and white dress with a bustle, enhanced with layers of gray shawls, pink peonies in full bloom sewn on to every layer, and two curly locks framing each side of her rubenesque face. In the throng of elegant, dusky colors, the only attraction more salient than the sparkling of guests' jewels was Sunrise Walsh's fiery orange-yellow, sleeveless dress and black cape and opera gloves. From her position at the second tier railing with her family, she scoped the main floor for Eli, and when Paul noticed her search, he alerted his grandson. When Eli first caught sight of her, his countenance changed, stunned to awe at her dazzling beauty. Eli waved from the floor until she noticed and smiled with delight. Eli, like his brother Mikey, wore a simple black suit, white button-down shirt, and a skinny tie, Eli's in dark gray flannel, Mikey's in pale gray with a black and white Dominican shield at the bottom.

As friends greeted friends and inhaled the gaiety, the violist rang a bell into a microphone until silence alighted in the lighthouse. The president of the Lighthouse Preservation Society welcomed the guests and reminded them what was in store for the evening. She introduced the choir, comprised of students from Greengate Grade School's choir and Saint Catherine High School choir, who sang an original tune composed for the occasion, moving many to tears. Next, Gracie delivered her speech on the history of the lighthouse, reminding attendees of notes on the original construction of the edifice, features of its design and architecture, functions of the rooms and other buildings on the grounds, and the recent changes made fifteen years ago during the lighthouse rehabilitation project to which so many of the residents had contributed. Next, the ninety-five-year-old Blake Carroll regaled the gathering with stories of his father and uncle's experiences living on the grounds and his own personal anecdotes. Finally, Father Soplido spoke about Saint Catherine of Siena, the town and lighthouse's namesake, the history of the statue of Saint Catherine atop the lighthouse, and the significance of the black and white Dominican shields forming the molding on every floor's ceiling. He concluded with a beautiful blessing on the Saint Catherine's Cove Lighthouse and all the benefactors of the lighthouse through the years. When Father Soplido finished, the president of the Lighthouse Preservation Society encouraged all to enjoy the half-hour steamboat excursion to view the characteristic and to remain for cocktails and *hors d'oeuvre* in the heated tent afterward. At this, the string orchestra began to play, and mingling resumed, along with dancing.

Gracie, from the railing above, made eye contact with her grandparents, who responded with waves and thumbs-up. Claribel then turned to Paul to share her praise of the ceremony. Paul could barely agree before resident after resident, friend after friend, inched over to greet him, to check in on him, to compliment him. Mikey found the parents of a few of his friends and caught up with them while Eli ascended the staircase to confer with the choir. In the dilatory movement of the throng, Lucretia, Nora, Roy, and Marni managed to find Paul and Claribel in order to direct them to the entrance of the lighthouse for the photo.

"Oliver wants to get home, so we should do this before he needs to leave," Lucretia announced.

Hands waving and names called sufficed to corral Drew, Oliver, Peony, and their photographer, Poppy, to the lighthouse entrance. The shrubbery outside the lighthouse, though night had fallen, glittered in the glow of the lights strung around trees and emitted from lighthouse windows. A climbing rosebush crept along the wall, its buds still pink despite the dying stems and foliage. As Poppy stepped back and organized the portrait, Lucretia pulled Paul to the side, clandestine in the passing people and attentions turned to posing.

"Paul, could I have a moment?" she asked, interlocking her arm with his good arm.

"Of course," he said, stepping aside with her.

"I wanted to thank you—and I didn't want to let another moment pass *without* thanking you."

When Paul looked into her eyes, he noticed a grieving of sorts, a sadness despite a smile that brimmed with joy.

"Thank me for what?"

"I never thanked you for something you did a long time ago, and it's been bothering me that I almost—expired—without ever having thanked you. And here we are taking this photograph that I've had on my mind all day for some reason, and I got to thinking, 'I have to thank Paul tonight.'"

Paul, unsure of where she was going, knew not to interrupt. He smiled back at her, awaiting her thanks.

"That day after school in the library when you invited me to the high school baseball game—that was the day I met all of you. Oh sure, I had known you all in school, but that was the day I became friends with you. And those friendships have lasted over fifty years. And to think of all the things we've seen each other through over the years! It's amazing to me. And I wouldn't have had those cherished experiences and friends if you hadn't included me that day, if you hadn't invited me. And I just want to say thank-you for that, because it opened the door to thousands of happy moments for me."

She teared up, but the joy never vanished from her smile.

"Oh, Lu," Paul said, but he did not know what to say. "I should be better with words, but, golly—"

"You don't have to say anything. And you know what else? Thank-you for being just as welcoming and kind to this day as you were back then. You're a good friend, Paul Scrivensby. I think that's why I was so defensive of you when Derek Braynard huffed and puffed about you."

"And that's why you almost got us killed when you thought you saw him Tuesday morning!"

She laughed. "It had to have been him. How many beige sports cars zoom through Saint Catherine's Cove?"

They chuckled as they eased back into the fold, arm in arm.

"Well, Lu, the pleasure was all mine. You've brought a lot of joy to our lives."

With Petunia by her side, Poppy positioned everyone and stepped back to take the photo. The longtime friends smiled jovially, each anticipating its permanence on the wall of the coffee shop and parlor. In five quick snaps, the shoot had finished.

"People are heading to the steamer. I think it's time to walk over," Peony intimated. When she spoke, as the portrait's subjects disassembled, everyone noticed the wind had picked up considerably.

"Maybe they can leave early and return early," said Marni, in response to the sharp wind.

"Paul," checked Nora, "we won't wait for you and Claribel, right? You're going to help Eli with his—courting?"

"That's right," Claribel confirmed. "We will see you for the reception in the tent afterwards."

As they strolled into the lighthouse gardens a few feet off the main entrance, the rumble of thunder thwarted all conversations to a lull before they resumed again.

"So much for a storm coming after midnight," Lucretia said.

"The forecasts haven't been right for a while now. I don't know why I put any stock in them anymore," Paul said, another rumble cluttering his last words.

"Why don't you head to the steamboat so you're not outside, and we'll head back inside the lighthouse. That might be a northern," Claribel testified. "And I'm feeling it."

"Good-luck with Eli," Peony said as she joined the procession down the promenade to the marina.

When the others reentered the lighthouse, much more vacant now, the string orchestra's tunes continued to sound before the chatter filling the air. Eli was leading the choir up staircases to the top of the lighthouse. Mikey stood with his grandparents, grinning at the sight to come.

"Is the helicopter situation taken care of, Grandpa?" asked Mikey.

"They confirmed," he responded.

"What helicopter situation?" asked Dr. Drew.

"The Lighthouse Preservation Society hired a helicopter to hover over the lighthouse and lake during the display of the characteristic. They'll be filming and taking photos. I simply inquired if they couldn't hover a littler earlier to record Eli and Sunrise." He grinned, acknowledging his joy in the recording of this event.

"I see," Dr. Drew said. "I'll let you get to Eli then. I'm going to meander around here until everyone gets back from the steamer."

"You're not going on the steamboat?"

"No. I'd rather stick around here." Dr. Drew stepped toward the entrance when Mikey took a few steps with him, stopping him when he called his name.

"Dr. Drew, do you have a second?"

"Sure. What's up, Mikey?"

"I know Grandpa told you my good news, but I just wanted to thank you for helping. You didn't have to drive him there and sit in on the meeting. I really appreciate all your help through this, and I wanted to make sure you knew I am really grateful."

"It was my pleasure, Mikey," Drew responded. "You know, you're a good boy, and you should be proud of that. You should be proud to be so much like your good grandfather when he was your age."

"Thanks, Dr. Drew," Mikey said, looking at the floor, honored but feeling undeserving of the comparison.

"I haven't seen all of my own grandchildren grow up the way I have seen Paul's. My Kelly's kids are around your ages. They live in River Forest, a suburb of Chicago, and go to Dominican schools in the area, too, as you did—all except Zach and Bridie, who already graduated from high school and are in college now. Zach's a year older than you, and Bridie is your age. It's always been a wish of mine that you would all be friends one day. You're all great kids—intelligent, fun-loving, and good-hearted kids—and I think you'd all get along."

"Maybe I can meet them some day."

"I'm hoping they'll be spending more time up here, and I'd like it if you can." He placed a hand on Mikey's shoulder as he said, "Congratulations again, Mikey. I'm glad it all worked out for you." Looking Mikey in the eye, he closed with, "Now I'm going to enjoy some cocktails so that I'm nice and smashed by the time everyone gets back from the boat ride." Then he exited the lighthouse. When Mikey saw his grandparents with their heads together, he left the lighthouse, too, not wanting to interrupt their discussion of Eli and Sunrise.

"They're going to be starting any minute," Paul said.

"Do you have your camera?" Claribel asked.

"I have mine. Do you have yours?"

"I do."

"All right," Paul said. "Then what I would like to do is stand below the watch room gallery on the pier and take pictures from below. I was upstairs not too long ago and saw Drew standing on the pier. It gave me the idea that that might be a nice angle. You can go up by Eli and take pictures on the gallery while I shoot a few from the pier."

"Then you'll miss the whole thing," Claribel said, frowning.

"I'm sure I'll hear it just fine from below." When he said this, thunder rumbled loudly. "Well, *maybe* I'll hear it. On second thought, why don't you take the pictures from the pier, and I'll go to the top. That way, you can take a few and then run back in if it gets too cold or starts to rain."

"Paul, there's no way you can take all those stairs, especially with your arm. I have no problem with stairs, and I can sneak right in if it gets too cold up there. You take photos from the pier, and take them right when Eli and Sunrise appear on the gallery so that you can hurry back indoors."

"Are you sure?" Paul asked.

"I am sure. Now we better get to our places. They'll be starting soon."

Claribel hurried to the staircase to ascend flight after flight to the watch room gallery where Eli had taken Sunrise. The choir stood to the side, and Blake Carroll in the watch room awaited them to finish. As Claribel passed, Blake stuck his head out.

"Claribel Wheeler," he greeted her. "Is little Paulie Scrivensby ready to begin?"

"That's Eli, Mr. Carroll. Paulie's grandson."

Oblivious to her correction, he ducked into the watch room.

Paul exited the lighthouse, buttoning his suitcoat with one hand as the sharp wind struck him. In addition to the thunder rumbling, he heard the water crashing against the rocks below and the din of the nearing helicopter in the air. He scurried through the illuminated lighthouse garden and down the promenade staircase until arriving at the pier. Only twenty-some feet above, he could hear more clearly the water growing more turbulent, and he could see the steamer setting out farther into the lake in order to position herself for the characteristic display; she tilted widely on the distressed lake water, and Paul caught himself hoping she would return soon. Grasping for his camera in his sling under his buttoned suitcoat, he neared the railing of the pier when he stepped on something funny. At his feet, he saw an abandoned oar lying ownerless on the pier deck, and he pushed it with his shoe toward the railing. Not a moment after brushing it aside, splashing water soaked it from between the pier's floorboards, alerting Paul to the height of the waves' reach.

Once in position with his back to the wooden railing, he looked to the top of the lighthouse. As the helicopter approached, he saw Eli and Sunrise near the gallery railing; Eli stood before the choir. Even from the distance, Paul could see Sunrise blushing to a shade that matched her carnelian dress and name, and Eli grinning widely. The gentle nightingale and the vibrant firebird had perched on the gallery deck, anticipating the song amongst the choirs of voice and thunder. Then he saw Claribel step onto the gallery, her back to Paul with the wind lifting the ends of her long scarf, holding her camera, ready with anxious enthusiasm. Paul raised the camera to his face to take a few shots when the song began.

The choir began humming the introduction to Yaz's "Only You," a pop song from the eighties, and as the lyrics began, Eli led the choir. Before long, the entire choir swelled with the lyrics, accompanying Eli in his serenade. Paul and Claribel snapped photographs as the helicopter hovered above, recording the scene. Sunrise brought her hand to her mouth amid the wonder, oblivious to the thunder and flashes of lightning; her attention and love rested solely on Eli who, backed by angelic voices, sang the well-practiced song like a nightingale. No one could help smiling widely, from each member of the choir to Blake Carroll in the watch room.

As the song came to a close, Eli's solo ended, but the choir continued to hum the melody. While they hummed, he walked to Sunrise, whose hand never left her astonished face. Eli gently took her hand, shaking as he lowered it, closed his eyes, and kissed her. It was a short kiss, but it was their first.

The choir cheered, and Claribel, who had captured it in a photo, turned to Paul below to show her elation at the moment. Paul saw her through the view finder of his camera and snapped a photo of her. And he saw as her gaze drifted, as her smile turned to terror, as she mouthed the word "Paul" and bolted from his sight. Wonderstruck by the turn in Claribel's expression, he lowered his camera, hoping to see the gallery in its entirety, and found standing three feet before him Derek Braynard.

They locked eyes for a long three seconds before Derek shifted his gaze to the lake and slowly walked past Paul to the railing. Paul glanced up to the lighthouse gallery to see Eli and Sunrise waiting to exit as the choir filed out. Youthful screams punctured the din of chatter when rain began to fall on them. Paul hardly knew the rain struck him as he turned toward the railing where Derek looked out at the steamboat, now dawdling a good half mile from the shore. The passengers, covered, lined the side of the vessel in anticipation of the characteristic. The helicopter headed toward the steamer for better recording positioning of the lighthouse. A gust strengthened the ever-blowing wind, slamming Derek and Paul in the face as they peered out, splashing water onto the pier from under the planks.

"So your grandson gets to return to school without consequence," Derek said, staring out.

It was raining. Paul had taken his photos. The serenade had finished. He had no reason to remain on the pier and turned to depart.

"Some things don't change, I guess," Derek said. "Scrivensbys get to do whatever they want and don't care who they hurt."

Paul stopped. "Why I am not surprised you're still bitter? You managed to stay bitter about something that happened over fifty years ago when we were kids. So why would I expect you to get over something that happened only days ago?"

"You make it sound like it's that simple—to get over it—just like that."

"It might not be easy, but it *is* that simple. It takes a choice and some dedication. And I'm hoping you will make that choice and stick with it because I won't have you targeting my grandson at school anymore."

Derek's voice did not reflect the weather, the waters, his resentment. In an eerie monotone, he said, "I saw the photo shoot outside the lighthouse tonight. My, how you have all banded together over the years. I suppose that's what friends do. But I bet none of you thought twice about me after I left town."

"What's this got to do with—"

"You got all the accolades for your career. I travel the world writing for *Beyond Frontiers* and *Terrain Non-Ex* and other major publications, and no one in this town cares a lick. I climbed mountains for days. I got dropped into a lake from twelve thousand feet. I write about it for adventure and nature enthusiasts around the world, but no one in Saint Catherine's Cove knows. They know about your little column, though. They know about your controversial commentary on—" he mocked upheaval and shock with a feigned gasp— "class! Gracious me!"

Paul listened to this tangential rant and said nothing.

"Well, good for them. And good for you. Your career needed upheaval, a little attention. It's a little late, but better late than never. And one day I'll participate in an excavation and write about an artifact we unearthed that explains how the Egyptian pyramids were built, and no one in Saint Catherine's Cove will notice."

"All right, Derek. I get it. The only thing I want to make sure you comprehend is to steer clear of my grandson."

"It's moot, Paul. I won't be going back to the university."

Paul wanted to walk away, not only to discontinue conversation with Derek but to find cover; however, his curiosity had been piqued by the comment. In the distance, through the strengthening rain, they saw the steamboat tilt dangerously to the accompaniment of faint gasps from her passengers. Splashes from the breaking waves, ever growing in size, soaked their shoes from beneath the planks of the pier had the rain not done so already.

"Once the committee had reached its decision on your grandson and President Cringle made it clear he backed the outcome, he said in no uncertain terms that my days at the university were numbered. He said, 'this doesn't bode well for your tenure here.' The long and short of it is that he believed you over me. He believed I was motivated by a vendetta against you and not the facts that your grandson insolently reviled a professor in a paper and belligerently refused a minor reprimand."

"President Cringle believed the truth, Derek. That's the long and short of it."

With his back to the rocky façade of the cliff, Paul had not seen Claribel descend the staircase and rush to the pier. Her footsteps turned both men around to find her. Gusts of wind tousled her long scarf, and as the rain pelted her, she clenched her arms with her hands.

"Claribel Wheeler," Derek said. "Excuse me—Scrivensby."

"Claribel," Paul said, "you shouldn't be out here right now. Come on. Let's go inside. I've had enough of this—talk—anyway."

Derek could see Claribel's concern for her husband from the panicked arrival, from the quizzical countenance, from the impulse to draw nearer to him.

"I was just telling your husband that the way he presented his case for your grandson cost me my job as dean." He released a contrived chuckle. "Thought I had something good going for me, I have to admit. But I was told it doesn't 'bode well' for me."

"Can you believe that, Claribel?" Paul said. "The president of the university had the audacity to believe that Dean Braynard was motivated by a vendetta against me. How unfortunate, Derek, that the truth got in the way of what you had going for you."

Derek rolled his eyes. "Had a feeling you'd see it that way. So I'm not going back. I resigned, and no one asked me to reconsider. No one said I was over-reacting and that we could work something out. So you win again, Paul. You took my job this time."

"Took the job from you 'this time?' And last time? It was me?" asked Claribel.

Derek did not respond. He could not, so broken was he by the rejection, and too damaged to intimate that he felt he had a claim to her at one time.

"Derek, you need to know something. You are wrong to blame Paul for whatever is happening with your job right now. You know that. If you're honest with yourself, you know you have no one to blame except yourself for targeting Mikey and how you went about persecuting him."

Even in the rain, Paul and Claribel could see Derek turning red, in part from shame but mostly from anger.

"But you need to know that you were wrong to blame Paul for what happened all those years ago, too," she said.

"Claribel," Paul interjected. "You don't have to do this. You don't owe him anything. Let's go inside."

"Paul didn't happen to ask me to May Fest before you could do it," she persisted, knowing she had his full attention. "I convinced him to ask me because I knew your intentions. You and I started talking, and I realized you wanted something more than friendship—and I didn't. Paul didn't know at the time why I wanted him to ask me. He did it as a friend. Only afterwards I told him I had wanted him to ask me so that I wouldn't be able to go with you. It was stupid, and we were kids then, but that's the truth."

The former dean stared at her, unable even to glance at Paul, who, if Derek believed Claribel, was an innocent pawn in his own oblivious way. His mouth had dropped open at the revelation, but now it clenched shut as ire filled his eyes.

"You've spent all these years blaming Paul when you should have been blaming me. He didn't do anything wrong. It was me."

"You don't owe him an explanation, Bel," Paul said, stepping to his wife.

The step toward his wife to comfort her and the note of despondency in the way he spoke to her, for Derek, corroborated her story. She wasn't concocting a tale to take the target off her husband's back; she was clearing her conscience.

"So what?" Derek said softly, then, with the rancor in his voice intensifying, "So what do you want from me? Forgiveness?"

"No," she said, somehow calmly amid the storm. "I don't need forgiveness from a man who avenged himself on my innocent grandson for a grudge he's held from when we were kids. I want you to know how misguided you've been all these years—to this day. I want you to let this grudge against my husband go. It's misplaced."

While her disgust with him was unconcealed, her sincerity and gentleness went neglected by Derek, who fixated on her not wanting forgiveness from such a man as he. And as the thunder roared, his anger swelled.

"Apparently, you're as big a bitch now as you were back then."

Claribel, unrattled, did not expect Paul's reaction as he stepped in front of his wife as if to face off with Derek. She pulled his free arm gently toward her, as if to indicate, "Don't bother," when he shook his head in disgust and said simply, "You need to leave." He wanted to be resilient, to walk away unoffended by the attack, but the attack was directed at Claribel, not himself. "You've overstayed your welcome."

Derek's glare at Paul hardened. "Was I ever welcomed here?"

"Come on, Claribel. He wants to stay, fine. But we're not. Let's not waste a moment more on this guy."

He turned to his wife, and putting his arm around her shoulder, began the process of whisking her to shelter from the rain and cold, but Derek grabbed him by the arm Paul used to hold Claribel and yanked him so aggressively that he flung Paul beyond himself into the wooden railing of the pier.

"Paul!" Claribel shouted, rushing to him.

The monotone of Derek's voice did not hide the anger behind it when he declared, "You don't get to walk back to your perfect life and leave me—leave me to walk back to the shambles of a life *you* ruined for me. Not when you're the one who wrecked it!" And without a second's hesitation, Derek punched Paul in the face, causing him to stagger.

Claribel could react with but a gasp before Paul, barely having regrouped, swung his weak left hand into Derek's face. While the blow did not bother Derek much, the force propelled him backwards and his sole slipped on the wet deck, causing him to fall. He picked himself up sloppily and charged Paul, and when he cocked his arm to deal another blow, Paul kicked him in the stomach with the bottom of his shoe, knocking him backwards again. Beyond Derek, Paul saw three figures on the promenade staircase hurriedly descending, and only the vibrant color of a fiery dress revealed to Paul that one of the persons was Sunrise.

As Derek fumbled to regain his footing on the slippery deck, he noticed the abandoned oar. He reached for it and, by the time he rose to his feet, was wielding it as a weapon.

"Derek, don't!" Claribel shouted.

But Derek brandished it such that Paul and Claribel were backed into the pier railing with no way to escape without a whack. He swung the oar into Paul's sling, and Paul dropped to his knees, clutching his arm in pain. Claribel crouched to hold him when Paul determinedly forced himself to his feet, panting and awkwardly resting his free elbow on the low railing while withdrawing his suspended arm into his body. Unrelenting, Derek swung the oar again, this time in a backhand motion from over his shoulder, but he wasn't expecting Claribel to intervene. Stepping in front of Paul to block him from the blow, she took the full force of the hit. Her back slammed past Paul into the railing, and the momentum hurled her over it. As if he weren't in a sling, Paul grasped madly for a hold on her arm, her leg, one of the strands of her scarf, but grasped only the turbulent wind. His hands clutched nothing as he watched her land backwards into the waters below.

He couldn't rift his eyes from her body crashing into the choppy waves, her arms flailing, and the strands of her scarf thrashing every which way. His eyes remained fixed as helplessness sunk him into the railing until the voice of Eli shook him from his trance.

"Grandma!" Eli shouted as he jumped onto the railing and not a second later leapt into the lake.

"Eli!" Sunrise screamed, as she ran to the railing.

If it weren't for the rain and the wind, Paul might have heard Claribel gulping for breath, the horror-struck gasps from the passengers on the steamboat, the loudening helicopter as it switched from a hover to a pursuit. Paul turned to see the terror in Derek's eyes, in his blood-shot eyes, as he tried to process what he had just done, what he had never meant to do. His eyes clenched, squeezing tears and terror out. He swung the oar over his shoulder and screeched, "You did this! You did this to me!" And he whirled it at Paul, striking again his injured arm.

Mikey had arrived on the pier with Eli and Sunrise and grabbed Derek, swinging him around, trying to wrest the oar from him. A wave crashed this time over the railing, and all parties maintained resolute balance. Derek fastened his hold on the oar and swung it into Mikey's torso, only Mikey absorbed the blow, grabbed the oar with both hands as it struck him, and yanked it from Derek. Tossing the oar to the deck, he had little time to deflect an uppercut from Derek. Mikey dodged it and took an immediate swing at Derek, landing a fist in the face. As Derek staggered, Mikey punched him in the face again, and then again, until Derek collapsed on the pier deck.

Sunrise had crouched beside Paul, talking him conscious, but even the woozy Paul could tell that her attention was divided between him and Eli struggling to save his grandmother's life in the lake below.

"Grandpa!" Mikey shouted as he crouched beside him. "Are you okay?"

"Your grandmother—Eli—" he panted.

Bright lights from the helicopter struck them as it hovered above. Dr. Drew descended the staircase and, once at the bottom, stopped for a second at the arrestive scene before him. Seeing Mikey and Sunrise crouching around Paul compelled him to hustle toward them.

"Get off the pier! This could be a surge!" he shouted as another wave landed on the pier, crashing through the railing.

The steamboat had come close, and a life preserver had been precision-thrown into the water. Eli had managed to grab a hold of his grandmother and worked with all his might to swim her to the preserver bobbing on the turbulent water. He tried to shield his grandmother from the walls of waves collapsing on them, tried not to inhale the water as the waves submerged him over and over. He felt his grandmother clutching his ribs and his arm as she fought for her life to hold on to him, slipped, and regained a slippery hold. Peony and Lucretia were shouting "Claribel" and Eli's father was shouting "Mom!" When the life preserver cleared a wave and presented itself within reach, Eli inhaled the first second he could and flung his grandmother toward it, knowing she had all along been working with him to hold on, unwilling to let his father lose his mother, as Eli had. He flung her toward it so that she could grab hold, flung with all the energy he had left, with his last bit of might.

And as he separated from the life preserver—and from his grandmother—Paul heard Sunrise scream his name over and over, each scream louder as the waves thrashed him and carried him, and the name of the boy resounded in the screams from familiar voices on board the steamer, terror-ridden and forlorn calls for Eli. Paul tried to hoist himself up to see, to save, but collapsed, unable. Before he lost consciousness, he saw Dr. Drew, who had been rushing toward him, avert his path and jump the railing into the lake in response to the sudden calls for Eli. The grandfather could barely murmur "Eli," but his whisper floated through the percussion symphony around him, like a gentle nightingale amid a tempestuous choir.

CHAPTER 20

A bench in Samuel Park was no place for Paul to be this afternoon, the afternoon of his retirement toast. The temperature, only a degree above freezing, urged him to hustle the stark, empty streets home, to dress himself in the fragrances of cinnamon caramel sauce and baked apples, to warm himself with the bourbon his grandson had enjoyed on the sly. But he could only sit on the bench under the nigh leafless maples and watch occasional gusts of wind scatter the yellow and scarlet leaves into beds of deadening flowers. He reached inside his pulled-tight wool coat and grabbed some folded papers from an inside pocket—the speech he had been working on a week before. Before he opened them, he ripped them in two, stared at the halves, and replaced them in his pocket. A sudden gust of wind stirred the leaves, scratching them across the pathway in the park. The wind cut into his skin, but he felt immune to its pain; after all, he had only one week ago encountered worse. The gust, long as it lasted, could not, he noticed, wrest a lone leaf from the maple above him as it clung tightly to the branch, a hint of green still in its veins. This wind, albeit colder, did not compare to the storm winds of last week.

Returning home for a bourbon and Cointreau crossed his mind before the thought of bourbon reminded him of his grandson Mikey, who had sneaked a glass a week ago. Mikey was not expected back in Saint Catherine's Cove before Thanks-Giving. In a way, Paul found himself paying homage to his grandson's park get-away for quiet thinking, praying, and mourning, a secret location he had learned of only days ago. Yet he could not think, did not pray, and dared not mourn.

Instead, in a thoughtless daze, he stared at the sole maple leaf effortlessly belonging to its branch, easily holding on despite the concerted torrents of northerly winds.

"Grandpa," he heard and turned to his right.

"Gracie," he responded. "It's too cold for you to be out here."

"I came to find you," she said. "I saw you leave and followed you down here. I wasn't sure why you were taking a walk at four o'clock in the afternoon when you have to be at the lighthouse for your toast at five. I thought you said you didn't even have a speech prepared."

"No, I don't have a—" He stopped himself and rephrased. "I'm not prepared. Not prepared one bit."

"Is that why you're out here? To collect your thoughts? To think of what to say?" He did not answer. "I just wish you would do it where it's warm. What would Dr. Drew say?"

"Wouldn't it be nice if Dr. Drew were here to say it for himself?"

Gracie knew that Dr. Drew, one among several concerns of her grandfather, preoccupied his thoughts, perhaps thwarting any motivation to pen a short speech, yet she wished that the ceremony designated in celebration of his life-long career as a writer not be wasted. So she extended a hand to her grandfather and invited him home. "Come on, Grandpa. I know you don't have much time and have other things on your mind, but I'll help you with your speech on the walk home. I just had to give one on the Saint Catherine's Cove Lighthouse, if you recall, and you helped me with mine."

Paul forced a smile as he rose, taking her hand. He knew what she was doing and could not let his granddaughter down. "One of the few moments from that night not riddled with disaster."

Gracie, more animated as she took on the role of speech coach, tossed ideas and topics to her grandfather on the walk home—"be sure to thank those who helped you along the way," "talk about how you came up with ideas for your column," "oh, and tell a story about working in New York"—but she concluded with the advice of "remember we're all here for you, so just speak from the heart and it will be good."

When they entered the house, Paul half-expected to hear Claribel getting ready upstairs, and leaving Gracie to her coffee in the kitchen, walked into the solarium. Almost four thirty in the afternoon and dusk alighted on the lakeside town. Still he could see the stark branches of oaks and elms and ashes and maples lining the streets and parks, depleted of their foliage now, swaying with each wind, and in the absence of their leaves, he could spot the lighthouse.

He accepted the futility of penning a speech at this late hour as he envisioned Peony, Lucretia, and Nora reaching for their coats, Roy and Oliver sipping the last of their apéritifs, the front doors opening, the engines starting. So he spent the next five minutes staring, envisioning, deflecting, avoiding, understanding, reasoning, resigning—as he wondered if that one maple leaf were still holding effortlessly fast to the branch.

"Gracie," he called. "Ready?"

"Yes, Grandpa!"

And she drove him to the lighthouse, arriving a few minutes before five o'clock's gray-falling lake dusk. Blake Caroll's ghostly wave greeted them, as did his weak but poignant smile. Paul realized not too many people remained who could remember him as a boy, and the smile on Blake's face reflected that he saw the boy still. Paul speculated he still saw Drew that way, too—as a boy, then a young man, then—.

He and Gracie passed the garden beside the lighthouse, the dusty florets of the climbing rosebush drying now, fragrancing the garden like a sachet. Here, only a few nights ago, with expectations of merriment and a storm ripping across the lake, Paul and his closest friends had taken a photo. Pee had hung it a few nights ago on the wall adjacent to their table in the ice cream parlor, where, they imagined, it would remain for years and years, when, one day, Petunia might pull it from the wall for a closer look, smile lovingly at it with nostalgic mourning, and hold it to her heart. In a few steps, they had passed the garden—and the memory—and entered the lighthouse where Paul's guests awaited. No staircases to ascend this time, and no gallery exposures—the toast would take place on the heated main floor of the lighthouse.

A few claps, many smiles, and pleasant salutations welcomed him as Gracie led him to the front of the gathering where a low platform had been placed. Opposite the podium and platform, three rows of folding chairs had been arranged by the planning crew of friends. Just when Paul realized that Stephen, the editor-in-chief of *The Current Front* stood among the guests, he felt a hand slip into his from behind him, a grasp he recognized easily and enjoyed for its comforting presence.

"Don't worry about a thing," Claribel whispered. "You can make this evening as long or as short as you want. I'll follow your lead." She kissed him on the cheek, and then he stepped onto the platform and stood at the podium. His guests unfastened from clasps of mingling clusters and stood before him.

"I can't tell if everyone's here who's supposed to be here— who's supposed—" and under his breath, he said, "who would have been here—who's *supposed* to be here." Then louder, he resumed, "And I see there are some people I wasn't expecting to be here." He smiled at Stephen and then Eloise, Father Soplido, and even his good New York friend Rick Mendel, standing next to his daughters, as his guests laughed lightly. As Claribel wrapped an arm around Gracie's waist, he surveyed the gathering for Eli, and then berated himself; he knew Eli would not be present. He let his stare settle again on the comfort of Claribel holding Gracie.

"The plan," he continued, "was that my grandson Mikey was going to read a paper he wrote at school—the McGuinty School of Journalism—on responsibility, and then I was going to say a few words before the toast. It was a beautiful paper, and when he shared it with me, I asked him to read it here tonight. But, you see, Mikey thought it was important to do something, something he considered more important than being here tonight, and I agreed with him and gave him my blessing. Drew, on the night of the Lighthouse Ceremony, had told my grandson Mikey that he wished his grandchildren and my grandchildren might become friends, so as soon as his classes ended for the weekend yesterday, Mikey drove down to Chicago to connect with Drew's grandchildren. As you know, he had met them and took them under his wing when they came up after the—accident—just over a week ago, and he thought it was important that he be there for them now." Paul saw cheerful smiles dilute, and merry eyes glisten as if sprinkled with a wind-touched spray of lake water. "So, with Mikey out of town, I guess all that's left is for me to say a few words—and I have nothing—"

"We're here, Grandpa!" said Mikey, hurrying through the lighthouse doorway. Behind Mikey hurried in four of Drew's grandchildren, and behind them, to the heart-stopping joy of Paul, came Eli and Sunrise. Mikey, Drew's grandchildren, and Sunrise immediately intermixed with those already gathered, but Eli stopped in the doorway as soon as he made eye contact with his grandfather at the podium. And then Eli slowly grinned, a bashful, for-no-good-reason-embarrassed grin, and Paul reciprocated, having made the same one himself many times, understanding that it simply rose to the top of no-other-possible reflexes. A moment later, Paul's son Michael entered, placed an arm around Eli, and led him to the front of the gathering, next to his brother, sister, and grandmother.

"I'm not sure what to say," Paul said. "Mikey, you weren't supposed to be here, and Eli, you were supposed to be at home recovering since you only got discharged yesterday."

Mikey glanced at his grandmother before proceeding. "Well, Eli's presence here is the surprise, but I was supposed to be here all along. I told you I was going to Chicago to hang with Dr. Drew's grandchildren, which was true, but I was really going there to bring them back here for tonight. It was important to Dr. Drew that they be here for you, in his place."

Paul's eyes welled with tears at this, and as if instinctively, Drew's grandchildren encircled him gently and in unison gave him a hug.

"I drove them up here earlier, and we arrived in Saint Catherine's with a little time to kill. So Zach and Bridie asked if we could check in on Eli, which we did. Apparently, Sunrise had the same idea because she was there when we arrived. A doctor also showed up at the house when we were visiting, and he informed us that Eli could come tonight!"

"It was a last-minute ruling," Mikey's father added.

"So we waited for him to get ready and all headed over. That's why we were a little late."

"I'm glad you're here at all," Paul said. "Thank-you," he added firmly, directing his gratitude to Drew's grandchildren. "Thank-you for coming all this way for me."

"We feel like we have a new family," Bridie said. "We didn't want to miss it."

"You *are* family now. And thank-*you*," Paul said, this time to Eli, Gracie, and Mikey. "I'm grateful you are all here. I'm grateful I still have you all." Then, his concern alighted on Eli. "Are you sure it's okay for you to be out?"

"The doctor was okay with it as long as I get right back. Look at me—I have five layers of clothing on!" His comment about layers referenced his extended stay in the hospital for hypothermia, the same diagnosis that initially plagued Dr. Drew due to his heroic leap into a storm-sieged Lake Superior. The comment also incited a bout of gentle laughter.

"If you're ready, Mikey, go ahead and read your paper. Then I'll say a few words, and we can all be on our way," Paul said.

"Not before the toast!" shouted Peony.

Paul chuckled. "Not before the toast." Then he stepped aside so that Mikey could situate himself at the podium. From inside his sport coat, his grandson pulled his folded paper and placed it on the podium.

"In order to be readmitted to school, I had to rewrite a paper on responsibility. I took it very seriously. We were supposed to give our thoughts on responsibility so that we could connect them to journalistic responsibility in a class discussion, which I missed." He grinned bashfully as the stigma of his suspension embarrassed him. "Once I had rewritten the paper, I read it to Grandpa, and he started to cry—"

"He read it while Eli was in the hospital! I was already emotional," Paul interjected to the amusement of his family and friends.

"—and he asked me if I would read it at his toast. So, here goes." Mikey looked at the paper and smoothed the creases with his hands. Then he read.

"I set out to ponder a question I was posing to myself for the sake of this assignment: 'what are we, as human beings, responsible for?' I entertained different answers like, 'we're responsible for taking care of the earth,' and 'we're responsible for raising our children right,' and 'we're responsible for doing our homework and taking our education seriously.' The answers I was coming up with seemed empty or missing some crucial concept I couldn't put my finger on. 'Why is taking care of the earth or tending to studies anyone's responsibility?' 'Why is raising our children right a responsibility?' After all, so many don't raise their children at all, or they believe that providing for them equates to being responsible.

"All around me, at the time I was reflecting on this, were my grandparents, their friends, and our families. Little did I realize that all around me were answers to questions like 'why be responsible at all?' and 'why take on new or even unnecessary responsibilities?' My father was working hard and happened to be on a business trip overseas when word reached him that I was in trouble in college, but work—synonymous with providing for his children—took the backburner when he reorganized his schedule and flew back to be with me. My sister could have turned down that one-more-thing-to-do, to turn a paper into a speech and deliver it in front of a few hundred people, but instead dedicated extra hours and hours to making sure it was great. My brother never gave a second thought about jumping into a turbulent lake to rescue his imperiled grandmother. My grandmother fought to live through a battle with cancer, and after winning, makes sure her family is well-nourished, especially with their favorites like shepherd's pie. My grandfather, while in the throes of a media frenzy over his column and later his press conference at the hospital, set everything aside to drive to my college to help me through a tough situation, as did his friend Dr. Drew. And after the tragedy on the pier, amid an entirely new media frenzy, he neglected all contact with the press to be with his family and friends in the hospital and at home, seeing us all through a difficult time. Example after example before my eyes led me to realize that I wouldn't find an adequate answer to my question, and that, more significantly, I wasn't asking the right question. I tilted my head for a new perspective. I cupped my ear to hear more clearly. And my question became, 'What are we responsible *to*?'

"From those closest to me, I am learning that I have a responsibility to my body, to take care of it and nurture it so that I am as productive as possible with the parts that make it up. I am learning that I have a responsibility to my mind, to enlighten it with worthwhile knowledge, to exercise it through critical reasoning, to sharpen it through study, so that I can put it to *good* use. I have a responsibility to my life, this life in this time in which I have been placed, so that my choices fortify my integrity and bolster my character. I have a responsibility to my religion, to my university, to my family, to reflect them in how well I live this life and in gratitude for all they have instilled in me. I will have a responsibility, one day, to my career, to represent it not as a writer but as a good writer. I am realizing that I have a responsibility to my soul—this unique creation that needs grace and virtue and love for blooming, for brightening the lives of others. And I have a responsibility to my God, Who created it—us—all. I have a responsibility to this body, to this mind, to this soul; I have a responsibility to this, my own life; I have a responsibility to my religion, my schooling, my family; I have a responsibility to others known to me and unknown; and I have a responsibility to all these things and people because I realize I didn't have to have them—they are all gifts. To assume that having all this and being all this is just the way it is or to meander through life as if none of this is precious would eclipse the value of responsibility to anyone or anything in my life. To recognize that I don't have to have any of these things—even this life— compels me to recognize that they are gifts, special ones to be taken care of, and to which I have a responsibility.

"So while there are many values worth embracing in this world, I can't neglect responsibility as one of the most important. Many shirk responsibilities altogether let alone voluntarily take them on. But many others, making lives better for others and making their little worlds better places, are the ones I want to emulate, the ones undeterred by their responsibility to the gifts they have been given."

Using the palm of his hand, Mikey smoothed the crease in the paper again. He had finished reading his short reflection, and his grandfather, this time, smiled.

"My paper doesn't address *how* to show our responsibility to these things, but I knew a genuine apology to my professor was the right way to show that I am responsible to the blessing of people in my life, as was reaching out to Dr. Drew's grandchildren, as he had requested. I want to reflect my family and this community well by the choices I make, by how I conduct myself, and I learned that from everyone here. So, thank-you."

As the small gathering gently applauded in unison, Oliver said, "You are representing us beautifully, young man," and Roy added, "You represent the best of us, I think." Then Peony added after a jovial laugh, her hands still clapping, "I think he's too good to reflect us as we really are. Let's be honest!" As everyone responded with chagrined laughter, Lucretia noted to Paul, "Your grandchildren certainly won't need any help carrying on your legacy of class."

Paul smiled at the prospect of raising the controversy on class again; his November column and the piles of letters and the overheard conversations about it seemed the distant past. Yet he recognized the truth of Lucretia's statement and mused that, if he and his friends had done anything right, it was, at the least, raising an awareness of the need and the value of good behavior.

"All right, Paul," said Peony. "It's your turn."

Mikey stepped off the platform and found his place next to Eli and Gracie. The moment between his exit and Paul's ascent to the podium revealed the retiree's reluctance. When he finally raised his eyes to those gathered, the embarrassed smile faded slowly, replaced with an expression of stunned wonder and doubtful accomplishment.

Standing on the platform, albeit displaying himself before mostly family and friends, he felt exposed for the first time in days on account of constant efforts to conceal himself from the press and the masses after the episode on the pier. The helicopter above, after recording Eli's serenade, caught much of Derek's attack on the Scrivenbys and all that ensued afterwards; the helicopter team, along with those on the steamboat, assisted with the rescues. By the next morning, local and national press camped outside the hospital as well as the Scrivensbys' house. Although suffering from injuries himself, Paul had spent a vigil at the hospital, returning home with the assistance of his son only to shower, change, and fill a duffle bag with a few items to assist with his next prolonged stay at the hospital. He entertained no questions and dodged inquiries at every turn, as did the rest of his family. Father Soplido and other friends worked together to buffer the families from unwanted interrogations while checking in on Paul and the other patients frequently.

Of course, *The Current Front* had contacted him, and he relied heavily on their sympathetic public relations staff to rein in the wildness of frenzy already begun by the press, who had wasted no time in airing the footage from the helicopter. His friends at *The Current Front* understood Paul had much more important issues with which to preoccupy himself, including the health and well-being of those closest to him.

Claribel, after her admittance to the hospital, despite her extended exposure to the cold, turbulent waters, surprised everyone with the quickest recovery, anxious to be at her husband's side as he transferred his attention and prayers back and forth between Eli's bedside and Drew's. Eli's family kept him surrounded with love through an extended unconsciousness from having struck his head on rocks, and through a serious bout of hypothermia. Dr. Drew, in the best physical shape, suffered the most, especially as his already precarious hypothermia took a turn for the near worst by bringing on arrhythmia and heart complications. His weakened condition depleted him of energy, and his overtaxed heart had a difficult time keeping any beat let alone an arrhythmic one until he slipped into cardiac arrest. With his family in from Chicago outside the hospital room door, along with the Scrivensbys and his Saint Catherine's Cove friends, Dr. Drew, after nearly a minute, was resuscitated and closely monitored as his heart struggled to continue beating. Over several days, while the hypothermia subsided, the heart issues, requiring attention and care, kept him in the hospital, too weak to crack decorum-defying declaratives. Paul, too, suffered injuries from the fight with Derek. After days of refusing treatment, he finally consented to x-rays and closer looks. His arm sustained no breaks but instead more painful bruising, extending his healing and sling-wearing by weeks.

Although the press had eventually moved on from the territory they had staked outside the hospital and his house—without comment from Paul—he had caught in the newspaper and on television stories about the occurrences of that evening, the evening of the lighthouse's sesquicentennial celebration. While journalists and reporters offered little on Claribel, Eli, and Drew's recovery, they zeroed in on Derek Braynard's remanding into custody, delving into his history with Saint Catherine's Cove, his career as a journalist, and his position, now revealed as a "former post," as Dean of the McGuinty School of Journalism. Interviews with the helicopter pilot and photographer, President

Cringle from the university, and medical experts fleshed out stories as the same footage of fighting on the pier, jumps over the pier, and rescues near the pier undergirded commentaries.

Paul Scrivensby, after a lifetime in journalism, for the first time had felt he had his fill of the press. He needed a break yet could not enjoy the lull before inevitably resuming with press conferences, interviews, and, of course, writing a few pieces of his own. Or could he? Before an intimate gathering of family and friends, for a few minutes devoted solely to him, he certainly could enjoy the moment, couldn't he? And suddenly, the joy at his and Drew's grandchildren's arrival that had initially filled his heart, began, he allowed, to overfill his heart, to overflow into his body, rising and rising, whereupon, as he pulled away all floodgates, it reached his mind, allowing it, too, to fill his thoughts and memories and imagination. And somehow, that little, lone leaf clinging intently to the maple, the one with the touch of green, appeared in his mind—that last leaf to remain—and blew away. The smile returned to his face, more glorious than cheerful, with a joy beaming from his glistening eyes. The leaf stood for something other than he had supposed, and he knew that when he returned to that place in the park tomorrow morning, it would be gone, and the now bare tree, when he returned to it in several months, would be singing in the spring breeze with budding foliage.

"I gave myself a few minutes because that's all I wanted. I put that limitation on myself, and maybe I didn't need to. But that's still all I want to give myself, and you. Gracie and I brainstormed about what to say today, and we covered everything from memories to thank-yous. And I thought about my column—how I spent a lifetime offering my perspective on various issues and occasionally imparting advice. This group of people—this world of Saint Catherine's Cove—is the basis for my values, my perspective, my occasional advice, so I don't need to share, I think, any of that with you. But as a writer, maybe a metaphor is inevitable: I'm not interested in starting the final chapters of my book, my life; all I want to say is that I'm looking forward to starting a *new* book, to writing a whole new set of chapters, with each of you. Or better yet, not a book—a column! 'Partly Paul' is drawing to a close, and I'm starting a new column series under a different name. I never liked 'Partly Paul' as a title anyway. And the first column starts right now, with this beginning, not this end. This new column I'm writing—well, I'm just the author and the narrator—but I promise it will be all about you. My three grandchildren, who have a much deeper understanding of themselves than I did at their age, nudged me, in their own beautiful ways, to this new goal. And a conversation with Drew helped me to see that I want to spend my retirement making it about anyone but myself, and if I stick to my guns on this, I'm guaranteed the best years of my life."

He looked down and saw Mikey's composition still lying on the podium, his grandson's words in fresh ink, brimming with tradition-rife perspective and youthful sentiment and pulsating life. Forcing a lump from his throat, he smiled, squinting his glistening eyes at his loved ones, responding to the love in theirs.

"Everyone, grab a glass!" shouted Claribel, sensing her husband's wish for the relief of transition.

"I made punch out of Paul's favorite! I combined his bourbon and Cointreau, added a little champagne, and, lo and behold, it didn't come out all that badly," announced Lucretia. "So we have the champagne for celebration and the bourbon for Paul all in one. Fill up your coupes, friends!"

One by one, Lucretia ladled the champagne punch into Paul's guests' coupes, the fresh sparkle still misting over the punch bowl. And once everyone had a glass in hand, Paul stepped aside to share the podium with Claribel.

"Please raise your glasses, everyone," Claribel said, "as we toast to—" and she stopped, curtailing the sentences she had planned. And looking at Paul and then all before them, she said, "as we toast to Paul's new column!"

Everyone raised a sparkling coupe, clinked glasses, and said in unison, "To Paul's new column!"

Paul exchanged hugs and pats and celebratory words with kith and kin on the main floor of the lighthouse. Amidst the festivity, he noticed Stephen, the editor of *The Current Front*, ascend to the podium while his son, Michael, holding something wrapped, stood beside him. Paul listened as Stephen regained everyone's attention.

"I have a surprise gift for Paul, and if I could get everyone's attention for one moment, I'd like you to be the first to see it— before the world does!"

Peony yelped at the mystery of his words, yet everyone had a vague idea of where Stephen might be going with this.

"Paul thought the last that *The Current Front* might see of him was his final column in the December edition, but we have a surprise for Paul. Thanks to the help of Eloise Bernardi, Father Fernando Soplido, Claribel Scrivensby, and the entire staff at *The Current Front*, over fifty percent of the December issue will be devoted to—in honor of—Paul Scrivensby, from articles about him to—" and he pulled the wrapping off the large, rectangular package Michael was holding— "the cover!" Before Paul and all his guests, Stephen revealed an over-sized, framed cover of the December issue of *The Current Front*, featuring a previously black-and-white, newly colorized photograph from Paul's first months at the periodical. Amid wordless utterances of delight and congratulations, Stephen continued, "Paul, you will always be one of *The Current Front*'s best treasures, and you will always be welcomed back. On behalf of the entire staff, we hope you will visit us often because, frankly, the office just hasn't been the same without you."

Paul walked to the podium and gave Stephen a hug and a "thank-you, Stephen!" Then he leaned in for a closer look at the cover, noticing the wrinkle-free version of himself, the headlines, and the strong, solid font of the words *"The Current Front."* Stephen handed him a copy of the soon-to-hit-the-stands December edition.

"Hot off the presses, Paul. Happy reading," Stephen said.

"Really, Stephen, thank-you."

"Looks like the first column of your new series might begin with a look at the December issue," said Stephen. "Your own words, the final column, are on the last page of the issue."

Paul continued to entertain congratulatory words from his family and friends as the darkness settled. He watched Eli and sent nervous glances to his son Michael every few minutes, subtly insisting he bring Eli home and back to bed. Observing his father's cue, Michael rounded up his youngest son along with Sunrise and brought them home. Mikey and Gracie escorted Drew's children to the car to drive them to the hospital for a check-in on their grandfather. New friends Father Soplido and Eloise departed with New York friends Stephen and Rick as they discussed how nicely Eloise's article complemented the features in the December issue. Paul, left with the remaining friends and family, passed Blake Carroll, who waved and offered, "Congratulations, Paulie Scrivensby," as they passed.

As they approached their cars, a woman walking a dog down the sidewalk neared. Paul recognized her as Mrs. Janes, who, while he was being honored a few weeks back at Greengate Grade School, vociferously declared her opposition to Paul's November column on the decline of class.

"Mr. Scrivensby," she called when she recognized him, her eyes observing the over-sized magazine cover he was carrying to his car. "No doubt that will be hanging outside our auditorium soon," she said.

Thinking back to how the school planned to honor him when the December issue came out, he realized he had to agree. "I'm hoping it will be a smaller version. I think I've had enough attention to last the rest of my life, and if a smaller image of mine is walked by unnoticed for the next few years, I'd be all too glad." He chuckled.

She did not.

"Well, I bet you've learned a valuable lesson after everything that's happened," she said, intent on inserting a point. That she had been wanting to express a thought was clear from the way her carriage changed upon recognizing Paul, and that her thought might not be pleasant manifested in the scowl that formed upon seeing the periodical cover. Her coworker, Lucretia, instinctively loyal, sidled up to Paul to hear what Mrs. Janes had to say.

"What's that?" inquired Paul, too happy to brace himself for admonishment of any sort.

"In light of all this life-or-death stuff involving that psycho on the pier, you must feel petty to have put so much emphasis on something as insignificant as class in one of your last columns. I hope you've learned that there's so much more important stuff than trying to be classy."

Lucretia stepped forward, feigning casualness, and parted her lips to utter a quip. Then she bit her lip and placed a hand on her hip, refraining from retort.

"Thank-you, Mrs. Janes, for reminding me of a valuable lesson," Paul said cordially.

"And for presuming he needed to hear it," Lucretia said, matching Paul's cordiality.

Mrs. Janes scoffed and continued walking her dog down the block. Paul and company exchanged grins and continued walking, some to their cars, some toward home.

Claribel whispered to Paul, "Maybe the 'Partly Paul' column hasn't ended. The class controversy continues."

"I'll take it," Paul said.

"Seeing Mrs. Janes reminds me," Lucretia ruminated, "I still haven't mailed my thank-you card to little Peter Unterbrink."

Then Peony's voice sounded. "How about pie and ice cream at the parlor!" she shouted.

"What about dinner?" shouted Lucretia.

"Who needs it? Come on! It's a celebration! Afterwards, we can bring a piece of pie to Drew at the hospital and eat it slowly in front of him while he's full from hospital food," responded Peony, laughing loudly.

Maybe it was for the pie and ice cream or maybe it was on account of the lure of Peony's contagious laughter inviting them to laugh with her, but they all knew to head to the parlor, dinner or not.

"Why not?" Paul said. "We can start paging through the December issue."

THE END

ACKNOWLEDGEMENTS

This work developed into a novel from what I had initially written and completed as a novella. The words "THE END" had originally appeared after the first part on class. After several readings and with input from others, I continued the story, expanding on characters, their worlds and perspectives, and interrelated themes. Although in some ways it feels as if there is more to say, to include, to develop—I have learned many authors feel this way about their "completed" stories—it embodies a fullness now that I have come to appreciate.

I am grateful for all the support I have witnessed during this undertaking, from words of encouragement to understanding of the need to step away and write. I thank family, friends, and peers who have helped me and cheered for me. Sharing of perspectives, knowhow, and enthusiasm has been a great aid to me throughout this process. I thank them all.

In particular, I thank Mom and Dad, Anna, Nellie, Gina, Alan, Mike, readers and editors of my drafts, and the CW team.

ALSO BY J. SHEP:
  AFTER ME (2024)

FOLLOW J. SHEP ON FACEBOOK.COM/JSHEPAUTHORPAGE
BOOK GROUP QUESTIONS AND IDEAS AVAILABLE AT
WWW.CHRISTOPHERWHISPERINGS.COM
TEACHER RESOURCES AND CLASSROOM DISCUSSION PROMPTS AVAILABLE AT
WWW.CHRISTOPHERWHISPERINGS.COM